BRO

Brock, Darryl.

If I never get back

$18.95

DATE			

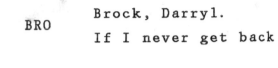
© THE BAKER & TAYLOR CO.

IF I NEVER
GET BACK

IF I NEVER
GET BACK

A NOVEL

DARRYL BROCK

Crown Publishers, Inc.
New York

Published by Crown Publishers, Inc., 201 East 50th Street, New York, New York 10022

CROWN is a trademark of Crown Publishers, Inc.

Manufactured in the United States of America

Library of Congress Cataloging-in-Publication Data

Brock, Darryl.
  If I never get back/by Darryl Brock.
    1. Cincinnati Reds (Baseball team)—History—Fiction.   I. Title.
PS3552.R58I3   1989
813'.54—dc19   89-1346

ISBN 0-517-57345-8

10 9 8 7 6 5 4 3 2 1

First Edition

For Lura

ACKNOWLEDGMENTS

———————◇———————

In a sense this tale emerged from my historical rummagings as if it had always been waiting there. It pleases me that most of the characters were doing in 1869 what I have them doing, and that many events—even minor ones—occurred as I have shown them. Some, of course, did not.

Information and inspiration came from a generous number of sources. In 1985, while traveling the country and retracing the Red Stockings' tour routes, I was aided by reference librarians in dozens of cities. Special thanks to Thomas R. Heitz, librarian at the National Baseball Hall of Fame; to W. Lloyd Johnson, Executive Director of the Society for American Baseball Research, and to others of my SABR colleagues for their energy and expertise; to Dahlia Armon of the Mark Twain Papers at the University of California at Berkeley; to Elaine Gilleran of the Wells Fargo Bank History Department; to Bill Bloodgood of the Oregon Shakespearean Festival; to Jon Carroll of the *San Francisco Chronicle;* and to Karlyn Barker of the *Washington Post.*

I am indebted to Jack Finney for blazing a literary trail; to Peter S. Beagle, the sagest of guides, for his counsel and steadfast friendship; to Gemma Whelan, my Irish connection; to Julie Fallowfield and James O'Shea Wade, my agent and editor, whose patience and craft shaped a dream into existence.

Most of all I am indebted to my wife's perceptions and loving enthusiasm; this work is dedicated to her.

PROLOGUE

*A*s a child I spent hours gazing at landscapes in the patchwork quilt my grandmother tucked around me. Farms and hamlets grew up in remnants of Grandma's print dresses. Grandpa's work shirts sprouted towns. Older, unfamiliar patches formed mysterious hinterlands. Over the years, imbuing each patch with mood and legend, I envisioned myself fording rivers in fabric hollows and scaling cloth peaks, traversing the ridged boundaries of thread to adventure with the imaginary folk of all my patchwork provinces.

Once or twice I was able to stare downward with such mindless concentration that I felt myself actually sinking into the topography I had created: it broadened and opened beneath me as though I were descending slowly in a balloon. All around, hazily at first, bright forms—orange houses, lavender pastures, blue hills—materialized and quickened with life.

Just as I began to drink in the sensations of this new world—the odors of grasses and blooms, the rustlings of birds, the shouts of children playing ball in the distance—I pulled myself back with a wrenching effort, and afterward lay trembling on my bed. What would happen, I wondered, if I ever went in all the way?

PART ONE

THE GREEN FIELDS OF THE EAST

———————◇———————

Nelly Kelly loved Base Ball games
Knew the players, knew all their names,
You could see her there every day,
Shout "Hurray" when they'd play.
Her boy friend by the name of Joe
Said to Coney Isle, dear, let's go,
Then Nelly started to fret and pout,
And to him I heard her shout:
Take me out to the Ball game,
Take me out with the crowd.
Buy me some peanuts and crack-er-jack,
I don't care if I never get back.
Let me root, root, root for the home team,
If they don't win it's a shame,
For it's one, two, three strikes,
You're out at the old Ball game.

JACK NORWORTH and ALBERT VON TILZER

. . . step to the bat, it's your innings.

MARK TWAIN, A Connecticut Yankee
in King Arthur's Court

—◇ 1 ◇—

T he Amtrak crawled out of Cleveland. I sat sweating in my new dark suit, staring out at the blackened brick walls from which milky light was beginning to ooze. Maybe I could hold it off. What had I been thinking about? The TV. Concentrate.

She opens her mouth wide: NNNNOOOOOOOOOOOOOO!!! But I have no intention of hitting her. I shoulder past to the console squatting near the vaulted window of her hog-rich parents' Burlingame home. On-screen is Anchorman, her lover, smarmy voice and trademark eyebrows embellishing the tripe he intones from the TelePrompTer.

I get my back into it, thrust upward with my legs, muscles knotting . . . no workouts for too long . . . a frenzied snatch-and-lift . . . I stagger sideways and heave . . . picture window explodes . . . shards of glass cascading . . . TV in flight . . . cabinet folds inward as it crashes on the flagstone . . . muted cracklings precede one large red spark . . . the long rumble down the hill, pieces flying . . . Stephanie screaming . . . for an instant . . . one pure rushing instant . . . I was King Fucking Kong. . . .

Milkiness encroaching. I reached for the pint of Scotch in my coat. Almost empty. The pale light was seeping in through my ears.

Rock bottom. If not here, couldn't be far off. What I didn't know was whether to feel scared or relieved.

The TV . . .

Maybe she picked him on purpose, knowing how I detested the breed: electronic jackals in symbiosis with their brain-dead viewers. Mincing on the scene, crews running interference. Checking makeup. Asking their two stupid questions. Broadcasting the shoddy results hours before our stories hit the streets.

It was when she told me she was moving in with him that I assaulted the tube.

[5]

It proved costly. With the divorce came a custody judgment barring drunken violent me from seeing our daughters more than once a week.

Booze gradually came to fill a lot of empty places. I was a wretched part-time father. I alienated my friends. Jeopardized my job. Screwed up everything.

Strangely, my father's death had seemed to offer a certain opportunity, a rite of passage to manhood.

"I can't imagine how they tracked you down." Stephanie's cool measured words—her telephone voice—sounding in my brain. "They called here for you. I told them our situation. If you need to miss a visit, I'll think of something to tell the girls."

By burying him I would ascend some pinnacle of maturity. There, viewing my thirty-two years with new wisdom, I would find significance and a tenable position.

"Take a month if you need, Sam." City Editor Joe Salvio giving me a fishy smile, significant look. "Pull yourself together . . . skimpy interviews . . . facts not checked . . . get back to your old form!"

Or your ass is dead.

So this morning I had picked up the suit I'd ordered, flown to Cleveland, and cabbed to the Cuyahoga County Morgue. Without ceremony they slid the cold-storage drawer out and raised the sheet. Shivering in the refrigerated chill, I peered into the sallow face for the first time, seeking traces of myself. There was no cosmetic work: skin sagged from his neck, hair sprouted from his nostrils, snowy stubble matted his jowls and collapsed cheeks.

Did you fill your days? Did you love anyone?

I stared at the swollen nose. It was bulbous—like mine before college boxing flattened it—and purplish, crosshatched with tiny broken vessels.

Did you ever think about me?

". . . like a chunk of pumice. . . ." The voice of the man from the coroner's office buzzed. ". . . enlarged twice normal and severely cirrhotic . . . yellow and fibrous as dry sponge . . . sure as putting a gun to his head, just slower. . . ."

I had a fleeting urge to reach down and lift one of the wrinkled lids. What color were his eyes? Shouldn't a son know?

Burial was expensive. I opted for cremation, my hand shaking as I signed as "nearest surviving relative." I asked where he'd been living. The answer was vague; no address. I went back in for a final look. Beneath the odor of preservatives I imagined his stench rising about me. I turned away and heard the drawer slide in.

So long, Pop.

[6]

Outside, the afternoon heat hung like a force field. I stood uncertainly, swallowing hard, then headed for a liquor store.

Lately the milky light came often. Enveloped in it, confused by it, I seemed to experience multiple dimensions. Without disappearing, things around me receded into the pale haze as distant images and voices swirled to the foreground. Most of them I recognized as my own memories. But not all. The experience was unnerving, sometimes almost terrifying. Drug overload. Or maybe I was going crazy.

The idea of taking Amtrak back had been to give myself time to savor the experience, see the country. But what was to savor? A long look at a corpse? I tilted the pint up. They say drinking runs in families.

The woman across the aisle was staring at me. I leered and winked. She pursed her mouth and looked away. Hell with her. The last of the whiskey slid down. My stomach churned. My vision blurred. I pressed my hands to my eyes. The milkiness was close.

The delay—something about a tie-up outside Toledo—was announced not long after we'd cleared the last dismal suburb and were barreling across open country. I'd been watching the fields rush by ablaze with wildflowers, their beauty a mockery.

The train's rhythm flattened as we slowed. We curved onto a siding and glided to a halt beside a weather-beaten loading dock rising like a low island from a sea of weeds and nettles. Waves of heat radiated from the wooden platform though dusk was settling. Insects swarmed in spirals. The compartment's doors opened with a hiss. A steward announced that we would be held up awhile; we could stretch our legs. I looked around. Nobody seemed eager to leave the air-conditioning. I stood unsteadily. Had to go outside. Had to do something.

My shoes clumped on the long platform. I retreated inside the sounds, tried to focus on the grain of the boards. Sweat filled my armpits. I felt a chill in the thick, heavy heat.

At the far end of the dock a small wooden ticket office stood darkly limned against a glowing backdrop of greenery. Drawing closer, I saw a rusted weather vane tilting from the peak of the roof. Strips of sun-bleached yellow paint curled from the wallboards; cobwebs sagged like nets from the eaves. Somebody had scrawled SUCKO on a square of plywood covering the single window.

"*Daddy?*" *A child's voice; my daughters' faces.*

I walked on, faster.

The rear of the depot looked out on a meadow green from spring rains and bordered by a row of tall sycamores. Near the edge of the platform wild clover exploded in bursts of pinks and whites. From their midst a cacophony of buzzings and dronings suggested that life was indeed very pleasant. If you were a bug.

A wave of dizziness passed over me. I shut my eyes for a moment, a mistake.

"Won't you live with us anymore?" Hope asks, her voice quavering. "Mommy says you won't." I look down at her helplessly. "Daddy?" she urges. Behind her, Susy stares with huge round eyes. "Don't go, Daddy!" she cries suddenly, and rushes to me. I press her in my arms, feel her small shoulders trembling. I struggle to find words that will tell her I don't want to go—never wanted to go.

My eyes burned. For a long moment I didn't know where I was. Shapes moved in a pattern before me. I blinked. Circling in the middle distance, blackbirds played tag in the slanting light, their scarlet wing patches flashing like epaulets as they wheeled and darted over the field.

. . . light glowing on the sallow face . . .

"No!"

I must have said it out loud. The sound reverberated in the evening stillness. My head pulsated. I pressed my hands to my temples and leaned against the depot wall.

"Why do you have to go, Daddy?"

Did he think about me?

"Are you coming home, Daddy?"

I reached into the pocket where the bottle had been. My fingers closed around my watch. I pulled it out and pressed the hidden latch that opened the silveroid case, eyes fixed on it, trying to drive the milkiness back.

Years after losing Grandpa's railroad watch I'd found this one in an antique store. The name P. S. Bartlett inscribed on the works identified it as a model first made in 1857, and its serial number dated it in late '60 or early '61. The seventy-five-dollar price was steep, considering it lacked the key for winding and setting. I paid a locksmith fifty dollars to make a replacement; it came out too modern-looking but did the job. With brass polish I buffed the case to a high sheen and took pleasure that the watch kept perfect time.

But now the hands said six-thirty. Hadn't it been nearly eight before I got off the train? I saw the secondhand not moving in its tiny inset. Funny, I'd wound it that morning. Pulling the key from its hole on the top—where stems were fixed in later models—I fitted it over the winding knob.

At the edge of my vision was a fluttering. Two redwing blackbirds landed on the dock a few yards away. Their wings beat the air, one squawked while touching down, and their feet scratched nervously on the platform.

They were real, not my imagination.

When their wing markings began to vanish, I shook my head to clear my vision, although every detail was registering: the yellow borders of the patches slowly disappeared, then the red centers, leaving both birds completely black.

I stared at them.

Then, soundlessly, still hopping about on the platform, the birds themselves began to grow hazy. They didn't fade, exactly, or dissolve, but seemed to fill and overflow with pale light until the spaces containing them held only the light and nothing more.

The milkiness climbed around me.

Another bird materialized and flew very near my face, a dark fluttering form flashing before me, wings thrashing. It shot past. Then, for a distinct instant, emerging from the white light, I saw a human figure. It was draped in a uniform coat—military, or some kind of conductor's, long and faded, with parallel rows of brass buttons—and one arm was stretched toward me. I thought it was moving, as if in flight, but I couldn't tell whether approaching or receding. In the background, on a hill across a stream or narrow river, a group of people stood in hazy tableau, looking at me.

The world tilted. The sycamores grew smaller. Beyond them the dusk light bronzed and the sky shrank to a narrow band. I clutched at the depot wall but couldn't hang on. The platform rose abruptly and crashed against my face. Blackness engulfed me.

The next thing I knew, pain was pulsing behind my eyes and I couldn't see. I tried to climb to my feet, reaching one knee and falling back again, nauseated. A loud, insistent hissing probed the air somewhere inside or outside my brain. Groping on the platform, my hand encountered the watch and returned it to its pocket.

Gradually the depot wall reappeared, blurred and grainy. I made out the two blackbirds on the platform where they had been, their wing markings again visible. I took a deep breath and touched my face where it felt swollen. My fingers came away bloody.

Moments later I was mystified by the sight of cordwood around me. It was split in three-foot lengths and stacked neatly against the depot, the sawed ends looking fresh cut. Nearby, a loading cart rested on enormous iron-rimmed wheels. Where had that come from? I turned and peered at the wall. The peeling yellow paint was gone, replaced by whitewash. Was I in the same place? I scanned the field. It seemed unchanged. Then I looked again. Had those cornstalks been there? That rail fence? The puddle of water in the foreground?

Suddenly the shapes of the trees looked different and the heat felt stickier.

Then I heard the hissing again, loud and shrill, cutting the air, and I realized with a start that it came from the opposite side of the station.

Christ, I'd forgotten my train!

I struggled to my feet and made my way along the platform. My throbbing head forced me to move slowly. When I reached the front corner of the station, I stopped altogether, transfixed by what I saw.

The silver Amtrak train was gone.

In its place, coming the other way, a black locomotive rumbled slowly toward me, bursts of steam spraying from its skirts. Behind it stretched a line of creaking, swaying wooden coaches. I stared, mute and disbelieving, as it bore down on me. A scarred red cowcatcher curved downward from the swirls of steam. Behind it, a long ebony boiler gleamed like a polished boot. Brasswork glinted on the headlamp—enormous, square, shining in the thickening darkness—and on the elegant bell and myriad pipes and fittings that wound like lace around the boiler. Fragrant hardwood smoke curled from the diamond-shaped tip of the stack. The noise was deafening. I backed up and leaned against the station wall.

The cab passed, the engineer twisting to stare at me from his square window. Behind him came a tender piled high with cordwood like that stacked on the station platform, BALTIMORE & OHIO on the tender's side in block letters.

I tried to make sense of it: a steam locomotive pulling a train out of Currier & Ives. Someone must have spent a fortune restoring it, and yet it looked oddly work worn. The passenger coaches drew near, silhouettes moving inside.

A wispy elderly man in grimy overalls and a striped trainman's cap stepped onto the platform carrying a sputtering lantern.

"Some sort of historical thing?" I asked when he drew near.

"What say?" His eyes were yellow in the lantern glow.

I cocked a thumb at a passing coach. "What's the occasion?"

"Don't follow." He raised the lantern. "Something happen to your cheek?"

"Took a spill," I said. "What's this train about?"

He looked blank. "Just the reg'lar run from Shelby Junction. Stops here for wood 'n' water. Leaving for Cleveland now." He held the lantern at arm's length, scrutinizing me.

"Okay, if you say so. What happened to Amtrak?"

"What?" He frowned, looking down at my pants.

"The Amtrak out of Cleveland—where is it?"

"Ain't nothin' by that name comes through here."

"What do you mean?" My head throbbed. "I was on it."

"I guess you know more about 'er 'n me," he said wryly, "so go ahead—climb back on."

"I can't," I said through clenched teeth. "It's gone. Again I'm asking, where is it?"

"You ain't makin' sense," he said doggedly, shaking his head. "First off, what're you doin' out here, mister?"

"What difference does it make?" I snapped. "I flew into Cleveland this morn—"

"Flew?" he interrupted, eyes narrowing. "You say flew?"

"Yeah, I—" He turned abruptly and strode away, the lantern trailing a pungent paint-thinner odor. I stood dumbly, then pursued him and caught his arm. "What's wrong with you? I'm just—" I caught a lungful of the lantern's acrid fumes as he swung it around. "Jesus Christ, what're you burning in there?"

He struggled to pull away, then stood rigid. "No need to curse me, mister; it's just coal oil." His arm trembled in my hand. "The station's closed up now. I'm the yardman. I got nothin' you want. Please turn me go."

I released him and watched him scuttle around the corner. He looked badly frightened. Coal oil? What the hell was going on? Then I remembered the blood. I probably looked like an ax murderer. Slow down and think, I told myself.

Maybe somebody was making a movie. I didn't see film equipment, but a couple at the far end of the dock looked like costumed actors: he wore a stovepipe hat and swallowtail coat, she a bonnet and long bustled skirt. They were waving to someone on the train.

I started toward them. A voice suddenly boomed over the slow clacking of the wheels. "You! Hullo!"

I looked around.

"Up here!"

He leaned out a window of the last passenger coach and waved in my direction, a straw boater shading his features.

"Hurry up!" he called. "We're pulling out!"

"You talking to me?"

"You out from Cleveland?"

"Yeah."

"We've been waiting for you!"

The cars were gaining speed. I tried to walk faster. "Where'd the other train go?"

"Other train? Next one's in the morning." He waved his arm. "Jump aboard! I've got your ticket! I'll fill you in!"

I hesitated. A train going the wrong way—even this museum

piece—was better than staying here, I decided. With luck I could catch another Amtrak out of Cleveland in the morning. And it was time somebody filled me in.

As I clutched the handrail at the rear of the car and stepped upward, momentum swung me onto the metal steps far faster than I expected. Nausea swept over me for a moment. Pressing hard against the door, I watched cinders from the smokestack wink like fireflies in our wake. There was something familiar in the moonlight silvering the rails and the depot's solitary light receding in the distance; I had a fleeting, déjà vu sense that I had passed this way before.

"Where'd he go?" said a muffled voice inside.

I gathered myself and pushed through the door into a small compartment smelling of kerosene smoke. A sooty lamp glowed dimly on the opposite wall, illuminating a wooden table and chairs, a hat rack, and tarnished brass bowls that I guessed were spittoons.

"Jupiter! I was afraid you'd fallen off!" The man in the straw boater appeared in the opposite doorway. He adjusted a key on the lamp and brightened the compartment. "Here's your ticket."

As I took it he jumped backward. "Hullo, you *did* fall off!"

"Just a scrape." I said, eyeing his wide floppy tie. It and the boater lent him a Fourth of July look. He was in his midthirties, I guessed. He had thinning blond hair and a pudgy face made owlish by round steel-rimmed spectacles. He wore a strangely cut linen coat, badly rumpled, with wet splotches under the arms.

"Expected you in Mansfield proper," he said, wiping his brow. "Which are you—Jacobs or Jones?"

My head pounded in the compartment's stale heat. I could imagine nothing sweeter than lying down. "I'm a little confused," I said. "Who are you?"

"Thought you'd been told," he said officiously. "Millar of the *Commercial.*" He pumped my hand. "I have all you'll need: this afternoon's tallies, all the boys' histories. I confess I haven't started my own piece yet—we're having a little celebration here—but you're welcome to a look-see when I do. Had to play in a field today as Mansfield's new grounds were flooded. Did you get the score off the wire, Mr. . . . ?"

"Fowler."

"That's singular—they said they'd send either Jacobs or Jones." He was looking at me closely. "Where'd you come by that suit? Is that what you wear in Cleveland?"

"Wait a second," I said. "*Who* sent somebody from Cleveland?"

"Why, the *Leader.* You're in their employ, aren't you?"

[12]

"No, I'm . . ." I tried to arrange my thoughts. "I'm with the *Chronicle,* on leave "

"*Cleveland Chronicle?*" he said skeptically.

"No, the *San Francisco Chronicle.*"

His jaw dropped. "San Francisco?"

"Right."

"You came all this way to cover us?"

"Cover you?" I stared at him. "Who *are* you?"

He looked startled.

"Look, I missed my train. Next thing I knew you were yelling at me to climb aboard this relic and saying you'd explain. So let's hear it."

He shook his head. "There's been some mistake, Mr. Fowler," he said. "I'm sorry. May I have the ticket back?"

"As soon as I have an explanation."

He pursed his lips tightly and extended his hand. "Please return it."

"Listen, I've had one hell of a day." I waved at the compartment. "This is all pretty weird, to put it mildly."

He kept his hand extended.

"Talk," I told him.

"You've been drinking," he said abruptly. "I smell it on your breath."

"Millar," I said, taking a step forward, patience gone. "Fill me in—like you said!"

"I'm bringing Mr. Champion in here." He edged back nervously. "He'll know how to deal with you."

The door clicked behind him. I slumped onto one of the chairs and rested my feet on another, too exhausted to worry. The train's jiggling and clacking heightened my overwhelming sense of dislocation. Staring numbly at a tobacco-spattered wall, all I knew for sure was that I was moving. And that I needed desperately to sleep.

"HAPPY BIRTHDAY, ANDY!"

It was shouted by male voices from a distant part of the car. My eyes snapped open. Moments later I heard a single tenor voice.

> *"Oh, once I was happy but now I'm forlorn,*
> *Like an old coat that is tatter'd and torn,*
> *Left in this wide world to fret and to mourn,*
> *Betray'd by a girl in her teens.*
> *The girl that I love she is handsome,*
> *I tried all I could her to please,*
> *But I could not court her so well*
> *As that man on the flying trapeze."*

And the chorus of voices boomed:

[13]

"Oh, he flew through the air with the greatest of ease,
This charming young man on the flying trapeze. . . ."

More verses followed. And more. I drifted off again, only to be awakened by pronounced New York accents just outside the compartment.

"I mean it, Acey, no more."

"Ain't every day you're twenty-three, Andy. Let's celebrate it!"

There was a belch, then laughter.

"We've celebrated plenty. You know the rules. Harry'll bounce us if we're caught out. Tell him, Sweaze."

"Let's chew on it some in the smoker," said a third voice.

I sat up, feeling no better for having dozed. Seeing the first man who entered didn't help matters. Like Millar and the couple at the station, he was dressed for the wrong century.

"Well, how's this!" He stopped short as he saw me. "We got a visitor."

The other two crowded in. They were all well-built, compact men— none topped five nine—with deeply tanned faces. The one who had spoken looked to be in his late twenties, older than the others by a good five years. His hair was glossy black and he sported bushy muttonchop whiskers. The others were smooth shaven and wore high stand-up collars; they looked like they'd stepped from a barbershop quartet poster. They scrutinized me with considerable interest.

"Care if we sit?" Muttonchops asked politely, his dark eyes spaniel soft. There was a hint of the dandy about him, with his striped cravat knotted carefully and a flower peeping from his buttonhole.

I sighed and waved at the chairs, wanting to sleep.

"May we know your name?" asked Muttonchops.

"Sam Fowler."

He nodded in a friendly way, spaniel eyes roving over me. "I'm Asa Brainard." He gestured toward the taller and chunkier of the smooth-faced men. "This gent's Charlie Sweasy."

Though bantam-sized, Sweasy looked like he was constructed of solid slabs, enlarged deltoids swelling his coat, muscular thighs stretching the fabric of his pants. Meatball, I thought. He reminded me of undersized guys I'd known in college who'd pumped themselves up with steroids and lifting. Even Sweasy's bulgy face seemed to strain against the skin. Just now it regarded me with a beady stare. I felt myself disliking him.

"Who fixed yer noggin?" he demanded, thrusting his chin out, head cocked roosterlike. The flat, East Coast tones held a hint of Irish brogue. A gap between his teeth added a sibilant hiss. A cocky little shit, no doubt about it.

"Did it myself," I said shortly, meeting his stare.

"That so?" He studied me. "I'd say it rendered you homely enough to tree a wolf." He laughed, a series of nasal snorts.

Maybe what he wanted, I thought, was a solid boot in the ass.

"Our lad of the hour," Muttonchops/Brainard went on—his whiskers moved as he spoke, little shag rugs rising and falling—raising his voice over Sweasy's snorts and nodding toward the smallest of the three, who grinned at me, looking for all the world like Huck Finn's understudy; his face was splashed with freckles, his hair was carrot red, his eyes green as glass. "Andy Leonard, who's toasting his birthday and his good fortune in collecting no broken fingers today. We're taking a little nip of the rosy. Maybe you'd like to—"

"Acey, there's a curfew!" Andy Leonard broke in.

I studied him curiously, intrigued by some quality about him. His surface boyishness was instantly engaging—a cinch for Most Popular in his graduation class. But something deeper spoke to me from the wide-set green eyes, the forthright gaze, the quick smile. I'd want a brother like him, I thought. The idea pleased me. Huck Finn, my brother.

"—join us," Brainard finished smoothly. "Care for a stogie?" He opened a silver case and displayed a row of fat cigars. "Genuine Conestogas . . . the cash article."

"Don't smoke," I said. "But I could use a drink."

"Very good." With small scissors Brainard snipped the ends from two cigars and turned to Sweasy. "Your phossies handy?"

Sweasy grunted and flexed as he worked a brass match safe from his tight pants. He extracted a wooden match and struck it against the bottom of the cylinder. It was about twice the thickness of a kitchen match and emitted a powerful sulphur odor. Drawing on his cigar, Brainard produced a flask from his jacket and passed it to me. "Not exactly store-bought," he said, "but the finest readily had in Mansfield—although it mayn't do for you."

Sweasy snorted. "Hell, Acey, I saw you buy it off them tramps down at the railroad. Ain't nothin' but forty-rod poison!"

I took a healthy swallow. It bucked and burned down my throat. "What *is* this?" I asked, eyes watering.

"Rye." Brainard grinned. "Gets smoother with practice." He tipped the flask and a gurgling sound followed. Sweasy did the same. Andy hesitated, then followed suit, giggling afterward.

"Now, Sam," said Brainard tentatively, "if you don't mind, I'd like to ask about your garb. I'm a clothes fancier—"

[15]

"That's equal to saying Grant's an army fancier," Sweasy said, emitting another nasal snort.

"—and I'm curious as to where you got your outfit. Can't place it. Ain't exactly a sack cut, though it bears a resemblance. Don't look full enough to take a waistcoat."

"My clothes are fascinating lately," I said. "Which is something, considering what you guys have on."

"Guys?" said Andy Leonard.

"Andy's from Jersey," said Brainard, winking. "Thinks everybody oughta talk like him."

"What's at fault with Jersey?" demanded Sweasy.

"Why, not a single blessed thing," Brainard said, his ironic tone lost on Sweasy, who sat back, mollified. Brainard turned to me. "You were about to say where you came by that suit—and also them hard slippers with no buttons?"

Whatever Muttonchop's act was, he had it down pat. I wondered where it went. "Well, the suit's Brooks Brothers and the loafers are imitation Italian—"

"Eye-talian?" said Sweasy, tensing again.

"Sam's trying to come a dodge on us," said Brainard, shooting me a sly glance. "I was in to Brooks Brothers last winter. They don't make coats with them little lapels or pants with them crimps you got down the front. You claim them duds was cut for you in New York?"

"They're off the rack," I said. "In San Francisco, where I'm from."

"Frisco?" said Brainard. "*Brooks Brothers?*"

"Right. Say, how's the whiskey?" The second slug went down easier. "Thanks," I said. "Now, exactly what in hell are you guys up to?"

"Hey, now, we didn't mean to rile you," Andy broke in, looking worriedly at Sweasy. "We shouldn't even be here. Harry, our captain, wouldn't like it one bit. But we're not up to nothin', honest. We're just ballists headin' to the next town."

"You're what?"

"Ballists," Andy said. "Base ballists."

"Baseball players?"

He nodded. "First nine of the Cincinnati club. Acey pitches, Sweaze fortifies second, I'm generally in left—except today I had to handle Acey's swift ones. The club made a starring tour to the East last year, just like now. Maybe you heard of us." He paused and reflected. "Well, maybe not, out on the Pacific Slope."

"You're pros?" In my weariness I felt a quickening of interest. In earlier, sweeter years, baseball had been my first love.

"Professionals, you mean?" said Brainard.

I nodded.

"You talk funny out in Frisco." Andy grinned at me. "Yep, we're signed on for the whole season. First time it's happened anywhere. Some folks think it ain't right, though, so we don't generally go around puffing ourselves."

"Whose chain are you in again?"

"What?" Sweasy frowned.

"You're minor leaguers, right?"

"What's that?" Sweasy snapped. "Juniors?"

"Don't *sound* like us," Brainard said wryly.

"But the only pro Cincinnati club I know of," I said, "is the Reds."

"Right," said Andy proudly, "we're the ones. Ain't nothin' in the shape of a ball club can lay over us."

"*You* guys play for the *Reds?*"

"Guys," Andy repeated. "That's a dinger!" He laughed. "Some call us Reds, or Red Legs. Most say Red Stockings, though. So you *have* heard about us?"

I shook my head, beginning to wonder if I'd blundered into a carload of loonies. "Look, what's today?"

Sweasy muttered. Brainard's spaniel eyes regarded me brightly, as though I'd introduced a fun guessing game.

"That's easy," said Andy. "June first—my birthday."

"When were you born?"

" 'Forty-six."

Which *was* loony. It would make the kid more than forty, not twenty-three.

"Just what year do you think this is?" I demanded.

He looked at me strangely. " 'Sixty-nine."

My brain seemed to sputter and stop.

"What's the matter?" he asked. "Eighteen sixty-nine. Something wrong with that?"

Eighteen sixty-nine. I looked at their clothes, the kerosene lamp, the spittoons. "Very wrong," I muttered, starting to rise. "Either with me . . . or . . ."

Footsteps sounded outside the door. "All right, Millar, all right," rumbled a deep voice, drawing near. "I'll take care of it. Enough of your pestering."

Andy's face went pale. "Land alive, it's Champion! The game's up! I'm off the nine!"

Brainard reached for the flask on the table, then snatched his hand back as a man's large figure filled the doorway. Stooping, the figure moved purposefully into the compartment and stood before us, blocking the lamplight. I squinted upward. Above the dark suit blazed a pair of pale blue eyes. A Roman nose of impressive proportions was trained upon us. Thick black hair blended into the ceiling shadows. A black goatee looked pasted to the pale skin of the lantern jaw.

"Why are you men here?" he rumbled. The blue eyes flashed past me to fix upon the others. "You were to retire by now."

Slowly, with elaborate nonchalance, Brainard produced a watch. "Why, how the time got away, Mr. Champion," he said blandly. "Sweaze and I were extending Andy our personal felicitations, and then we set to congratulating ourselves on being members of your tip-top nine, and then commenced discoursing with this gent who knew our repute clear out in Frisco, and—"

"Yes, Mr. Asa Brainard, that's all very well." Champion bent ponderously and picked up the flask. A gold chain drooped below his ample stomach. All he needed to model for the old cartoon figure of Plutocracy, I thought, was a vest with dollar signs. Sniffing the flask, he said ominously, "And whose is this?"

There was silence. Andy stared morosely at the floor. Brainard and Sweasy exchanged a glance. Then, in rough unison, they answered, "His."

Grinning malevolently, Sweasy pointed at me.

◇ 2 ◇

Champion's big jaw tightened. Looming over us, he turned slightly, unblocking the lamplight, and I got a good look at him. He was more thick-bodied than fat, probably only in his late thirties, but deep lines edging his eyes and crosshatching his brow made him look older. "Well?" he said, blue eyes boring into mine. "Is that true, sir?" The rumbling voice had a sharp-edged prosecutor's tone I didn't care for.

Andy hung his head like a schoolboy caught by the principal. What the hell, I thought, things couldn't get much crazier.

"It's mine," I said, picking up the flask. "They didn't touch it."

Andy's head rose quickly. Sweasy stared. A smile pulled at Brainard's lips.

"I trust I have your word as a gentleman," Champion said at length, eyeing the blood caked on my face; then, "Millar!"

The plump journalist squeezed in behind him, face twitching. My own White Rabbit, I thought; he'd ushered me into this topsy-turvy world. Then, like Alice, I'd been left on my own. I glanced around the table: Muttonchops, Meatball, Huck. Who were they? Who was this colossal stuffed shirt, Champion?

"Yes, sir?" Millar piped.

"Is this the man?" Champion demanded.

Millar blinked rapidly behind steel-rimmed lenses. "That's him."

Champion swung toward me with almost theatrical quickness. "Sir, would you please account for your presence in this car? And your refusal to return the ticket mistakenly given you?"

Again, the prosecutor's tone. I sighed and explained that I'd collapsed on the station platform and missed my train.

"After taking spirits?" he said pointedly.

"There's more to it," I said, irritated. "But okay, I'd been drinking. Is it a crime?"

He stared at me distastefully.

I felt anger rising. I'd had enough weirdness. I briefly considered hitting something. Very hard.

"I presume you can reimburse us?" he said finally.

"Hell yes!" He seemed to flinch at the words as I stood to reach for my wallet. I must have looked menacing. Champion stepped back with alacrity, looking surprised that I stood as tall as he. The others watched in fascination. He untensed when he saw I wasn't coming for him, then frowned as he noted my unsteadiness.

"Need sleep," I muttered. Seeing his gaze on my Visa card in its plastic sheath, I covered it and handed him two twenties. "That's excessive," he said, then looked closer. "Federal Reserve Note. What is *this?*" He shook his head. "I thought I'd seen every variety of greenback since the war, but these take the cake!"

"Those good in Frisco?" asked Brainard.

"Gold, sir!" Champion said, handing the bills back. "This won't do."

My anger dissolved in weariness. "I don't have anything else." I sat down shakily. "I'm just trying to get back to Cleveland."

At that point Andy said, "There's an empty bunk above me. I'll take it on myself to look out for him."

"He's drunk," Champion said flatly. "I'll not risk our good reputation—"

"I think he's had trouble and feels sickly," Andy said. "He could stand some help."

"I won't allow—" Champion began.

"We can't put him off the train," Andy persisted. "I'll make good his fare."

And that was all I remember. Later I learned that I passed out and pitched face forward from my chair, effectively ending the discussion.

I slept for three days. Andy claimed that my eyes were open when he guided me in and out of train compartments and hotel rooms. But I recall nothing but a succession of vivid dreams. Stephanie figured in a lot of them, as did my girls.

But the best ones were about Grandpa. And me. About things that happened long ago. The dreams took old pictures from my memory and made them live again. . . .

I am beside him on the bleachers at the high school diamond. It is the sun-washed afternoon of my first game. Grandpa wears his khaki windbreaker and his blue legion cap. He has promised me this for weeks. I'm too excited to sit still. Everything before me is wondrous—the grassy field, the infield dirt, the bright uniforms, even the chalked lines of the diamond. I look out at the teenage players warming up as though they are gods. More than anything I want to be one of them, to wear a jersey and spikes, to throw and catch and swing the bat. When they trot past they greet Grandpa respectfully—he supports the team each year—and he introduces me to them. I am shy and enormously proud. "Give a good account of yourselves," Grandpa tells them. "Do the Post proud."

The innings pass. I am entranced by the pop of the ball into gloves, the infielders' chatter, the crack of line drives, the dirt-spilling slides. Already I know that I am in love with the game.

"Will I play for the legion team someday?" I pester Grandpa, wanting his promise that I will be as good, as worthy, as these older boys. Already I sense that certain things will come hard for me. I am moon-faced and hulking, the butt of barbs and jokes at school.

"Could be," Grandpa says, promising nothing—his stock reply.

But afterward he takes me downtown, grasping my hand—the iron-haired man in his sixties linked with the eager boy of seven—as we cross busy streets. He leads me to a sporting-goods store where he buys me a glove and ball. At home he shows me how to oil and mold the pocket. I can't believe the glove is mine. I've never owned anything so valuable.

At dusk we play catch on the front lawn. With each toss he seems younger. He talks of waiting in hushed crowds outside the telegraph office in Philadelphia during crisp autumn afternoons in the century's first years—awaiting inning-by-inning scores of World Series contests pitting his beloved Athletics against McGraw's fearsome Giants and Christy Mathewson, the greatest hurler ever.

Catch and throw. Catch and throw.

"That's a strong arm you've got, Samuel." He is not given to praise. The warmth of his words makes me feel tall and powerful.

"Like Christy Mathewson's?"

"Could be."

Grandma has kept the food warm. "Only damn fools stay out tossing a ball after dark," she informs us. During supper she looks at me with mock sternness. But I detect a glint of something else in her eye as she asks, "Why are you grinning like that?"

That must have been one of the times when Andy claimed I laughed out loud in my sleep.

In my dreams Grandpa read aloud to me again. It could have been any of the nights I was growing up. His voice nasal but firm, his horn-rimmed bifocals in place, reading from Huckleberry Finn or A Connecticut Yankee or Life on the Mississippi—always Mark Twain, his favorite. By the age of ten my mind was filled with jumping frogs and buried treasure and riverboats. By the time I reached high school

Grandpa had read nearly all of Twain's works to me. And by then I'd decided I wanted to be the kind of journalist Twain had been. I'd travel about, composing humorous accounts and satirical sketches that flowed marvelously from my own experience. In the process, of course, becoming wise, rich, and beloved.

It hadn't worked out that way. In J school, at Berkeley, my thesis on Twain's formative years as a reporter won honors. Then I hit the real world and in the next decade encountered precious little in the way of Twainesque romance or riches. I became a second-banana reporter for the *Chronicle*, a major daily newspaper. And there I remained, stuck on an unwanted crime-and-disaster beat. Juicy features went to others while I punched out depressing police-blotter stuff on the green-glowing terminal I detested. The rewrite people duly snuffed individual style—not that I showed a hell of a lot. I was scooped routinely by electronic media. Worst of all, reporters with less experience were promoted over me. I couldn't see that they possessed superior talent. It all hurt. The dream faded.

None of which was Grandpa's fault. Never one to go halfway in important matters, he'd even given me Twain's name. Born James Fowler, Jr., I became Samuel Clemens Fowler on my first birthday. Grandpa made the change some six months after my mother, his daughter, was killed, her car demolished by that of a drunk GI just home from Korea.

My father disappeared with the insurance settlement. He never returned. For the next twenty years—the rest of their lives—my grandparents acted as if he hadn't existed. Grandpa had always wanted a boy to raise. And to name for Twain. When I entered college he offered me the chance to change it back.

I hadn't wanted to.

Something was shaking me. I opened my eyes. "Wake up, Sam." Through a blur I saw somebody with red hair smiling at me. "You're makin' pretty good chin music."

Chin music? I lay in a soft bed, gray light streaming around me. Slowly, picking through jumbled images, I raised my head. "You're Andy, right?"

He grinned. "Big as life and twice as natural."

"Where are we?"

"Rochester."

"Rochester?" I sat up groggily, trying to focus. Grandma and Grandpa had been alive again. It was hard to let that go. "Not Cleveland?"

"We played there," Andy said. "Warmed the Forest Citys."

"Yeah?" Who or what was that?

"Then we went to Buffalo and whipped the Niagras," he said. "You slept the whole time."

Buffalo, I thought, where Twain had set up housekeeping after his marriage. . . .

Andy was watching me. "Everything hunky?"

I pushed back flannel sheets and swung my legs out. My headache was gone, but I felt badly out of sync, weighed down by a fuzzy sensation. It was something like jet lag. But worse.

I looked around. Nearby stood a tall maple wardrobe and a dressing table with a constellation of mirrors. Across the room was a cathedral-shaped cabinet holding an assortment of doors and drawers. Beside it perched a brass spittoon.

"This a hotel?"

Andy nodded. "Congress House, next to the depot. We pulled in last night about nine."

"Where's the bathroom?" I descended to the floor. My balance seemed okay. "Gotta piss six quarts."

"Which d'you want first?" he asked, grinning. "We can bring you a tub—or maybe they got a special room like the highfalutin places—but you ain't fixin' to pee in your bathwater, are you?"

I felt like a tourist. "Where's the john?"

"The joe?" He laughed and produced a chamber pot from the large cabinet. "Ain't no commodes in Frisco?"

I used the pot self-consciously. "Andy, what year did you say this is?"

"Eighteen sixty-nine."

Twain was alive, I thought.

"What's the matter with you, Sam? What year you think? You gone and done a Rip van Winkle?" He laughed hugely, enjoying himself. "Slept through whole years—like you slept through days and nights lately?"

I couldn't help smiling. "Guess I'm a little mixed up."

"Maybe you got amnesia. I've heard as how folks bump their beans and lose track of their past." He looked at me challengingly. "Can you recite yours?"

I considered it—and saw no end of complications. "It doesn't really seem . . . connected to me now."

His face sobered. "Why, I believe that's a prime sign!"

"Anyway, thanks for taking care of me."

"You saved my job," he said emphatically. "Acey's a veteran and Harry needs him, but Harry thought I was too small; I'm only on the nine 'cause Sweaze wouldn't sign without me—see, we've played together since we were kids in Newark. If Champion'd wanted to teach a lesson by letting one of us go, I'd surely be that one." He took my hand and shook it warmly. "You made yourself a true pal, Sam."

There was no hint of self-consciousness in his smile or in the clear green eyes that looked straight into mine. I was warmed and a trifle embarrassed by his directness.

"I'm freezin' for hash!" he said. "How about it?"

"What?"

"Sorry, you got to remind me for a spell that you're . . . you know. What I said was I'm hungry. Want some breakfast?"

I realized suddenly that I was ravenous. I also realized that I had qualms about venturing from that room.

"Is there time to clean up?"

He lent me his straight-edged razor, first honing it on a leather strap, and produced a basin of water from one of the commode's compartments. I saw in a mirror that the blood had been cleaned from my face and a bandage plastered to my cheek. I soaked it off and stared at an angry-looking gash, thinking it odd that I remembered no pain from it.

Ring's Verbena Cream reeked of perfume and produced a thin, bubbly lather. Handling the long blade clumsily, I nicked the edge of the gash and looked around for a styptic pencil. Andy handed me alum to stem the bleeding. Maybe I'd like to splash on some witch hazel, he said, and started out to borrow Brainard's. "You want Acey's macassar oil?" he called from the doorway. "For your hair?"

"Uh, no, I'll pass."

When he was gone I tried to take stock of my situation. Was this another dream? Was I hallucinating? It didn't seem plausible. Andy was real. It all felt real. But if I had actually jumped backward in time, why? And how? Was my old body still on that station dock? Had I died and somehow been reborn here? I recalled the shadowy, beckoning form I'd glimpsed just before passing out. Had that meant something? There must be a rationale to all this, a purpose. If I looked for clues surely I'd figure it out. But the whole thing was scary, like plunging into a void. Even with Andy's help, how was I going to cope?

As I gingerly scraped the razor over my face, I puzzled over a strange sense of familiarity—then remembered Grandpa attacking his whiskers with his old ivory-handled razor while singing his World War I songs. I felt closer to him and Grandma than I had in years. Why? The dreams? But if this were actually happening, then I'd landed in a time before Grandma and Grandpa were born. Was it possible for me to exist before they had?

I rinsed the lather away and stared at my image. Apart from the gash and considerable puffiness around my eyes, I didn't look different. The eyes actually seemed clearer. More than forty-eight hours without booze. When was the last time that happened? So far my brain was free of the milkiness.

Free . . . was I? Had I jettisoned everything, even my daughters? Had I been catapulted into another existence?

A train whistle sounded in the distance. Stepping to the window, I looked out into an air shaft topped by a rectangle of overcast sky. I heard a jumble of indistinguishable sounds. Could it really be 1869 outside? The Civil War, I remembered, had ended in 1865. Lincoln was dead, Reconstruction in progress. Who would be in office now? Grant? And in England, Victoria?

Incredible.

I sat in an upholstered chair on which flowers competed with the denser floral designs on the wallpaper. In the past—the future—I'd enjoyed novels and films about time travel. I looked around the room. Somehow I'd imagined the light of an earlier time as being softer, tinted perhaps, as in old photographs. But this looked like any other. How could a June morning in 1869 be so . . . ordinary? I took out my watch and opened it, wondering how late I'd slept—and saw with sorrow that the glass face was cracked and the key missing.

Andy burst in. "Here!" he said, thrusting a bottle at me. "Hurry! They'll eat everything!"

The witch hazel stung my face, its sharp aroma reminding me of the barbershop where Grandpa used to get his hair trimmed.

"You looked like the blue devils had you when I came in," Andy said.

"My watch key's missing. It must have fallen out on that station dock."

"Outside of Mansfield?"

"Yeah, I guess so."

"Hmm, that's curious, Sam. Happens I found one on the ball grounds in Mansfield that very day, in the grass behind home plate. Stuck it in my uniform for luck, on account of it being my birthday an' all." He pulled his white uniform pants from a traveling bag and unbuttoned a small pocket. "I believe it accounted for my home run yesterday—only one we got against the Niagras. I knocked that ball damn near into Lake Erie!" He laughed. "Harry was on third. You should've seen his eyes bug. Here, see if this'll work in your timepiece."

It was small and silver, and its oval grip felt good. It fit the winding knob easily. After a few turns the watch begin to tick. I slid the key snugly into the hole on top.

[25]

"Looks like you got your missing part," Andy said. "If it ain't the original, it's a close match."

I held it out. "I can't keep your lucky piece."

He pushed my hand away. "Don't it strike you queer that you'd have the watch and I'd have the key?" He looked at me quizzically. "Tell the truth."

"Yes, it is queer," I agreed. "Trouble is, *everything's* queer."

He put his hand on my shoulder. "It's awful how things stand for you, Sam. Look, you hold on to that key. It'll bring me luck, long as you're around." He scratched an ear, reflecting. "Want to know somethin' else curious? I had a notion even back on that train that you 'n' me were drawn together special—that you were *supposed* to help me out of that fix, same as I was to look out for you. Ain't that a dinger? D'you feel it too?"

I hesitated, embarrassed again. "When I first woke up, I thought you were my brother. Which is weird, since I never had one."

"I've got sisters," he said. "Wouldn't it be grand to have a brother?"

We looked at each other.

"C'mon, friend Sam, let's eat!" He whooped and steered me toward the door.

In the long dining room downstairs, black waiters in gold jackets cleared dishes and delivered trays to a dozen tables. I recognized Sweasy among a group sitting at one.

Andy halted behind a muscular young man with a shock of bushy hair who was bent over a *New York Tribune*. Looking curiously over his shoulder, I saw that the articles carried no banner headlines but merely one-column captions. I made out CUBAN REVOLUTION, and, next to it:

THE INDIANS
Continuation of the Outrages in Kansas—
A Panic Among the Settlers.

"This is George Wright," Andy said. The young man looked up, displaying a prominent hawk nose and white teeth that flashed in a grin. He immediately put me in mind of a very young Joe Namath: cocky, likable, all-jock, probably had to fight women off.

"How'dya do," he said pleasantly, accent heavily New Yorkese. He seemed to take my presence for granted.

We shook hands. I nodded at his paper. "What's that about Indians?"

"Nothing new," he replied. "The usual depredations."

In Kansas?

"I've a pal in the army," George Wright said. "Says you newspaper fellers puff the frontier, make up them bloody tales. I guess you'd know about that."

So Millar had told them I was a reporter. "Your friend's probably got a point," I said.

"Figured so." He flashed the Namath grin again, then his attention shifted. "Say, pass those battercakes!"

"George is the country's kingpin ballist," Andy said as we moved toward two vacant chairs at the crowded table. "His older brother Harry talked Champion into paying George top money to play for us. Nearly two thousand dollars! I guess it riled Acey some, but we're lucky to have George at any price."

Two thousand didn't seem very much, I thought.

"I see he even scrubbed the blood outen your shirt," a sibilant voice rasped as we were about to sit. "You've about turned my partner into a nursemaid!"

I looked into the unfriendly eyes of Charlie Sweasy. He had risen from his chair and stood rocking on his feet, flexing his shoulders. A prize meatball.

"Wasn't no job to wash the shirt," Andy said; then, quickly, "I told Sam about us comin' up together in Newark, Sweaze."

Sweasy's eyes bored into me as if checking for weaknesses. I felt myself tensing. It was amazing how fast this little guy pushed my buttons.

"I'm goin' by," Sweasy said, shoving abruptly past me into the aisle.

"Your buddy's a sweetheart," I told Andy.

"Sweaze gets in a pucker sometimes, but he'll come around square, you'll see. Here, meet Dick Hurley." Andy gestured to a sad-eyed, droopy-mustached individual just rising to leave. His dark hair was parted in the center. If Hurley's face were paler, he'd have looked remarkably like Edgar Allan Poe, I thought. The same haunted quality in the dark eyes.

"Shhhh." Hurley dramatically raised a finger to his lips. His eyes were bloodshot; a solitary coffee cup sat before him. " 'Sit patiently and inly ruminate the morning's danger.' "

"What?" I said, startled.

" 'So many horrid ghosts,' " he intoned. " 'O now' "—he tilted the finger so it pointed at a man farther down the table—" 'behold the royal captain of this ruin'd band. . . .' "

He was quoting, but I had no idea what. Maybe Hurley thought he *was* Poe. In my present state I didn't appreciate it. Things were disjointed enough. "Okay, I give," I said. "What're you doing?"

Hurley looked smug, as if my ignorance were no surprise. "*Henry the Fifth."* The bloodshot eyes held mine for a moment, then again he pointed. I turned and saw a well-built, handsome, bearded man reading a letter several places down, opposite Millar and Champion. "But soft," whispered Hurley, "there ruminates noble Harry himself." With that he walked away.

"Dick's a study in waking up," Andy said.

"He always quote Shakespeare first thing?"

"Like as not. He's smart as a whip, took his university course at Columbia. He can recite for hours. Sweaze says he's just showing himself, but I think it's like music." He lowered his voice. "Trouble is, most nights Dick drinks an awful lot."

Andy turned to the man Hurley had indicated. He was now folding his letter into an envelope bearing a three-cent stamp. "From Carrie?" asked Andy.

He looked up and nodded. He was older and more rugged-looking than the other players. Chestnut hair and whiskers framed the chiseled planes of his face, which looked made of brown stone. But striking among his features were his eyes: soft deer-brown orbs with startling depths, incongruous in the strong face.

"It arrived this morning," he said. "She inquires particularly about you, Andy. Says she longs to hear you singing in our parlor again."

"Your missus is a peach, Harry. Hope I find one like her. Sam Fowler, meet Harry Wright, our captain."

He rose and we shook hands.

"He's a big 'un, ain't he, Harry? Got some use for a change first baseman?"

I would learn that "change" meant "backup" or "relief." Wright appeared to consider Andy's suggestion seriously, though he had been joking. "Have you played the game?" The quiet voice carried faint British accents.

I was impressed by his calm authority. And by a sense of integrity in the wise brown eyes that seemed to promise he would recognize and respect one's best qualities. I found myself wanting to earn the man's respect right away. Andy said later that Harry affected almost everybody that way.

"I did play a little ball," I said cautiously. "Years ago."

They both immediately glanced at my hands. Wright smiled. "Years indeed. Andy tells me you're from Frisco. Do you know the Shepard brothers?"

"Uh, I don't think so."

"I played with them on the Knicks before they went west."

Was he putting me on? "The Knicks?"

"Knickerbocker Club, New York. I understand the Shepards established the Pacifics in your city. Is it a sound sporting club?"

"I . . . didn't play at that level." I saw no point in relating that my high school and legion games took place almost exactly a century in the future.

"If you care to accompany us to the grounds this afternoon," Wright said, "I'll arrange a seat at the scoring table. Mr. Millar can answer your questions."

Millar nodded glumly across the table, clearly not overjoyed by the assignment. But next to him Champion was beaming.

"Our California visitor," Champion rumbled, "can thus report our hospitality as well as our sporting deeds."

No talk of drunkards now, I reflected. Not when old Stuffed Shirt thought he was dealing with the press.

"Thanks." I looked at Millar. "I'll probably have thousands of questions."

The breakfast we sat down to was the most amazing of my life. Bowls of porridge similar to oatmeal were served with fresh strawberries and thick cream. Then platters of steaks, eggs, fried potatoes, and hot biscuits. Then more platters of buckwheat cakes and fried bread. And still more heaped with thick slices of pie. They kept coming, overlapping, so that you could finish the pie and start all over again with porridge if you wished—and were able. I thought I was a big eater, but when I finally leaned back, Andy was reaching for another steak.

"Don't you have to play a game today?"

He laughed and wielded his knife. "Not till three."

"What happens in the meantime?"

"Well, the Alerts—they're the Rochester club—offered to drive us around to see the sights, but with the weather bein' what it is, I doubt many of the boys'll turn out." He glanced up. "Well, if it ain't ol' Acey and Innocent Fred."

I followed his gaze and saw Brainard approaching with a stocky, barrel-chested man whose bowed legs gave him a rolling gait. Brainard was a picture of elegance in a blue cutaway coat with satin lapels, plaid waistcoat, and tapered gray trousers. A carnation graced his lapel. His jet hair and whiskers gleamed with oil.

"Top o' the day, Sam." He sat opposite me, dark spaniel eyes friendly, as casual as if we breakfasted together every morning. "This is my sidekick, Fred Waterman."

Waterman's high balding forehead and bland expression gave him the unctuous quality of a church deacon. But his eyes glinted with devilish humor as we shook hands. He must have heard about the flask.

"What position you play?" I asked.

"Third sack." His handlebar mustache moved with the words. "Some at change catcher—though Andy can have that." He grinned, revealing tobacco-stained teeth. His gaze traveled slowly over my suit.

My fuzziness was by no means gone, and his scrutiny bothered me. For a moment I toyed with the notion of simply blurting out that I was from another century and needed their help. But what could they do? They'd doubtless figure I was demented anyway. And back here, I remembered, crazy people were thrown into hellhole sanatoriums.

"Do you suppose," I asked Andy as the others loaded their plates, "you could loan me enough to buy some clothes?"

"You bet," he said with no hesitation. "How about Acey helping fit you out? He always cuts a dash."

"Sure, if he wants."

"Whadaya say, Acey? Freddy?"

Waterman shook his head. "That's Acey's territory."

Brainard considered. "Don't care if I do," he offered, which turned out to mean "count me in." He appraised me. "I think I know just the place."

"Not too high-toned," Andy warned. "All of us ain't in the dimes."

"Pinchpenny ne'er served any," Brainard countered. "A true gent ain't gonna stint on his appearance."

"That's a soft snap for you, Acey, with your fat star salary."

"Maybe we should forget it," I said.

"Don't let him squeeze our scheme," Brainard said, as if the idea had been his. "The way Andy kicks you'd think he was on his case note. I'll pitch in if the cost gets steep." He looked at me shrewdly. "Besides, you figure to pay us back, don't you?"

"Certainly," I said. And wondered how.

"I got a hunch about you, Sam," he said as we walked out through the lobby, where a number of men sat smoking cigars and reading newspapers on horsehide divans. "Can't say why, but I think our little investment will pay off."

"I've felt that about Sam right along," said Andy.

"I hope I don't let you d—" My words were lost as I stepped through the front doors and was assaulted by the street. My first impressions were of swarming people and animals and conveyances. Water standing in puddles from earlier showers was sprayed in slicing arcs by passing vehicles. I saw a woman gazing mournfully at the mud-coated hem of her long dress.

Noise resounded everywhere—a din of yelling voices, clopping hooves, rattling iron-rimmed carriage wheels clanking and skittering over the wet cobblestones. From the nearby train house emanated rumblings and belches. Opposite us stood a brick building bearing a large sign.

CENTRAL MILLS
FLOUR & FEED

Shrieks of heavy grinding machinery sounded inside. The air around us was awash with whitish particles. I had trouble drawing a deep breath.

"What is this stuff?"

"Wheat dust," Andy yelled. "Rochester's called the Flour City, you know."

The air was cleaner on Front Street, where we walked along the Genesee. Barges rode the green channel and smoke poured from funnels of river freighters. I couldn't see how so many churning craft avoided colliding. A chorus of bells and horns reached our ears. Along the docks stevedores swore and shouted, swarming over drays and wagons and carts, while teamsters cracked their long whips over the backs of horses and mules.

"Busy place," I said.

"Thing's 're boomin' along the canal, too," Andy said. "It comes into the Genesee just a few squares down."

We turned up from the river toward the commercial district. The brick sidewalks ended. I stepped around muddy puddles and piles of manure. Stenches worked the thick air. Garbage lay in stinking heaps before buildings, hogs and chickens picking through it. The morning was humid but fairly cool. I wondered what olfactory assaults hot weather would bring.

"This place is filthy," I said.

Andy looked surprised. "Air's a sight better here than in Smoky City."

"Smoky City?"

"Cincinnati."

"You're sayin' Frisco's clean?" Brainard said.

I pictured lower Market. "No, but these hogs . . ."

"Hogs eat slops," Andy said. "Clean the streets."

So much for that. The enormous distance between us was once again borne upon me. What was I doing here?

At length Brainard found the tailor he had in mind. There I spent what seemed hours holding up bolts of material while Brainard cocked his head and muttered, "Can't see it, let's try another." Finally we agreed on tan broadcloth for a daytime suit, to include a frock coat, and another of dark English wool, with tails, for evening.

"Have them done up today," Brainard told the tailor. "We leave on the night train."

"Two dollars extra," the tailor said. "Forty-six in all."

"Here's five eagles," said Brainard, glancing at the gold coins Andy handed him. "Keep the change." He chuckled at Andy's indignant look.

I was amazed. Less than fifty bucks for two suits. With waistcoats and vests, tailor-made in hours!

We boarded a green horse-drawn car to return to the hotel. Inside were benches for about twenty passengers. A wood stove in the rear had been lit earlier and still trailed wisps of smoke. Because of the wet streets, straw had been spread on the floor for safer footing. A strong animal odor rose from it.

"What's that smell?" I asked.

The glance they exchanged suggested I lacked some fundamental marbles. "It's a mild concatenation," Brainard said, adjusting his carnation, "of odoriferous effluvia."

"Say what?"

"Horseshit."

Andy explained that as manure dried, the resulting dust was impossible to sweep from cobblestones. After rains, the straw in public vehicles became permeated with it, therefore smelling like horse stalls.

"I never would have thought of that," I said.

"I suppose Frisco's got smooth paving everywhere," Brainard said sarcastically.

His tone irritated me. "Damn right it does!"

— ◇ 3 ◇ —

After a snack and nap at the Congress House, Andy bounded out of bed and stretched. Seeing his compact body ridged with muscle, I realized I hadn't been in decent shape in years. He pulled on bright red leggings over shins scarred from spike wounds and adjusted elastic bands at the bottom of his pants just below the knees. Except for the scarlet C scripted on the jersey, the uniform was solid white. He cinched up his wide leather belt and pulled on a white linen jockey cap. Then, holding a pair of high-topped calfskin shoes on which he'd screwed brass spikes, he stood in the middle of the room poised like a gymnast. His green eyes sparkled.

"The ladies are some for our uniform," he said, grinning. "It's a rouser."

Except for the heavy material and the jersey's pointed lapels and long cuffed sleeves, it looked pretty standard to me.

"What about it gets to the ladies?" I said.

"Why, the new knickers and stockings." He pointed to his legs. "Up to last year nobody'd seen the like. Harry says they used to call him the 'Bearded Boy in Bloomers' and 'Captain of the Bloody Calves.' But this year the Cleveland club's already out in blue stockings, and I hear the Mutuals might switch over. You're travelin' with the Beau Brummells of baseball!"

I smiled as he cracked up at his own wit. "Let me get this straight," I said. "You guys are the first to wear baseball pants and colored sox?"

"That's what I'm saying—what everybody knows." He shook his head. "Sometimes you're *way* out of touch, Sam."

I couldn't deny it. "Are you in a league? With a regular schedule?"

"No, Harry and the other captains jaw about it, but right now there's just the association—the National Association of Base Ball Players. It meets every winter to set the rules. This is the first year it's allowed all-professional clubs."

"And you're one," I said.

"We're the *only!* The rest split up their gates and pretend they're still amateurs. Shoot, everybody's known for years that the top stars— like George Wright, or Al Reach of the Athletics—got paid on the sly. Ask George, he'll tell you he's never worked a lick outside of ball."

I thought I heard a note of envy. "So you're all under contract?"

"That's right, signed on back before the season begun. All out in the open. Harry and George get the most, of course. Acey and Fred make out pretty good, and so on down to Mac, Hurley, Sweaze, and me—the new ones."

"Who's Mac?"

"Cal McVey, our kid right fielder. You'll meet him. Anyhow, Mrs. Leonard's boy Andrew ain't chuckleheaded. I signed on for seven hundred dollars, and I'm happy as pie. Without this, I'd be sweating in some factory."

I had a troubling thought. "How long's your season?"

"April fifteenth to November fifteenth. Why?"

Seven months. He earned only twenty-five dollars a week. My suits cost half a month's wages. Good grief.

"Nobody's kicking about my play either." Andy looked at me defiantly, his voice rising. "I may be small, but I cover my field good as any man, and if it's pluck that—"

A knock came, then Harry Wright's calm voice. "Coaches are here."

"I'm for it!" Andy yelled, springing for the door.

Six small carriages drawn by pairs of matched horses were lined in front. Liveried drivers perched on tiny seats above upholstered passenger benches. The tops were folded down, leaving the shallow compartments open to the sky, which showed dark cloud masses building in the west.

I wanted to ride with Andy, but Millar guided me to the rear carriage where Champion waited with the Alerts' officials— bewhiskered burghers who stared at my clothes—and we set off clopping and bumping and rattling up State Street.

The ride was rougher than any auto's. A sense of unreality overcame me again as I looked out at vendors pushing carts and shopkeepers staring from doorways and a welter of bell-ringing claxon-sounding vehicles—including several odd-looking wooden bicycles— that swarmed around us in no pattern I could discern. People were waving gaily to us. The cheery atmosphere put me in mind of a sailing regatta—and then I was seized by the wonder of it all: it was Friday,

June 4, 1869! I was riding by open carriage through Rochester, going to see America's first pro ball players!

Shouts went up: "The Cincinnatis! The Red Stockings!" People thronged the sidewalks. The players waved to them, their uniforms bright splashes of color in the gray afternoon; they grinned at the shouts and taunts of boys in ragged knickers who chased them barefoot through the streets.

I felt a little like a boy myself as we passed the white-foaming falls in the Genesee and angled left past Brown's Race. As the river's noise faded I thought I heard singing.

"Team song," said Millar. "Each player has a verse. Listen, they're starting Harry's."

> *"Our captain is a goodly man,*
> *And 'Harry' is his name.*
> *Whate'er he does is always 'Wright,'*
> *So says the voice of fame.*
> *And as the leader of our nine*
> *We think he can't be beat,*
> *For in many a fight old Harry Wright*
> *Has saved us from defeat."*

They broke into a booming chorus:

> *"Hurrah, hurrah,*
> *For the noble game hurrah!*
> *Red Stockings all will toss the ball*
> *And shout our loud hurrah!"*

"Singing on their way to play ball," I said. "Amazing!"

"No more so," Champion said defensively, "than men singing on their way to battle."

He had a point. It *wasn't* more amazing than that.

Our passage slowed as we entered Jones Square, a block-long public park lined with elms, and crowds pressed around us. I craned my neck to see the diamond.

"How many?" Champion said suddenly.

Millar said he guessed about three thousand.

Champion glanced nervously at the storm clouds. "Another Yellow Springs and we're in deep."

Millar explained that the tour's opener against Antioch College, four days earlier, had been rained out—posing a problem since gate receipts had to meet travel costs.

"You don't have enough to cover rainouts?" I said.

"The truth is we're vastly in debt," Champion replied. "We've borrowed against future receipts to pay the ballists while they trained. We plunged thousands into erecting a new clubhouse and stands. If this tour fails, it will spell disaster."

"Our grounds are the finest in the country," Millar asserted.

"And doubtless the most expensive," Champion said. "The lease alone costs two thousand a year."

I nodded gravely; newsman on his job.

"But beyond those concerns, Mr. Fowler, is the larger issue of whether the national game can succeed as a profession."

"You've got to be kidding," I said.

"That phrase is unfamiliar," Champion said, a bit huffily. "As you may know, baseball with standard rules was developed by gentlemen's sporting clubs only several decades ago. The old amateurs did all they could to keep control of their game. But its popularity during the war weakened their control, and a newer element—sharps and their ilk—brought drunkenness, brawling, and wagering to contests, the very things the old clubs feared. Of late, matches have been deliberately thrown off by players in the hold of gamblers. The game's integrity is in grave question."

"Where do the Red Stockings fit in?" I asked.

Champion smiled wanly. "So far, it appears that we threaten both amateurs and gamblers—the latter because salaried ballists are harder to bribe."

I nodded, wondering how much he was overdramatizing.

"We are a novel experiment, Mr. Fowler. People, some of them unscrupulous, are watching us carefully to see whether the national game can be put on an honest business footing. That is why our men must give their very noblest performance at all times. They must be incorruptible—"

He looked at me.

"—and sober."

I got the point.

"Don't worry, baseball will survive," I told him, mindful of my era's enormous stadia, fawning media coverage, and millionaire players.

"Your assurance is gratifying," he said tartly.

On a field still wet from the early downpour the Alerts warmed up, moving crisply in white uniforms with long pants bearing navy stripes that matched their flat Civil War–style caps; each tunic was emblazoned with a red A. Using both hands, they seemed to catch the ball as effortlessly and painlessly as if they wore gloves. How could they do that?

"They look good," I said to Millar. "What are our chances?"

"*Our?*" He gave me a pained look. "We've won all six of our matches so far—three at home and three on tour—and should take this one. The Alerts are veterans, but this is only their opening game. Still, they'll want to be the first eastern club to topple us."

We had been surrounded by working-class males of all ages in shapeless pants and collarless shirts. I'd seen no women among them. Closer to the diamond, things began to change. On the arms of men dressed more or less like Brainard—"swells," Millar called them—women glided demurely, faces blurred by veils on tiny hats, torsos encased in rich, heavy, elaborate, bustled dresses; scarves fluttered about their necks, and their gloved hands brandished parasols with practiced ease.

I stared at them, fascinated. They looked formidable, mysterious, utterly unapproachable—and desirable. Were Victorian women as repressed as they'd been made out? A fact-finding mission seemed called for. My brain concocted erotic fantasies. Even though I was still disoriented, I was undeniably horny.

The ladies took seats with their escorts in a covered stand behind home plate. Officials herded other spectators toward what Millar called the "bull pens," roped-off sections behind the foul lines where men stood shoulder to shoulder. Ringing the outfield behind a low fence were horse-drawn vehicles ranging from carts to omnibuses.

I sat between Millar and Hurley at a long table outside the first-base line. Hurley, the team's sole substitute and keeper of the score book, looked a bit healthier than he had that morning at breakfast.

A crescendo of admiring oohs began to rise from the crowd. In the center of the diamond, four Stockings—Andy, Sweasy, Waterman, and George Wright—stood tossing a ball rapidly among themselves. It reminded me of a Harlem Globetrotter warm-up routine. The ball blurred behind their backs, around their heads, over their shoulders, under their legs, the four of them feinting, stretching, diving, laughing at their own sleight of hand, urged on by the crowd's response: applause, delighted cries, and finally full-throated roars as George Wright capped the exhibition by hurling the ball straight overhead, higher than it seemed a ball could be thrown. He stood nonchalantly under it until the last possible instant, when, with no other movement, he cupped his bare hands and made a basket catch, waved the ball aloft with a flourish, and, joined by the others, followed it downward in a sweeping bow.

The crowd ate it up. So did I.

"Not bad, I'm thinkin', for country-club lads," said a loud voice edged with Irish brogue. "Sure an' it's a fact, two of the four tricksters sprang from the very soil of the Emerald Isle!"

I looked around and saw a tall, hatless, smooth-shaven man approaching. He was almost handsome in a bluff way, with thinning red hair and the beginning of a paunch.

"Uh-oh," muttered Millar.

"Who's he?" I asked.

"Red Jim McDermott," said Millar. "A sharp, one of Morrissey's crowd."

I pondered that as I scrutinized him. A pair of calculating baby-blue eyes belied the jovial smile.

" . . . the same country lads that just thrashed the poor Niagras sevenfold, forty-two to six, in but seven innings!" McDermott guffawed to the Rochester reporters at the other end of the table. His style seemed to lie in delivering pronouncements at top volume, then looking around shrewdly to check reactions. His tone suggested that we were brothers in a fraternity of greed. "Worst drubbing in Buffalo ever—and by these same western eclectics, for the love of Jaysus and Mary." His glance swept over us.

"Our boys play a lively fielding game," a Rochester reporter argued. "They won't drub us."

"Well, now," said McDermott, "the pool-selling lads appear to agree. They've set the scoring at only three to two, Reds."

"That so?" said the reporter, rising and starting for the third-base side. "Then I'm getting in now."

"And what d'ya Ohio lads think?" McDermott faced Millar. A diamond pin twinkled on his shirtfront. "You set for a tussle?"

"We'll play our hardest," Millar said shortly.

McDermott smirked. "There's some think one or two might throw off a little today."

Millar stiffened. "By Jupiter, we'll give a square account. Our boys aren't corruptible . . . like some."

"Sure, an' I'm a wee angel meself to believe it." McDermott guffawed and looked around for support. "You're tellin' me Acey Brainard's not placed a wager in his life? Nor taken a man's honest earnings in a billiard parlor?"

"Go ahead and bet your money," Millar said. "It's not our concern."

"Well, it's a blunt thing to be saying." McDermott's smile faded as he leaned down and stared into Millar's eyes. "But that's exactly what I intend—and my money sure as hell won't be on you."

He straightened and moved away slowly.

"What was all that about?" I asked.

Millar let his breath out. "Last year I wrote about McDermott and his ilk's control of sporting events. The *Clipper* reprinted it in New York. I'm not his favorite."

"What was that three-to-two stuff?"

"He's betting we won't outscore the Alerts by a ratio of three runs to two." Millar's pudgy jaw tightened. "I hope we lay all over 'em. I hope that loudmouthed mick loses his shirt!"

I regarded him with new interest. I was about to ask how gamblers could operate so openly when the crowd stirred. Harry Wright and the Alert captain had selected an umpire, a respected local player. The contest was about to begin.

I was surprised to learn that the visiting club didn't automatically bat first. Instead, the winner of a coin toss decided. But, since nobody had thought to bring a coin, the umpire finally spat on a flat stone, flipped it in the air, and pointed to Harry. "Dry!" called Harry. It landed wet side up. The Alerts chose the field.

I've watched hundreds of baseball games, but I'd never seen anything like what followed. I suppose I'd thought of old-timers as smaller, less-skilled, even comical versions of their twentieth-century counterparts. I began to get a different impression as the first inning unfolded.

George Wright marched up to home plate—an actual iron plate, painted white—and grinned cockily at the Alerts' pitcher. He dug in, waved his bat ("grasped the ash," Millar would write later), and called, "Low!"

"What's he saying?" I asked.

"George wants it between his knees and belt."

"You mean he *calls* his pitch?"

"Of course. 'High' would mean belt to shoulders." He explained that if the ball didn't pass through the designated zone, the umpire would warn the pitcher and begin calling balls. The batter (Millar said "striker") took first after three called balls, or four in all. Strikes worked the same way, with the hitter first warned, then allowed three more.

There was no pitcher's mound. The Rochester hurler, his sleeve rolled to reveal a brawny pitching arm, stood poised inside a four-by-six chalked box only forty-five feet from home, instead of the sixty feet six inches I was used to. He wound up elaborately, holding the ball over his head statuelike, then dipping into a submarine delivery much like a softball pitcher's. The new ball flashed in a barely discernible blur over the short distance. George swung and lofted a foul. The catcher, without shin guards, chest protector, mask, or mitt, was stationed a good forty feet back. The ball hit the turf far beyond his reach, but he hurled himself in a futile dive.

"Hustle's fine," I said. "But that's ridiculous."

Hurley turned and gave me a funny look. He said dryly, "Foul bounds are out." Which turned out to mean any foul caught on the first bounce. Crazy rules, I thought.

"What's the story on their pitcher?" I asked Hurley.

"He's some swift," Hurley said appreciatively. "But we fatten on swift tossing."

"No, I mean why doesn't he come in overhand?"

Again he looked at me oddly. "That's throwing, not pitching."

Millar explained that according to the rules, a pitcher's hand couldn't rise above his waist during the delivery, with no twists of wrist or fingers allowed.

Which would mean no breaking balls. It didn't take a genius to see that with those restrictions, plus hitters getting four strikes and calling their pitches, this was a wildly offensive version of the game.

There was a sharp *whack!* as George lined a ball into the left-center gap.

"He'll make his third," Millar said, as George rounded first with impressive speed. But the Alerts played the ball promptly and held him to a double.

"They're pretty quick out there," I said.

"The wet grass slowed the ball," Hurley said. "Wait'll you see Andy run, if it's quick you want."

George, still grinning, stole third on the next pitch with a dirt-spilling hook slide as smoothly modern as any I'd ever seen. He scored moments later on a sacrifice fly that the center fielder juggled and nearly dropped.

"Aren't there a lot of errors using just your bare hands?" I asked Hurley.

"What else'd we use?" he said. "George stunts with his cap sometimes, that what you have in mind?" He gave me the look again. "I thought Andy said you'd *played.*"

"Muffs are a natural element of the game," Millar said pontifically. "Even Harry makes a few."

At that moment, as if to demonstrate the point, the Alerts' left fielder dropped Waterman's lazy fly. The stocky Red Stocking then stole second and third, his bowed legs churning with surprising quickness, and scored on a fly before Harry grounded into the third out.

I tracked the Stockings I knew as they took their positions: Andy sprinting to left as if he feared being late; Harry jogging to center with casual grace; Waterman straddling third, hands on hips, cheek bulging and mustache tilted by an enormous chaw; George tossing pebbles at shortstop; Sweasy crouching near second, making shrill sounds and spitting through the gap in his teeth.

Brainard sauntered to the pitching box with a toothpick dangling from his lip and made a single warm-up toss to the Stocking catcher. He used a corkscrew motion in which his left leg twisted in front of his right, rocked back, and then came forward as his arm whipped from behind his back with impressive velocity. His follow-through, a series of dancing steps, took him to the very front of the box. The ball blurred to the plate even faster than the Rochester hurler's had.

Millar informed me that Brainard had broken in as an outfielder with the old Excelsiors and also had played second base for several New York and Washington clubs before coming to Cincinnati. As a change pitcher he hadn't been particularly effective until the end of last season, when he'd learned to control the "chain lightnings" that made a formidable counterpoint to Harry's "slow twisters." Now Brainard was the team's starter and recognized as one of the country's best.

The Alerts' leadoff man topped a dribbler that Sweasy couldn't charge fast enough to play. I watched Hurley enter a tally by his name in the "Slow Handling" column under ERRORS IN FIELDING. The sophistication of the score book amazed me. Symbols existed for everything—including K's for strikeouts.

After an out, the third hitter blooped a single over Waterman to left. Andy sprinted in with remarkable speed—Hurley was right, he could *move*—to contain the runners. But the next Alert squibbed a soft fly behind first, which the Stockings' tall blond first baseman lumbered after and muffed badly. Both runners scored, the batter reaching second. Millar looked glum. Hurley muttered.

Brainard's next pitch seemed to have less velocity. The Alert striker poised and whipped his bat. There was a resounding *tock!*

"Oh blazes!" Millar groaned. The ball soared and grew small in the darkening sky.

Harry Wright had turned and was sprinting over the grass, back to the diamond. As he bore down on the waist-high rail fence bordering the outfield, spectators spilled from vehicles behind. I held my breath, fearing he'd hit it headlong. A step from the fence Harry took the ball over his shoulder and swiveled at the same instant; scissoring his legs high, he vaulted the fence as easily as a boy going over a hydrant. I could hardly believe what I'd seen. The crowd applauded him as he climbed back onto the field. He tipped his cap and threw the ball in, making it all look nonchalant.

The score was 2–2 after one inning. The Rochester reporters

seemed excited. So did the crowd. The favored Stockings were vulnerable after all. Across the way the pool sellers, having done extensive business at the three-to-two ratio, were now taking even money on the Alerts.

With the sky overhead blackening, Andy stepped to the plate, jaw clenched and knuckles white on the bat.

"Over the fence!" I yelled. "A homer, buddy!"

"Over the fence here is but two bases," Millar said snidely. "Didn't you hear the captains?"

"C'mon, Millar, don't be a jerk."

"Just what does 'be a jerk' mean?" His glasses flashed at me. "You're not exactly the cheese, Fowler."

"What?"

Andy ended our brilliant repartee by slamming a low pitch between third and short. I cheered as he sprinted to first.

Then the skies opened.

"This way!" somebody yelled. We dashed across the square toward the residence of an Alert official.

For the next hour, as rain drummed on the roof and players and reporters shouldered closer to the glowing stove, I listened to their gossip and made mental notes to check with Andy. Somebody was deemed "plucky withal and safe with the willow" and "led the scoring with five and two over." Another needed "something stirring to be earnest—a pretty player but loose." What did *that* mean? Another was "an uphill stem winder who never showed the white." And so it went.

There was also talk of the Stockings' win over the Niagras, a team the Alerts would face. Somebody produced a *Buffalo Courier* and quoted a reference to the Cincinnatians as "rather a burly set of men."

Sweasy cracked, "They must've overlooked Andy." It got a laugh. Andy's smile, I thought, looked a trifle forced.

When the downpour ended we trooped back to the diamond. Pockets of water shimmered everywhere on the infield. As numbers of spectators returned, I heard Champion urging Harry to get the field in playing shape or else they'd have to refund gate receipts.

I swept water from the base paths with a short-handled broom and helped drain the batter's and pitcher's boxes. We spread sand and sawdust as fast as it could be carted to the diamond. The outfield remained a marsh.

The game resumed with Andy on first. The Alerts soon fell prey to the slippery conditions. Solid hits by Brainard, Sweasy, and George were abetted by errors, resulting in five runs.

The rain held off. The game moved quickly, with few of the lazy rituals or stalling tactics I automatically linked with baseball; the teams changed positions promptly and went about the business of hitting or fielding. Millar said that most contests—even those with scores resembling football totals to me—ended in less than three hours.

By the end of the sixth the Stockings led, 14–4. A laugher. And yet excitement mounted on the sidelines. The pool sellers seemed to be writing slips faster than ever. I was about to ask Millar the reason when my attention was caught by a pale, blade-thin, black-whiskered man leaning close to McDermott, behind the third-base line. He was tense and grim-faced, unresponsive to McDermott's frequent guffaws. There seemed an aura of menace about him. I pointed him out to Millar.

He lifted his spectacles, squinted, replaced them. "I hope I'm wrong," he said. "I think it's Le Caron."

"Who's Le Caron?"

"Fowler, if you truly work for a newspaper—"

"Just tell me, okay?"

He sighed. "Henri Le Caron's likely the most brutal rough ever to emerge from Five Points. Rumor has him working for Morrissey and McDermott now, but I think he's not been seen publicly with either before."

Wondering at the powerful visceral reaction I felt to the man, I said, "How do you know it's him?"

"He was pictured in *Leslie's* and others earlier this year. It made a ripe scandal when he left prison only months into a long sentence."

"What had he done?"

"Stabbed three men to death in a gambling hell."

My stomach tightened. "Oh."

"Not uncommon, of course, but because the mayor and police officials happened to be sporting there at the time, things got a bit dodgy for him. Till Tweed and that rotten Tammany bunch pulled strings."

"Boss Tweed?" I stared in fascination at the thin, dark man. "What was his connection?"

"Le Caron came out of the Dead Rabbits." Millar glanced at me significantly. "That give you the picture?"

It didn't, of course, and I had to pull it from him. What I learned was that political bosses like Tweed intimidated foes and controlled expanding immigrant neighborhoods partly through gangs of street hoodlums. A member of the most-feared gang, Le Caron had fought his way upward in Manhattan's infamous Five Points slum—as had John Morrissey, former bare-knuckles boxing champ and current representative in Congress—in bloody struggles for dominance. But where Morrissey had gravitated to mainstream channels of power, Le Caron had remained what he was. I studied him as Millar talked. I'd never knowingly gazed at a murderer. For a moment, when Le Caron's dark eyes seemed to flash directly into mine, I felt a faint chill.

On the field the Stockings' impressive defense was stifling the Alerts. Waterman smothered drives at the hot corner with his arms or body, snatching the ball and rifling what Hurley jokingly called "finger breakers" to the blond first baseman, who took them casually, possessing, I decided, no pain threshold whatever.

The Stocking catcher also seemed indifferent to pain. Reacting with a cat's quickness, he snagged everything, even tipped balls, with sure-handed ease. Unlike the Alerts' receiver, he stood upright, not crouching. Since I'd played mostly catcher myself, I found the technique intriguing—and suicidal. The guy's body must be a mess.

But the Cincinnati star was unmistakably George Wright. I'd never seen a better shortstop, with or without a glove. He ranged over the field spearing balls most players couldn't have reached with butterfly nets. He leaped high to knock down liners, drifted gracefully beneath pop-ups, glided deep in the hole to launch white streaks that nipped runners at first. Andy was right. They were fortunate to have him. At any price.

In the bottom of the ninth the Alerts went to bat trailing 18–7. The Stockings' lead began to look less comfortable when Brainard, tiring, allowed a succession of hits, some of which found outfield gaps for extra bases. By the time two were away, a pair of runs had scored and the bases were loaded.

Millar squirmed and drummed his fingers on the table. Three more Alert runs would bring the score to 18–12, a 3–2 ratio. We would still win the game in all probability—but McDermott would cash in on a far larger scale. Sensing momentum shifting their way, the Alerts were keyed up. So was the crowd. I checked out the gambling booths and saw McDermott whooping it up. Le Caron was no longer in sight.

There was a lull as Harry trotted in from center to huddle with Brainard. "Harry'll pitch now," Millar mused. "And yet I can't imagine he wants Asa in the field, wet as it is. Brainard's slow afoot."

"Can't Hurley go in?" I asked.

"After the third inning, the rules allow replacements only for injuries."

"Third inning? Why is that?"

"So clubs can't influence betting odds by holding out ace ballists for critical moments. Players on the field may exchange positions any time, however."

"I get it," I said. "That's why 'change pitcher,' 'change catcher.' "

He nodded distractedly. "Asa's staying."

Brainard stood rubbing the filthy ball—it had been in use the whole game—and eyeing the Alerts' cleanup man, a stocky outfielder named Glenn who'd hit him hard all afternoon. The crowd was standing and cheering. The gambling element formed a bellowing fist-waving mass that pushed hard at the third-base restraining rope. Waterman eyed them warily. A few broke through and were pushed back roughly by blue-uniformed cops. One man slipped and toppled backward into the mud. McDermott, standing nearby, laughed uproariously at the sprawled figure.

"They're drunk," Millar said contemptuously. "Whiskey sellers been over there all afternoon. Shouldn't be allowed—we don't at home. It brings out the worst side of the worst element."

I'd seen the vendors with their large baskets on leather straps; most of them sold hard candy, peanuts, and lemonade. But the biggest business that cool afternoon had gone to those hawking "Spirits!"

After the police restored order, Brainard twisted into his windup, arm flashing, feet dancing. The ball sped in at knee level. Glenn swung hard and sent a low skittering drive up the middle. In the crowd's instantaneous reaction I heard Sweasy yell, "Shit!" He'd shaded toward first and had no chance. Neither did George Wright at short. But he sprinted after the ball anyway, reflexively pursuing some unseen possibility. The runners, off with the pitch, tore around the bases. Glenn pumped toward first.

Nobody could believe what happened next.

The ball struck the second-base bag, bounded into short center—and did not bound again. It landed squarely in a puddle. And that was where George caught up with it. Running full tilt, bending low, he plunged his left hand down as if snatching at a fish. Simultaneously he pivoted toward first; the effort cost him his footing, his lunging body toppling forward. Twisting in midair, he flung the ball in a spray of mud and water, threw it with his wrong hand, his *left* hand, under his body—and splashed face first into another puddle. How he got anything on the throw was hard to imagine. But he did. The ball rocketed to the first baseman, who stretched and took it a split second before Glenn's straining foot kicked the bag.

"Out!" yelled the umpire, raising the classic thumb.

The game was over.

For a moment silence enveloped the diamond. Then the Stockings broke from their positions, jumping and whooping, running to George, who climbed slowly from the quagmire, a tar-baby figure, his white teeth gleaming through a layer of mud.

Millar and Hurley leaped from the table and dashed on the field.

Champion strode after them. I started out too, then hung back, made shy by the awareness that I was not one of them. I'd almost forgotten it in the excitement.

The crowd applauded George graciously. The Alerts formed a huddle and boomed three cheers for the visitors. I tried to imagine Steinbrenner's Yankees hip-hurrahing the Red Sox after dropping a close one. The Stockings returned the cheers, lifted George from the mud, and placed him on their shoulders.

> "We are a band of ball players
> From Cincinnati City.
> We go to toss the ball around
> And sing to you our ditty.
> Hurrah, hurrah,
> For the noble game hurrah. . . . "

I looked on silently, envying them their joy, their accomplishment, their belonging. My glance wandered to where McDermott had been standing. He was gone. His absence caused a strange disquiet in me and I scanned the area behind. The long table was empty now except for the score book and the metal box holding the Stockings' share of the gate receipts.

The cash box.

Moved by an uneasy premonition, I stepped toward the table. And that's when I saw Le Caron edging through the crowd, angling toward it. He seemed to be keeping a wary watch on the diamond. Probably just paranoia on my part, I told myself, but nonetheless I circled the opposite way through the crowd, on a diagonal to him.

The table stood several yards inside the restraining rope. The box lay in reach of anyone who dared to duck inside, take two long strides, then turn and vanish into the crowd. Le Caron edged to the rope and took a quick glance at the field. I knew then that he would make the attempt.

If I'd had time to think, I might have hesitated. Tension knotted my stomach and bunched my shoulders. I stepped to the rope as Le Caron darted inside. He seized the cash box. I came up under the barrier as he turned, and clamped my hand over the wrist bearing the box.

"Wha—!" He struggled to wrench his arm back. I yanked his skinny wrist hard. The box tumbled free and burst open on the ground. Le Caron was wiry, snake quick in his movements, but not strong enough to pull free. He stumbled toward me and I spun him like a dancing partner, twisting his arm behind him and jamming it toward his neck. He gasped in pain and tried to twist away. I pulled him back by ramming my left forearm against his windpipe.

[46]

"I'll cut you," he wheezed, reaching across his body with his free hand. I shoved his arm higher and he froze.

"Shut up or I'll snap it!" I said. I had no idea what to do next.

"What's this ruckus?" a loud voice called. "What're you doing to him?"

McDermott pushed past hushed onlookers and ducked under the rope. He wasn't guffawing now. In fact, he looked as grim as the sap he gripped.

"Ask him," I said, wheeling so that Le Caron became a shield. He raised his foot to stomp mine, but changed his mind when again I thrust his arm to the breaking point.

McDermott crouched and started for me, then stopped and stared over my shoulder.

"Is there a problem?" A calm British-inflected voice spoke behind me. I took a quick look. Harry Wright stood with a bat resting on his shoulder. He looked relaxed, but his eyes were locked with McDermott's.

"He went for the cash box," I said.

"Liar!" spat Le Caron. "The bastard jumped me!"

"I'm thinking there's a mistake," McDermott said, sounding more affable. "I happened to see it all. Your man misjudged this lad's intent. Sure, an' he acted in haste. We need to set this square."

"Let him go." Harry stepped up beside me, bat still cradled.

I released Le Caron and stepped back quickly. He straightened, rubbing his arm. I watched him closely. The menace I had sensed at a distance was magnified now. Partly it was physical—the sallow face pitted with pox scars above the black beard, the teeth greenish and rotten-looking—but it was more: the man radiated some sort of evil, strong as a force field. I'd never felt anything like it. His glittering black eyes fixed on mine.

"It was no mistake," I said. "He was stealing—"

"Are there other witnesses?" Harry asked.

We looked around. People were already edging away; those remaining claimed to have seen nothing.

McDermott smiled, his eyes cold. "Your lads showed well today. Be a shame to ruin it now." He took Le Caron's good arm. "We'll see you in Troy. It's my thought your paid ballists will get their due against the Haymaker lads."

"You'd be well advised," Harry said, "to keep a proper distance from our table, to avoid—"

"—misunderstandings," McDermott finished. "Your meaning's taken. I've a word of advice, too—instruct your big boyo there to consider before assaulting others. Trouble lies in that for him." He shook his head dolefully and turned away. Le Caron's mouth twisted in a thin smile, his eyes still fastened on mine; then he followed McDermott into the crowd.

"If Red Jim's companion is who I suspect, you've made quite a pair of friends," Harry said, stooping over the box. "Fowler, did you realize that all of our money, over five hundred, is here?"

Champion strode up, frowning. "Who were those men?"

Harry explained what had happened. "Our guest showed rare courage," he concluded. "Or exceptional foolhardiness. In any event he saved the day."

Champion rubbed his jaw, no doubt considering how close they'd come to packing for home. He extended his hand. "Fowler, you've done us a most valiant service."

I'd had the thought earlier that maybe the best thing for me would be to try to hook on with a New York daily newspaper. Now as we shook I waited for what I hoped would come.

"Is there a service we can perform in return?"

Ah, good man. "How about letting me travel with you—I'll repay the costs—until we get to Manhattan?"

"That's ten days." He glanced at Harry, who nodded. "Very well. From the funds you rescued we can surely advance you that much, to be repaid at your earliest convenience." He gazed at me thoughtfully. "Meanwhile, considering the nature of our forthcoming contests and your proven capacity, there is a task you might handle."

"Sure, what?"

He handed me the cash box. "Safeguard this."

I wasn't wild about it, but under the circumstances my choices were limited.

"I might have something for you also," Harry said.

"Oh?" What had I let myself in for?

"You mentioned that you'd played baseball."

"Well, yes, but—"

"Look up Charlie Gould, our first baseman. See if his extra uniform fits you."

4

Gould wasn't too happy about it. " 'Lo, Fowler," he'd said, his gravelly voice amiable at first. We shook hands. I said I'd heard that he was the only native Cincinnatian on the nine. He beamed. Then Andy told him what Harry wanted—and he nearly crushed my hand. As if the grip weren't enough, his fingers seemed coated with iron.

"You put something on those things?" I asked, prying myself loose.

"Benzoin."

"Charlie's our human bushel basket," Andy said. "Holds any ball he can reach."

"I saw him today."

Gould's pomaded mustache bristled. "Harry's lookin' for a change player?" He sized me up. At six three, I had him by a couple of inches.

"Don't have a clue," I said.

Gould's gray eyes were set a fraction too close, giving him a perpetually worried look. Flaxen ringlets curled over his temples, and below his curved blond mustache was an elongated Vandyke. He stood with military stiffness, frowning. With obvious reluctance he handed over his spare uniform. I'd have empathized with him if my hand weren't still smarting.

Andy introduced me to the other two players I hadn't met. Cal McVey, the youngest Stocking at nineteen, glanced up and mumbled, "Hi'dy." His short-cropped sandy hair complemented long-lashed brown eyes and peach-fuzzed cheeks. His father made pianos in Indianapolis, where young Mac's baseball skills had first caught Harry's attention. Andy claimed Mac could coax music out of anything. He seemed a nice, shy kid, but I wouldn't have wanted to wrestle him: his torso looked powerful; rolled-up sleeves revealed massive forearms. He and Gould—and Sweasy on a smaller scale—formed the club's muscle contingent.

The final Stocking was Doug Allison, the catcher I had marveled at during the game. Up close he looked like a hayseed, with coarse auburn hair standing up in cowlicks. He had apple cheeks, a lopsided grin, and nearly as many freckles as Andy. I stuck out my hand.

"Cain't just now," he said in a high nasal twang, shaking his head mournfully. He held a hand up. The fingers were gnarled, the joints huge and red, the palms swollen purple.

"Don't you ever wear a mitt?" I said.

"To practice sometimes lately," he replied, a bit shamefacedly, "Here, could you pass over that arnica?"

Andy handed him a bottle of bitter-smelling yellow oil. I watched in fascination as Allison peeled off his shirt and oozed the stuff over a multicolored mass of welts and bruises covering his chest and arms.

"Ouch," he said.

Ouch indeed, I thought.

Framed in the windows of our parlor car, the sun was an amber ball plunging behind low, wheat-covered hills as we rolled out of Rochester on the New York Central. I sat playing whist, quite the dandy in my new pleated frock coat and ruffle-front silk shirt with green stripes—the latter a gift from Brainard. A high starched collar squeezed my neck. Knee-cramping stirrups stretched from tapered trouser bottoms under my insteps.

"Deuce of trumps'll do," Sweasy chortled, slapping down a card. "You boys don't win much."

In two hours' time and half the distance to Syracuse, I'd lost every bid I attempted. Waterman, my partner, an intense competitor, shuffled the deck with a sharp crackle. "I'd have a thought before studyin' the tiger with Fowler in some faro joint," he said sourly.

"Come again?" I said.

Waterman grunted.

"Freddy thinks you'd be advised not to visit a gaming house," Sweasy translated, grinning maliciously. "Leastways, not with him."

A few seats ahead, the rookie McVey blew "Camptown Races" on a harmonica. Andy was right, he was pretty good. Next to him, George Wright started to sing, off-key.

"Appears you owe us four thousand dollars," Brainard said, studying the point totals.

"Add it to our bill," I said.

Sweasy studied me. "As a card operator you're a piece of work."

"Piece of something," Waterman muttered.

I yawned and smiled. Since my encounter with Le Caron they'd begun to include me in their "sizzling." A tacit form of acceptance—except from Sweasy, whose barbs verged on outright insults.

George finished warbling and flashed his toothy grin. Earlier I'd heard Millar ask him about his game-ending play. George just shrugged and said, "I could always throw with either arm."

The younger Wright was something. Supremely self-confident, he was, at age twenty-two, probably the highest-paid player in the nation. Even when his cocksureness bordered on arrogance, it was impossible not to like him. How easily things came to a select few, I reflected. Things maddeningly beyond the reach of the rest of us. There was a time when I'd have given anything to possess half the raw talent of a George Wright. I'd had to work my ass off to be just a notch above average. Some boyhood dreams die hard. Maybe I still wanted to be a baseball hero.

Millar appeared among us. "Asa? Mr. Champion asks you to lead off the singing."

Brainard rolled his eyes.

"He requests his favorite."

"I guessed it," said Brainard. "Sent his messenger boy to whistle me up like a low hound."

"Woof, woof!" barked Sweasy.

Brainard stood in the aisle beside McVey and sang "The Man on the Flying Trapeze." I realized his was the tenor voice I'd heard before. The stylish pitcher was a man of several talents.

"That song new?" I asked Sweasy.

He nodded. "Just come out last year. Sheet music's selling like johnnycakes—in the hundreds of thousands."

I couldn't resist. "Climbing to solid platinum?"

Sweasy blinked and scowled. "How's that?"

"Never mind." I felt perverse satisfaction.

Most of the Stockings, aside from Brainard and Andy, proved to be wretched vocalists. But that didn't stop them from harmonizing fiercely on choruses and turning the whole thing into a sort of competition.

Brainard finished and pointed to Gould, who rose with ramrod stiffness and, to my astonishment, affected a Chinese accent and sang a song in pidgin, the chorus of which began, "*Oh ching chong opium, taffy on a stick . . .*"

"Ever hear the like?" Andy asked from across the aisle.

"Never," I replied.

Things did not improve. Doug Allison twanged out a racist minstrel piece called "Nancy Fat," then Sweasy hissed his way through "The Girl That Keeps the Peanut Stand," distorting maudlin lyrics with suggestive winks and leers. Harry then sang "Captain Jinks" in a pleasant baritone; I finally knew the words to a chorus. Harry then pointed to Andy.

"The Emerald Isle!" called Dick Hurley. "A hundred verses of 'The Blarney Rose'!"

Andy laughed, shook his head, and sang, Jersey accents giving way to a broad, comical brogue.

> *"Mike Finnigan, a patriot,*
> *He swore that he would raise*
> *A mighty corps of musketeers,*
> *That all the world would daze. . . ."*

At the chorus, Mac, Sweasy, and Hurley stood up and they all joined arms.

> *"To see us march as stiff as starch*
> *And listen to the cheers,*
> *Fairer boys yez niver saw*
> *Than Finnigan's Musketeers."*

I noticed that not all of the Stockings were joining in with equal enthusiasm. "Those guys always stand up like that?" I asked Waterman.

"Micks, the lot," he said dryly. "Andy was born in County Cavan."

"That so?" I said, and suppressed a yawn. The day was catching up with me. The kerosene globes hissed faintly overhead, swaying beneath the vaulted enameled ceiling, splashing pools of yellow on walnut-paneled walls and burgundy seats. Rhythmical clacking underlay all sound. Next to my head rattled a steamy window. The darkness outside seemed remote. The voices comforted me. I realized that nobody here had heard a radio or recording. Music came to them directly, only from others. Why didn't people sing together in my time?

"Sam's my pick!"

My eyes jerked open. Andy was pointing at me. "No," I said. "I can't." They shouted me down. I stood, my mind a blank.

"Something from the West," prompted Andy.

I stood dumbly next to McVey and finally blurted out the first song that came to mind:

> *"From this valley they say you are going;*
> *We will miss your bright eyes and sweet smile. . . ."*

I beckoned for them to join, but they didn't. When I reached the chorus they were leaning forward, listening intently.

"Come and sit by my side if you love me,
Do not hasten to bid me adieu,
But remember the Red River Valley
And the boy that has loved you so true."

There was silence—then ringing applause. "More!" yelled Andy. Others echoed him. They seemed to mean it.

"But that's all I know."

They insisted that I sing it again. McVey played softly behind me, and they sang harmony on the chorus.

"That's quite lovely," Champion murmured, astonishing me by dabbing at his eyes with a lace-edged handkerchief. "Won't you give us just one more Western tune?"

I racked my brain. "Okay, but this time one we all know."

"Oh give me a home where the buffalo roam,
Where the deer and the antelope play . . ."

Again they were silent. In the hush that followed, Andy remarked that it was the noblest song he'd ever heard.

"You warble like a bullfrog in heat," Brainard said, leaning in close as I sat down. "But those're prize ballads. We'd make a pile if we printed 'em."

I looked to see if he was joking. He wasn't. "But I didn't write them."

"Who did?"

"Haven't the foggiest."

"How'd you come by 'em?"

"They've been around for—" I paused. "Well, they're not original with me."

"They are hereabouts." He examined the gold rings on his fingers. "How you calculate the odds of their bein' entered with the government?"

"Copyrighted? I suppose if nobody's heard them, they aren't . . . yet."

He looked at me. "There's our chance."

He was entirely serious. "I could use some cash," I said. "But stealing songs isn't my idea of how to get it."

"Sure as sin somebody's gonna cash 'em in. Why not us? Besides, how's it stealin' if nobody's laid claim?"

I didn't have a ready answer. Viewed from his standpoint, the future glittered like a treasure vault. By tapping my foreknowledge, wouldn't I merely be nudging things along predestined channels? In this Darwinistic age would a Vanderbilt or Rockefeller or Carnegie hesitate in my shoes? Was the Gilded Age ready for Scott Joplin? Gershwin? The Beatles?

S. C. Fowler, Sheet Music Czar.

It had a certain ring.

But actually, wouldn't I be changing the past instead of merely retracing it?

Then a more bizarre idea occurred to me: What if I'd passed this way before? What if I'd already created the songs myself—and possessed no recollection of doing it?

Time as overlapping circles, then, not a line.

"You thinking about it?" Brainard demanded.

"I most certainly am."

"And . . .?"

"It's complicated."

"Hell, Sam, it couldn't be simpler." He snorted. "You're thinkin' too damn hard."

Maybe he had a point. Things were already complicated enough.

We reached Syracuse after midnight. The air was clear and cold, the dark sky strewn with pale blue stars. Inside our hotel on Clinton Square the feather beds were thick and soft. I sank into mine, drew up the quilt (Andy called it a "bedrug"), and said good night.

"Your first day awake with us was some sockdolager," Andy said. "You handled them sharps slick as grease. I've heard a thing or two about McDermott. He's a rough customer. Lucky for us you were along."

I was exhausted but pleased. Some sockdolager indeed. God, what a day. Just before plummeting into sleep I wondered if I would wake up in the twentieth century. I suspected not. Did I want to?

Just then I couldn't have said.

Saturday, June 5, exploded into my consciousness. A thundering crash sent us bounding from bed. Naked, shivering in the morning chill, we peered from our window at a chaotic scene. A four-horse brewer's wagon had smashed into a butcher's cart, overturning both vehicles. Carcasses from the cart lay strewn in grisly lumps. Horses screamed and struggled in their traces as the drivers cursed. Some beer barrels had burst on impact; others rumbled cavernously over the cobblestones.

Andy turned away. "Wisht we hadn't looked. Seein' empty barrels on a beer wagon always brings good luck, but this here . . ."

I yawned and scratched. "You believe in that stuff?"

He shrugged. "Like the tinker said of the wee folk, you don't have to believe in 'em to know they're there."

Gray skies and cloudbursts had pursued us. Later that morning, between showers, Andy and I boarded a mule-drawn omnibus with Cal McVey, the muscular rookie, and the Wrights. We headed up Salina Street. Bells on the mules' collars jingled cheerily as we clopped through the gloom toward the city's northern edge.

George displayed stereopticon cards he'd purchased at the hotel. They pictured several of the mineral springs that lent Syracuse the nickname Salt City. George said he collected the views everywhere he traveled. I realized suddenly that picture postcards didn't yet exist.

As we rode I noted how different George Wright was from his older brother: cocky and gregarious where Harry was self-effacing, even shy; wisecracking where Harry was sober. There was no strong physical resemblance either. George's shock of dark curls and large hooked nose contrasted with Harry's lighter coloring and regular features. Though twelve years younger, George stood nearly an inch taller and weighed ten pounds more. What they shared, I decided, was a quality of alert tolerance in their eyes and unmistakable authority in their manner. Harry was more a leader, but George too had powerful presence. I'd learned from Andy that their father was the resident professional at a posh Staten Island cricket club. He had coached Harry as a boy, who in turn coached George. The brothers were true rarities in America—second-generation pro athletes.

At a commercial spa near Onondaga Lake, we soaked ourselves in hot, salty baths for five cents apiece. I stood shoulder-deep in the steaming water, face dripping, muscles relaxing.

McVey stared at my cheek when I removed the soaked bandage. "That don't appear to be healing normal."

"Afraid you're right, Mac." I winced at the sting of salt. That morning the gash had shown yellow and purple on its edges, dark pink in the center. The translucent scab that had formed didn't seem to be thickening. Had exotic nineteenth-century microorganisms infiltrated my system? If so, I was in trouble. Antibiotics were over fifty years away.

The sky was clearing when we returned to the hotel. It looked like the game would be played, though no word had come from our opponents, Syracuse's Central City club. Concerned, Harry and Champion went to investigate. I left Andy to his nap and tagged along. So did Millar. We climbed into in a small hackney coach that Champion flagged.

"Where's the field?" I asked.

"Fairgrounds," Harry replied.

Arriving, we saw that there'd been a major foul-up. Grass waved knee high in the outfield. Sections of the fence had collapsed. A pigeon shoot was in progress. Nobody knew of a baseball game.

Champion's face darkened. From Millar I'd learned he was a formidable trial lawyer in Cincinnati. Just then he looked like he wanted to indict the whole city.

"I'll conduct a practice," Harry said with forced heartiness. "It'll sharpen our mettle for Troy."

"Won't sharpen our finances," Champion said.

Harry turned to me. "Dick Hurley's our single replacement. Should misfortune strike in Troy, Fowler, we may need help." He smiled grimly. "Against the Haymakers, injuries aren't exactly rare. We'll see your goods this afternoon."

Great, I thought. Cannon fodder. How nice to be wanted. But I felt a flicker of excitement. Rec-league softball had been a tame substitute in recent years. Baseball, the real game, carried a quotient of fear. I'd almost forgotten that.

Hours later, in baggy sweats and calfskin shoes borrowed from Mac, I tramped around the damp practice lot, a long, weed-stubbled expanse sandwiched between a smelly gypsum plant and a fenced-off cow pasture. Dwindling energy had narrowed my fears to a single focus: avoid total humiliation.

"You're gettin' it back," said Andy, standing on first base beside me. A low throw from Waterman had just glanced off my fingers. "It's easy to tell you've played."

"Right," I muttered. My hands throbbed. My legs were dead. My throwing arm ached when I raised it. "If I survive."

In Captain Harry's workout, each regular played his normal position except when hitting. Hurley and I worked our way around filling vacant spots. At the plate everybody got a dozen swings and ran out the last hit. Harry called situations—"runner on second, no outs"— and we played accordingly.

Very little escaped Harry Wright. He halted practice frequently to give pointers on individual plays. If he suspected somebody of slacking, he'd comment, "You need to show a little ginger." That was all. Andy claimed that Harry had never been heard to utter even the mildest profanity. I tried to imagine it in a twentieth-century manager.

Harry was not impressed when I showed off by throwing overhand curves and knucklers in warm-ups. In fact, he put an emphatic end to it when Andy and George wanted to learn. But he seemed to appreciate the fact that I knew my way around a ball field. For my part, I quickly realized that the Stockings were damned good—by far the best I'd ever been on a diamond with.

Harry drilled us endlessly on defensive covers and backups. His system was as complex as any I'd experienced. Basically, he employed two field captains: Allison flashed hand signals to position the basemen, while Harry, in center, directed outfield traffic as well as brother George, who galloped far and wide from shortstop. On a high fly Harry called not only who should attempt the catch, but who should crouch nearby to pounce should the ball be muffed—a very real possibility, I soon discovered.

The ball itself, while only a fraction larger than the modern regulation version I was used to, was remarkably more elastic. Manufacturers produced two general types: lively and dead. Harry practiced with a lively ball and reserved the others for games. His idea was to increase batting confidence in practice, at the same time honing defensive skills. He was doubtless right—where his veteran players were concerned.

With me it was another story.

Harry initially stationed me in right. When the first ball came lofting out, I moved under it with reasonable assurance, reached up to take it—and was shocked when it caromed off my hands like a tennis ball and bounced six feet in front of me. I then mortified myself and put the others in stitches by kicking it out of reach as I bent for it.

"No muffins here!" Sweasy's voice pierced the field. "We're a first-rate nine! Catch the ball!" He looked around with a proprietary air, as if speaking for them all. Andy's grin faded to a worried frown.

I felt my face redden. Fuck you, Sweasy.

After more embarrassments my hands began to give with the ball. I snagged several flies and uncorked low, one-bounce pegs to the plate; my arm was stronger, if more erratic, than Mac's. I knew that my lumbering pursuit of drives in the gap impressed nobody.

When Hurley's turn came to hit, Harry sent me to first and Gould to right. Sweasy turned his back on me and busied himself at second while George and Waterman warmed me up. Their medium-speed throws stung, but I held them and felt a glimmer of confidence.

"Striker's in," Harry called from the pitching box. Brainard, ill, had begged off practice, and Harry was handling all batting-practice pitching chores.

Hurley grinned and pointed his bat at me, the club's only lefty. He sizzled several shots down the line, then deliberately chopped the ball off the turf in front of home so that it bounced high outside the first-base line. I jogged after it, wondering at the strange maneuver. Then I heard Sweasy screaming, "Fair foul!"

I didn't realize then that a ball hitting in fair territory remained in play even if it went foul before reaching a corner base. Some strikers—Hurley and Waterman on the Stockings—were adept at knocking fair-foul balls beyond the reach of fielders. Which accounted for corner basemen often playing on top of their bags; they had a lot of foul territory to worry about.

"What kind of headwork is that!" Sweasy shrilled. "Look sharp! Get your finger outa your butt!"

I ignored him. Which increased his output. Harry shushed him and briefed me on the rule. Sweasy paced and muttered.

Hurley next topped a roller to the right. I started for it, then retreated to the bag as Sweasy moved in quickly. He short-hopped it neatly between Harry and me, pivoted leisurely—and suddenly whipped the ball with all his strength, exploding it directly at my face.

"Let it go!" yelled Harry.

Let it go! echoed a voice in my brain. I reached for it. The ball slammed through my fingers like a hurricane flattening trees. Pain mushroomed in my left hand. For an instant I stood motionless, teeth clenched. With an effort of will I retrieved the ball, rolled it to the box, and resumed my position. Only then did I glance down. The large joint of my index finger was a bulging red knob, the skin already stretched shiny and smooth.

Sweasy's act was not lost on the Stockings, who stood silently at their positions, wondering, I supposed, how I would respond. Harry asked if I was okay. Not trusting my voice, I nodded.

Hurley's last turn came. Harry yelled, "Swift man at first, one out." Hurley pulled a sharp bouncer along the line. I took it cleanly on the bag and turned to throw out the imaginary runner. Sweasy dashed to cover second. I set myself, strode forward, and rifled the ball from behind my ear, catcher-style, following through with every ounce of my weight. I'd never thrown harder in my life. The ball rocketed from my fingers. I pictured it knocking Sweasy's head off.

He saw the effort and must have grasped my intent. He looked as if he intended to wave the ball past with a bullfighter's scorn. But he had badly misjudged. It zoomed in crotch-high, then made a wicked upward break. I saw his eyes widen. In desperation he flipped backward, catapulting as if struck by the ball's oncoming air cushion. His cap flew off. He hung horizontally in midair. His head and shoulders crashed to the sod, knees flopping wildly behind. The ball streaked over him into the outfield.

He sprawled on his back. The impact must have taken his wind. Waterman and George were doubled over in fits of laughter. "Like a chicken!" Waterman howled, pointing. "Sweaze flew like a chicken!" The laughter spread. Even Harry smiled.

Sweasy climbed to his feet and started toward me, face scarlet. "You son of a bitch!"

I flipped him the finger.

Ignoring Harry's shouts, he clenched his fists and charged. I set myself, arms braced, waiting. He halted only inches away, stocky body quivering.

"Go ahead," I said, watching him carefully. "You better make it your best shot."

Sweasy had to crane his neck to glare at me. Rage had not erased the fact that he gave away half a foot and thirty or forty pounds. He took a ragged breath. Then Harry and Allison reached us.

"That's enough, Charles!" said Harry.

Our eyes remained locked.

"You have no quarrel." Harry's tone was that of a father lecturing a child. "Fowler returned what you offered full measure."

Sweasy let out his breath slowly. "I guess it showed sand," he muttered.

"What the hell does that mean?" I snapped.

"Settle yourself, bub!" Allison stepped before me. "He's sayin' you got some grit to you. Here, let's see that."

The hand that gripped mine looked like it had been caught in a machine. Allison's knuckles were grotesquely enlarged, fingers flattened and bent. He probed my injured joint, grinned, said, "Welcome to the national game, bub."

Thanks. He made it sound like I'd passed some sort of test. Great. The protruding finger hurt like hell. No way I was going to sleep that night. Did aspirin even exist? Too bad Sweasy hadn't swung. I'd've enjoyed popping the little bastard.

Harry was eyeing me. "Go up and strike," he said.

I borrowed Gould's heavy black ash bat that he called Becky. I had trouble gripping Becky's leather-wound handle. I had far more trouble timing Harry's pitches—Allison called them "dewdrops"—high, arching tosses at variable speeds that seemed to bend in flight. I missed the first ones completely, fouled the next weakly.

"You're elevating your front shoulder," Harry said.

On my final swing I connected squarely, getting my weight behind the bat and driving the ball. Shock waves danced up my arms. Andy watched the ball soar high over him. It hung against the sky, then plummeted into a distant cow pond.

"That was a Joe Darter," said Allison behind the plate. "Two to one George couldn't sock it farther."

"Thirty cents," Harry called, walking in.

"What?" I said. "Is he betting?"

Allison laughed. "You gotta pay for the ball."

"Are you serious?"

"Yes sirree, Mr. Champion's orders."

"I prefer daisy cutters to sky balls," Harry said, stroking his goatee thoughtfully. "On the other hand, few grounds could have contained your last blow. How are you against swifter pitching?"

I shrugged modestly.

"Fisher of Troy is one of the swiftest. I wish Asa were here to test you." He looked around. "George!"

I stepped back in and swung hard at three fastballs delivered by George Wright.

Whiff. Whiff. Whiff.

Harry clucked sympathetically.

Having foolishly admitted catching in the past, I agreed to a check-out behind the plate, first requesting a glove and mask. I had to describe the latter.

"Let me hear this square, bub." Allison cocked his head and grinned. "You want your face inside a bird cage?"

"Okay, forget it," I said hurriedly as he turned to broadcast it to the others. "But I've got to have a mitt."

"I'd understand better if Asa were tossing." Harry shook his head, but sent the freckle-faced catcher to fetch his glove.

I didn't know whether to laugh or cry when Allison returned. The "glove" he'd confessed to using with such embarrassment was exactly that—a kid-leather glove with the fingers cut off, no thicker than a cyclist's.

I put it on silently, a matter of principle. Allison proceeded to render a clinic in state-of-the-art catching, 1869-style: how to anticipate the spin on Harry's twisters when fielding them on the bounce far behind the plate; how to move up close (too damned close, with no protective gear) behind the striker with men on base; how to cup my fingers to minimize sprains and breaks, and to shield my face and neck with my forearms. Allison accepted my squatting position when I showed him I could rise and snap throws off quickly. My arm matched his, but my reflexes were vastly slower. Foul tips whizzed past me before I could begin to react. With visions of my face being caved in, I wasn't unhappy when Harry finally called an end.

"You better hope everybody stays healthy," I said. "I'm a wreck."

"Your instincts are passable," he said, as gravely as a doctor. "You manifest a great deal of training. Some of your techniques—well, I've never seen their like." He paused. "But, Fowler, you've let yourself

[60]

deteriorate. Slow in the field, tender-handed as a baseman, ill-timed at striking—"

"You always mince words this way, Harry?"

"—but you'll do in a pinch."

"Look, I never said I was . . . what?"

"You don't budge when threatened." He gave me a look I couldn't read. "That could prove of worth."

A suspicion struck. "Did you set Sweasy on me?"

"Not my style." He sounded weary. "Sometimes Charles gets his back up like a cat."

"What's his problem with me?"

"Andy, most likely." He shrugged; dismissal. "The fact is, he tried to back you down but couldn't. We'll need that sort of pluck against the Haymakers on Monday."

"They're a rough crowd?"

"You'll see."

"Where'd you learn the game?" Andy asked later. "What clubs you been on?"

"High school," I answered. "A little my first year at college." I'd nearly said Berkeley.

"You went through all the grades? Course I figured you'd know your letters tip-top, bein' a newspaperman, but college . . ." His voice trailed off in wonderment.

"Didn't you finish high school?"

"Hell, Sam, I didn't even start. Figured I was lucky to pile up six years. So'd my family." He laughed. "Nobody on the nine's got more, 'cept Harry and George with eight—and Hurley, of course. Say, when I send off letters will you polish 'em?"

"Sure."

"What college did you take your course at?"

I rubbed my head as though trying to recall. Berkeley probably didn't even exist yet. "Yale?" I said tentatively.

"Why, they field crack nines at Yale College!" Excitement brightened his voice. "No wonder you're up on so many points of the game."

"Now wait, I'm not sure," I cautioned.

"Must be, though." He beamed proudly at me. "Sam Fowler of Yale. Ain't that a dinger?"

"It certainly is."

We left Syracuse at midnight, bound for Troy in a close-packed sleeping car. I nursed my finger with arnica and frequent sips from a

[61]

tall bottle of Mrs. Sloan's Soothing Sirup. Soothing indeed! The patent medicine blended laudanum—tincture of opium—with a 30 percent alcohol solution; it sent an aggressive glow from my belly to outlying regions. If I couldn't sleep with this stuff, forget it.

Andy had humored me—I was positive he regarded my injury as trivial—by helping me find a druggist. While he investigated "Proprietary Remedies," I roamed the rest of the store, boggling at the weirdest bottles, jars, and vials I'd ever seen.

I bent to examine labels, fascinated. Most left specific ingredients to the imagination, but were hardly bashful about promising results. Sufferers of "rheumatism, contracted cords, asthma, deafness, neuralgia, sore throat, piles, and afflictions of the spine" would be "permanently cured" with Dr. Park's Macedonian Oil—an amazing bargain at fifty cents. Another boasted: "People who vomit at the very thought of pills actually relish Minerva's Liver and Stomach Lozenges," which "act like a charm in dyspepsia, bowel complaints, liver diseases, and general debility." I was startled to see bottles of something called Burnett's Cocoaine. They turned out to contain "the Best and Cheapest Hairdressing in the World."

Andy beckoned me to the cash boy's station. Cash registers didn't exist; businesses hired kids to spirit payments off to secret niches where cashiers made change. As I pulled out my wallet, my eye fastened on a card tacked to the counter. In Italianate script it read:

CLAIRVOYANT AND PHYSICIAN
Mme Clara Antonia
Business and Medical Clairvoyant

A correct diagnosis given of all diseases, without one question asked of the patient. Consultation in English, French, and German, and has her diploma. Spiritual guidance in sickness and health.

Jesus, I thought, I wouldn't want medical problems in this century.

"What're you studyin'?" Andy said.

I showed him. His lips slowly formed the words. "I know her," he said. "Clara Antonia lectures all around the country. My mother turns out, gives her money."

"Your mother? Why?"

"You'd say it was like believing in the wee folk," he said. "An' you don't hold with that, remember?"

He was teasing, I think.

Andy stirred in the berth below. I gazed out the window as we churned through the dark city. Unaccountably, the New York Central had put tracks in Syracuse at street level; now we rolled along a main thoroughfare. I stared up at occasional glowing windows that glided by like ornaments in the night. Who lived behind those curtains? Why weren't they asleep? I pictured Hope and Susy in the illuminated rooms, imagining that I had just turned on the light to look down at their sweet slumbering faces. Oh, lord.

Somewhere inside my drug-induced torpor lay a terrible ache, a void. I desperately missed the world I had left. What was I doing here?

The loneliness of the night seemed limitless. I imagined a woman's softness touching me, comforting me. A woman to love. I felt even sorrier for myself. Miles farther on into the darkness and into the soporific charms of Mrs. Sloan's Soothing Sirup, I finally stopped feeling anything.

$$\diamond\ 5\ \diamond$$

We arrived in West Troy with the rising sun at six in the morning. Eyes sagging, brain woolly, body aching, I paraded with the others onto the platform, where we stood huddled in the crisp air for over an hour. Nobody from the Haymakers showed up.

Champion paced fretfully. "A deliberate insult!"

"They acknowledged our telegram?" Harry asked.

Champion nodded, mouth pinched.

We boarded the first scheduled streetcar this hushed Sunday. A conductor in natty gold braid stood on the rear platform beside the brake and took our two-cent fares. As I faced him, my mind suddenly filled with the ghostly figure I'd glimpsed as I collapsed on the station dock. Suddenly I seemed to be stepping up simultaneously into a bright yellow horsecar and a dark green cable car—with twentieth-century San Francisco bustling all around me, vivid and real even as an overlay on the Troy surroundings. The illusion faded almost at once, but I had felt the first hints of the milkiness: it was like peering through a wall suddenly grown translucent. Too much Mrs. Sloan's, I thought—and hoped that was all there was to it.

Out on the front platform the driver slapped leather reins against the horses' haunches—a sharp, fleshy sound—and we set off along the broad street. My hands trembled all the way to the Troy ferry building, an elongated wooden labyrinth. Another fare put us aboard a skiff rigged with a light sail; oars were secured below the gunwales.

"Yez can row, for speed," the skipper said.

We ignored the oars, drifting leisurely on the Hudson's calm gray surface. I began to relax again. Mist rose around us. To our right, the massive Watervliet Arsenal bristled with cannon. Directly ahead, the low forested hills of Troy City looked under attack by phalanxes of brick buildings swarming up from the water's edge.

"What's that?" I pointed to a huge new structure.

"Ironworks, I think," Waterman said. "Ask George."

I did. And got my ears filled. In the twenties, George said, a Troy housewife snipped the soiled collar from her husband's shirt to avoid washing the entire garment—and thereby created a new industry. Detachable cloth collars, later celluloid, had poured forth to an eagerly waiting nation.

Now Troy was a booming steel-manufacturing center, not yet superseded by Pittsburgh. The city's flood of wartime manufactures had included the metal plates that girded the *Monitor*.

The smokestacks were quiet this morning, but as we drew close I saw them looming everywhere, thrusting above the factories like black fingers.

We checked into the Mansion House, a small inn near the river that boasted a fine table and comfortable beds. I lay down on mine, took out my Mrs. Sloan's, and had a healthy pull.

"What are you doin'?" Andy demanded.

"Hair of the dog."

"I don't want you drinkin'."

I was silent.

He stood over me. "I mean it."

"For Chrissakes, Andy—"

"It was runnin' your life, wasn't it, Sam?"

"I don't believe that's any of your—"

"It *is* my concern." His green eyes glittered. "Drink killed my father. I'm not temperance, Sam, but it's time to put things on the square. You fall into the bottle, you say good-bye to me."

I stared at him, Mrs. Sloan already starting to muddle my brain. "Killed *your* father?"

"Drink did it. You understand what I'm sayin'?"

"Yeah," I said. "I understand."

In the afternoon I awoke to a babble of noise. Andy rose from a writing table.

"What's the commotion?"

"They discovered we're here."

"Who?"

"Townfolk, already in a sweat."

I looked through the window. A throng of people worked at stretching a banner across the street: UNIONS OVER CINCINNATI! The Haymakers, Andy said, were officially the Unions of Lansingburgh, a suburb north of Troy City. Cheers erupted as a dummy with red feet was elevated on pitchforks and suspended from the hotel's eaves, where it dangled at the end of a noose.

"They're pretty intense," I said.

"Wait'll the sporting crowd shows up. This is our biggest match before we get to Brooklyn. Last year the Stockings came here and drubbed the Haymakers twenty-seven to eight. They been freezin' for revenge ever since. Built a crack team—same as we've done."

"Who's favored?"

"Oh, the pool sellers'll always puff the East club. 'Specially since the Haymakers think they're going to take the whip pennant this year."

"What's that, the championship?"

"Yes, the flag. The top club keeps it till they lose twice in a match of three. Then it goes to whoever beats 'em. The Haymakers think it's as good as flyin' over their grounds already." He laughed. "We'll have somethin' to say about that."

Again I felt excitement at the prospect of a tough clash. "You nervous about tomorrow?"

He shrugged. "Are you?"

"A little."

"I'll likely fret some." The green eyes regarded me calmly. "It's natural. But there's a prime thing to keep in mind."

"What's that?"

"We didn't come all the way out here to get warmed."

I smiled at his single-mindedness. "I'll try to remember that."

We spent the day quietly. Andy and the other Catholic players went to Mass, while Harry, Champion, and a few others took in an Episcopal service. Brainard, Sweasy, and Waterman disappeared to explore more secular pursuits.

I occupied an overstuffed divan in the Mansion House lobby and tried to make sense of the news. The *Troy Times* carried a piece on the Stockings' victories in the young season, lifted almost verbatim from Millar's stat-laden press release. Why were sportswriters always nuts about numbers?

The front pages were devoted to a national peace jubilee scheduled in Boston the following week. Grant and his cabinet would be there. Choirs fifteen thousand strong would sing in the week-long event. Overseas, England's Parliament was hotly debating disestablishing the Irish Church, while in Cuba the guerillas continued their struggle against Spanish rule. From the Far West—grouped with items from Calcutta and Madagascar—General Custar [*sic*] had telegraphed to scotch rumors of his demise at the hands of the Pawnee.

I wrestled with the problem of foreknowledge, remembering that the blond cavalry commander met his fabled end in June 1876, almost exactly seven years ahead. Should I try to warn Custer? Use any argument that might spare all those lives? Would he listen? Did I have the right to interfere with events? Minding my business suited my temperament and seemed more sensible, but even doing nothing I risked altering history. My presence here was doubtless an alteration in itself.

Had I asked for any of this?

The Haymakers sent neither delegates nor carriages on Monday. We ate shortly after noon. The atmosphere was tense. Sweasy tried, "Say, 'd you hear the one about the Yankee peddler and the farmer's fat daughter?" In unison, Waterman and Allison told him to shut up.

Up in our room I spread out the accessories Harry had given me: a jock strap of stiff webbing with attached tie strings, a thick leather belt, red stockings, and elastic bands.

By wearing the belt—it was so wide and rigid it felt like a girdle— low on my hips I managed to make Gould's pants stretch below my knees. The flannel jersey felt heavy as a blanket. My wrists extended from the sleeves like a scarecrow's and the shoulder seams cramped my armpits. With spiked shoes in hand—mine half a size small—we walked on stockinged feet, a silent procession moving down the boardwalk to the horsecars. Bands of ragged boys and older tobacco-spitting youths swarmed around.

"Youse jakes'll get whipped!" they yelled. "The Haymakers'll lay over you milk-and-water bastids!" They hurled dirt clods with insults and darted close to spit at the windows. A street scene out of Dickens. When Champion wasn't looking, Sweasy gave them the finger.

We moved along River Street through North Troy, an industrial scape with steel mills, carriage works, and steam-powered knitting factories. Many of them were letting workers out early to see the game; they lined our route, faces pallid, some already lurching drunkenly. The streets resonated with animals and vehicles, pedestrians, shouts and curses and cracking whips. Sweating cops on horseback tried to free intersections.

We crawled past a cemetery, past the huge Ludlow Valve Works, into Lansingburgh. Tree-shaded lanes ascended from the Hudson. Lining them were Dutch Renaissance mansions with steep roofs and narrow windows, and bristling with gables, towers, and ironwork.

We reached open land. The Haymakers' grounds lay in a natural amphitheater formed by sloping hillsides. Fences hadn't been erected, but the crowd formed a dense barrier around the playing area. Millar estimated ten thousand on hand, and more were flooding in. Already the noise level was formidable.

George Wright grinned at me, excitement flashing in his eyes, and said, "How's this for high?"

It *was* a high. Imagine the most exciting day of early summer when you were young and everything was vibrant and the world teemed with possibilities. That was the afternoon we had, clear and sparkling, breezes heightening the air's crispness. Perfect for baseball. I felt like I was thirteen again. We pushed through the crowd. Before us lay the field, a green mat surrounded by swirling color and sound.

Harry stopped and grouped us. His eyes met mine, moved briefly to those of the others. "We know what these fellows are," he said, his words barely audible. "Let's show them our ginger today." Head high, he turned toward the field. We marched in single rank, eleven abreast, in rough step. Andy was on my left, Hurley my right. Our crimson stockings flashed across the grass. From the crowd came an anticipatory roar.

Into the grinder, I thought.

And I had a sudden and very clear realization that there was nowhere else I'd rather be.

The Haymakers were not in evidence. We spread over the diamond to warm up. George and the others began their flashy routine, but here it brought jeers. George pirouetted and tipped his cap. His cockiness buoyed me. The hotter things were, the happier he looked. He was a truly joyous competitor—or just plain crazy.

Andy tossed blades of grass to assess the wind. He asked me to throw balls over his head for him to take going away. His accurate return throws bounced in gently, away from my sore hand. Nearby, in the shade of a large wooden grandstand, a cluster of canvas-topped booths lent a carnival touch. Near some I recognized pool sellers from their pads of wager slips and unceasing cries of odds—which currently favored the Haymakers at better than two to one. I asked Andy who operated the others.

"Thimbleriggers," he said scornfully. "Punchboard operators, three-card monte sharps." With visions of quick wealth they systematically separated factory workers and farmhands from their meager coins and bills.

The gambling element sported gaudy outfits, twinkled with diamond stickpins, twirled ivory-handled canes and umbrellas, and showed off an array of ultrafashionable headwear from stovepipe "plugs" and fedoras to derbies and boaters. Among them prowled bejeweled women in satins, silks, and velvets. Their faces were white with powder, their lips blood red, their eyes predatory.

A momentary hush descended on the booths. People fell back as a cream-colored barouche drawn by matched white mares approached. A man stepped out looming powerful and dark, his jaw shadowed blue though smooth shaven, his eyes deep and probing beneath thick brows. His tan suit was elegant and he carried a gold-knobbed walking stick.

He offered his arm and a woman stepped out, skirts bunched, boots gliding down the coach's steps. I stopped breathing as I tried to memorize her. Ringlets of ash-blond hair peeked from a scarlet cap, glinting pale gold in the sunlight and framing her oval face. A gray satin dress with scarlet trim set off alabaster skin and large blue-violet eyes. Her mouth was wide and sensual, her lips full. She smiled. The afternoon took on even more radiance.

"Who are they?" I asked Andy.

"Congressman Morrissey," he said. "I've never laid eyes on even the half of *her* before."

I resolved on the spot to find out about Morrissey and his companion. Especially the companion. As they promenaded to the grandstand she looked toward the diamond. For an electric instant my gaze touched hers. I stared, transfixed. She glanced away, then to my surprise tilted her chin and turned back to meet my eyes. Some spark of intense blue-violet energy flashed. I wanted her desperately—and was sure she knew. She tossed her head and laughed—a glimpse of white teeth and pink tongue—but I couldn't tell whether at me or in response to Morrissey.

"My lord," Andy whispered. "Ain't she some dry goods? Did you see her lookin' at me?"

"At *you?*"

"Sure as sin she was sparkin' Mrs. Leonard's boy. Ain't she some belle? Ain't she . . . *darling?*"

It sounded almost sacred. I glanced at him. He looked goofy. No matter that she was light-years out of his league. No matter that she was on the arm of one of the state's most powerful men. No matter that she'd actually been looking at me. Poor deluded Andy.

"Here, what's this!" Harry yelled.

We threw with guilty haste. Then a loud voice sounded nearby. "So he's a damned revolver!" Red Jim McDermott stood pointing at me with grim satisfaction. "For a fact we'll be investigatin' this, have no fear!"

Harry moved over quickly. "Investigate what?"

"Faith, an' you needn't play-act, Mr. Holier-Than-Thou Wright. Fleshin' out your nine with a revolver, is it? You'll get what you deserve!" He strode after Morrissey.

[69]

Harry frowned at me. "You came from another club?"

"Are you kidding? Do I look like I've been playing?"

"Yale," Andy reminded me.

"You're wearing our colors now," Harry said. "Yale is no concern to me, but if you were affiliated with any but a college club during the past sixty days, the Haymakers can claim this match by forfeit."

"No problem," I said. "McDermott could scour the globe for fifty years and find no trace of me playing ball." Or anything else about me, I thought.

"Given Red Jim's temperament," Harry said, "that's a good thing. Very well, I believe you."

A roar burst forth as the Haymakers careened on the field in carriages decked with bunting and streamers. In the grandstand a brass band began to play. Girls in farm dresses held pitchforks to form an archway through which the Haymakers ran to home plate. They wore long brown corduroy pants, black spiked boots, and white jerseys. I didn't like their looks: a burly, hard-eyed lot, bigger than us.

A man with a megaphone stepped forward to announce them one by one. Hurley accompanied the introductions with sketches of those likely to cause us trouble.

"STEVE BELLAN, CENTER FIELD." An olive-skinned, black-haired athlete who smiled calmly as he sized us up.

"Esteban Enrique Bellan," reported Hurley. "Comes from a rich Havana family. Played at Fordham when I was with Columbia. He's a safe hitter, not heavy. Quick on the base paths. He'll rip you if you don't watch his spikes." Hurley spat a stream of tobacco. "Course all the Haymakers'll do that."

"They will?"

He nodded judiciously. "Especially if they're playing to win—like today."

Great, I thought.

"WILLIAM 'CHEROKEE' FISHER, PITCHER." A dour bullet-headed individual with gimlet eyes, close-cropped blond hair, and droopy mustache.

"They say he can split a board with his tosses. He pitched for the Buckeyes in Cincinnati last year and hates the Stockings, but has yet to beat us. If you ever strike against him, be set to low-bridge. Fisher can be dead wild when it suits him."

"Wonderful," I said.

"MART KING, THIRD BASE . . . STEVE KING, LEFT FIELD." Hulking, moon-faced brothers with massive shoulders and biceps bulging from their rolled sleeves.

"Mart's the younger and meaner, already big as a firehouse. They

[70]

live for home runs and fancy catches. Generally spoiling to fight, too; give one of 'em a queer look and both of 'em 'll lay into you quicker'n powder."

"CLIPPER FLYNN, RIGHT FIELD." In his late teens, body whippet lean, features chiseled a bit too fine, loving the figure he cut as he mugged and winked at the stands, drawing young girls' giggles and their escorts' glares.

"He's easy bought, it's said. Got caught using a false name with the Putnams in 'sixty-seven. He's plucky enough, though not the ace he thinks. He's heavy at bat and runs hell-to-split." Hurley spat again. "I'd give a half eagle to watch Andy humble him in a footrace. Then I'd render him an Irish hoist—my boot to his ass."

The Haymaker captain was announced last. The crowd rumbled in anticipation. "WILLIAM CRAVER, CATCHER." He thrust a massive fist upward, an animal-like man with a thick torso set on squat, powerful legs. A black mustache curled up the sides of his oblong jaw. The smile on his meaty lips was not reflected in cold, wide-set eyes that scanned us above a mashed-in nose.

"Will Craver's every brand of trouble you can imagine. During the Secesh war, when most of us were home playing ball as lads, he signed on as a drummer boy. Saw four years of hell and came out twisted. Temper's short as piecrust now, and he's said to take pleasure from seeing pain—'specially when he's the cause of it."

I reflected on that for a long moment. "Sounds like he needs a padded cell, not a ball field."

" 'Padded cell'?" Hurley looked amused. "Don't mistake me, Craver's a first-rate ballist. Strikes with the heaviest. Throws down runners like operating a gatling gun. He's steady and fearless."

Sure, I thought, psychos often are.

"Crooked, though," Hurley added. "Owned by Morrissey and McDermott—but hell, the whole club is. And he'd never blink at hippodroming."

"At what?"

"Playing to the odds, maybe even losing, to cash in."

"You mean he'd throw this game?"

"No, they're backed by the big sporting money today; he'll play square. They're freezing to humble us, too."

I gazed at the burly figure. "He's built like a bull."

"He's called 'Bull' Craver by some. But I wouldn't care to say it to his face." Hurley looked at me expectantly. " 'Cheated of feature by dissembling nature . . . I that am not shaped for sportive tricks.' "

"*Richard the Third?*"

[71]

"Not half bad!" He seemed startled. "You show rare promise, Fowler."

While Harry and Craver met, the band blared marches. The music was ill-suited to baseball, suggesting to me more the supercharged atmosphere of college football.

"Will they play the anthem?" I asked.

"The which?"

" 'The Star-Spangled Banner.' "

"Oh, the national ballad. What for? This is a ball match, not the Senate."

At least one bit of jingoistic idiocy hadn't yet lodged in the national psyche, I thought.

The captains' negotiations dragged on. By the rules, home teams proposed umpires; visitors approved. Harry flatly rejected Craver's first choice. The rules also stipulated that a visiting club provide the game ball subject to a host's concurrence. Craver refused our dead ball, insisting on a Ryan Bounding Rock, the liveliest ball in existence, certain to maximize the Haymakers' slugging over our fielding edge.

The captains finally parted. Harry returned and said, "P and S." Which turned out to mean we'd be using a Peck & Snyder New Professional Dead Ball, livelier than ours, less elastic than the Ryan. Harry bent over the score book to enter the name of the compromise umpire, one J. Feltch, from nearby Cohoes.

From its outset the game was a war. Harry won the toss and sent the Haymakers to bat. As Brainard ambled to the box, toothpick in place, the jockeying began.

"There's Brain-hard, the gut-bellied tit!"

"His pitching motion comes from planing privy seats!"

"He could use it to jerk off his whole nine!"

They guffawed and poked each other. Brainard paid no attention. Bellan, their leadoff man, stepped in and watched a rising belt-high fastball split the plate.

"Warning!" shouted the ump. "Next I'll call!"

"Call what?" Allison demanded.

"Wide."

"WHAT!" Allison jumped in the air. Brainard rolled his eyes and studied the sky.

Bellan took three more pitches—an ominous sign of things to come: thirteen Haymakers, including leadoff men in virtually every inning, would walk that afternoon. Whenever Brainard protested— technically illegal, since only captains were supposed to dispute umpires' calls—the Haymakers launched fresh verbal assaults.

Suggesting that Brainard's "jimjams" (wildness) had genetic roots, they proceeded to stock his family tree with startling possibilities.

Finally the pitcher turned in exasperation and said, "Go to damnation!" Champion recoiled in shock at our table. A different reaction came from Bull Craver. He stepped from the Haymaker bench and snarled, "Shut your goddamn flyhole, Brainard, or I'll shut it quick!"

"These guys are incredible," I said to Hurley.

"They're low is what."

"Yeah," I agreed, "on the evolutionary scale."

Again he looked at me in surprise. "You know Darwin's work?"

"Where I come from," I said, "it's old stuff."

Bellan stole second and took off for third on the next pitch. Allison rifled the ball to Waterman, who made a sweeping tag. The ump ruled Bellan safe. Waterman spat a brown stream into the dust between the official's shoes.

We got a break on the next play. When Fisher walked, Bellan, forgetting a recent rules change, trotted home, accustomed to advancing on walks as modern runners do on balks. Allison promptly tagged him. The Haymakers protested, to no avail.

Mart King, swinging hard enough to fell a tree, bounced a ball back to Brainard and slammed his bat to the turf, shattering its handle in a shower of splinters. Brainard abetted his fury by delaying until King was two strides from the bag before throwing him out. The hulking Haymaker glared at him. After another walk, Clipper Flynn stepped in with a theatrical stance, bat cocked like a rifle, face profiled to the grandstand.

"Oh, ain't he the cheese?" said Hurley disgustedly. "Puffing himself before the home folks."

Flynn swung at the first pitch. The ball rose on a line toward left. At shortstop George vaulted high. With an outstretched hand he knocked the ball down, scrambled after it, and threw with all his strength. Ball and runner converged on Gould, who reached with an outsized left hand. The ball materialized in it almost magically and Gould jammed it into Flynn's neck, thrusting him bodily from the baseline before his foot could strike the bag.

"Out!" the ump yelled.

The Haymakers screeched and charged the official. Flynn clutched his throat and wheeled angrily toward Gould. He reconsidered as the blond first baseman stared at him, mustache bristling.

"How's that to start!" Hurley chortled. "Dropped a duck egg on the bastards!"

I knew by now that holding an opponent scoreless in an inning carried the emotional weight of, say, a rim-rattling slam dunk or a quarterback sack on a crucial down. Newspapers invariably reported the number of "whitewash" innings.

The crowd was properly subdued as George moved to the plate. "Hi, Cherokee," he said, grinning. "We miss you back home—ain't nobody we enjoy lickin' so much."

The glum pitcher responded with a fastball at George's head. Its speed was terrifying; I barely saw a pale blur. With lightning agility George bailed out and hit the dirt. He climbed back up, still grinning. "I guess you recall me, too."

Fisher threw at him again, this time targeting his knees. George skipped backward. Fisher scowled. Another blazer, even faster, at George's throat.

"Christ!" I jumped to my feet. "He's trying to cripple him!"

Harry pulled me down. "We'll not descend to their level."

"But your brother—"

"George knows what he's about; he's faced determined men since he was twelve. We play as gentlemen. That language won't do."

I felt like a child. How did the man generate all that force without raising his voice?

George picked himself up again. "You've lost a little spunk off your hot one, Cherokee."

Fisher scraped his spikes in the box and this time threw *behind* George's head—a murderous ploy since a hitter's reaction is to fall back—but George seemed to expect it. He bent forward, placed his bat neatly on the plate, and strolled to first.

Wondering how Fisher could be so flagrant, I asked if a batter was awarded first after being hit by a pitch.

"Only on a fourth wide," Hurley said. "Otherwise strikers'd jump in the path of every toss, especially slow ones."

No wonder, then. The rules gave Fisher a license to head-hunt.

Rattled by George's daring leads, unable to hold him closer, Fisher uncorked an 0–2 pitch six feet over Gould's head. With the runner on, Craver was close behind the plate. Gould alertly swung, just as he'd practiced in Harry's drill. By the time Craver chased the ball down, George perched on third, Gould on second.

"You cut a fine figure from over here, too, Cherokee," called George.

Fisher tunneled the next pitch in the dirt. Craver swore and sprinted after it. George trotted home. Gould scored on Allison's infield hit, but our rally ended when Waterman stumbled—I'd have sworn Craver tripped him coming out of the batter's box—and was thrown out easily.

Stockings 2, Haymakers 0.

In the second Craver smashed a scorcher to left, stole second—he covered ground with surprising speed—and was doubled in by Steve King. King in turn scored on a hit, then Sweasy snatched a low liner and doubled the runner to end their threat. In our half, Flynn chased down Andy's deep fly, Brainard singled and was forced by Sweasy— who misread Harry's signals and tried to steal, only to be gunned down by Craver. A whitewash for them. The crowd perked up.

Stockings 2, Haymakers 2.

Things got worse in the third. Mart King hit a pitch so hard that he shattered a second bat. The ball screamed through Waterman's legs for a double down the line. Overconfident, the big Haymaker was nailed by Allison on a lumbering attempt to steal third. But a succession of walks and hits followed. Craver came up again and skipped a grounder toward short. As George charged it, a runner slowed in front of the ball. It hit his leg and caromed into left. Haymakers circled the bases.

"Interference!" I yelled. "Runner's out!"

"No," Hurley said, scoring the play in his book.

"But it was deliberate!"

"Doesn't matter, ball's alive."

There were times, I reflected, when I might as well be watching a ball game on Mars.

The Haymakers took a 6–2 lead. We fought back in the bottom half, hits by Allison and Harry scoring two. Andy went to the plate with Harry on third and two out.

"Give it a ride, buddy!" I yelled.

Fisher surprised him with an off-speed ball that Andy swung under and blooped down the right-field line. Sprinting over, Flynn extended one hand casually—and fumbled the ball. Andy had already rounded first and Harry had scored when the umpire suddenly yelled, "Foul!" To my astonishment, Harry pivoted and sprinted back for third. Flynn got the ball there ahead of him. The ump thumbed Harry out.

"Good grief," I said. "You mean to tell me you gotta get back on *fouls?*"

"Do I look like *Beadle's Dime Book?*" Hurley snapped. "Why don't you learn the damn rules?"

On the field Harry protested the tardy foul call. It did no good. Three innings gone.

Haymakers 6, Stockings 4.

The gambling booths were bustling as men shouted and jostled, drunks staggered, and odds makers chanted, "Haymakers! Three to one!" The cries grew strident as the number willing to bet on us dwindled.

I scanned the crowd for Morrissey and the woman. They sat in a cluster of extravagantly plumed spectators. His dark head was tilted back, laughing; she leaned against him, smiling and petite. God, she was something. As I stared I became aware of another figure. McDermott, the red-haired gambler, was pointing at me. They followed his arm to look in my direction. McDermott clenched his fist in a slow challenging gesture.

Had she not been looking, I'd have moved my lips: *Fuck you.*

The fourth was a disaster for Andy. He fumbled Fisher's leadoff fly and then threw wildly. Fisher sprinted all the way around. Berating himself, Andy later misjudged Craver's hooking shot, which allowed another run. Only brilliant heads-up play by George, who deliberately dropped a pop-up and launched a double play—no infield-fly rule existed, naturally—kept the lid on for us.

Haymakers 8, Stockings 4.

The pool sellers boomed a new litany: "HAYMAKERS! FOUR TO ONE!"

Struck by a tantalizing idea, I asked Brainard whether the odds referred to the ratio of runs.

"No, just who wins," he said wearily. "They think we'll fold up our tent, so they'll risk four dollars to every one on us."

"Are we gonna fold?"

He glanced up sharply. "What brand of question is that?"

"I'm asking your opinion."

"What's it matter?"

"Depending on your answer, I might want to borrow fifty to bet on us."

"Hush, Sam," he whispered, his eyes darting. "I can't spot you cash for that. Champion'd be fit to—"

"I'd take all risk," I broke in. "At those odds I could double your fifty, pay Andy back, and still have money to spend."

"Double my fifty, you say?"

"Yeah, you got it?"

"Not here." He glanced at the cash box. "But you do, close at hand."

"Cover me if we lose?"

He reflected. "You got collateral?"

"Hell, Asa, when we win you'll get—"

"I'd settle for 'Home in the Valley' and that other ballad."

"I told you, they aren't mine."

He shrugged and worked a clod from his spikes.

"Damn it," I said. "Look, you think we'll win?"

He nodded slowly.

"Okay, what the hell. But just one song: 'Home on the Range.' For your fifty—and only if we lose."

"I guess that's hunky with me."

"Done."

Suppressing a paranoid vision of Brainard throwing the contest to claim the song, I counted the day's take. Nearly a thousand. I palmed five gold eagles and closed the box. "Gotta hit the privy," I told Hurley. "Keep an eye on the money."

I borrowed a sweater from Millar to cover my jersey and headed for a rear booth out of sight of our table. My timing was perfect. When I returned with a betting slip tucked inside my belt, the odds were tumbling before a barrage of Stocking blows. Capitalizing on two hits each by Andy, Brainard, and Sweasy—and several atrocious errors by Mart King—we stunned the Haymakers with ten runs.

But they came at a price. As Andy sprinted home the second time, a premonition told me to watch Craver. He stood disgustedly, hands on hips, just behind the plate. When Andy crossed before him he shifted as if to take an incoming throw. His spike crunched down on Andy's heel. Andy staggered, his leg buckling for an instant. When he came to the bench, he was limping.

I started up, my brain on fire. Andy blocked me and said, "I'm all right."

His face was pale. I bent to look at the wound. His stocking was ripped just above the heel of his left shoe. I saw a splotch subtly darker than the crimson fabric spreading over his Achilles tendon.

"Get your shoe off, we'll ice that."

"No, it'll swell. I'm just scraped." He stared into my eyes. "Don't try to keep me from playing, Sam."

I reluctantly returned to the table.

The Haymaker sluggers, righties all, were pulling Brainard hard now. Craver lashed a drive to left center that Andy, practically hobbling, could not intercept. By the time Harry retrieved it, three runners had crossed the plate. Following a conference, Harry moved to left, Mac to center, and Andy to right.

"Why doesn't he take Andy out?" I demanded.

"Needs him as a striker," Hurley said calmly.

The Haymakers soon struck again—in several senses. With another run in and the corners occupied, the first-base runner took off on Brainard's pitch. While Allison whipped the ball to Sweasy, Craver broke from third on a delayed steal. Sweasy handled it with textbook perfection, stepping in front of second and pegging back to Allison.

But before the catcher could turn for the tag, Craver lowered his head and blindsided him. The ball shot straight up as Allison folded to the ground. Craver touched home while the other Haymaker sprinted to third. When Allison regained his feet, his eyes were glassy. Like Andy, he refused to come out.

Stockings 14, Haymakers 13.

We were at game's midpoint, clinging to the lead. For us it was becoming a question of attrition. In the fifth, Fisher quick-pitched George, got a prompt return from Craver, then hurled the ball squarely into George's back as he protested to the ump. No longer smiling, George retaliated by slamming a drive inches from Fisher's head and hook-sliding safely into second on a daring challenge of Bellan's strong arm. Later in the inning, Andy, mouth set in a grim line, clubbed a pitch into the right-center alley—normally at least a double for him, but now he held up after limping to first. Brainard and Sweasy followed with hits; we came out of the frame with three runs.

Stockings 17, Haymakers 13.

In the sixth Harry took the pitcher's box, Brainard's arm stiffening from hundreds of pitches. The switch proved disastrous. After the predictable leadoff walk, Bellan and Flynn smashed triples into the ring of spectators around the outfield. Craver stepped in later with runners on and drove them home with a ringing blow to center. An infield hit moved him to third. It didn't take a genius to see what would come. "Double steal again," I told Hurley.

Sure enough, Craver barreled toward the plate like a runaway train. Sweasy's throw came late this time, and Allison stepped safely aside. Craver laughed at him as he scored their ninth run of the inning.

Haymakers 22, Stockings 17.

In our half George stretched a looper into a double and scored on Brainard's hit. Andy singled up the middle—and hobbled so slowly that Bellan in center nearly nipped him at first. Harry finally replaced him with Hurley. Andy protested, his face drawn, his bloody legging bulging ominously.

"Better not to risk a serious injury," I told him, patting his shoulder. He knocked my hand away and stalked off.

Brainard returned to the box in the seventh, throwing erratically and giving up two quick scores. The crowd's jeers and swelling volume seemed to parallel our dwindling confidence. Brainard muffed an infield dribbler. Sweasy dropped a ball and had to be restrained from chasing Bellan when the Cuban spiked his toe rounding second. Harry misjudged a sinking liner in center. Waterman capped things by taking a bad-hop smash squarely in the balls, writhing on the turf within the sheltering circle we formed.

Andy took over Hurley's score book chores. He didn't resist when I packed his ankle in ice from a lemonade vendor. The swelling looked bad.

"Sorry, Sam," he muttered.

"No problem."

We watched glumly as Craver drilled his sixth hit. When he reached third they pulled the double steal again. This time, on Harry's instructions, Brainard took Allison's peg in the pitcher's box and threw it immediately back. Craver slid furiously, spikes high. As Allison made the tag, Craver kicked him hard, sending him reeling to the turf. Pants torn, thigh bleeding, Allison scrambled to his feet. He still held the ball.

"Safe!" yelled the ump.

Waterman and Allison charged him. He took refuge behind Craver, who stood mockingly on the plate. Waterman crouched and cocked his arm. Harry grabbed the third baseman before he could swing. It was a while before things calmed.

An outrageous idea started to form in my mind, something I'd once heard or read. I turned to Andy. "I think I know a way to use that delayed steal against them."

"How?"

"I'll need a prop," I said. "Watch the box."

Minutes later I was back with a piece of sponge I'd paid a hack driver a nickel to tear from his seat. Outrageous price, but my bargaining position was poor. I set about trimming it to the desired dimensions.

George carried us in the seventh with two amazing fielding plays, one an over-the-head snatch of a fly to short left, the other an off-balance throw from deep short after backhanding a skidding grounder. We needed the clutch plays badly. We were in trouble.

Haymakers 29, Stockings 22.

The crowd's cheers and the pool sellers' hawking cries battered our ears. Undaunted, George led off the bottom of the seventh with a double over third. Gould lofted a high pop that the Haymaker second baseman lost in the sun. Waterman's fair-foul chopper paralyzed Mart King at third, scoring George and putting Stockings at the corners. Allison stepped in.

And then it happened.

He topped a roller in front of the plate. Craver sprang for it, spun, and dove at Gould, who slid in ahead of his tag. Snarling, teeth bared,

Craver bounded to his feet. Allison was halfway to first. Craver cocked his arm. The ball thudded against the rear of Allison's skull. He toppled without a sound. Fisher retrieved the ball and tagged him as he lay unmoving.

Gould and I carried him to the shade beneath the grandstand, where at length he sat up groggily. On the field both clubs surrounded the ump, who finally ruled Allison out. At that point Champion wanted to withdraw from the field. Harry would have none of it.

"We'll take their measure," I heard him argue as I returned. "Here on their grounds with their chosen official. We'll show them what it means to have ginger."

Andy and I looked at each other with the same unspoken question: Would all the ginger in the world be enough for us to take the Haymakers?

"Fowler!" Harry called. "Sam Fowler!"

"Here!" My voice sounded strange.

"We need you now," Harry said. "You're in for Allison."

$$\diamond \ 6 \ \diamond$$

Timely hits by Harry, Waterman, and Hurley sparked a prolonged rally that saw us score nine runs. One out still to go in the bottom of the seventh, nine runs in, and we'd retaken the lead, 32–29.

Andy nudged me. "You're the striker, Sam. Lay into it."

Trying to hide my nervousness, I popped a wad of "gum" in my mouth. Earlier I'd tried to buy chewing gum only to learn that it didn't exist. All I'd found was a commercially sold blend of spruce gum and chicle that tasted like tree sap. Now I chewed furiously.

At the plate I dug in, waved Gould's black Becky menacingly, and took a deep breath. Fisher regarded me with no visible affection. Craver spat at my shoes. "Here's a prime-sized gump," he growled. "He'll buy the rabbit, Cherokee."

I tried to concentrate on Fisher. Gump? Rabbit?

"You callin' it?" asked the ump.

Shit, I'd forgotten. "Low."

I scarcely saw the ball as it darted from an upsweep of hand, arm, and shoulder; it flashed suddenly in the sunlight like a rippling fish. I'd intended to look at one. Instead I swung—and missed by a foot.

Craver laughed scornfully. "Give the gump another, he's narrow gauge."

I worked my gum, trying to concentrate. Fisher's speed was overwhelming. Could I get around on him? I checked the defense and saw Mart King playing deep at third base. Hmmm . . .

As Fisher wound I squared around and slid my right hand up the bat, cradling it with thumb and forefinger, extending it like an offering. The ball's sharp impact drove it back against the cushion of my palm. The ball trickled down the third-base line.

I dug for first, sure that I could beat it out. Awareness quickly came that I was the only one moving. Even the Stocking base runners stood

[81]

staring at the ball as it died halfway to third. Then hell broke loose again as the Haymakers stormed the field, claiming I was out.

"What's wrong?" I asked Harry as he ran past. "That was a perfect bunt."

"Is that what you call it?"

I realized then that not only had I executed a bunt, I'd invented it.

The ump finally compromised, agreeing to count it a strike. The afternoon's cumulative strain showed on Harry's face. "That was a singular maneuver," he told me. "Don't ever use it again."

Craver shared a number of personal observations with me as I stepped in again. Least offensive was his reference to me as a "milk boy." He seemed to harbor doubts about my masculinity.

"Chill out, Godzilla," I suggested. It shut him up temporarily.

I swung hard at the next pitch, but the result was a slow bouncer taken easily by the first baseman. I kicked a rock halfway across the diamond. Why couldn't it have been storybook? Knock the ball halfway out of the galaxy, get carried off the field by my teammates, tumble into bed with that sensational blonde.

At our bench I secured the sponge under my belt, pulled Allison's glove from my pocket, and started for my position.

Andy grabbed my arm. "Sam, you're not truly gonna use that!"

"The glove?" I said. "Sure, why not?"

"Oh, lord."

I understood moments later. The Haymakers pointed and guffawed, a reaction which spread through the crowd. Flynn minced in dainty circles, fitting his hand into an imaginary glove. Craver roared, "First the milksop—what'd he call it?—*bunts* the ball. Now he's turned out like some Nancy boy with his little pinkies in a . . . *glove!*" It was too much for them; several actually rolled on the ground.

I went out to the box to check signals with Brainard. It didn't take long. One finger for the "chain lightning," two for the "snake ball" delivered with surreptitious lateral spin. It was so noisy that we could scarcely hear one another. The jibes were taking a decided tone:

"WHERE'S YOUR BONNET, MARY?"

"AIN'T YOU THE SIZABLE PEACH!"

Brainard shook his head in disgust. "These country reubens're even lower than I thought."

"What are they saying, that I'm gay?"

He looked at me incredulously. "I guess not!"

I realized my mistake. "You know, homosexual . . . queer?"

To my surprise his cheeks turned hot pink. A topic clearly beyond discussion.

"CUT THE JAW MUSIC, GIRLS!" Craver's voice boomed, bringing waves of laughter.

At first I was amused, thinking that in more ways than one I'd come a long way backward from San Francisco of the 1980s. But as it continued for long minutes, my anger began to rise. I resisted an urge to raise my offending glove hand and flip off the entire place. But it would only stir them more. As Harry'd said, why descend to their level?

Tension built sharply in the eighth. Down by three, the Haymakers knew time was running short. When Flynn led off with the predictable walk, every soul in the park knew he would challenge me with his speed: stealing second, he would put himself in scoring position and out of double-play danger. Harry came in for a consultation. We'd try to discourage their running game by showcasing my arm at once. Harry would play shallow in center—a calculated risk with Craver up—to provide a backup in case I overthrew.

The powerful catcher stepped in, waggling his ass and digging his spikes deep. I crouched behind the plate, keeping a wary eye on Flynn on first.

"Don't get too near, sissy boy," Craver warned in falsetto. From the side, where the ump stood, came a muffled laugh. I focused on my tasks in the next seconds.

As Harry had instructed, Brainard's first pitch zoomed well outside. I stepped out for it quickly. We'd guessed right: Flynn was off, sprinting for second. Craver threw his bat to distract me. It missed the ball, which smacked into my hands only an instant before Craver's shoulder bumped me. I swore and shoved past him, set my feet, and threw to second. Flynn slid headfirst. The ball came low and hard—a hell of a throw, everything considered—and Sweasy plunged it savagely into the small of Flynn's back.

The ump, dashing out near the pitching box, spread his arms. "Safe!"

Flynn bounced up, face contorted, hair flying, and said something to Sweasy, who sprang at him; they tumbled to the turf, clawing like cats.

My shoulder suddenly felt as if a boulder had fallen on it. Bull Craver spun me around, his livid face inches from mine. "You goddamn sissy bastard," he sputtered, spit flying into my face. "You push me like that, you'll—"

I didn't wait for the rest, but thrust my arms out, jolting the heels of my hands against his chest. He stumbled backward. With a high incredulous howl he communicated the joy he'd have in dismantling

[83]

me. He gathered himself to leap, only to be enfolded in the burly arms of Mart King.

"Not now, Will!" King yelled. "After the match!"

"I'll bury 'im!"

"Grand—but after!"

While I waited for Craver to stop foaming I took in the formidable torso, the hamlike fists, the brutal face.

"I'm going to say this once." I put all the authority I could muster into my voice. "I've been in the ring. I know how to fight. If you force me to prove it, you're going to get hurt."

They both stared at me. "What ring?" said King.

"In college."

"College!" Craver snorted. "You milk-sucking whoreson! Soon's we whip you tit suckers, I'll cave your goddamn homely face in."

"I'll be waiting."

"You'll wish you'd hid in a shithole."

"You lay a hand on any of us," I told him, "I'm gonna knock your fucking head off."

It felt delicious to say it.

Sweasy and Flynn had been separated and were glowering at each other near second base. Craver picked up his bat and gave me one more homicidal stare. I set up on the inside, hoping Brainard's fastball would drive him off the plate. But Craver was not to be intimidated; whipping his bat with vicious precision, he powered a drive just inside third that Hurley, in left, played perfectly, holding him to a single. Flynn scored. The Haymakers trailed by only two.

Steve King popped up for the first out. The next hitter grounded to Sweasy, who flipped to George at second. Craver bore down on him. George vaulted over the searching spikes and sidearmed the ball to Gould. Double play! We'd held them off. I jogged from the diamond, thinking I hadn't done badly. Now maybe we could cushion our slim lead and salt the contest away.

It didn't happen. Frenzied eruptions from the crowd followed each of our meager offensive thrusts: Harry down on an infield trickler; Hurley a foul bound to Craver; Brainard an easy fly to Flynn.

One, two, three. How they loved it!

Stockings 32, Haymakers 30.

I could feel the game's momentum swinging to them. All of us felt it. We took the field grimly in the ninth, knowing we had to hold them.

Brainard stared at the ball for a long moment and then called us to his box. Picking at the stitches, he said, "They switched the damn ball on us!"

Harry examined it, then summoned the ump. Brainard figured they'd made the switch in the eighth, pitching a dead ball to us while removing the original ball's cover and inserting a Bounding Rock, then restitching it in time for their ups. If Brainard hadn't spotted shiny threads on the discolored surface, it would have worked.

The Haymakers denied everything. A confusion of arguments ensued, each club claiming a forfeit on the grounds of unsporting conduct. The crowd stamped and whistled and booed. Finally a new ball was agreed upon and play resumed.

To our dismay their leadoff man—in this case the speed-burning Bellan—again walked on four pitches. Brainard stalked around the box angrily. I went out to steady him. He had almost nothing on his pitches now.

"How do you feel?" I asked.

"Like a double play!" he snapped. "Get the hell out of here!"

Fisher fouled off several pitches and finally sent one spinning high behind the plate. I wheeled and dug hard, saw the ball bounce far ahead, dove anyway, and before it bounced again managed to thrust my gloved hand—let them savor it!—between the ball and the grass; my fingers clutched it for the out. Remembering the stupid foul rule, I threw quickly and nearly doubled Bellan off before he could dive back to first.

"That's the ginger, Sam!" yelled Harry. Praise poured in from the others.

But my satisfaction vanished on the very next pitch—a bouncer in the dirt that got by me so far that Bellan stood on third by the time I retrieved it. Shit!

The tying run strode arrogantly to the plate in the person of Clipper Flynn. He swung viciously and pulled a mammoth drive that hooked foul just before clearing the outfield carriages. Then he lined a shot that nearly tore Waterman in half. The scrappy third baseman somehow clutched the ball to his stomach for the out. We took a collective breath. Two down. One more and the game was ours. Just one more. The crowd was growing silent.

Up to the plate stalked Craver, bat twitching in his hand. His face was set in grim lines. We said nothing to each other now.

Remembering that he'd drilled a tight pitch last time, Brainard teased him with one six inches outside. Craver watched it pass. The ump issued his usual warning. We faced a tough decision: work Craver cautiously and risk putting the tying run on; or challenge him, taking our chances against his powerful bat. We decided to come at him. Brainard loosed a beauty that danced along the outside corner.

It was the wrong choice. Craver's upper body swelled as he whipped the bat like a toy. The ball exploded and climbed the sky, soaring over the outfield. Harry and Mac turned and gave chase into the crowd of carriages and spectators. Mac shouldered desperately among them. He emerged with the ball and heaved it in with all his might to the cutoff. Craver, rounding third, abruptly retreated to the bag.

The tying run stood only ninety feet away.

Steve King strode to the plate. I called time and went to the pitching box. "What now?" Brainard demanded. I waved for Harry to join us.

"Let's walk him," I said.

Harry's eyes widened. "On purpose?"

I nodded.

He shook his head. "It isn't done."

His propriety irritated me. "So what? Let's do it anyway. Their shortstop's on deck; he hasn't hit anything all afternoon."

Harry pulled at his whiskers, his soft eyes probing mine. "But that would set up the two-stage steal again. Even if Craver held third while the other advanced, they'd be in position to score the tying *and* lead runs with a single strike."

"But Craver *will* try to score," I argued. "He's done it all day—and I want him to once more. I have a way to get that last out we need." I told them what I had in mind. Brainard shook his head in increasing wonder.

"The rules don't provide for it," Harry said, his face troubled.

"Do they forbid it?" I said. "And do they provide for Craver knocking us around whenever he wants?"

After a moment Harry turned and jogged toward his position.

"That means we're on our own." A smile glinted in Brainard's eyes. "I say let's give 'em a stir, Sam."

We walked King on four lobs far outside the striker's box. The crowd bellowed. I was showered with new abuse, not all of it verbal: ripe fruit and several bottles thudded nearby. I had outraged their notions of how the game should be played. First the bunt. Then the glove. Now an intentional walk. Too much.

King edged off first. Craver moved down the line from third and called, "Now I'll see what you're made of, milk boy!"

You will indeed, I thought.

I withdrew the sponge from my belt and squeezed it into my gloved hand. As Brainard twisted into his windup, I watched King at first. Sure enough, he was off with the pitch. The ball came in hard and high; the batter made no attempt to swing. I caught it cleanly and rose to throw. From the corner of my eye I saw Craver poised to sprint. I plucked the sponge from under the ball and hurled it as hard as I could toward second, having trimmed it to the approximate circumference of a baseball. Brainard sprawled flat in the pitching box as though to get out of its way.

At the instant it left my hand Craver lowered his head and charged. "No!" the hitter yelled. Craver kept coming. I concealed the ball in my gloved hand, my heart pounding, and forced myself to look straight ahead until he was only a few strides away. I'd moved slightly up the line toward third inside the baseline. Craver could have passed with no contact. But I could tell that wasn't what he had in mind: his forearm swung upward as he barreled straight for me. I stepped away and with a right hook planted the ball against the side of his head. The solid impact was very satisfying. Craver grunted, lurched sideways, toppled to one knee.

I showed the ball to the ump. He looked perplexed. "Runner's out," I prompted, and tossed it to him.

Then Craver was up and charging, his eyes crazy. Concentrate, I told myself, trying to resurrect basics from more than a decade before: chin tucked on shoulder, weight distributed on balls of feet, rocker steps. I could almost hear my coach's litany: "Hands up! Chin down! Breathe!"

I stepped inside Craver's wild charge, rocked forward and jabbed sharply, exhaling with a snort as I punched. There was a popping sound and blood gushed from Craver's nose. He stopped and stared stupidly at droplets spattering to the ground. A hand clutched at my shoulder. I shook it off. There was shouting, a sudden confusion of straining bodies. I glimpsed Mac and Mart King struggling on the ground; Brainard and Fisher flailing at each other; Sweasy astride Flynn, clutching handfuls of long hair.

Craver came at me again. He brushed aside a parrying jab and jolted me with a right that exploded on my cheekbone, his fist slamming squarely into my unhealed cut. It felt as if my face had split like fruit.

I staggered back. Darkness hovered at the edges of my vision. Andy appeared suddenly, incongruously, on Craver's back. The big man tore him loose, backhanded him, tossed him roughly. It afforded me precious seconds. I backpedaled and shook off my wooziness as Craver advanced, managing to halt him with another jab to his nose. Eyes glazed with pain, he reached out blindly. I crossed a right over his outstretched hands. He raised them reflexively when my fist thudded against his eye. I drove a left into his gut. His hands sagged again. Balanced, breathing in exaggerated puffs, I hooked him twice, then got my shoulder behind a straight right that staggered him and almost sent him down. Looking as if he couldn't believe what was happening, he glared at me, one eye already swelling shut.

"Had enough, asshole?"

He crumpled to one knee and said nothing.

I moved closer and asked him again.

He'd decoyed me. With unbelievable swiftness a boot materialized in his hand and swiped upward at my face. The spikes grazed my chin as I wrenched my head back. I kicked at him wildly and threw everything I had as he came to his feet. I drove fists into his body, neck, face. Blood and sweat sprayed in a pink mist. Snarling, spewing incoherently, he kept coming as I circled him. Finally he stood weaving, his chest heaving with sobbing breaths.

I sent him spinning with a sloping left, then stepped forward to finish him—and my arms were pinned from behind by another Haymaker. Craver lurched forward, punched me on the forehead, then clamped me in a headlock. Even half-conscious, his strength was superhuman. I panicked as I felt my neck giving; desperately I gripped the encircling arm and wrenched it forward. We were so slippery with sweat that I popped free, nearly at the cost of my ears. As he wheeled I crashed a right squarely to his mouth. He fell forward, head sagging, and landed heavily on hands and knees. For a long moment he teetered, spitting blood and fragments of teeth. Then he fell sideways to the sod.

I raised my head wearily and saw a circle of staring players. "Mother of God!" said Hurley. "Where'd you learn to fight like that?"

I shook my head, too exhausted to talk.

The King brothers lugged Craver off the field. The silent crowd looked on disbelievingly. The ump had little choice but to rule Craver out—he'd never touched the plate. The Haymakers' frantic search of the rules turned up nothing to serve them.

Following the conventions of the time, we took our last ups, even though we'd won 32–31. Hits by George, Gould, and Waterman, plus halfhearted fielding by the Haymakers, gave us five more runs.

Knots of silent spectators dotted the field, staring as if we were alien creatures. It gave me the willies. For one frightening instant I thought I glimpsed the dark figure of Le Caron near the grandstand; then I realized it was only a cluster of shadows.

No songs or cheers followed this game. The Haymakers departed quickly. While Mac, looking no worse for his tangle with the behemoth Mart King, packed our two dozen bats into their huge sail-cloth bag—the rookie's traditional chore—I pulled Millar's sweater on over my jersey and headed for the booths, shoved in at the head of a line, and showed my betting slip.

"There's a problem, chum," said the pool seller, a thin-faced, fast-talking man.

"No problem," I said. "Fork over two hundred."

"Wait, you see—" He stopped and peered at me. "Ain't you him that whipped Will Craver?"

"Yeah, and if you don't—"

"You circled him like a cooper 'round a barrel, hammering his every side." He flicked jabs at an imaginary opponent. "Why, it's an honor to serve him who took Bull Craver's measure." He extended a wad of bills. "Him that's wrecked every grogshop hereabouts, and most men in them too."

I counted the money.

"If'n I was you Ohio boys," he confided, "I'd keep a sharp eye out."

"The crowd gets nasty?"

"Naw, they're sheep. It's the wolves I'd fear."

I pocketed the money. "Gamblers?"

He winked slyly. "Red Jim was here at the commence of each inning, laying down three thousand without fail—a thousand for each Red Stocking out, he boasted."

"So he lost . . ."

"Twenty-seven thousand."

"Good God."

"Word is it warn't all his, neither. Some's from John Morrissey— there's one unlikely to stand for losing—and some straight from the Fenian treasury. If either part's true, ol' Red Jim's on the anxious seat right now."

"Thanks." I reflected that I'd be on it too if I didn't make myself scarce. "By the way, who was the woman with Morrissey?"

"Name's Elise Holt." He looked wistful. "Leg-show queen, one of them British Blondes."

Leg-show queen?

"Somethin' to nibble, ain't she? Here's my advice: Don't trouble yourself thinkin' about her."

"Why not?"

" 'Cause she'd fix your flint 'fore you could *begin* to spark her."

The fight boosted my status considerably. To Harry I was now Sam instead of Fowler; George sought me out to share his choice stereopticon views; Mac and Gould, the team's enforcers, let me know they'd accept my assistance in a pinch; Waterman allowed as how he might be willing to play cards with me again sometime; Brainard, wearing a shiner, insisted we begin his boxing instruction at once; Sweasy was relatively inoffensive; and of course Andy was proud beyond all measure. "Ain't Sam a dinger?" he demanded repeatedly. Hurley topped them all by coming up with a dandy quote from *Pilgrim's Progress:*

> *"How doth the Fowler seek to catch his Game*
> *By divers means, all which one cannot name?"*

It was all very warm and flattering, although I felt guilty about the fight. An old pattern. At Berkeley, even winning the 190-division Pac-Ten title, I'd had to work myself into a rage to perform, as against Craver (or, for that matter, Stephanie's parents' TV). But when the rage passed I felt only shame. Victorious, I'd exploited sick emotions. Defeated, I'd unleashed them for nothing.

My coaches said I lacked a killer instinct; at some level I had to *want* to put opponents away. But I could never really get into it. And so I put out of mind that Craver was a bullying animal, even that he'd injured Andy and Allison. I dwelt instead on his lack of training, thinking I'd had a huge advantage. Stupid, I know, and probably self-defeating as hell.

Under the best conditions I'm hardly a cheery riser. The next morning I set new records in mood foulness. My body felt as if it had been systematically hammered. My hands were mittens of flesh: the knuckles looked like they'd pounded nails; the fingers were too swollen to bend. My forehead was purple. My gashed cheek was seeping again. I'd slept fitfully. I didn't want any more beefsteak for breakfast—invariably overcooked, with a thin slab of bone in the center, swimming in butter and laden with coarse black pepper. I was fed up with baths in cramped zinc tubs. I wanted a decent shower—which mystified Andy, to whom all bathing except after games was strictly a once-a-week concept. And I was tired of remembering to say "dinner" when I meant "lunch" and "valise" when I meant "suitcase." I broke my goddamn collar button, too.

The day's start, however, was nothing compared with its end.

We entrained shortly before noon. The sky was clear when we left Troy, but cold winds and showery squalls hit during the short hop to Albany. Crossing the river from Rensselaer—situated, George informed us, directly over the fort where "Yankee Doodle" had been written—we saw a flotilla of enormous side-wheel steamboats working the Hudson. Fulton's *Clermont,* the first steam-powered craft—a hundred feet long and twelve and a half feet wide—docked at Albany during its maiden cruise in 1807. Now, George reported enthusiastically, leviathans like the *Isaac Newton* were four hundred feet long, seventy-five wide, and forty-seven deep, with sleeping accommodations for seven hundred passengers.

The others looked suitably impressed. Yes, I thought, let's hurry up and destroy the rivers faster.

We passed through a patchwork of foundries and shipping yards crammed with cattle and lumber. As the Erie Canal's eastern terminus, Albany was a major export point by water and rail—George had a card picturing the *DeWitt Clinton,* one of the nation's first trains, which had chugged out of the city and into history only thirty-eight years previously.

It was all so new, yet already happening so fast.

Albany's Nationals, our afternoon opponents, took us to their clubhouse on North Pearl, where we suited up. My uniform was still damp and ill smelling. With Andy out and Allison questionable, there was a strong chance I'd play. I chewed gum and concentrated.

I could have relaxed. The contest was so one-sided that few of the spectators who braved the forbidding weather were around by the end. A solitary pool seller did little business. There was no sign of Morrissey, McDermott, or Le Caron.

It went only seven innings. Hurley made the most of his chance to play by pulling two homers down the right-field line. Gould smashed another. George and Hurley each banged out seven hits. Harry made a one-handed catch in center, and Sweasy, Waterman, and George stole three bases apiece. Huddled together over the score book, Andy and I managed to keep warm. After the Haymaker game, this was like schoolyard exercise. We won 49–8.

The Stockings' record was now a neat 10–0.

Amid talk of the tough games awaiting us in Brooklyn, we ate a hearty supper at the Delavan House, a noisy establishment at Broadway and Steuben, "junction of all railroad lines." We would soon board another train, this one for Springfield, Massachusetts, where we'd play the next day, then on to Boston for three contests.

It happened just after I stepped out the door of the Delavan House. I heard a voice—"Say, there!"—and turned to see a figure beckoning to me with a lantern. He stood in darkness at the end of the long veranda. A slouch hat shadowed his features. "Could you hold this light? I'm trying to fix my horse's shoe."

Something about the voice was vaguely familiar, but I didn't think about it then. "Sure." I looked around; the others were still inside. "I've got a minute or two."

"Much obliged," he muttered, head down, as I approached the corner of the porch. "Here, you take the lamp and steady her head, I'll—"

Then he stepped back. In the lantern's halo I recognized McDermott's features. A grin curved his mouth; his eyes were shadowy pockets. Behind him a thin dark figure moved quickly. I stood frozen, lantern in one hand, reins in the other. There was a dark glint of metal. Then a bright flash. A terrible sound—something between a crack and a roar—reverberated around me. I was slammed back against the porch, spun around by a sharp impact on my left side.

They're killing me!

Without conscious volition I heaved the lantern. It exploded in flames on the planks midway between the dark figure and me. For an instant I glimpsed Le Caron's pocked skin and glittering eyes. Then he was gone, and people were swarming around.

The next hours are confused in my mind. I recall seeing my frock coat drenched with blood and thinking it was ruined. I remember being lifted bodily by Mac and Gould, being examined by a young nervous doctor—gunshots evidently weren't his thing—and, later, just before the team left, being startled by the sight of tears in Andy's eyes.

Jesus, I must be dying. . . .

And then feeling oddly comforted that he cared that much.

I awoke in a sun-splashed room, sweating and stiff. Pain radiated above my left hipbone.

"Shit," I groaned.

"The eloquent voice of suffering." Across the room, sitting in a straight-backed chair, Millar regarded me. "The club departed last night," he said sourly. "I was assigned to stay."

"Am I . . . ?"

"Yes, you'll certainly survive. The bullet passed through flesh—of which you have a sufficiency—without coming near your organs." He sounded as if he wanted to add, "Worse luck."

In my brain Le Caron's face flickered again in the lantern's glow. I felt a jet of fear. "Are we still in Albany?"

He nodded. "You're safe enough. The police department's next door. I alerted the hotel staff not to allow anyone up here." He stood and stretched. "I'm to put you on a train to New York as soon as you're fit to travel."

I began to shake, a most unpleasant sensation. They'd tried to kill me. My teeth chattered—something I thought happened only in books—and I couldn't quiet my violent trembling.

Millar paced irritably and grumbled at not being able to write his dispatches.

I bent my legs and felt a spasm of pain. The shaking gradually stopped. "I'll do 'em for you," I told him. "They're all the same: 'Smiling George Wright, striker nonpareil of the Crimson Hose, waved his willow wand and dashed a splendid blow to the outer gardens. Making his third, he showed pluck withal by—'!"

"What's lacking in that?" Millar demanded.

"It's flowery tripe."

"And of course you're inferring that your own prose—which remains conveniently unseen—is superior?" His eyes were bright behind the steel-rimmed spectacles. "Fowler, my father covered river news around Cincinnati for fifty years. He taught me the profession. My sporting coverage has been commended by Henry Chadwick himself, so I don't care to hear your rude—"

"Who the hell's Henry Chadwick?"

"Who *is* he?" He looked incredulous. "Only the country's foremost sporting writer, the originator of scientific scoring, the most prolific voice—"

"Okay, okay," I said wearily. "I believe you. You're wonderful. I'm sorry."

He nursed me, grudgingly but well, for the next day and a half, changing the poultice on my wound, injecting me with quinine, helping me to the commode, ordering meals, bringing newspapers in, and generally keeping me company.

My body was behaving strangely. My cheek resisted healing, but the bruise on my forehead vanished almost at once. Similarly, the bullet's passage scarcely pained me the second day; when we changed the bandage I saw the puckered flesh already beginning to congeal. The young doctor marveled at my recovery; finding no sign of infection, he said I could travel as soon as I wanted.

That afternoon, while Millar purchased train tickets, I walked slowly uptown until I saw an awning bearing the sign FIREARMS. I'd never owned a gun in my life. Forty minutes later I walked out with a snug-barreled Remington derringer. The proprietor, a swarthy war veteran who vaguely resembled Richard Nixon, had shown me how to load its rimfire shells in the twin chambers. My fingers enveloped its rubber-grip handle; I could almost palm the whole weapon. I hefted it. Heavy for such a little thing, maybe three-quarters of a pound. Death at my fingertips. I aimed into a barrel of sawdust and pulled the trigger. A tongue of flame shot from one of the nickel-plated barrels. The sawdust jumped. There was a satisfying recoil as the weapon kicked against my hand.

"Ain't accurate more'n a few feet," the proprietor said disparagingly. "Gambler's gun, for under the table. You intend on hitting something, you'll want a long-barreled Colt. Hell, a body could damn near dodge the bullets outen that derringer, they travel so slow."

"It'll be fine," I told him, wondering if I could actually fire it at anybody. "Where's the safety?"

He snorted. "You see one?"

I didn't. There wasn't. I bought it anyway.

By telegram Harry wished me fast recovery and reported wins over Springfield, 80–5, and the Lowells of Boston, 29–9. In a separate dispatch Andy warned me to stay alert; somebody had been around asking about "the ballist with a bandaged cheek."

Late that evening—Thursday, June 10, forty-eight hours after the shooting—Millar walked me to the train station. I tried to appear nonchalant, but couldn't stop my heart thumping or my eyes darting nervously. When somebody wants you dead, it tends to dampen your faith in humanity.

I was to go directly to the Stockings' hotel and wait for them to arrive three days later. Millar, bound for Boston, had booked me through on the Penn Central. But, fearing that line would be watched, I took a roundabout route.

By midnight I was cursing my decision. Evasion was one thing, rattling and lurching along an interminable milk run through the Catskills was another. It wasn't until nearly one A.M. that I got off at Binghamton, the transfer point for the Erie. A long journey to Manhattan still lay ahead.

I sat glumly in the empty waiting room, debating whether to spend the night in town. It seemed like a good idea. My side was acting up a bit. My head felt a little weird. Then I heard something drumming against one of the high windows and saw some kind of bird thrusting itself almost comically against the glass as if trying to fly through it. Then, to my astonishment, it *did* seem to fly through, for suddenly it was inside, whooshing and rustling and careening in circles. I watched it make two passes, then I crouched as it dove at me, a light-hued feathery mass, wild eyes staring. Water bird, I thought, but couldn't be sure; it brushed my collar—or maybe just the air close by—and vanished through the doorway. I stepped there in time to see it winging away over the trees lining the tracks.

No longer drowsy, I peered up at the window. No opening was

evident. How had it gotten in? I played with the idea that it had come for me. A silly and yet compelling notion. Maybe the bird had been lonely and sought company. Its flight had looked almost purposeful. Maybe it was a message. Was I to follow, along the tracks?

A wheezing, asthmatic porter lugged my bag through the narrow aisles of the sleeping cars. He stopped at my berth—a fold-down shelf with two blankets behind a thin curtain. I fished through my pockets for a tip. Coins spilled to the floor. I handed him a dime and bent to retrieve the others. In doing so I glimpsed a corner of what appeared to be a letter lying against the baseboard, concealed by folds of drapery. I pulled it out. It was a thick packet tied with lavender ribbon and scented like the sachets I remembered in Grandma's dresser.

I slipped the ribbon free. Enfolded in half a dozen sheets of stationery was a clipping from the previous week's *Plymouth Pulpit,* of Brooklyn. It was the text of a Henry Ward Beecher sermon entitled "Heaven's Golden Promise." I set it aside and unfolded the letter. Each sheet was crested with a circular monogram of leafy twigs forming the intertwined letters O and L. The handwriting, in purple ink, was small and neat.

My Dear Youth, I read, and felt a remote memory stir.

> *You entreated me so mercelessly (you are wicked, though I know you never intend it) not to 'send you away empty in heart and hand,' as you put it (as if I were capabel of sending you away!) and so I am staying up to write this.*

The salutation, the misspellings, the ink—a preposterous suspicion began to form in me.

> *I have realized, as perhaps you have not, that Father has of late come to tolerate your bold glances in my direction, or is perhaps mearly resigned to them. I say this not to scold you, as you are wont to accuse me of in your 'wicked' moods, but to indicate how much Father has come to accept you since the beginning of our engagement. In your absense he speaks most proudly of you. Already he has subscribed fifty copies of the book for his friends the moment it is published. Speaking of that, you must not become to critical of Mr. Blish. You have labored so hard, my darling, I know that you will reap the harvest of your effort. Remember, 'The poet and the beetle, each his task to perform.'*

Succeeding paragraphs dealt with family members, friends, and a cousin marrying in Hartford the following month. I scanned them impatiently, looking for the proof I wanted. At the end of the letter I found it.

> *You mustn't carry out your silly promise! Becoming ill cannot hasten my throat to recover. I scarce know when you are develling me. The idea of you not sleeping in underclothes and going without socks is enough to worry my poor throat sicker! Is that your purpose? You will only succeed in bringing back the cold you had last month—and then you will be low-spirited again! That is more than I could bear. Please carry my loving cautions with you—and write in great detail all that you think of Reverend B's sermon. (I believe it his finest this year.)*
>
> *Your loving Livy*

My hand trembled as I stared at the signature and realized for certain that I held a letter to my namesake from the woman he would marry, Olivia Langdon. What was it doing here? Could Twain himself have dropped it? I felt a giddy rush of excitement. He might have passed through this aisle, stood in exactly this spot.

$$— \diamond\ 7\ \diamond —$$

*F*rail daughter of a millionaire coal magnate, apotheosis of gentil-
ity and respectability—everything, in short, that to Twain
meant "making it". . . .

I was surprised at the details that flooded back. Livy would become
his censor, his respectability filter. I'd argued in my J school thesis that
she symbolized Twain's great sellout; that in settling for bourgeois
security, he forever cashed in his bohemian credentials, sold short his
creative freedom. Never again to be an independent satiric visionary—
an artist—he fittingly became the superstar crony of plutocrats.

Well, hurling thunderbolts at Livy Langdon from grad school was
one thing. Holding her letter now was quite another. I felt a feverish-
ness beyond anything research was likely to evoke. Livy, only twenty-
three if I had calculated correctly, was very much alive and being
courted by Twain. I remembered that he was some ten years older,
which would make him about . . . my age.

I pushed through the cars till I caught the porter. He knew of no
passenger list, but suggested I stop by the saloon car, where some
gentlemen still held forth. I retraced my steps and found the car near
the end of the train. At a counter along one wall several forlorn men
were drinking; another slumped facedown, his hat mashed on the
counter. Card games were in progress at two tables, the players
low-voiced, intent.

I stood in the doorway peering through clouds of smoke. In my
mind was an unsmiling daguerreotype image of Twain as a young
man. I tried hard to match it to the faces I saw. Impossible. I walked
inside, my excitement slowly dissolving. None of these could possibly
be Twain. I was about to leave when I saw the door to the toilet swing
open at the far end. Out stepped a slender man with bushy auburn hair
and a thick mustache that drooped beneath a Roman nose. His eyes

met mine briefly; in that instant all doubt vanished. I was looking at Mark Twain.

I had an impulse to rush to him, hug him, tell him . . . what? That I'd grown up reading books he hadn't yet written? That I'd been named for him?

I watched him sit alone at the most distant table. He was smaller than I expected; medium height, not short but small-framed, with narrow shoulders. He wore a dark, rumpled suit; his tie was unfastened. Beneath the tousled hair his skin looked pale in the lamplight. He produced a pipe and rummaged through his pockets for matches. I took a deep breath and stepped forward.

"Mr. Clemens?"

His eyes reflected blue-green as they met mine. His hands paused in their search. His mustache twitched. Something in his face changed, a quick masklike adjustment. Pensive and even melancholy in repose, the features were abruptly charged with sly alertness. "Yes?" He peered at me. "Are we acquainted?" The reedy voice held a pronounced drawl.

I held the letter out. "I think this is yours."

"Sweet Jesus," he breathed, snatching it and crushing it to his mouth. He breathed its scent, eyes squeezed shut. "Hang my head and carry me home to die!"

I stood awkwardly as he pulled out a handkerchief and honked into it.

"Forgive me," he said. "As a general thing my feelings're more cordially reserved. I've hunted high and low for this infernal letter. What a relief to have it!"

I told him where I'd found it.

"Must've dropped from my pocket. Sit down, sir! Allow me to stand a drink. This night's built for pleasuring after all. Hell, I'll stand us a dozen!"

He came back with four whiskeys, two apiece. Sorry, Andy, I thought, but this is a very rare occasion.

"You knew I was Clemens," he said. "How's that? Most sound me by a certain nom de plume. I can't recollect—Washoe, the Pacific Slope, the Lyceum circuit? Have we met?"

"Not personally," I said. "I'm Sam Fowler."

"One Sam to another, I'm obliged." We clinked glasses and drank. He gestured at the letter. "I'd be a ruined proposition if my darling thought I cared so little for her as to misplace that. Course, I'd gladly go through Hades in a celluloid suit to make up for it. Not that she'd demand it. She's the dearest, gentlest, sweetest—oh, the *best* woman I can picture. Why such a noble and delicate creature as Livy consented to a conjugal matchup with the likes of—" He stopped suddenly, pulled the ribbon from the letter, and scanned its sheets.

"Why, there're no full names here, just as I reckoned. How'd you know it was to me?"

"Isn't it signed Livy Langdon?" I said.

He shook his head, eyes narrowing slightly over the hawk nose. "It addresses Youth and is signed Livy. Took months to convince her there's no comfort to me in signing Olivia Louise Langdon, a practice that nigh put me into lunatic spasms. Presently I'm working to repair her spelling. When I've done that, I'll relax with something easy—like bringing the Pyramids over brick by brick."

As I laughed he gauged my reaction with a deadpan expression, the performer checking his material.

"Why Youth?" I said.

" 'There is no word for failure in the bright lexicon of youth,' " he recited dryly. "One of the sayings Livy keeps in her infernal little inspiration book. It's part of her scheme to haul me out, scrape my keel, and refloat me." He winked foxily as he produced a box of matches. His pipe emitted thick clouds and a swampy odor. He eyed me keenly. "Now, you didn't answer me about the letter, did you?"

"I can't really explain it, Mr. Clemens," I said. "Call it a hunch. To tell the truth, I know a lot about you. You're quite famous, you know."

"Call me Mark," he said, looking pleased. "What exactly do you know?"

The whiskey eroded my caution. "Well, for one thing, I know how you first saw Livy—her brother showed you her picture."

His eyebrows lifted. "And where was that?"

"On your cruise around the world."

"Bay of Smyrna, summer of 'sixty-seven." His drawl sounded almost dreamy. "Even in that ivory miniature she was the loveliest of visions." He shrugged and sucked on his pipe. "But you could be pals with young Charley Langdon or any other close to the family."

"I know your engagement date."

"Oh?" He frowned slightly. "You do?"

"February fourth." I'd proposed to Stephanie on the same date. "It's inscribed in Livy's gold engagement band—and probably inside that one on your finger, too. Want another drink?"

"How'd—?" he began, staring hard. "Yes, I guess I do!" After they came he said, "What part of the country you from, Fowler?"

"San Francisco.

"Freddy Marriott!" he exclaimed. "That's who you pumped! And yet I don't see how Freddy would've known of the rings. . . ."

"Your first daughter will be Susy," I said, laughing, enjoying the power of it; in a way my whole life had been a preparation for this. "I'll give my second girl that name."

"That's very curious," he mused.

"Later you'll write a wonderful book about a boy on a raft and—"

"Hold on," he interrupted. "You're not the first to tell me—I mean, about the girl Susy."

I was speechless for a long moment. My sense of power evaporated, replaced by sharp and poignant sorrow: Susy, his favorite, would die in her early twenties, a terrible loss to Twain and his family. I had no right to be doing this.

"Who else told you?" I said.

"Spiritualist woman, a Lyceum stager with Redpath, same as I was. Went by Madame Antonia, something like that."

I remembered the card in the drugstore. "Clara Antonia?"

"That's the one." He looked at me quizzically. "She also told me I'd run into a spiritual counterpart from another dimension. Said it with tolerable gravity. Even seemed a mite troubled to be informing me. It gave me pause at the time, though I didn't exactly hang fire over it."

My pulse quickened. I *was* following a path, I must be. "What would you say," I asked him, "if I told you my full name was Samuel Clemens Fowler, and that I'd come here from another century?"

He sipped his whiskey. "My historical double?"

"I don't think—well, in a way, maybe."

He regarded me impassively. "What century'd you have in mind?"

"Oh, say the next one—the 1980s, let's imagine."

"They still know about me up then?"

"You'd be surprised."

He ran his hand through his hair. "And folks say *I* suffer from overblown imagination. Would you care to know what I'm wondering?"

"Whether I'm crazy?"

"No," he said, hooded eyes alert. "It's manifest you're a lunatic. I'm wondering if somehow you managed to steal that letter off me."

"I didn't, I swear. Anyway, why would I return it?"

He nodded slowly, seeming to agree.

From whiskey we moved to champagne cocktails. Then sherry cobblers. Then brandy smashes. Twain showed the skeptical bartender how to make what he called "Californy Concoctions." They carried names like Santa Cruz Punch, Eye-Opener, and Earthquake. He bought rounds for the car, celebrating, he said, the prodigality of his love. We raised our glasses to Livy.

Later he let himself be coaxed up beside the bar, where he slouched with thumbs hooked in his vest and told stories in a flat drawl. His style was that of a frontier Jack Benny, I thought; he maintained an unshakable deadpan, pausing often for effect, feigning puzzlement when interrupted by guffaws—a frequent occurrence.

From somebody else his material might have bombed—a preacher who spilled faro cards hidden in his gown during a sermon; a huckster who charged admission to see an eclipse from a topless tent—but Twain made it work. His cappers were tall tales—"stretchers," he called them—about a corporation of mean men who docked an explosives worker for time lost in the air while being blown up; or a champion liar who claimed that his horse outran the edge of a thunderstorm for eighteen miles while his dog swam behind the wagon all the way.

Well into morning, when most of the others had gone, Twain and I sat bleary-eyed. He leaned forward conspiratorially. "Sam, want in on a proposition that could make us richer than Solomon?"

"Sure." I remembered that he loved get-rich-quick schemes, and that several would prove ruinous.

"I mentioned Freddy Marriott earlier. He puts out that infernal *Advertiser* in Frisco. You read it?"

I shook my head, glad I hadn't told him I was a reporter. "What about him?"

"Later this summer Freddy'll announce news so grand it'll make the Pacific Railroad blush. He worked with Henson in England, you know, and never gave up the notion of aerial transport. Using every dime from his paper, Freddy's been hiring engineers on the sly." Twain gave me his foxy look. "At last he's developed a flying steam carriage!"

If it was meant to shock, it failed. I stifled a yawn and said, "You believe that?"

"I'm satisfied *Freddy* believes. He's happy as a lord, laughing at all the doubting sapheads. A working model goes on display next month. Then he'll offer stock in his new company."

"A company to build and sell flying machines?"

"Nope, Freddy figures imitators'll swarm in like insects, soon as the word gets out. He couldn't do much to stop them. He's primed for something bigger."

"Bigger than airplanes?"

"Aerial carriages," he corrected, looking around to make sure we were alone. "Freddy's going after a monopoly on transcontinental passenger service."

"What!" I almost laughed out loud. "He intends to fly people coast to coast?"

"These are revolutionary times, Sam," said Twain firmly. "What sounds lunatic one year is thundering reality the next. Those who don't take risks swallow the dust of those who do. Think of the hidebound wretches who didn't invest in steamboats and trains, canals, the telegraph—a host of modern inventions. There'll soon be steam trolleys and Lord knows what else. Anyway, Freddy's letting his friends know about it now, so we can get in before things go sky high." He paused to make sure I caught the pun. "I'd be of a mind to plunge, if I had cash at the ready. Picture the returns!"

I didn't get much of a picture. "Why are you telling me about it?"

He looked hurt. "As a favor, my man! For the service you did. You struck me as a likely gent for a brave new game."

"Maybe so, but I don't have the cash either."

"A damnable shame. Well, when you get back to Frisco"—he gave me a penetrating look—"that is, if it happens to be in *this* century, maybe you'll see fit to hunt up Freddy and look into it. Are you headed back soon?"

I explained that I was meeting the Stockings in New York.

"Ah, baseball. The game's everywhere now, puffed up like a dimeshow marvel. I've stood reg'lar watches on Elmira's bleaching boards, observing our two local clubs trying to humble each other. Played myself as a boy in Missouri—called it town ball then. One afternoon Tom Blankenship struck a ball through Widow Holliday's kitchen window. Overturned a painkiller bottle from the sill. The widow's old yellow cat, Last Judgment, took a stiff wallop of the stuff and streaked out to settle accounts with every dog in the township."

I laughed, again aware of his scrutiny.

"You look done in," Twain said. "Let's get some sleep."

It seemed only seconds after I'd fallen on my bunk that the shout came: "Jersey City! All off!"

We crossed the Hudson—here it was called the North River—on one of the small side-wheelers packed along the Jersey docks. I climbed to the observation deck, hoping to see the Manhattan skyline, but fog formed a dense curtain. The ferry's pealing bell was answered by invisible craft on all sides. I stared into the mist and wondered what lay ahead for me. As the Desbrosses Street dock loomed, I felt my elbow touched.

"Been here before?" Twain's reedy drawl.

"No," I said, which was almost true. I'd attended a conference once, gotten a few first impressions.

"This island held the noblest fascination for me when I arrived sixteen years ago, a printer boy with ten dollars sewn in my coat. Stayed the whole summer of 'fifty-three. Saw the World's Fair at the Crystal Palace. A spectacle! Did you know six thousand attended every day? Double my hometown's population." He knocked his pipe against the railing. "Fell in love with Manhattan like she was a woman. Now it's different. Traffic's an abomination. Prices are higher'n perdition—lodging alone's triple what I paid then. By the way, where're you staying?"

I pulled a slip of paper from my wallet. "Earle's Hotel, Canal Street."

"Why, that's right near the St. Nicholas. How'd it be if we took in a few sights together? I'm a mite weary of folks I generally see."

"You're on," I said, delighted.

"Buy a money belt," he said. "The cash you're carrying in that fancy billfold won't be with you six blocks in a Seventh Avenue car or downtown Red Bird bus."

"Muggers?"

"Them too, but I meant pickpockets."

We walked down the ferry ramp. The dock was noisy with workers on freight platforms, baggage wagons rumbling over planks, horsecars gliding on rails. Twain hailed one of the lined-up hacks.

We slanted onto Canal Street and clattered beneath a flimsy-looking iron trackway running along Greenwich. It stood fifteen feet above the street. "What's that?" I asked, reminded of erector-set constructions Grandpa and I had made.

"The new Ninth Avenue Elevated," Twain said. "Runs from Battery Place clear up to Thirtieth and Ninth. Experimental, cars pulled by cable." He explained that steam trains weren't permitted below Forty-second: noise and smoke terrorized horses; cinders posed a fire hazard.

I craned my neck as we crossed Broadway. Paved sidewalks were overhung with broad awnings. The streetlamps were globes topped by brass balls. Pedestrians swarmed among bicycles—I'd learned they were fairly new and known as velocipedes—and round-topped public minicoaches and swifter carriages and carts and horsecars. There were no traffic signals. One cursing cop tried to keep it all moving. Traffic wasn't bad this early, Twain remarked. To me it looked awful.

I peered around the driver, trying to see everything. A maze of telegraph wires stretched overhead. Buildings were encrusted with ironwork, and the tallest stood only five or six stories. In the distance a steeple soared above its surroundings. It was Trinity Church, Manhattan's tallest structure at well over two hundred feet. But it would soon be surpassed, Twain said. The walls of the new St. Patrick's on Fifth Avenue would stretch some three hundred and thirty feet heavenward.

A horrendous clanging sounded. Pedestrians and vehicles gave way to form a corridor in which an ambulance emerged, its grim-faced driver wielding a whip on a single straining horse. The cab's shades were raised; I glimpsed an attendant struggling with his patient, a bald man thrashing spasmodically. I stared in morbid fascination. Violence and death were close to the surface back here; it lent existence a certain tenuous vitality.

The lobby of Earle's Hotel held worn horsehair furniture, tarnished spittoons, and an oppressive portrait of the Duke of Wellington, whose painted eyes followed us. Twain rumbled disapprovingly and suggested I stay with him at the St. Nicholas. I said it was presently out of my price range. He reflected on that, nodded, and said he'd return later.

My room was drab but reasonably clean. I examined my wound. It was still stiff and tender, but had virtually healed. The gash was unchanged. Weary and a bit hung over, I tried the bed and was soon making up for lost sleep.

Manhattan's built-up portions extended to 130th Street, near the Harlem River, and held over a million people. Twain seemed determined for me to see most of them. He started by escorting me along Broadway, tipping his hat to people staring at him, beaming and responding when they called, "Hi, Mark!"

He showed me the famous gray-stoned Astor House at the corner of Barclay. Built thirty years earlier, it had been considered too far uptown, Twain said. Now it was too far down, its glory stolen by the Metropolitan and St. Nicholas, whose homey comforts Twain preferred, and which in turn were being supplanted by mammoth new establishments farther uptown. At Madison Square we strolled into one—the Fifth Avenue Hotel. It covered a square block and held six floors. Twain showed me its steam-powered elevator (he called it a "perpendicular railway"); so many used it for fun that the management had installed in it a gas chandelier, plush carpeting, and a divan. Every room contained the latest comforts: central heating, private baths, speaking tubes for room service.

We hired a hack and toured the white-fronted palaces of consumerism along the fashionable "Ladies' Mile." There, lavishly outfitted women left liveried coachmen to wait while they shopped in Lord & Taylor's emporium at Twentieth or Arnold Constable's at Nineteenth, both having recently opened their pale marble facades to the public.

I told Twain I wanted to visit a state-of-the-art department store. He chose A. T. Stewart's cast-iron palace at Ninth, just east off Broadway. Its exterior white metal, ornately sculpted, was designed to look like marble. Blue awnings shaded the window displays. Inside, the scale was grandiose. Eight floors spanned two and a half acres. Two thousand employees dispensed stock to meet life's physical requisites, from baby clothes to funereal "black goods." A central rotunda framed an enormous domed skylight. A double staircase linked all floors. An organ played solemnly—appropriate, I thought, for a marketplace shrine.

We looked in on the vast sewing room, an entire floor, where rows of women—more than nine hundred—hand-stitched every bit of clothing sold in the store. Noticing that they didn't work from patterns, I questioned the floor manager, a silk-hatted martinet who gave me a fishy look and informed me that not only did no such absurdity exist, but that Stewart's was far too exclusive to consider it.

"Forget about airplanes," I told Twain. "Just market paper sewing patterns all over the country."

"Do I look prize fool enough to try 'n' get any two females to make the same thing?" He snorted. "It'd never work."

With some surprise I saw women among the clerks at Stewart's. Until then I'd seen only men employed in stores. Hiring women, Twain said, began during the war, when manpower was short. Girls also worked among Stewart's two hundred cash children. They were very young and looked poor and tired. No wonder. They worked fourteen hours a day.

"Aren't there any child-labor laws?" I asked Twain.

"Not to speak of," he said. "That a fault?"

"Of course," I said.

"But if there were, how'd I've learned my printing trade? My father died when I was ten. I left school and went to work—and then my true education commenced. How would you have it different?"

I didn't know. Without social legislation, few choices existed.

We lunched in a basement saloon off Printing House Square. Thick pork loin sandwiches, wedges of cheese, fried oysters—tasty and absolutely free, but so salty that a number of nickel beers were required to wash it all down; no fools, the pub owners.

Afterward we strolled through City Hall Park, where the *Tribune* and *Times* buildings stood side by side. Excavation was under way at the southern end for an enormous new post office. We sat on a bench and enjoyed the scene. Birds sang in the trees. Squirrels chattered. Children laughed and screamed. Strolling couples bought balloons, checked their weight on scales, peered through telescopes, and blew into a strange-looking contraption that measured lung strength.

"Hokey pokey, penny a lump!" cried a vendor.

"What's he selling?" I said. "Coal?"

Twain looked at me sidelong. "Ice cream, you saphead."

I bought two cups of sherbet. "Hey," I said to the vendor, a stick-thin boy, "You know 'I scream, you scream, we all scream for ice cream!'?"

"Oh, ain't you the trump," he said, giving me a withering look. "That's precious old, mister."

At least the sherbet was good.

The foot of Broadway resounded with a welter of languages. Peddlers abounded. Knife grinders rang bells and pushed their carts. Barefoot children stood beside steaming pots shouting "Here's sweet hot corn!" Others shouted, "Roasted peanuts!" and "Strawberries, fine, ripe, and red!" Still others hawked apples, flowers, pencils; one even had french fries—"Saratoga potatoes"—and I bought some eagerly, the first I'd encountered. Everywhere we were besieged with cries of "Blackin', sir? Shine, sir?"

"Every street arab buys a brush and foot box," Twain grumbled, "and sets up boot-blacking."

Over the sidewalks hung meat and poultry crawling with flies. We skirted cut-rate furniture and dry goods piled on the walks. Rank odors came from tables of smoked meats and fish, decaying fruit and vegetables. Twain said most of it had likely been picked off the ground at the Fulton and Washington markets. Pointing to ragpickers trudging behind small dog-drawn carts, he informed me that they had to pay license fees, yet some made as much as seven dollars a week and bought farms out West. I didn't believe it.

" 'Ere you, mister!" An urchin girl poked matches at me. I bought a penny parcel—and threw them down when I saw lice crawling on my fingers. In the Alger novels of this time, I remembered, ragged kids got ahead through luck and pluck—saving a rich child from drowning or returning a fat wallet—but these sniveling, rot-toothed waifs looked too malnourished to save anyone, especially themselves. And a wallet dropped here would vanish in microseconds.

"Something's got to be done about these kids," I said to Twain as we moved on.

He snorted. "There's a mortal confusion now of workhouses, jails, charity asylums, hospitals—all for the unfortunate."

"Shouldn't the government take responsibility for people's welfare?"

"You'll never make *that* old cat fight," he retorted. "The people are responsible for their *own* welfare."

"But those kids are living on pennies!"

"How's the government at fault? Look, Sam, here they got a *chance* to make their mark. Sure, some'll end up as ragged bummers, some as flash girls. But they all had a chance. That's it. Why you think so many come pouring in here from all over creation?"

I shut up. What struck me as basically harsh struck him as basically fair—at least as fair as anything else.

[106]

Bumping back up Broadway in a coach, we halted behind a crew paving over the cobblestones with asphalt. My eye was caught by a theater marquee across the street. Niblo's Garden proclaimed the presence of LYDIA THOMPSON'S BRITISH BLONDES! I asked Twain about it.

"They put clipper-built girls up on the stage, prancing with barely clothes enough on to be tantalizing." He confessed that he'd seen the first of the leg shows, *The Black Crook*, at Niblo's three years before. "Since then, imported blondes have become all the rage. But it's still the scenery and tights that're everything—except for one new blonde who's supposed to be a genuine dazzler."

"Elise Holt?"

"That's the one. How'd you know?"

I explained where I'd seen her. He drew me out with questions, and I found myself telling him about Morrissey, McDermott, Le Caron, the money, the shooting—everything.

"Whew," he said. "Morrissey's not to trifle with, and them others don't brace me up either. You carrying that gun?"

I patted my coat pocket.

"I had no thought of being teamed with such a desperate character," he said, stoking his pipe. "Feels like Virginia City all over."

We started moving. Near Fifth Street, Twain suddenly pointed at the facade of a small building beside the Metropolitan Hotel.

*** WAVERLY THREATRE ***
*** THREE DAYS ONLY ***
*** PARIS or THE JUDGEMENT ***
*** ELISE HOLT BURLESQUE TROUPE ***

"Jesus, that's her," I said excitedly. "Think we can get tickets?"

"Pretty late for a Friday," he said. "I'll see to it tomorrow. Strikes me that a dedicated journalist should make every effort to stay abreast of things. So to speak." He shot me a look from under his eyebrows. "Bear in mind that by no stretch would this *ever* be a fit topic for Livy's ears."

"Of course not," I said.

Next morning I got a note from Twain saying that business had occupied him, but he'd meet me that night at the theater. Feeling at loose ends, I wrote a letter to my daughters telling them that even if I missed their birthdays—Hope would turn five early in July, Susy three a few weeks later—I loved them and would come home as soon as I could. I included their zip code in the address just in case, put a three-cent stamp on the envelope, walked it to the post office—no mailboxes yet—and dropped it through a slot, feeling silly and yet closer to them.

By the time I strolled up Broadway in my black evening suit, my spirits had rebounded. I'd slicked my hair, scrubbed my teeth with Burnett's Oriental Tooth Wash, and put on gleaming new high-laced shoes. Around me throngs of people stepped briskly in the deepening dusk, speaking in animated voices. Lamps from theaters and concert saloons splashed the sidewalks with brilliant colors. Bursts of music and applause floated from lobbies. The lamplighters were out with their ladders, making the streetlights glowing yellow balls. Stagecoaches' lights of red, green, and blue formed tracers as they bumped over the cobblestones. Excitement bubbled in me. I was on my way to the theater. With Mark Twain, no less.

He stood in the lobby of the Waverly, natty in tails, silk stovepipe, and polished gaiters, surrounded by admirers. When I pushed close he muttered, "Let's clear out."

Our seats occupied a small gilt-framed box flanking the stage. The Waverly's interior was intimate—cramped, to be less poetic—all its surfaces festooned with draperies and gilt molding. In the orchestra seats were a few fat burghers whose overdressed wives looked self-conscious in the mostly male audience. The fifty-cent sections were boisterous. The house held about three hundred, and standing room was vanishing fast.

The curtain rose. A hand-lettered sign said that we were about to see "A Pretty Piece of Business," which turned out to be a comedy skit. Following it were two sisters who danced in remarkable unison, like music-box figures. The audience grew restless.

Finally the feature. By the most forgiving standards it was awful. Performed to Mendelssohn and Meyerbeer, set with flowery painted backdrops depicting ancient Greece, a sequence of frothy numbers built to the goddesses' contest for the golden apple. Buxom women in platinum wigs wore garish clinging gowns, one Viola Crocker, as Venus, parading herself especially sinuously. Her heavy curves were much appreciated by the house. To me she looked almost alarmingly overweight.

I'd had about enough when Elise Holt finally sauntered on as Paris. Although ostensibly a male—she played the wisecracking, cigar-smoking soubrette—Holt alone wore flesh-colored tights. Her well-curved legs and hourglass torso showed to maximum effect. The blond curls peeped from under leafy garlands; the oval face was powdered and rouged. The audience paid rapt attention. So did I.

She looked larger onstage than she had at the Troy ball grounds. But beside the others she was petite. She danced with jaunty grace. Her throaty voice sounded more suggestive than musical. Unlike the fleshy women, Holt exuded sensuality without seeming to try. It occurred to me that she was very like a 1920s flapper—liberated, mannish, sexual—almost sixty years before her time.

"Witching little thing," Twain remarked. "Vital as a St. Rupert's drop."

"Fantastic body," I said.

He glanced at me. "And dressed with meagerness to make a parasol blush."

As an encore, the cast performed a wild full-stage cancan. "A wilderness of girls," Twain called it.

He was hard to read on sex. The glitzy peroxide and tights seemed to have amused more than titillated him. I remembered his writings as being sexually repressed, standard for the age. But it might have been a facade. Or imposed by Livy.

Twain lit a cigar outside. "You fancy the little blonde?"

"Doesn't everybody?"

At a flower stall he purchased red roses and sent them backstage with a note. "Let's see if this stirs anything."

We stood by the stage door. After most of the performers had departed, Holt appeared, bundled in furs, flanked by a man and a woman.

"Miss Holt," drawled Twain, tipping his hat. "If you'd be kind enough to join us, we'd be honored by your company at Delmonico's."

She looked at him, brows knit. The other woman whispered. Holt smiled vaguely; either she didn't know of Twain or didn't care. "The flowers were lovely," she said, starting past. "Thanks ever so much."

Damn, I thought, and stepped in front of her. "I enjoyed your performance here and in Troy."

Startled, the blue-violet eyes scanned my face and rested briefly on my cheek. "Why, you're the one who provoked that row at the match!" She laughed, low-pitched and throaty. "I enjoyed *your* performance, sir."

"I'm Sam Fowler," I said, grinning. "Come have a drink with us?"

"That's kind, but I'm afraid not." She gestured at the man. "My fiancé."

The guy gave me a tight smile. Fiancé? Where the hell was he during the Troy game? Or did she only go to ball games with high-rolling Congressmen?

Holt must have guessed my thoughts. A warning flashed in her eyes: *Be quiet.* I nodded slightly, smiling. " 'Night, gentlemen," she said crisply.

"That's that," I muttered, watching her move away.

We walked several blocks in silence.

"You fancy female companionship?" asked Twain.

I thought about it. "More than ever."

We took a hack out Fifth Avenue toward Murray Hill, where Commodore Vanderbilt was planning to erect a magnificent railway depot to serve all Manhattan. In Twain's view it would be too far uptown.

"Where does 'uptown' start, anyway?"

"About Twenty-fifth or so."

"That's not so far, then."

"Too blamed far to walk from the St. Nicholas."

We descended in front of a tall brownstone on Thirty-fourth.

"House of ill repute?" I said.

"A palatial bagnio," Twain replied. "Parlor houses are prospering between Union Square and Central Park, but I guarantee you won't fault this one."

"You sound pretty knowledgeable."

"One of fame's advantages," he said mildly. "Entering doors that are otherwise shut."

A peephole clicked open. Twain was recognized. We stepped into a garnet-and-gold hallway. Recessed niches held a life-sized marble Diana and a bronze Cupid. A dandy with oiled sideburns ushered us into a large, overheated drawing room. I looked wonderingly at a profusion of crystal chandeliers, exotic plants, plush divans, and art objects. There were carvings and vases and busts—nearby on pedestals rested Cleopatra, Minerva, and, oddly, Milton—and on the walls oils by Hogarth, Rembrandt, Reynolds, Van Dyck. The dandy informed me archly that the carpets had been specially woven on Smyrna looms to match the Damascus hangings. Bursts of birdsong came from a gilded aviary. Incense hung heavily in the air. Water bubbled in a marble basin after flowing through an aquarium.

"My God," I breathed, loosening my tie, sweating in the hothouse atmosphere where everything seemed overripe. I wanted to peel off my clothes—maybe that was the idea.

"Pleases the eyes, don't it?" Twain said, looking about languidly as he settled on one of the divans. "I'd have no kick about this as a steady thing."

I was about to say it would drive me crazy when a cultivated voice said, "Gentlemen." We looked up. A stout woman enveloped in yards of lace and satin, ablaze with diamonds, regarded us regally. We rose and bent in turn over her jeweled fingers. All convivialities of her home, she assured me, were at my disposal.

[110]

"Since it's manifest you prefer the finest company," she said, beaming at Twain, "allow me to say that our young ladies are finely bred. You will enjoy their discourses."

"I'm sure I will." I eyed a Rubenesque young thing floating around a corner in a filmy gown.

"Precisely," she said, and disappeared through the leaves of an enormous dieffenbachia, her departure not unlike, Twain remarked, a lit-up paddle wheeler forging through an overgrown channel.

"How much will these Rabelaisian delights cost us?" I asked.

"Cost *you*," he corrected. "I'm sworn to reform myself. Oh, the night could run sixty, seventy dollars, but for that you'd get *all* you could concoct—and more."

"I'll limit my concoctions." I had at most fifty dollars left from my gambling winnings.

Twain bought drinks, smoked a cigar, and departed. I wasn't alone very long. A red-haired woman appeared, plump and rouge-cheeked. Her name was Opal, she said, and asked if I would care for champagne.

"Well, I think I would."

She smiled and suggested showing me the salon. "Do you enjoy Chopin?"

At a grand piano, playing a nocturne with effortless facility, sat a young woman with chestnut hair and pale eyes. She was wonderfully slender—doubtless viewed as a freak, I reflected—and her skin was flawless. She looked up at me. She smiled. I smiled back. Opal vanished discreetly. A waiter appeared with champagne and two glasses. The young woman finished playing.

"Thank you, kind sir." She sipped from the fluted glass and studied me over the rim. "I am Charlotte."

"I'm . . . impressed."

She took my arm and guided me to a loveseat. She sat close, her hip brushing mine. Her eyes regarded me intently. Her voice was cultivated, devoid of the flat eastern accents I'd grown used to. She was careful to ask little about me. We talked of San Francisco and its weather, topics about which she seemed knowledgeable. She asked if I would like to chat in a cozier quarter of the mansion.

Her room was almost as lush as the parlor. A silk canopy overhung a huge bed swimming in folds of blue satin. In an alcove stood a sofa carved with arabesques. She led me to it.

"Do you enjoy Molière?" She laughed delightedly at my expression. "I am reading *Le Misanthrope*. Do you know it?"

I tried to remember it from college. "Well . . ."

She lifted a volume from her table and read a passage aloud in fluent, musical French. "Alceste's friend, Philinthe," she translated, "tells him, 'My mind is no more shocked at seeing a man a rogue . . . than seeing vultures eager for prey, mischievous apes, or fury-lashed wolves.' "

She spoke slowly. Her pale eyes stared into mine. In them I saw tiny reflections of a flickering gas jet on the wall behind me.

"Sam," she said huskily, stroking my hand, "a gentleman *needs* to be a rogue on occasion."

That did it. I pulled at her dress as she tore at my shirt, and things became like a movie passion montage—you know, naked bodies churning and tumbling and dissolving from one position to another. Charlotte knew her business and gave every appearance of liking it. Once when I thought I was hurting her—she was anything but a heavyweight—she hissed and clawed at me when I slackened.

I couldn't get enough of her smooth flesh against mine. I pressed her hard, ran my hands over her, stroked and kneaded, took the warmth of her into me. Toward dawn, after the last climactic shudder, after the last glass of brandy, she held my head to her breasts and rocked me like an infant.

"Dear Sam," she whispered, "you needed this terribly."

A high sighing sound escaped me; she pressed me tighter.

"I haven't felt like this since I was first married."

She laughed gently and said, "I help many marriages."

"I'll bet. What about you? A beautiful woman who reads Molière and plays Chopin. Why aren't you out shopping the Ladies' Mile, spending a rich husband's money?"

She smiled faintly. "I was ruined for that life."

"Ruined?"

"Seduced by a gentleman."

"So?"

"You don't understand? We were to marry. I let him have his way. Then he no longer wanted me." She shrugged. "It occurs commonly."

"And you're *ruined?*"

"Why do you say it so? You know perfectly well no respectable man would have me."

"How old are you?"

"Twenty-four." She shrugged. "It all took place five years ago. I don't look backward or carry regrets. I've saved my earnings. Someday I'll have a mansion of my own."

"Ruined, for God's sake," I muttered. "What a time to live!"

She kissed me. "Is there another?"

◇ 8 ◇

Central Park's greenery glowed in the afternoon rays. Twain and I halted our carriage some distance from a gazebo where a band tuned noisily for the Sunday afternoon concert.

"You don't look the worse for wear," Twain noted. He wore an ivory-colored linen waistcoat and white silk necktie. A pair of dark glasses—"green spectacles"—perched on his nose.

"Could hardly feel much better," I told him.

We spread a blanket and settled.

"There's a good deal about you, Sam, that don't add up if studied very close."

I felt myself tensing. "What do you mean?"

"Now don't get riled. It's just that I've *been* studying you. I can't help it, it's my nature. I pride myself on knowing folks. When I talk about the pilot trade back in my rivering days, I generally lay the claim that I ran afoul of every type imaginable. But God's truth is, I never met one quite like you—though there were a number who didn't let on much about themselves."

"You think I'm hiding things?"

"Think it? I *know* it! What's more, it's like you're studying how to behave. Sort of like I did when I came here at fifteen, not knowing how to act at all, lookin' around for signals but keeping quiet and hoping nobody'd notice."

He looked at me speculatively. "Now, mind you, I'm not criticizing. A man's business is his own. As a general thing I'm partial to them who consider before starting their jaws. And I've observed you enough to see that you manage all right. In fact, for a greenhorn, you make out tolerably."

He waited for the band to finish a clamorous passage.

"Now, I've considered this, Sam. I've learned to trust my estimation of my fellowman, and I'm seldom wrong in my judgments."

[113]

I smiled at his earnestness. "What's on your mind?"

"I want to pass on a tale told to me after a lecture up in Elmira last year. I happened to stick in a warmhearted piece about a certain John Irishman. Well, the next day an old codger appeared at the Langdons' front door and stirred up such a ruckus to see me that the servants finally gave in.

"I went out and sat on the porch swing and smoked while he poured out everything he had to say. He was Irish himself, and he talked so thick it was hard to decipher him at points. But I got the gist, and once he wound up and pitched into it, he had my hair fairly standing at attention.

"Started off telling me he could feel death coming. Didn't want to depart with his secret untold. Naturally, I asked what the secret was, but he told me to be patient, it was a mite complicated. And so it was.

"Late in the war, after the two sides stopped exchanging prisoners in 'sixty-three, a surplus of Secesh captives forced the building of more Yankee prisons. In May of 'sixty-four one opened for business in Elmira, right down on the Chemung River. Well, they hadn't even got barracks up yet; the prisoners lived in tents. During the summer things went along, but once the cold flowed in it was mortal hell. Boys perished from exposure. Smallpox broke out. In the spring of 'sixty-five the Chemung flooded, dysentery got bad, and then to cap it all, they got hit with erysipelas."

"With what?"

"You'd maybe know it as St. Anthony's Fire. Head turns red and swells, high fevers and delerium. It spreads like perdition when those with it can't be isolated—like in a cramped prison. The Rebs got to dyin' so fast—one out of three during the worst of the pox—that for a spell they were carted off to the cemetery nine at a time, that being how many coffins the ambulance wagon held. It went on around the clock.

"The old-timer knew all about this 'cause he worked in the death house. That was a shack just off the hospital, where he packed the boys in their boxes and did whatever precious little else to prepare 'em for their Maker.

"Now, another consideration during all this is that the Yankee guards were the New York Ninety-ninth Regiment—mostly Fenians who'd survived Meagher's Irish Brigade in places like Antietam—and they got this plum of a job for the duration.

"Now the Irish, you know, are thick as thieves, and gambling comes as natural to them as breathing. The guards held regular games and often let prisoners in on 'em too. There were a good many Irish Johnnies—people forget that when they claim migrants alone won the war for the North—and sizable amounts of money changed hands, sometimes up in the thousands."

"How'd the prisoners get money?"

"Oh, they were allowed to receive drafts—drawn on Yankee banks, of course. Some lived fairly high. One in particular, who went through the faro and poker sessions like wildfire, got assigned to burial detail. His name was . . . well, I don't rightly know it, but he came to be called O'Shea. Mark that, Sam, it's critical. Before long, working together as they did, O'Shea and the old-timer got to be like father and son.

"Meanwhile, at night, O'Shea and ten others set about digging a tunnel from inside the hospital. By the time they'd burrowed under the stockade walls sixty feet distant, the smallpox siege was at its peak and they decided to make a break right away. But two nights before their target time, O'Shea was cleaned out in a poker game by a Yank sergeant named Duffy. It was generally suspicioned that Duffy cheated and that he'd stockpiled considerable funds since coming to Elmira. O'Shea was bitter. He confided to the old-timer about the game, and also about the breakout. He swore he'd square himself with Duffy before he escaped.

"Then a number of things transpired. The breakout went as planned. Eleven boys were counted missing. Eventually ten were re-captured, and security tightened down considerably. But the eleventh, who had trailed the others through the tunnel, was never seen again. Can you fathom which?"

"Got to be our man O'Shea."

"The same. Now here's where it gets right interesting. Duffy was found in his tent, his throat slit. Next to him, a large oak chest had been prized open. Scattered around like chicken feathers were bank drafts and currency—Secesh notes—in the thousands. But missing were thousands *more* in greenbacks and gold! Upwards of twenty thousand, near as they could estimate."

"U.S. dollars?"

"Yes, partly in greenbacks—that's what Yanks were paid with—but mostly in gold eagles and double eagles."

"Duffy must've been one hell of a cheater," I said.

"Likely so, but there'd often be several thousand sitting in just one pot. Look at it that way, and it's not hard to calculate him salting away quite a load over a year and a half."

"What happened to O'Shea?"

Twain chuckled. "For five years now a lot have wondered that. The Fenians are especially curious, since they claim first rights on the money. Rumors had O'Shea getting plugged by a guard the night of the breakout; or making it all the way to Richmond, only to be killed later in the war; or still living today like a god somewhere in the South Seas. In any case, the money never turned up."

He emptied his pipe and reloaded it leisurely.

"But you know where O'Shea is, I gather?"

"Don't crowd me," he drawled. "Story as good as this needs time to spin out to its proper length."

I lay back on the grass and watched wispy clouds trailing lazily against the sky. Soldiers' shapes moved among them.

"The old man was in his shack by the death house that night, nervous as a cat. You can fathom his shock when O'Shea staggered through the doorway, bleeding from a mortal wound. What happened was, he'd sneaked in on Duffy and delivered a good lick to his head, figuring it would hold him. But just when O'Shea'd cleaned out all the usable money from the chest and packed it in two big knapsacks, Duffy jabbed a blade in his back. He was trying to repeat when O'Shea grabbed it away and finished him. But it was too late for O'Shea. He died in the old man's arms.

"Well, the alarm sounded and Hades tore loose. In the confusion the old man made two trips to Duffy's tent—it was all he could manage to lift one knapsack—and brought the money back to his hut. He spent the next days mourning over the boy, scared to death they'd come in and find the money and blame him for Duffy's murder. He wracked his mind to figure some way out of his predicament."

Twain refired the pipe with maddening care.

"What he finally came up with was this: He packed O'Shea into an extra-long pine box—remember, O'Shea wasn't his name, but that's what the old man stenciled on the lid to cover his tracks—and he packed the money in quart jars all around the boy."

"But wouldn't they check the phony name against prisoner records?"

"I asked him that very question. He told me some prisoners never gave their rightful names at all, just said 'registered enemy.' Moreover, the prison hadn't made any plans for boys dying. First they buried them along the riverbank, till those got swept away in the flooding. At the height of the pox they used communal graves. It was all a tangle. So he didn't fret about discrepancies—'cause nobody was looking."

"Well, what happened?" I said. "Did the old man get the money back?"

Twain eyed me shrewdly. "Once I tell you, Sam, the two of us'll be the only ones alive who know. I want to make a proposition. If you decide to go for the money, I'd want half as my share. Discreetly done, of course."

"Why cut me in? If the old-timer's dead, why not take it all your-self?"

"I don't dare. If it ever came to light I was linked with a grave-robbing scheme, my standing with Livy's relations'd be blasted all to perdition." He sighed. "A sultan's treasure for the taking, and I can't make a stagger at it. You're the only one I've run into who might be foolhardy enough to take on the job, yet honest enough to trust."

I laughed at his assessment. "Okay, I promise. I mean, I want to hear what happened. Who wouldn't? But I can't see myself robbing a grave."

"I'll just leave it with you, then, and expect you'll keep your shutters up."

I nodded.

"Well, O'Shea's coffin was taken up to Woodlawn Cemetery above Elmira. There's a Confederate section there with over three thousand graves. They weren't even marked at the time, but luckily an army sexton copied the names off coffins and kept track of burial plots."

"I just thought of something," I said. "O'Shea's folks had no way of knowing what happened to him."

Twain nodded. "The old man felt poorly over what he was doing to the boy's family. His notion was to write them in Carolina, once he'd retrieved the money.

"But it never happened. What he didn't count on was the army keeping a guard posted in Woodlawn's military section day and night, all through the war—and after. It's still guarded, in fact."

"Couldn't he have said he was kin? Claimed the body and taken it away?"

"He tried," Twain replied. "They wanted proof. When he came back with trumped-up papers, somebody recognized him and started asking questions. That scared him off. He fretted for a long while, but came up blank. By the time I heard his tale, he'd given off doing it alone."

"So what did he want you to do?"

"Use my 'influence' with city hall to have the guard removed one night."

"Plant a bribe?"

"Most probably."

"Would it work?"

"Maybe, maybe not."

Ten thousand dollars. My half would set me up for a long time.

"Ponder it some," Twain drawled. "That money ain't going away. And if it *should* happen into our hands soon, why, we could

[117]

boost Freddy's flying machine and make ourselves rich as all splendor."

"That's quite a scenario," I said. "You got any moneymaking schemes *on* the ground? Yours're all above or below it."

He laughed, winked his foxy wink, and said no more.

The next morning Twain left for Hartford to attend the wedding of Livy's cousin and pore over final proofs of *Innocents Abroad* with his publisher, Elisha Bliss. Then he would accompany the Langdons to Elmira. He had intentions, he said, of journeying to California in late summer. He promised to follow the Stockings' progress in the papers. He said he'd see me again. We shook hands, and I watched his hack clatter away.

I returned to Earle's, already missing him. Could bare coincidence have thrown us together? Not likely. But what else explained it?

I retreated into the day's newspapers. Monday, June 14. I'd been back in time for two weeks. It seemed an eternity.

The Stockings were getting more coverage as the victory streak lengthened. After whipping Boston's champion Lowells and Tri-Mountains, they'd taken on the strong Harvard team. Powered by Waterman's early homer, they coasted, 30–11. Their record was now 14–0, and Manhattan writers drooled over the next day's clash with the Mutuals.

Seeing their names in print, I realized that they were my people, the only family I had in this world. I realized something else: I didn't want to stay in New York. Even in this slower time it was too big, too fast-paced, too impersonal for me. Maybe I could think of a way to stay on with the club.

At 8 P.M. they arrived at the New York & New Haven depot behind Madison Square. I watched as teams of horses drew the New Haven's straw-colored cars along rails in the street. The city's ordinance against steam vehicles forced the disconnecting of trains from locomotives fifteen blocks from the passenger station.

Andy ran up and hugged me hard, recoiling when he remembered my wound. I assured him it didn't hurt. Brainard and George and the others crowded around, marveling at my recovery.

As Andy brought me up to date at the hotel, I kept thinking inanely, He's the greatest little brother I never had. He said they'd rented boats in Springfield and rowed miles up the Connecticut River; played on Boston Common's lower parade ground and Jarvis Field in Cambridge; visited the penitentiary at Charlestown; cruised Boston Harbor on a revenue cutter; seen the Peace Jubilee's grand organ—the largest in America—with pipes so large a man could stand upright in them; been guests at a burlesque, *Humpty Dumpty,* filled with gorgeous women in tights soaring over the stage in swings.

"But not one of 'em a dinger like the peach we saw in Troy," he concluded. "I'm freezin' to cross *her* path again."

I didn't have the heart to tell him. According to the papers, Holt was leaving New York for Philadelphia anyway. I described meeting Twain, but Andy insisted that either I was telling him stretchers or I'd been taken in by a humbug. It must have bothered him to think I'd had high times while he'd pictured me suffering in bed.

Champion tried to keep everybody in the hotel that night. It worked with Allison, Hurley, Mac, and Gould—all from outside the New York area. But Brainard and Waterman vanished before supper, and Andy and Sweasy went out with friends from Newark. George took off for Morrisania, a village across the bridge from the Harlem flats where he'd grown up. Harry, ever responsible, stuck around.

I met with Champion and Harry later on. They asked me to recount the details of the shooting. "You're positive you saw McDermott and Le Caron?" Champion said. "But nobody else? No possible witnesses?"

I shook my head.

"We'd never get a conviction," he said. "You think it all stemmed from the cash box incident?"

"And the Haymaker game." I told him of McDermott's losses.

"I've heard the same," Harry confirmed.

Champion looked as if he wished it would all go away. "Are you safe here, Fowler?"

I took the big plunge and told them I wanted to stay with the club. I'd serve as a sub on tour. In Cincinnati I'd work on marketing and publicity innovations I was sure would prove productive.

"You wish *employment?*" Champion said incredulously. "But only the first nine are salaried. We're a *club,* Fowler. Our affairs are handled voluntarily, by members."

"I'd like to stay connected," I persisted. "I'll volunteer, if that's the only way. Meanwhile, I'd like to finish the tour."

"But your injury invalidates you as a substitute."

"I can play in a pinch."

"He's not asking much," Harry said.

Champion sighed and rubbed his eyes. "Very well, but no further incidents, Fowler. We can't afford trouble."

"I didn't ask to get shot—" I began, and stopped as Harry flashed a look that said to quit while I was ahead.

The next afternoon, in uniforms and topcoats, we took the Fulton St. Ferry across a dark, wind-frothed East River. Mist blurred our surroundings and rain swooped in occasional patters. To my left Champion grumbled about the wretched weather dogging the tour. To my right Millar polished his early dispatch for the *Commercial*. I looked over his shoulder.

> . . . the Knights of the Sanguinary Hose *can* carry off the palm of victory in each of these contests; but as to whether they *will*, we must let the caution of good old Captain Harry, who knows the tricks of the Eastern gamesters . . .

Knights of the Sanguinary Hose, I thought. Good God. "All I've been hearing lately," I said cheerfully, "is 'Wait'll you country-club bastards tangle with our Mutes.' " I saw Millar and Champion wince visibly at the word *bastards*. "Are they the toughest club we'll face?"

"Probably," Millar said, adding that if we got past the Mutuals today, the powerful Brooklyn Atlantics tomorrow, and last year's consensus champs, the Athletics, in Philly next week, we might finish the tour undefeated. But those were three formidable obstacles.

"The guys seem pretty relaxed," I said.

"It's friendly here, unlike Troy," Millar said. "Brainard and the Wrights played for New York clubs over the years. Waterman was a Mute only two seasons ago. Andy and Sweasy came up with some of the Mutes' young ballists."

"They recruit top players, then?" To me the Mutuals were starting to seem like the all-conquering Yankees of my youth.

"All the city treasury can afford," Champion said acidly. "Currently around thirty thousand a year, tied up neatly in the rolls of the street-cleaning department. How they pass themselves off as amateurs eludes me."

"Are they one of the oldest teams?"

"One of them," said Millar. "It's agreed that the Knickerbockers were first, but who came next is still debated. Around here were the Gothams and Metropolitans—"

"The Mets!" I exclaimed.

"Yes," Millar said, eyeing me. "And the Athletics in Philadelphia and the Excelsiors in Brooklyn. The Mutuals formed sometime around 'fifty-seven, in Tweed's old Americus fire department, Mutual Hook and Ladder Company Number One. They're Tammany's darlings, of course."

Under ominous skies the Williamsburg ball field—it bore the name "Union Grounds," like so many things now—blazed with color. At opposite ends of the grandstand the Mutes' and Stockings' flags flapped like medieval knights' standards. Besides the Mutes' rode the coveted whip pennant, signifying their status as reigning champions.

The Mutuals marched onto the diamond: somber, formidable figures in mud-colored long pants and tight-fitting jerseys with white dickeys. They were fully as big as the Haymakers and moved with quick grace warming up.

The crowd's buzzing struck me as knowledgeable—the speculative, anticipatory sound of people familiar with the game. I said so to Andy as I lobbed the ball, testing my side against the pull.

"They're in the know here," he said. "But they got nothin' over Westerners for lovin' it. In Cincinnati right now they're crowdin' up outside the tobacco shops, Ellard's Sporting Goods Emporium, and all the newspaper bulletin boards down on Fourth. They'll stand hushed for hours—and bust loose like Injuns when word comes we won."

World Series. I thought of Grandpa's stories of his vigils during the battles with McGraw's Giants. I remembered myself smuggling a radio to school and listening to games thousands of miles distant.

The sky brightened. The crowd swelled to six thousand. Our white uniforms sparkled on the field, the underdog good guys versus the sinister dark-clad Mutes. I wondered if the pool sellers saw it that way. I asked Hurley as we took seats at the scorer's table next to our bench.

"Odds favor the Mutes," Hurley said. "But only five to four. Our reputation's arrived before us. We're starting to attract sober attention."

Harry won the toss and sent the Mutes up. Brainard's first fastball brought a rising, expectant, full-throated sound from the crowd.

Within hours of its conclusion, this game would be judged the best ever played. Multitudes would claim to have seen it—far more than could fit inside the ballpark. The contest was hard-fought and low-scoring; at the end it was waged in an atmosphere of goose-pimpling, gut-gripping intensity.

It began with Charley Hunt, the Mutual left fielder, grounding to Waterman; jaw bulged by his ever-present plug, the stolid third baseman calmly played the short hop and threw him out. Jack Hatfield next grounded to Sweasy, who lobbed to Gould. Everett Mills topped another grounder to Waterman, who charged it cleanly but pulled Gould off with a high throw. Brainard walked the next Mute, then knocked down a smash up the middle with a snake-quick backhanded move for the third out.

It previewed what would come in most innings: threatening runners, tight pitching, clutch fielding. Brainard's fastballs, sinking today, were driven repeatedly into the turf by the Mutes' bats. In all they grounded out eighteen times against six flies. Conversely, Rynie Wolters, their pitcher, threw rising, medium-speed floaters that we clipped underneath, producing sixteen fly outs.

"Wolters reminds me of Jimmy Creighton," said Brainard, watching him work on George Wright. "Makes the ball look like it's coming up out of the ground. 'Cept Jimmy was swifter—swifter than anybody."

"Who's he pitch for?" I asked.

Brainard gave me an unreadable look. Andy nudged me and murmured, "He's dead."

Well, shit.

George popped to Hatfield. Not an auspicious beginning. Our star rarely failed to get on to start a game. Gould drove a scorcher into left center, but Hunt streaked over the grass and took it against his chest, like a football receiver. It brought an appreciative roar ("rapturous cheers," Millar would write). But the crowd quieted when Waterman took first on an error, hustled to third on a passed ball, and scored on Allison's bouncer muffed by the shortstop.

Stockings 1, Mutuals 0.

In the third we tallied again. George rocketed a double to left and scored on passed balls by the rattled Mute catcher, who had trouble with Wolters's rising tosses when he was close behind the plate. Otherwise, pitching and defense smothered all threats. The Mutes held us to five hits *total*—unheard of among top clubs—and managed but eight of their own.

The game moved quickly as goose eggs mounted. The crowd watched in deepening silence as we shut out their champions inning after inning. At the end of seven it remained 2–0.

I kept my eyes peeled for McDermott or Le Caron. If they were going to strike, it would happen while we were in New York. The derringer was in my topcoat pocket, close at hand. It seemed unlikely they'd attack in front of ten thousand witnesses. But I didn't rule it out.

Andy was playing superbly. On base in the fourth, he ignored Mills—the Mute first baseman was notorious for distracting opponents with amiable gossip—and promptly stole second. Taking third on a wild throw, he danced down the line, but Mac's fly stranded him. In the sixth, with two away and runners tearing from the bags, a

Mute batter smashed a ball so high that it vanished momentarily into low-hanging clouds. Hurley groaned, thinking it was gone. But Andy retreated to the fence, leaped high, and came down with the ball in his right hand. The crowd moaned in disbelief.

In the eighth, the Mutes got their leadoff hitter on with a scratch single. The next two hitters couldn't advance him. Then Mills sent a soft looper outside the left-field line. It looked as if Andy had a chance for the foul-bound out. He sprinted. The ball bounced on the turf. He dove, stretched out, one arm extended. His fingers clutched the ball— and fumbled it.

Hurley swore softly and I tried to shake off an uneasy premonition. Sure enough, Mills connected on Brainard's next pitch, lining it into right and scoring the runner. The next hitter grounded sharply to George for the force. We were out of the inning, but our lead was cut in half. And the chance for a historic accomplishment—shutting out the mighty Mutes—was gone.

Stockings 2, Mutuals 1.

Allison's leadoff single was the only spark in our half of the eighth. Playing smoothly and confidently now, the Mutes cashed in three quick outs. The stage was set for the ninth.

The silence falling over the diamond was eerie. I could hear coughs in the stands across the field. Then a solitary voice shouted encouragement, and a chorus took it up. It built to a crescendo as the Mute hitter stepped in. Suddenly the tension was too much. Hurley and I scrambled to our feet along with the crowd. The assembled thousands stood and yelled, waiting to see who would falter. Very quickly we saw that it wouldn't be the Mutes.

Brainard's fastballs still looked to have full velocity, but the first two batters poked singles over the infield. The next fouled a pitch behind third. Waterman sprinted and lunged, missed by inches, somersaulted, and slammed into a grandstand support. He staggered up, spitting blood and waving off George, who tried to attend him.

The Mute used his second life to push a heartbreaker through the box and past a diving Sweasy. The tying run came home. Mac's quick throw held the other runners at first and second, but there were still no outs. The crowd danced and stomped and screamed and waved and heaved food and trash and money and hats and umbrellas and coats and canes and scarves and parasols.

"Crap," I said.

"In a word," Hurley agreed.

The jubilance was choked moments later when the next hitter lifted a weak pop-up. Waterman moved in rapidly to take it.

"Two, Freddy!" George sprinted behind him to third base. "Two!"

[123]

Waterman settled under the ball, cupped his hands—and deliberately let it roll off his fingers. He snatched the ball from the sod, wheeled, and fired to George, who kicked the bag and rammed the ball to Sweasy at second. The chagrined runners were frozen. Double play!

The Mutuals argued vehemently that Waterman had caught the ball before grounding it, but the umpire ruled against him. When the confusion settled, the next Mute stepped in, swung hard, and tipped the ball straight back. Allison sprang high and speared it. He ran from the diamond yelling and holding the ball aloft triumphantly.

We'd escaped. I sat down and breathed again.

Stockings 2, Mutuals 2.

Andy was up. I moved close as he wiped his bat with his lucky rag. His face was taut. I knew he was still down on himself for dropping the foul in the eighth. Jaw muscles bunched, he stalked to the plate. I wanted to look away as he took his stance—feet wide apart, crouched slightly, choking up on the bat—and looked out at Wolters in the crowd's stillness. He watched a high pitch go by, then got what he wanted. He swung and drilled the ball on a low line toward left. The Mute shortstop jumped, knocked it down, threw quickly. Andy's legs blurred on the baseline. He left his feet and hurled himself at the bag as the throw came.

"Safe!"

"Yeah," I screamed. "OH, YEAH!"

Andy looked for Harry's sign. Steal. He broke for second on the next pitch—and slipped and sprawled. It took half the Mutes to run him down. Andy trudged to the bench, head low and cap pulled down over his eyes. I knew better than to say a word.

"Stir 'em, Acey!" yelled Hurley.

Working his toothpick, Brainard turned smoothly on Wolters's pitch and rapped the ball safely to left. To our surprise—and certainly the Mutes'—the slow-footed pitcher didn't stop. Hunt fielded the ball and threw it in without realizing Brainard's intent. Even so, the cutoff man had plenty of time to nail him at second. But the Mutes' alarmed shouts must have flustered him. He launched the ball ten feet over the leaping second baseman, allowing Brainard to puff into third.

We hooted and pounded each other. Wolters looked sick; it would take a miracle to hold us now. His very next pitch skidded on the plate and went through the hapless catcher's legs. Brainard trotted home with the winning run. I hugged Hurley till he sputtered, then lifted Andy and pummeled him till he laughed with the rest of us.

After police had cleared a few maniacs off the field we played the contest to the last out—a nonsensical practice. Sweasy slammed a triple through the Mutes' dispirited outfield and scored on Mac's infield out to add a meaningless run—except perhaps to bettors—to our total.

Stockings 4, Mutuals 2.

We stood together, arms entwined, cheering the Mutes, cheering Brainard, grinning and thumping each other, and then singing at the top of our lungs.

> *"Standing in the central box*
> *The "Brainy" one is found,*
> *He beats the world in tossing balls*
> *And covering the ground.*
> *And as the pitcher of our nine,*
> *He seldom needs to change,*
> *For those will find who play behind—*
> *Our Asa has the range!*
> *Oh, we are a band of ball players*
> *From Cincinnati City . . ."*

It occurred to me even then, in the midst of it all, that this heady feeling of belonging, of achieving together, of winning, was high up among the very sweetest things I knew. The others' faces showed something of the same. That happy circle in the middle of the Williamsburg diamond is burned in my memory.

9

That night Earle's Hotel reigned as New York's sporting center. Reporters and fans besieged us. Brainard, Waterman, and George were in heavy demand as stars of the victory. Harry was as euphoric as I'd ever seen him.

"Thirteen blanks!" marveled a bearded reporter I later learned was Henry Chadwick, dean of America's baseball writers, waving his notebook and citing the number of scoreless innings. "Magnificent contest! Most scientific on record!" He claimed it even surpassed the recent rowing championship between Yale and Harvard. "You western boys are rekindling the national game here, no doubt about it!"

The lobby buzzed with speculation about tomorrow's Atlantic game. And with debate over whether our 15–0 record topped that of the 'sixty-three Brooklyn Eckfords, who had won all nine of their match games, plus every first-class, second-class and amateur contest they had played—nobody knew the exact total—and as the arguments grew heated they included so many classifications and technicalities that I gave up and listened instead to talk of a fight that day in St. Louis. One Mike McCoole, the current American heavyweight champ, had defeated Tom Allen of England. Although illegal, boxing flourished and was passionately followed in both countries. Enormous sums of money must have changed hands this day, I thought.

Champion stood on a table and read a telegram that arrived from the directors of the club.

> "ON BEHALF OF THE CITIZENS OF CINCINNATI WE SEND YOU GREETING. THE STREETS ARE FULL OF PEOPLE, WHO GIVE CHEER AFTER CHEER FOR THEIR PET CLUB. GO ON WITH THE NOBLE WORK!"

George joined him atop the table and led cheers. Toasts were offered until Harry protested that we faced two more tough games in successive days.

During all of that I received a message of my own. A courier tapped my shoulder and handed me a sealed letter. I tipped him and tore it open.

> *Dear Mr. Fowler,*
>
> *Allow me to express my gratitude for the appreciation you showed following my performance. I will repay you with this vital information: I overheard Mr. M. talking to a certain gambler who will attempt to take your life after tomorrow's match. Beware passing through the crowd, for that is where it will come. I risk all with this note. Destroy it and never admit its existence.*
>
> *EH*

I stared at the thin sheet. The writing was frilly, its loops and flourishes incongruous with the stark message. EH: Holt. M: Morrissey. The gambler could only be McDermott. I twisted the paper nervously. Should I go to Champion? The police? Get the hell out of New York? But where? I didn't want to jeopardize my shaky standing with the club. I also didn't want to die.

Without explaining how I'd been warned, I huddled later with Andy. He called in Brainard and Waterman, and together we came up with a simple plan. I hoped like hell it wasn't *too* simple.

Sometime after midnight Andy and I were jolted awake by hammering on our door. Andy opened it. Sweasy and Hurley stood unsteadily outside. They smelled like a distillery. Hurley began to sing.

> *"Come, let us roam together*
> *O'er the soft and purple heather,*
> *From Ulster's dim gray mountains*
> *To Muskerry's fairy fountains. . . ."*

"He's spifflicated," said Andy. "We gotta keep him quiet."

" 'S as natural for Hibernians to tipple as pigs to root," Hurley proclaimed. " 'S your trouble, Andy, you think you're too good to be properly Irish anymore."

"That's true goods!" Sweasy said, scowling at me. He took a lurching step forward. "C'mon, you bastard!" He raised his fists. "You're bigger'n a shithouse, but I'm meaner'n a singed cat."

"Oh fuck," I said, and closed the door in his face.

"Get some sleep, Sweaze," said Andy. We listened as they lurched down the corridor. "Don't pay any heed," he said. "He's just jealous."

"Of me?"

Andy nodded. "See, me 'n' Sweaze've always been roomies. That's mostly what he's riled about."

"Well, hell, I never intended to break up—"

"I know you didn't. It was my idea, Sam. Like I say, don't pay it any heed. The tour only runs a couple more weeks. Sweaze an' me board together in Cincinnati. Everything'll be hunky by then."

"What was that Irish stuff?"

He looked uncomfortable. "Dick was just carryin' on. As for Sweaze, I reckon I've changed since we were kids. He's still the old way, an' he resents me coming to want new things."

"Am I connected with that too?"

"No, you're different." He did not elaborate.

The morning papers were flooded with descriptions of the victory. Several featured play-by-play accounts. One writer's use of "red-legged porkopolitans" baffled me, until George explained that it referred to Cincinnati's thriving hog industry.

Again we took the ferry at midday, but this time the weather was clear and sparkling. Sun sprites danced on the river; a breeze freshened the air. Sweasy, I noticed, wore colored glasses, and Hurley looked dead.

A noisy crowd of twelve thousand awaited us at the Capitoline Grounds in Brooklyn. I grew increasingly tense. Vehicles jammed the surrounding streets—Nostrand, Marcy, Putnam, Halsey—and spectators scrambled for vantage points. As we alighted from our bus, the Stockings formed a tight phalanx around me according to plan. Forging ahead, bats riflelike on our shoulders, we marched briskly to the diamond. Seeing one loony with binoculars clinging to the lightning rod of a church steeple, I thought it a very good thing that telescopic sights weren't yet around.

The Capitoline Grounds were spacious enough to hold two games at once. The grass was smooth and level as a billiard table. Banked inclines beyond the foul lines were jammed with wagons and carts. Blue-jacketed cops patrolled in substantial numbers—a comforting sight. The wooden stands were packed beyond capacity.

From a cupola waved the Atlantics' tiger pennant and banners from years the club had captured the whip pennant: '61, '64, '65, '66. They reminded me of Celtics' flags hanging from the rafters of Boston Garden. Andy informed me that Brooklyn had dominated New York baseball for the past decade, the local Eckfords taking the pennant virtually every year the Atlantics didn't.

Brooklyn and baseball. Grandpa and I listened faithfully to broadcasts of Dodger games in the years just before they moved to the West Coast. My first heroes were Pee Wee, Jackie, and Duke. How powerful I'd be, I used to think, with a name like Duke Snider.

It was ironic to learn from Andy that out on the field now, in ice-white jerseys and charcoal pants and caps, were men who had been his particular boyhood idols: Joe Start, known as "Old Reliable," the Atlantic first baseman; Dickey Pearce, the dodgy shortstop; and "Young Jack" Chapman, the left fielder.

In recent seasons the Atlantics had added talent: Tommy Pratt, a speed-balling pitcher; Lipman Pike, a true rarity as a power-hitting, left-handed second baseman; Freddy Crane, the whippet center fielder who threw his cap down before grabbing flies; and Bob Ferguson, whose showy one-hand grabs had earned him the press sobriquet "Death to Flying Things."

I was surprised when Dick Pearce came up to me. He was short and thickly built, with a brush mustache and intelligent brown eyes.

"I heard about your baby hit against the Haymakers, Fowler. Hoped you might show it off for me."

"Baby hit . . . oh, the bunt."

"That how it's called?"

After he assured me he wouldn't try it against us, I demonstrated squaring away and cushioning the bat. He watched me with a sharp professional eye. "I see it would take some little practice."

"Some little," I agreed modestly.

Later, when Pearce squared away at the plate during the game, I thought I'd been suckered. But he used the stance to punch a fair foul past Waterman, despite the latter's playing him a step in foul territory. There was simply no way to defense the maneuver, I realized. Pearce seemed even more adept at it than Waterman or Hurley, and for good reason: later I learned that he had invented it. With bunts added to his weaponry he would drive opposing infielders crazy.

The game itself, after yesterday's cliffhanger, was ho-hum. The Atlantics opened with hustle and confident chatter, but began to deflate when we blanked them in the opening frames. Meanwhile, our hitters jumped on Pratt's fastballs as if to make up for lean production against Wolters. We tallied five runs in the first and iced things with thirteen in the second. Coasting, we won, 32–10. The crowd, rising between innings in a foreshadowing of the seventh-inning stretch, seemed quite impressed by us, as did the Atlantics themselves. Later we heard that it was the worst defeat ever suffered by the proud Brooklyn club.

Allison, playing inspired ball, at one point lunged for a foul tip that caromed off his own neck. Pursuing the ball, he barreled into the batter, knocking him flat. Then, tumbling forward himself, he somehow kept the ball in the air with desperate tips and finally seized it as his chin plowed the sod. He rose to appreciative applause, grinning through clumps of grass and dirt. I considered, not for the first time, the possibility of Allison being not quite mentally balanced.

We moved in a tight orbit from the field. I'd seen no sign of McDermott or Le Caron or even Morrissey—rumor had him winning big on us yesterday—but my blood pumped rapidly. This was when Holt had warned it would come. I wrapped my fingers around the derringer in my pocket. We departed safely. There was no visible threat at the ferry. But I felt a pervasive menace, a sense of being watched by unfriendly eyes. One thing I knew: I wanted out of New York badly.

That night I ventured from our room only to eat, fearful that Holt's note had been some sort of ruse. Unable to sleep, I began a *Harper's Monthly* story called "The Murderous Gypsy Murillo: A Tale of Old California." It worked like a charm. I was asleep by the third page.

Except that we were back in Williamsburg facing the Brooklyn Eckfords, the next day followed the same pattern. A crowd of eight thousand turned out, even though we were prohibitive favorites.

The Eckfords came out fighting. Their pitcher, Alphonse Martin, who answered to "Phonnie" and "Old Slow Ball," baffled us with junk in the opening frames. Andy muffed a fly early on, and the Eckfords pushed across several runs. To my relief Andy fielded flawlessly the rest of the way, made a gorgeous over-the-shoulder catch, and lashed four hits. Brainard, relieved by Harry in the closing innings, held the Eckfords to eight hits. The final was 24–5. Our games now completed in New York, the crowd stood and gave us a departing ovation.

Bunched amidst the others, crouching to keep my head from posing a target, I imagined the sudden flash of a blade, the crack of a gun. *Move faster!* I urged silently. We made the trip without incident, although as we were entering Earle's I nearly jumped out of my shoes when a group standing in front of the pool hall next door raised cue sticks in mock salute to us. For an instant I thought they were leveling rifles. Gould wasn't amused either. He stopped and glared. They retreated inside.

That night I made it through four more pages of "Murderous Murillo," the highlight coming when "the tawny bosom of Rosa fired with dark yearnings on seeing the swarthy countenance of the savage Gypsy bandit framed in the flaps of her tent." There was a subtle hint that Rosa might even be uncorseted beneath her peasant blouse. Hoo boy.

To the delight of Andy and Sweasy, Champion scheduled a game against the Irvington club. We departed Manhattan after break-fast and crossed to Newark, a booming industrial and shipping cen-ter of over a hundred thousand, where smokestacks were eclipsing the earlier charms of graceful church spires and quiet colonial greens.

Champion also arranged for a team publicity shot at Huff's Photography Palace on Broad Street. Andy asked that I be included, but I begged off. The last thing I wanted was my likeness available to Le Caron or anybody else McDermott might send after me.

I wandered around, eyeing *carte-de-visite* portraits and stereo cards. On the walls hung samples of everything the studio advertised on the huge sign over its door: Likenesses of Distinguished Statesmen, Eminent Divines, Prominent Citizens, Indian Chiefs, and Notorious Robbers and Murderers. Also—Beautiful Landscapes, Perfect Clouds, and a Bona Fide Streak of Lightning, Taken on the Night of August 26, 1857.

The photographer, a fastidious German with walrus bristles and cantilevered belly, set up his forty-five-second wet collodion-plate exposures. He hissed at the players to be still, particularly Hurley, who turned his head repeatedly because George was snapping his ears.

The result, I knew, was destined for national distribution. *Frank Leslie's* and *Harper's* had approached Champion immediately after we toppled the Mutes. From the photo, artists would create the steel engravings used in printing. Having his era's *Time* and *Newsweek* already in line, Champion was eager to strike with others while we were hot. And just now we were very hot indeed.

I looked on in amusement. Everybody's hair was brushed, Harry's and Brainard's whiskers were oiled, Gould's mustache waxed. Collars were buttoned. Ornamental dickeys, each with scripted *C*, were on straight. George and Brainard sported cravats. George and Waterman wore their silver medallions awarded by the *New York Clipper* for leading their respective positions in hitting the previous season. They were posed in two rows, Harry sitting in the center foreground. Next to him Brainard held a ball, while Sweasy and Gould, on the ends, rested bats against their knees.

"You're all so beautiful," I said, mugging behind the photographer during his final countdown. When he turned around to hiss, Brainard brazenly flipped me off. We studied the matter later with a magnifying glass. Unfortunately the surreptitious finger did not record beyond the merest hint of a blur. History's loss.

The tiny thatch-roofed frame house in which Andy had grown up sat on a dirt street lined with box elders. A pig wheezed in the shade of the porch. Several bony cows grazed in a side lot. Andy ushered me through the front door. The atmosphere inside was close and hot, with a stale cabbagelike odor.

It was obvious that I was a guest of honor and that such occasions were rare. Behind a table covered with patched linen and set with crockery and pewter, the Leonards waited in line to meet me.

Andy's mother was tiny and birdlike, probably only in her fifties but ancient, her every movement tentative, as if she might take flight. Her rheumy eyes held mine with a quality of vague questioning as she repeated my name wonderingly and touched my hand.

Next was her brother Gavan, Andy's uncle, stout and red-faced and bald as a bulb. He pumped my hand and greeted me in dense brogue, something that sounded like "G'aarf bray!" I managed to understand, with Andy's help, that he'd taken off work early to see the celebrated nine engage in the glorious American game.

Andy's sister Brighid was only in her midthirties. She was a hair taller than her mother and had Andy's coloring, but gray already streaked her hair and crows'-feet bordered her light green eyes; she seemed weary, very weary. When I took her hand she blushed—and astonished me by dipping into a curtsy. I attempted to bow in response—my first ever—and it felt ridiculous. She explained apologetically that her husband couldn't leave the factory where he worked, but the children were home. And so they were: four of them staring as if a fairy-tale giant had stomped into their home. I suppose I was a giant. Nobody there even matched Andy's towering five six.

While he passed out gifts—the prodigal son come home—I looked idly at a bric-a-brac stand. A small wreath-shaped polychrome print caught my eye. On it were pictured eight men's faces. They bore the names O'Brien, Grattan, Fitzgerald, and others. At the top was "*Erin Go Bragh*" and at the bottom, "Justice to Ireland." In the center, on a field of green, appeared Erin herself—she resembled Columbia in militant feminism, but was probably plumper—garbed in flowing shamrock-bordered skirt and chain-mail doublet and trampling a prostrate English king. One shapely arm held a flag bearing the Irish harp; the other brandished a sword. She was nobody you'd want to mess with.

Beside the wreath was a framed twenty-dollar bond dated January 1866 and issued by an Irish "government in exile"; it bore portraits of Emmet and Tone flanking a bare-armed Hibernia exhorting what appeared to be a Union army soldier to take up the sword in Ireland's cause.

Behind it was a small green flag with a sunburst in one corner. Gold letters spelled, "Newark 1st Regt. Irish Army of Liberation. Ridgeway & Fort Erie, June 2, 1866. Presented by the Fenian Sisterhood of New Jersey."

I pondered all of that, recalling that I'd heard the term *Fenian* several times. Then my attention was caught by a group of miniatures;

daguerreotypes, I thought. They included a steely-gazed, teenage Andy in a baseball jersey with PIONEERS across his chest; a younger Gavan grinning beneath a jaunty derby; an even younger Mrs. Leonard— God, she'd once been a dark-haired beauty!—on the arm of a smooth-shaven, smiling-eyed man I assumed to be Andy's father. A studio logo told me the portrait had been made in Ballyjamesduff, wherever that was. I said the name silently as I stared at their faces, trying to imagine what their lives had been in that other land, that other time. My grandparents had kept only one picture of my father. It was a wedding picture. I had stared at it the same way. *Who were you?*

Then the last picture caught my eyes. Caught and impaled them. I tried later to sort out elements of the moment; I think my first discrete awareness was of the other eyes looking back: pale of iris, dark-lashed, metallic-seeming, gazing out at me.

Is it unusual to have an overwhelming sense of fatedness about an encounter? To feel from the very first instant that in some unfathomable way your existence is linked with another's? What I'd felt before with Andy and Twain now seemed almost minor beside this new sensation.

In her features were traces of Andy and Brighid and Mrs. Leonard. She was young, probably in her teens, at the time of the portrait. And a beauty, no doubt about it, with dark hair piled high, a straight nose, lovely cheekbones, lips in a trace of a smile. There was a haughty quality to that smile, a hint of stubbornness in the tilted chin, a willfulness in the eyes, a sense that she knew well who she was and would not be undervalued. Not quite arrogance, but on the road to it.

And then abruptly a door wrenched open in my mind. The material of her dress was familiar. Beneath its high ruffled collar, enough of the bodice was visible that I could see the pattern: columns of flowerlike bows trailing long ribbons intermixed with clusters of leaves and rosebuds. In the untinted photograph the material was light gray. In my memory it was pale yellow, dotted with pinks and greens—the only such patch on Grandma's quilt.

As my blood careened I tried to tell myself it was doubtless a popular design, had gone into any number of dresses and quilts. But I didn't believe it. A patch of that fabric had somehow become part of the quilt I knew as a boy. I was certain of it. And finally I had found the clue I'd been seeking to explain why I had come back in time: to deal with the person in that daguerreotype.

"Everything hunky?" Andy touched my shoulder. The expression, which I thought stupid, came from the slogan of a breath freshener named Hunkidori. He teased me with it frequently.

I pointed. "Who is she?"

"That's Cait, my other sis—"

"Margaret!" said Mrs. Leonard sharply. It came out "Mair-ghread."

"Mother, she doesn't go by Margaret now."

"We have no Caitlin," said Mrs. Leonard firmly, pronouncing it "Cat-LEEN." "Margaret's the name my Andrew picked, God rest him"—she crossed herself—"and as Margaret she was baptized in Holy Mother Church."

Andy stared at the floor.

" 'Twas only weeks before her marriage that the lovely portrait was made," chirped Mrs. Leonard.

Andy started to speak, then checked himself.

Marriage? Was a message intended? I turned reluctantly from the photograph. I wanted to steal it.

Time was short before we had to leave for the game. With long-handled utensils Brighid served pork and "praties" from iron pots suspended in the high open fireplace that had blackened the walls on either side. Gavan's spirited jeremiad on inflation accompanied the meal. I understood him better by then. Later I tried to reproduce a sample of his brogue in writing:

> When we first landed, yer honner, I made divil a cint but four dollars a week and find mesilf. But it was aisy livin' in a manner of spakin', as the troublesome prices din' keep elevatin' higher each time a soul turned aroun'. Be jaber, they'll soon drain all o' me heart's blood!

Charmed by the lilt of it, I found myself following sounds and rhythms more than words. But I paid attention when Mrs. Leonard announced, "General O'Neill stopped in to pay his respects with that handsome Captain O'Donovan"—Andy stiffened in his chair—"close by 'im, as ever. Sure an' they're two noble samples of manhood, Andy. The captain said that he was watching over Margaret, out in the West."

O'Donovan. The name resonated strangely in me.

"I wish he'd leave her the hell alone."

"Your tongue, Andy!" She crossed herself. "The leadership's travelin' about the country these days," she said. "Since the St. Patrick's circular from Head Center, it's been speechifyin' and money-raisin'."

Andy said sharply, "You didn't give away what I sent you, did you?"

She pursed her lips.

"Just a pittance of it, lad," said Gavan. "It's her joy, Andrew."

"It's a shameful scheme, is what it is!" He set his fork down with an impact. "They come sniffing in here and leave with—"

"Andy, don't," she wailed. "They're strugglin' for our homeland. Yes, yours as well—if ye'd but know it!"

"Even the Church can't stomach 'em," he said maliciously. "The whole lot're to be excommunicated."

"But it hasn't been done yet, has it?" she retorted, her tone equally spiteful.

"Mother, our lives are here now. We're not *going* back to Ireland. I'd like for it to be free, same as you, but I don't think it'll come by throwin' parades and wearin' emerald sashes and epaulets and phoenixes and sunbursts and shamrocks, and makin' endless speeches. I send money to *you,* for the family."

"You're a fine one to talk, with your fancy pantaloons and shameful stockings!" Her voice choked with sobs. "I want to go home, my work's done. You're the last one—and somebody I scarcely know. I don't want a life here, as you call it. I want to be with my Andrew, lyin' in the sweet ground beside him."

There was embarrassed silence.

Andy said tensely, "We shouldn't do this, with my friend here."

"Sure an' it is I'm sorry," she said, wiping her eyes. "But 'tis God's truth I'm not long for this life, and it's me wish, son, to go home."

Andy looked wretched. Gavan shifted uncomfortably.

"There isn't the money, Ann," he said softly. "The cost is divilish high. Even steerage'd require a year o' me wages."

"It's me wish! Sister Clara Antonia told me—"

"Oh, no," Andy interjected. "You're feedin' *her* again, too?"

"She has the gift—seventh daughter of a seventh daughter."

"I'm sure she took the worm test for you," he said sarcastically.

"No need of that," she replied calmly. "Though it's well known I gave it to every soul in this house. Small wonder the wee thing thrived with *you!*"

Andy threw up his hands in surrender.

"She said there'd come a deliverer. To release me from this life and send me to my Andrew—forever."

"Fine," Andy said wearily. "Did she offer to foot the expense?"

"That she didn't."

"Well, how about the society? Surely O'Neill'd jump to help a good Irishwoman in her time of need."

She said nothing. Her eyes met mine across the table. For a moment they were not filmy. Something happened between us. It was as if she'd asked a specific silent question.

"Your daughter," I said, fumbling for words. "Your other daughter . . . ?"

"Yes, my daughter," she agreed, smiling vaguely. Her eyes were filmy again. The subject seemed concluded.

As we rode the horsecar east toward the township of Irvington, I asked Andy why his mother's wish to return to Ireland upset him so much.

"Wouldn't it rile you," he answered, "if *your* mother wanted to leave, just when you were makin' something of yourself? Something for everybody to be proud of? Here I'm the only one earnin' money worth speakin' of, and she thinks I'm playin' a boy's game instead of followin' a trade."

"Still, wouldn't you send her back? If she really wanted it?"

He sighed. "I've come to believe it *is* her true desire."

I changed the subject. "What was that about a worm and having the gift?"

"Old Cavan beliefs. The gift is healing—laying on hands and such—and prophesying. The worm test tells whether a child has the gift. When the worm's placed in the hand and shrivels up, that signifies the child was born with the gift."

"But she said it thrived in yours."

He smiled ruefully. "Likely so."

I asked him to tell me about his family. It turned out he'd known his father scarcely more than I knew mine.

"I was three," he said. "All's I recollect was him there, skin white as paper, laid out amongst us. Brighid lifted me up to see . . ."

. . . lying alone, beneath the pale light . . .

". . . women keenin' and cryin', men drinkin' from jugs. . . . And that's all I can remember. Next we was on the boat, everybody moaning and throwing up."

"Coming here?"

"Yes, and lucky too. By then, 'forty-nine, a million had died. Blight set in, and the praties—'taters—failed three straight years. Folks swarmed to cities and died in the streets. We tried to hang on. Father wouldn't hear of leaving the land. But conacres—wee parcels he rented out—stood vacant. Finally our crops failed too, and since the linen mills and gypsum mines had closed long before, the game was up."

"What part of Ireland?"

"County Cavan, near Swanlinbar. Hills and lakes. Father couldn't leave. He died of heartache—and of whiskey bein' cheaper than meat."

. . . like putting a gun to his head . . .

Andy's tone lightened. "Old Hickory's folks lived in County An-trim, near us. I'm named for him, in fact. Andrew Jackson Leonard, same as my father."

"I'll be damned." I nearly told of Grandpa naming me Samuel Clemens. Instead I said, "What happened after he died?"

"Mother and Gavan sold the land for pennies—barely enough to cross in steerage. By the time we set foot at Castle Garden, Liam, my wee brother, was dead of consumption. Gavan found work as a tanner in Newark, so that's where we went. Not too many Irish there yet, though Sweaze's folk lived near. We had to learn the new ways quick. I had the easiest time, bein' the youngest. Mother never changed a lick, Irish to the core. Even Brighid's still a good half Old Soil."

"What about . . . Cait?"

He paused so long that I wondered if he were going to answer. "She's in Cincinnati."

My heart did a funny little beat. "So you're close?"

"These years we haven't a great deal to say to each other." A tired sound came from him. "It's a sadness for me." Again he was silent.

"What exactly are Fenians?"

He looked at me. "Why?"

"Well, you and your mother disagree about them. Also, somebody said it was Fenian money that McDermott lost at the Haymaker game."

"They're tryin' to get a free Irish nation," he said slowly, as if threading through a complex subject. "Over here it's called the Fenian Society, but it's properly the American wing of the Irish Revolutionary Brotherhood."

I envisioned TV-screen images: *IRA youths fasting . . . howling, rock-throwing mobs choking Ulster streets . . . Tommies in armored cars . . . bomb-blast carnage. . . .*

"A terrorist group?"

"You're talkin' Dutch, Sam."

"You know, operating in secret, using violence."

"Well, in Ireland they *tried* to be secret—but now they're all in jail. Over here they've been in the open all along, marching in their green uniforms and holding picnics and benefits to raise cash."

"Sounds tame enough."

"Well, they *did* invade Canada three years back."

I looked to see if he was joking. "Okay, I'll bite. Why'd they do that?"

"Intended to work a ransom game. Give England back its territory after Ireland was free."

"Andy, are you kidding me?"

"Rumors have 'em trying it again soon. Read the papers, you'll see."

"Isn't that pretty farfetched?"

"I dunno, Sam, tens of thousands of Irish boys fought in the war. On both sides. They're trained troops—that's what Fenian means in the old legends; from *Fianna*, for 'soldier'—and most still have their service weapons. In 'sixty-six, all trains runnin' north to the border were suddenly full of armed men."

"What did the government do?"

"Steered clear and let the Canucks handle it. Which they did, once the surprise wore off. But the society claims it'll be proper organized next time."

"How could we just steer clear?"

"Easy. England ain't 'zactly the cheese, you know, since they helped the Johnnies."

For some reason I had the sudden shocking realization that the nation wasn't even one hundred years old. There were people—many people—who carried vivid memories of Washington, Jefferson, Franklin. Incredible.

"Irish votes carry weight now," Andy continued. "Politicians're anxious not to rile us."

"Okay, but stand by and let part of the population—an immigrant army, at that—*invade a neighbor country?*"

"Governments can't control everything."

"If McDermott lost Fenian money," I said, changing tack, "he must be in trouble. But how'd he get it in the first place? Is he one of them?"

"No, but he lays in stores for 'em—stores not easily come by, if you take my meaning. Word is he's trusted by General O'Neill. Sits in on the councils in New York, privy to the inside workin's."

"How'd he manage that?"

"Dunno. He come out of the war with a medal—nobody knows for what—and puffed himself hard. For my money he's a chin artist and crooked as a crutch."

"What about the O'Donovan your mother mentioned? The one who came visiting with General O'Neill."

"He's O'Neill's chief of operations. Mean-tempered as an adder and short as piecrust. Even McDermott wouldn't want to cross him."

"And yet he takes care of your sister?"

Andy looked at me silently for a good ten seconds. "Sam, I can tell you're freezin' to know about Cait. I saw you studyin' that old picture."

"Well, okay, why won't anybody talk about her?"

"Me'n her were close once, the two youngest. Now we don't get along.

"But the whole family avoided talking about her."

"Cait's gone her own way."

"Well, if it's too painful . . ."

"Sam, I see how you came to be a newspaper feller." He slapped his leg in frustration. "You can't stop pumping!"

I laughed and said I'd ease up.

"No, I'll spill, but there's a lot to it. Goes back to just before the war, about when that picture was made. Cait was bein' sparked by John O'Neill's nephew, Colm, who'd never liked the name Margaret and so called her Cait. She'd loved Colm since they was little kids. They were set to marry. But when the fighting started, Colm took it into his head to fight for the Union like his uncle, then a cavalry lieutenant. Irish lads were pouring into the armies by the tens of thousands. Course, many didn't have a choice, as they hadn't cash enough to buy a substitute in the draft. Still, signin' on was the thing to do. Colm joined Meagher's Irish Brigade."

"How'd Cait feel about it?" I asked.

"Oh, she was *dead* against it. Said it wasn't his country, nor his fight. But Colm was a charmer, could talk anybody into anything. He had his way."

"What happened?"

"He got killed." Andy's tone was flat. "At Antietam. Holding the green regimental flag up even in death, we were told—though I always thought that part was malarkey."

I felt a strange tumble of emotions, a sense that things existed just beyond my understanding: dream wisps tantalizingly near consciousness.

"It changed Cait like day to night. She'd taken care of me as far back as I remember. But after Colm's death she didn't care about me anymore. Or anything else, exceptin'—"

"Wait a second," I said, charged with currents of excitement. "Didn't your mom say the portrait was taken before her *marriage?*"

"There wasn't none." Andy looked at me. "Cait had Colm's baby, but there was never a marriage."

"Had his baby? You mean, after . . . ?"

"A boy, born seven months after Colm died. Soon as the war ended, John O'Neill came around spreadin' the same old blarney. 'Cept now he was a Fenian general and instead of savin' the Union it was savin' Ireland. The war had all been a big training ground. Now all the boys that wasn't dead or maimed would have a go directly at the big thing—a free Ireland."

"Was that supposed to console Cait?"

"I don't know what happened between 'em directly," Andy said.

[139]

"But O'Neill was part of what changed her. She got a new purchase on life, a partial one anyhow. Along with the baby she had the Fenians. Took to 'em like religion."

"So that Colm hadn't died in vain?"

"That's my guess. She'd carry on his work, so to speak." He gave me a shrewd glance. "You're some quick."

"I gather you didn't think much of it."

"Mother sided with her, long as they'd pretend she was married. But I fought Cait every step, arguin' that the family came first, that she'd already given up enough; but she acted like I wasn't talking to her at all. Finally she moved out. And by then even Mother realized how far it'd gone—too far to ever change back. So we lost her."

"I'm sorry, Andy."

"Makes me sick. The politicians speechify, the generals make battle plans, the old women sew and give their pennies, the boys rush out to die, and the girls they marched off from ain't never the same."

I tried to think of comfort to offer.

"Colm was a fine lad," he said softly. "I looked to him as my hero. Cait was lively and vital and laughed so sweet it'd make your heart jump to hear her." He took a slow breath. "Well, she still looks enough like the girl you were studying' so close, Sam. But now she never laughs, not even with her son. And I don't care how many glorified speeches they make, Colm died like an animal led to slaughter."

My vision danced oddly. *McDermott . . . O'Neill . . . O'Donovan . . . Cait.* What was it about the confluence of those names that stirred a vague dissonance in me? "O'Donovan takes care of her and the boy now?"

"So Mother thinks," he said. "They work in the Fenians together is all I know. O'Donovan was Colm's pal, though most of us couldn't see why Colm let him be around so much. They went off to war together. It was O'Donovan who brought back the tale of the flag. I never fancied him, even before. I never liked the way he eyed Cait. But she's gone his way, not the family's."

I rubbed my eyes and saw the portrait again in my mind: the dark hair tumbled on her head; the lips with an echo of a smile; the prideful glint of something—mischief? challenge?—in her eyes. It was hard to imagine her perpetually somber.

"She's never married, then?"

"No, nor likely to; that part of Cait's sealed up."

"She must still be nice to look at."

"You're not the first to be taken with her looks, friend Sam."

Maybe so, I thought, but how many had grown up in another century with a piece of her dress on *their* quilts?

◇ 10 ◇

The Irvington ball grounds baked beneath a brilliant sun. It was the hottest day yet. Sunshades and straw hats dotted the crowd. The Stockings were loose and relaxed, out of New York with the winning streak—I with my life—intact. Andy and Sweasy got celebrity treatment. Surrounded by family members and reporters, they signed autographs, greeted friends, and gave youngsters tips. The rest of us were clearly secondary, even George—which probably accounted for his lackadaisical play: the star shortstop muffed several grounders and failed to hit with his usual authority.

There were no pool sellers here, no whiskey vendors, no fancily dressed sports. I stashed the derringer in the bottom of the cash box and stretched out, luxuriating in the sunshine, enjoying the game like a fan.

It wasn't much of a contest, despite the young Irvingtons' surprising fielding. We finished seven innings in two hours, all we could spare before returning to Jersey City and the evening train to Philadelphia. Scoring in each frame, we rolled to a 20–4 decision. Andy smacked two doubles and a single; Sweasy also doubled, all of which delighted the home folks. Brainard bamboozled the local hitters, striking out four. Allison was dazzling behind the plate.

The difference between Harry's well-drilled pros and the talented amateurs was dramatized when an Irvington player struck out with runners on first and second. Allison deliberately fumbled the ball, picked it up, and stared coolly at the batter, who suddenly realized that he had to run. Allison whipped the ball to George at second, and it went on to Gould for a double play. The shocked crowd applauded the tactic good-naturedly, unaware that we practiced it routinely.

Hurley played the final innings, and I hit for Harry his last time up. Feeling rusty, I drew admiring oohs with a sizzling foul shot outside third, then popped ignobly to short. But just being out there was enough this fine day. And wearing the Stockings' uniform was increasingly an ego boost. I had no trouble basking in reflected glory.

Before boarding our coach I joined Andy's family as he embraced them and said good-bye. I could see that they were proud of his performance on the field.

"We'll be back in September to take away the pennant," he told his mother, who looked about to cry. "I'll visit then. Or you *could* take the train out West beforehand, you know, to see me 'n' Sweaze and Sam . . . and Cait."

She shook her head, a tear trickling down her cheek. Brighid took her arm. Andy kissed her and turned away. Then Brighid surprised me by saying softly, "She fancies a moment with you."

"With me?"

"Aye." Brighid stepped away, and Mrs. Leonard edged close, birdlike, peering up at me questioningly. "Mr. Fowler?" The tiny voice was tremulous. "You'll care for my Andy?"

"Like a brother, Mrs. Leonard."

"He's a good lad." The words held a hint of fierceness. "Everything his father's heart desired. Why doesn't he see that I must go home?" With an effort she kept control. "I'll not see him again in this life, Mr. Fowler."

"Now, ma'am—" I began.

"No, 'tis dying I am." She clutched my arm with a feathery grip. "A matter of weeks. It's up with me."

I stared at her. "Why are you saying this? What can I do?"

"You musn't breathe a word to Andy, but I *must* go home. If I'm buried here, 'tis a certainty misfortune will strike my children. And their children, too. If they're to have their bright new lives here, Mr. Fowler, I must return to my Andrew."

I tried to understand. "Are you saying there'll be a curse?"

"Something like."

"But how do you know?"

She peered at me as if resolving a question. "Would you take it into your heart, Mr. Fowler, that I've laid eyes on you before this day? Sister Clara Antonia helped me to see you in a dream. You were our family's deliverer."

I looked down at the grass between my feet. It seemed bright and unreal. "How did I . . . deliver you in the dream?"

"It was unclear. There was a great store of money."

I felt as if I were being hurled along the surface of a wave, trapped in its momentum. "You're asking me to help Andy find enough money to send you home, is that it?"

" 'Tis my dying wish, and yet I wouldn't burden you, Mr. Fowler, were fate not a-playing with us all—and had I not seen the sweetness in your eyes. When Andy brought you in, I knew . . ." She reached timidly and touched my arm again. Her fingers felt like brittle paper.

It was that touch that nailed it down. Helping her seemed as right as anything ever in my life. "I'll do what I can," I said, putting my hand over hers. "I promise."

"May God bless you," she said quietly. "You're a fine man."

Harry was calling me. I said good-bye. Inside the coach I looked back and saw them all waving. Mrs. Leonard, dressed in black, seemed a small shadow in the sunlight.

"She ask you to look out for me?" Andy said.

I felt a keen, cutting sadness. "That's right."

He grinned. "Then who's to look out for you?"

I sat back and closed my eyes. It made no sense, the old woman reaching out to me like that. And the Clara Antonia business was absolutely mystifying. Yet the pull it all exerted on me was so strong, so irresistibly strong.

It happened with no warning. And, as in Albany, it began outside a railway station. We were standing on the Penn Central dock in Jersey City. While a Newark writer attempted to interview George, the rest of us volunteered his answers, hugely enjoying the reporter's frustration. A porter appeared at my elbow and said a telegram awaited me inside. Not until later did I think it strange that he hadn't brought it with him. Or asked my name.

I followed him, coat in one hand, cash box in the other. Just inside the doorway I felt a painful prod in the center of my back. At first I thought it was a cane or umbrella. I started to turn and felt my arm gripped. A voice close to my ear said, "This is set to shoot. Keep moving steady." A cold tide of fear rose in me as I recognized the voice as Le Caron's.

I suppose I should have made a move right there in the busy station. Wheeled suddenly and knocked the gun loose and punched before he could react, like in the movies. But terror had frozen my brain to a point where it didn't seem to be working at all, much less devising heroic scenarios. After a few seconds of absolute numbness, I remember thinking, Jesus, I'm going to die. Right here. In the evening. With the sun still shining. A deep, fatalistic dread encased me. The gun barrel jammed suddenly into my kidneys, bringing a spasm of pain edged with nausea. I moved, legs rubbery. My bowels felt like they were about to give way.

We went out a side door to where a hack waited. Le Caron prodded me inside it. He sat facing me. A long black barrel jutted from beneath a length of cloth, pointed unwaveringly at my chest. His eyes flicked toward the cash box.

"Now I got the money *and* you," he said, leering. "You meddling fine-haired bastard!" His breath reeked; I glimpsed broken, discolored teeth. "If you'da kept your goddamn hands off'n me, you wouldn't be in this fix."

I worked my tongue inside my parched mouth and managed, "Where're we going?"

"Depends," he said. "How much is in there?"

My brain showed signs of thawing. "Everything we've made on the tour," I mumbled. "You can't take it."

"How much?"

"Everything, thousands," I lied. Champion had already exchanged the hefty Brooklyn receipts for a letter of credit. The box held only our cut of the Irvington gate, maybe three hundred at most . . . and my gun. I pictured the nickel contours, imagined the satisfying weight in my hand, saw flame stretch from its barrel into Le Caron's sneering face.

"Open it."

"No." My voice held a tremor.

He moved the long barrel slightly. "I said open it!"

"I won't."

He snarled and smashed the gun against my collarbone. Through a curtain of pain I saw that he was vulnerable for an instant. But before I could react he'd trained the gun on me again. I doubled over in exaggerated agony. "Please," I groaned.

That tickled him hugely. "Oh, the big bastard don't fancy being hurt." He leaned back with pleasurable anticipation and motioned for me to open the box.

I clutched my right shoulder and kept my right arm stiff, as if it were paralyzed—which wasn't far from the truth. Moaning with each movement, I lifted the cash box to my lap and unlocked it with my left hand. I hoped desperately that I'd remembered which way the gun lay. Still using my left hand, I lifted the tray from the box and raised it slowly. "Why don't we work something out?" I said. "How about just taking a thousand or so and . . . ." Meanwhile I'd lowered my right hand. Praying that the tray would occupy his attention long enough to mask the movement, I eased my fingers into the box, felt the rubber-gripped butt of the derringer—thank God it was pointing away!—and, without trying to remove it, stretched a finger forward to the trigger.

"This don't look like no thou—"

BLAM! The box bucked. A tongue of flame spurted. Nerves at the snapping point, I bellowed and dove forward, hurling the box ahead of me. Le Caron screamed. There was a bright flash, a deafening boom. Then I was on him. With both hands I seized the arm holding the pistol and wrenched it backward until it gave way with a snap. The pistol dropped to the floor. Shrieking and twisting, Le Caron aimed a knee at my crotch that caught my thigh instead. Muscles straining, I jammed my forearm against his throat, pinning him. With my right hand I pounded his face. Blood foamed from his nose and mouth; his skin grew slippery. He wrenched sideways and tried to dive for his gun. I jerked him back by his hair, forced his head out through the hack's window, and drove my fist into his stomach like a piston until he went limp. For a moment, seeing his chest not moving, I thought I'd killed him. Then he sucked in a convulsive breath, retched, and vomited.

As I slumped there gasping for air myself it dawned on me that the hack wasn't moving. I tucked Le Caron's pistol in my belt and retrieved the derringer from the wreckage of the cash box, checking to make sure its other chamber was ready to fire. Keeping a wary eye on Le Caron, I opened the door. The horses stood placidly, whisking flies with their tails. The driver was nowhere in sight. Who could blame him? We were on rocky, uncultivated land. A hundred yards to the right the Hudson shone golden in the setting sun. I guessed that we'd come only several miles from Jersey City toward Hoboken.

Pondering what to do, I dragged Le Caron outside. His eyes were closed, his breathing ragged. I trembled, remembering the gunfire. How had we missed in the cramped space? Checking myself, I found that my hand had been sliced by the cash box; then I saw a round hole in the sleeve of my coat. When I propped Le Caron against a tree, blood seeped through his shirt. I tore it away. The derringer shell had torn through his armpit and exited below his shoulder. I tied the shirt over his wounds as best I could, wondering that he'd been able to fight so hard. I removed a long, ugly-looking knife from the sheath taped to his ankle.

I put the money from the cash box into a bag I found beneath the driver's seat, thinking that I needed to get back at once. The team must already be on the train to Philadelphia. Or had they delayed to search for me? Would Champion think I'd stolen the money? If only phones existed!

"You hear me?" I bent over Le Caron, gun leveled.

He mumbled and opened his eyes.

"I'll kill you next time, you fucker."

He spit phlegm and blood at me. My intimidation campaign was not off to a good start.

"What do I have to do? Shoot you right here?"

"Go ahead, shoot." He spat again; I felt wet flecks on my face. "You ain't got the balls."

I almost did shoot him. A crazy hotness spread through my brain. Loathing him and how he affected me, I raised the derringer and sighted on his face. I imagined squeezing the trigger, but couldn't do it. Le Caron's fixed stare gave way to a sneer.

I started toward the hack, then had another thought and ransacked Le Caron's pockets. Nothing there, but I discovered a leather pouch secured by a cord inside his pants. It held eighty dollars in gold and silver. I cut the cord free and tied his hands behind his back. I bound his feet with his belt—and discovered six fifty-dollar greenbacks folded into tiny pouches. I pocketed them. His black eyes glittered as I slit his pants and boots, yanked them off him, walked to the river's edge, and threw them in. He was naked beneath the tree.

"Enjoy the mosquitoes," I said, and climbed up onto the driver's seat. I felt his eyes burning into me a long distance down the road. Fortunately for me the horses were streetwise and docile; they ignored my jerky rein-handling and commands that probably would have smashed us into passing wagons.

It must have been the adrenaline wearing off. A giddiness overcame me. I'd just shot a man, beaten him senseless, taken his money, left him bound and naked. And I felt damn good about it.

The Stockings were gone. I found a police station and gave an abridged version of events, handing over Le Caron's pistol and the money—they were satisfied when it matched the amount Champion had reported missing—and was told to return in the morning.

I wired the Bingham House in Philadelphia, assuring Champion that all was well. Early next morning, after a miserable night in a fleabag hotel near the station, I was taken to Le Caron's cell. He jumped up when he saw me.

"That's him! The one that robbed me!"

"You're cute in stripes," I told him.

The cops were pleased with me. Le Caron was wanted for a number of indiscretions in New York. I signed a statement. They said I'd have to appear in court later in the week. That didn't sound good, but I let on that I'd cooperate.

Stepping into the bright morning, I made my decision. I'd thought about it most of the night. I knew of only one way to help Mrs. Leonard. And it might not hurt to keep a bit of distance from the club just now.

I sent another telegram informing Champion that a family crisis had arisen; I would rejoin them in several days. Then I went back to the station and bought a ticket on the Sunday train to Elmira.

I was going treasure-hunting.

The new white courthouse sat like a wedding cake on Lake Street, glistening in the sun, its Greek Revival portico and balustraded windows trimmed with stone frosting. I looked out one of its windows. Heat waves shimmered on the Chemung River two blocks away. Flies buzzed in the corridor outside the county excise commissioner's office, where I sat in a straight-backed wooden chair, waiting and sweating.

I'd arrived in Elmira Township late the previous afternoon and taken a carriage up to Woodlawn to scout the situation. It was unsettling to know that in time Twain and Livy, their infant son, and three grown daughters would be buried there. The grounds were hushed and cool, with shade trees and winding paths. But they held no military graves. Finally a caretaker set me straight: the Confederate section was in Woodlawn *National* Cemetery, adjacent to the municipal facility. In gathering darkness I trudged to the top of Davis Avenue and set out across fields. Beyond a row of young maples I found wooden markers—soldiers' graves, but Union soldiers. I hadn't gone ten paces among them before I was challenged by a guard in blue who cradled a rifle.

"Cemetery's closed." His New York accents seemed to fit the uniform. "Open tomorrow."

I asked him where I could get information about the Confederate graves. He said to see Sexton Vincent at the Baptist Church. I thanked him and retraced my steps. But before leaving I climbed partway up a nearby hill for a broader view. Above me, on its crest, stood a squat fortresslike structure with a posted sign: ELMIRA CORRECTIONAL FACILITY. A guard stared at me from a sentry box. A savage-sounding dog barked nearby. It all gave me a bad feeling.

I studied the burial ground. No fence. Just the one guard—no, there came another. I watched them talk in the glow of a lantern. One rolled a cigarette; they looked bored.

Did I dare try it that night? No, too big a risk. Even if they fell asleep later, how would I carry the loot? I'd need a horse and rig, tools, a light to work by.

So, obliquely, I was going through channels. I'd found Sexton Vincent—a gaunt, kindly, Lincolnesque man—at his church and obtained the information that Corporal O'Shea lay in plot #3117. Vincent sketched that portion of the grounds for me, indicating the grave's exact location.

"Were you related?" he asked.

"Acquainted," I said.

He said that even four years after the war, many still came searching for lost friends and relations. Most he could not help; I was among the fortunate few. I assured him that he was performing a valuable service. Precisely how valuable, I reflected, would soon be determined.

The Chemung County courthouse was proving more difficult. I'd gotten as far as the anteroom of Commissioner Costigan's office. There a clerk with the overbite of a woodchuck and clearly not enough work to do proceeded to belabor my ears with a capsule history of the township. Did I know why it was called Elmira? Well, back in '28, when folks were choosing a name, they recalled an early settler who'd yelled for her daughter in a piercing voice. Why not use the name they'd all heard so often? He looked at me expectantly. "Isn't that something?"

"Yeah," I said. "Something."

He went on about how the Chemung Canal was dug and linked with the Susquehanna River in Pennsylvania. How during the war the Woolen Manufacturing Company put half the town to work producing cloth for uniforms. How the new Elmira Rolling Mills and all the others were turning out tons of iron now, and soon the whole valley would be a paradise of industrial prosperity.

"What about the military prison?" I interjected.

He looked startled. "What?"

"Wasn't there a prison camp here during the war?"

"Why, yes," he said, shifting gears. "In 'sixty-four they converted old number three barracks into a grand, first-class facility. Folks visited from all around to take it in—and catch sight of the Rebs too, of course. Why, I remember booths selling cakes and lemonade and crackers and peanuts and beer and sometimes stronger potions—"

"Where was it?" I interrupted.

"Where? Why, right down below Water Street." He pointed southward. "Along the river, foot of Hoffman. Some of them Secesh boys like to cried at how kindly the folks hereabouts treated 'em. It weren't your general notion of a prison 'tall. Nothin' like them in Virginia, where our boys starved."

"Didn't a good many die here?" I asked bluntly.

"Pshaw," he said—the first time I'd heard anybody actually voice it—and looked indignant. "*That* old tune don't play. We treated them boys like they was our own, practically. They got the same food and provisions, got to move freely inside the camp, got to make articles and sell 'em to folks so as to earn their own money. . . ."

He droned on. I stopped listening and considered how to handle the

[148]

good commissioner once I got inside. The Army maintained only a skeleton detachment in Elmira now. Though guarded by federal troops, Woodlawn's military adjunct was under day-to-day municipal administration. I stared at the gilt letters on the door, aware of butterflies gathering in my stomach; if I blew this, they'd nail me for offering a public official a bribe. *Daniel J. Costigan.* Wasn't that Irish? Christ, they were everywhere.

At length the door opened and a burly man with a large paunch beckoned me inside. He had small piggish brown eyes and gray-streaked whiskers. His manner was brisk, the busy servant of the people. He gestured to a seat in a pool of sunlight, where I sat, sweating even more profusely. He retreated behind a battered oak writing table.

"How can I help you, Mr. . . . ."

"Snider, Ed Snider," I said. "People call me Duke. I'm here on a sentimental mission. One involving a lady's honor and her most cherished memories."

"Indeed?" His expression did not change.

"Yes, her cousin died here in the camp during the war. The family was loyal—they'd moved to North Carolina just before secession—and they promptly disowned the cousin when he joined the Rebels. But she gave him her most valued possession, a ring, to carry with him. She'd like to have it back now. It was her grandmother's, you see, and—"

He had begun to frown as I talked. Now he interrupted. "Sexton Vincent, here in town, was the camp's chaplain. He maintains wartime records."

"Yes, I've talked with him."

"And the boy was interred here?"

I nodded.

He placed his hands palms down on the tabletop. "Possessions of deceased prisoners were held for claim after the war, of course, but I don't believe such is still the case."

"Well, here's the thing," I said confidentially. "She feels positive the ring is still on his finger."

His small eyes listed to mine. "On his finger?"

"Yes, in the grave. She said the ring was so tight it couldn't have been removed in any . . . normal way." I mopped my forehead with a handkerchief. "She's positive that it's, well, still in place."

He shook his head slowly. "You must understand that those were times of hardship and confusion, Mr. Snider. Stealing was common, I'm afraid. A valuable ring, on the hand of a dead man . . ."

"I made that very argument," I said quickly. "She insisted that the ring was of so little value that nobody would go to the trouble of taking it. A plain band, no stone. Impossible to remove without ruining it." I packed my voice with nobility. "I pledged my solemn word of honor that I would help."

He eyed me lugubriously, as if assisting me were his fondest wish. "I trust she appreciates such gentlemanly aid," he said. "But I'm afraid the family will have to apply for the removal of the body in the proper manner. I can provide you the appropriate forms—"

I'd anticipated that. "No, I'm afraid it's impossible," I broke in. "You see, in all candidness, he was more to her than a mere cousin. They were lovers. She yearned to marry him when he returned. Now she's betrothed to another, and—well, you can see that discretion is called for. She simply wants the ring as a token of all that was dear to her before the cruel conflict." *Not bad,* I thought.

"A number feel the want of that," he said dryly, rising from his chair. "But you appear to be asking us to disinter a corpse in order to examine its fingers, without any sort of identification or proper authorization. That, sir, is stretching sentiment."

I pushed an envelope onto the edge of the desk. The small eyes fastened on it. He sat down again.

"More than sentiment is involved," I said. "The lady realizes this is irregular and is quite prepared to offer compensation." I slid the envelope across the desk. He picked it up. Four of Le Caron's fifties nestled inside.

He said quietly, "This is a good deal of money."

"Absolute discretion is required," I said, and explained that I wanted to handle the disinterment myself—the lady's wish—and that I hoped to accomplish it that very night. For the sake of all involved parties, of course, no one must ever know. I finished and waited, holding my breath.

For a long moment he sat stolidly. Calculating the risks, I guessed. He must have figured they were minimal. How could I ever prove anything against him? He tucked the envelope in his breast pocket. I breathed again.

"I believe I understand the delicacy of the matter," he said. "Which is the grave in question?"

I hesitated, then showed him the sexton's sketch.

"Hmm." He stroked his whiskers. "Not much traffic on that road at night, but a lantern would show a fair distance. I think you'd better do your work between, say, three and four, to be safe." He looked at me for confirmation; I nodded. "I'll have the boys off duty early. That'll agree with 'em, you can bet. Now then, you keep that site in good order. I'll send a man out early to touch up, but don't leave more signs than you have to."

I gave him my assurance. We stood. Neither of us offered a hand.

"All this for a lady, you say?"

"That's right."

He was silent for a long moment. I felt uneasy.

"Will you be staying around here afterward?"

"Leaving tomorrow."

He nodded judiciously. "Good idea."

"There can be another hundred," I said, worried suddenly that he held all the cards and I none, "if this goes right."

"That would be generous compensation," he said. "Most generous."

"You'll get it first thing in the morning."

"Fine." The small eyes roamed over me as if filing away every detail. "And let's not forget our rule of discretion."

I wanted badly to be out of that stifling room, away from his scrutiny.

"Certainly not," I said.

I spent most of the afternoon sitting among the tall reeds on the western bank of the Chemung, pondering and planning. I dangled my feet in the water and surveyed the site of the prison camp. Several dilapidated wooden barracks remained; they looked long deserted. An encircling fence with guard walks and a tower had collapsed at several points. Even in bright sunshine the place had a melancholy aspect. I tried to imagine myself held prisoner here in this shallow valley with its low rim of forested hills, struggling to survive blasting summer heat and winter freezes, knowing that any day I might fall to lethal fever or virulent pox.

I pictured the card games: soldiers and prisoners hunched over plank tables, faces intent, coins glittering. Did a fortune actually lie in that grave? If so, I'd be a rich man. I'd help Andy's mom. And what then?

Evening fell and the air began to cool. I wandered around town. On Baldwin Street, a half block above the river, I saw a brass business plaque: J. LANGDON, COAL DEALER. I asked a passerby where the Langdons lived and was directed to 21 Main Street, across the street from Park Church. Livy and Twain would be wed there, I remembered.

The mansion sat back from the street among tall elms. The grounds covered an entire block. The dwelling itself was enormous and spare, with a dull brown stone facade and narrow windows. I wondered if Twain were inside writing just then, or courting Livy in some obscurely romantic Victorian way. I liked that idea. Not least among the things I envied in Twain was his helpless submission to his sense of love.

After an early supper I set out to make the preparations I'd formulated. At a livery stable on the edge of town, near Elmira Female College, I arranged for a team of horses and a flatbed wagon. Then I asked about a driver. The proprietor brought forth his son, a pimpled lout who struck me as stupid and avaricious, a combination perfectly suited to my purposes. Telling him I'd pick the boy and the rig up later, I rented another horse, a small mare. I mounted unsteadily, feeling their amused looks, and rode from the stable. At first I felt very awkward, but my confidence grew as we moved along at a steady canter. Woodlawn was not far distant.

Sketch in hand, I examined the Confederate graves. A wooden marker near the end of the second row read:

CORP. K. O'SHEA
CO. F
25 N.C. REG
C.S.A.

I stared at the sod below with a thrill of excitement. So far everything had matched Twain's story. Was the money really only a few feet away? Part of me was repulsed by the idea of digging up the grisly remains. Another part wanted to begin the job right then and end my jitters. The profits might be great, but so were the risks. I turned away reluctantly, impatient for darkness. Glancing upward—and wishing I had not—my eyes encountered the gloomy monolithic hulk of the federal facility on the hill above.

◇ 11 ◇

A new moon limned the trees but seemed to penetrate no lower. We bumped and jolted over a road that looked like a channel of ink. The boy's name was Seth. He'd evidently been thinking.

"Ye're robbin' a grave, aint'cher, mister?"

Since the road went past the cemetery, and since we carried shovels and a lantern, and since I'd given him twenty dollars to keep mum about our night's work, it wasn't exactly a brainstorm on his part.

"*We* are *salvaging*," I corrected.

He sniffed. "Paw guessed it, soon's you hired the wagon team this time of night."

"Did he tell anybody?"

"Paw's closemouthed when it comes to others' business. That's 'cause he's a businessman."

It was too dark to see the boy's expression. Was he being subtle? "There could be a little something for your pop too, in that case," I told him.

"Paw'd like that."

We drove through the cemetery gate. It was about one-thirty. I'd come out an hour earlier to make sure the guards had gone. Now I had Seth stop the wagon while I climbed down and listened. Crickets chirped. An owl suddenly said, "Hoo-hoo, ho-hoo," sounding like, "Who cooks for you?" It startled me, even as my mind framed the answer: Nobody. Few lights still shone in the town below. I was deliberately jumping the gun on Costigan.

There was a bad moment when we reached the graves and lit the lantern. I was convinced that everybody for miles could see it. The owl hooted again, mocking. I saw lurking shapes in surrounding shrubbery and trees.

"You gettin' nerves, mister?"

I took a breath and commanded myself to relax. Weren't the

guards' lights visible each night? Why should ours cause suspicion?

"No way," I said. "Let's do the job."

We dug at opposite ends of the plot. The sod came up easily. Mounds of black loam began to encircle us. The blade of my shovel cut into the earth with a "shoosh," then dumped the soil with a "plup." I tried not to think about the blade going through into the corpse, maybe its face. Christ, what a thing we were doing. I thought of the fortune lying only inches away. I dug faster, my labored breathing mixing with the boy's. I began to sweat, a clammy sensation in the coolness.

Seth's shovel made a dull "plunk" against something solid several feet down. We worked harder. In a few minutes we had exposed the top of a long wooden box.

"Okay," I said, "let's pry it off."

But the badly rotted lid crumbled. We had to scrape it away. Underneath lay more dirt.

"I don't fancy this part, mister," said Seth. "What is it yer looking fer?"

"I'm not paying you to fancy anything," I snapped. "Dig around the edges—and be careful."

We exposed rotted fragments of canvas. Had everything been wrapped in a tarp, or just the body? We scraped gingerly. Once my shovel went too deep, and a fragment of something that might have been discolored bone appeared in the lantern glow. "Damn," I breathed, and covered it up. Seth swallowed nervously and said nothing.

Then there was a clink. My blade hit something that sounded like glass. At almost the same instant a shrill cry sounded overhead.

Seth jumped backward, whispered, "What's that?"

"Owl, I guess. C'mon, this is it!"

"Weren't no owl."

I bent low and scooped dirt with my hands. I pulled up a dirt-encrusted jar, roughly quart-sized. Rubbing it hard, I cleared a small area and brought the lantern close. Visible were the dark notched edges of coins. I restrained an urge to leap up and yell.

"This is it," I told Seth, still looking uneasily overhead. "Let's get 'em all."

We found twenty-two jars intact, one broken. Seth's eyes widened as he watched me pick bills and coins from among the glass shards. Since he knew, I went ahead and emptied the others into the two large canvas bags I'd brought for the purpose. Even without the jars, each weighed at least fifty pounds. How much would a hundred pounds of money buy? I wondered. We began filling the excavation.

Again the shrill cry sounded above, very close. It was a chilling blend of ferocity and terror—like the scream of a predator bird intermixed with human wails. My heart froze for a split second. Then I heard a more terrible sound: a branch snapping behind us. I smashed the lantern and dove into the grave, yanking Seth down with me. I snatched the derringer from my breast pocket. Beside me, the boy shook violently and moaned, "Lord! Lord! Lord!" A glowing light appeared in the maples bordering the road. "Stay out!" I yelled. "U.S. government property!"

"Douse that, you damn fool!" came an urgent voice, and the light vanished.

We waited, ears straining. After what seemed a long interval I heard crackling sounds to our left. I raised the derringer and snapped a shot off overhead. A pathetically feeble *splat*.

"You're trespassing!" I yelled. "Proceed farther and my men will open fire!"

"By authority of the Irish Army," a gruff voice shouted, "you're under arrest!"

That blanked me for a second. Who was bluffing here? I realized they must be Fenians.

"*Whose* authority?" I yelled, trying to think. One thing was clear: Costigan had set me up.

"We're armed, Snider!" the voice said. "You can't escape."

Seth loosed a quavering high-pitched moan. I clamped my hand over his mouth—and had a sudden desperate idea.

"Come after me, and I finish the stable boy!" I yelled, keeping my grip over Seth's mouth, pressing his head hard against my chest as he struggled.

"Shh," I whispered. "Your best chance is if they think we're not connected, understand?" After a moment he nodded; I removed my hand. "I'm making a run for the wagon. You tell 'em I headed *that* way." I poked his right arm urgently. "Got it?"

He nodded, trembling. I smelled his fear, a sharp, sourish, cheesy odor.

I stood cautiously and slung the bags over my shoulders. They were very heavy. I pocketed the derringer and picked up one of the empty jars. Bending low, moving as silently as possible, I started for the wagon. After a few steps I turned and hurled the jar as far as I could in the opposite direction. It smashed against a distant tree. Immediately I heard yelling and the thud of feet. A lantern flared, then torches. I was running, pumping frantically in the darkness, tearing and crashing along the row of maples.

"He's headin' fer the wagon!" Seth's voice shrilled over the noise of my passage. Christ! First Costigan, now the kid. Whatever happened to thieves' honor?

A bullet whizzed overhead, spattering twigs and leaves around me. I heard the bird cry out again, terrifyingly loud, and felt a feathery rush. I ducked instinctively, certain it was striking at my head. At the same instant a group of dark figures rose from around the wagon, and I realized they had been waiting for me. Frantically I tried to change course, reaching reflexively for the derringer. But I knew it was too late. With sickening clarity I saw the rifles leveling on me.

What happened in the next seconds is almost impossible to describe. A roar—not exactly a roar, but a sound, an emanation, a *suggestion* of a massed and horrible cry—came from the maples behind the riflemen. A figure appeared there. A figure in dark blue uniform with rows of brass buttons. It was stationary, but it emerged with the force of onrushing cavalry. Even in my agitated mental state I recognized it at once: the figure I had seen, its arm raised, when I collapsed on the station dock. It brandished a weapon now, a long gun—or was it a tree branch?—that threatened swift and certain annihilation. The arm holding it pointed directly at the group near the wagon.

They saw it too. "Holy Mother!" came a cry in high tones of terror. "They're comin' from the rear! Shoot 'em! Shoot the blasted thing!"

A volley of flame erupted into and through the figure. It didn't waver, its momentum seeming to gather instead. It advanced on the frantic riflemen, and yet the figure itself was unmoving as bullets tore into it. And that was all I saw. For the bird again screamed overhead. A warning. An imperative. The sound galvanized me.

I turned and ran the opposite way along the maples, the bags banging against my ribs and back, their weight slowing me maddeningly. As I exhausted the limits of my legs and lungs, I reached the mare I'd tethered in a thicket on the other side of the graveyard, a quarter mile from the wagon. I'd dubbed her "Plan B" as I walked back to the livery stable for the wagon team. Now Plan B would have to save my ass. I knotted the bags together, slung them over the saddle, and mounted. My face pressed into her mane, I urged her forward and tried not to imagine bullets crashing into me from the darkness.

We galloped from the cemetery, bursting through the maples. Branches clutched at me. I heard shooting in the distance. I pointed Plan B toward the hills to the northwest. She kept a steady pace across open fields and wagon ruts winding through the foothills. It took more than an hour to circle Elmira and approach it again along the Chemung. Plan B's hooves clopped on the packed dirt of Water Street. She was breathing hard, her flanks foam-lathered. My first impulse had been to make a long dash all the way to Binghamton or Corning, but she clearly wasn't in shape for it. Still, I felt reasonably safe. If my attackers had escaped the ghost soldier and were still searching for me, I didn't think they'd look for me in the center of town. We ambled toward Main Street.

My rapping echoed inside in the foyer as I stood outside the Langdons' front door. After several minutes a sleepy-eyed servant peered through a peephole.

"Emergency," I told him. "I've got to see Mr. Twain."

"Missuh Twain? There's no—"

"Clemens," I said. "Get Clemens here!"

"I don't 'spect it's proper to rouse Missuh Clemens just now, suh."

"Look, this is a crisis!" I tried to contain my frustration. "He'll never forgive either one of us if my news has to wait for morning! Bring him down and let him decide! Go, quick, and don't wake the rest!"

The peephole closed. I paced the long veranda in the darkness. At length the door opened. Twain appeared in robe and slippers, smelling of tobacco, hair disheveled, squinting at me.

"Sam? What in thunder are you up to?"

I drew him close. "I've got it!"

His face changed. "The money?"

I told him what had transpired at the graveyard.

"Holy Jupiter!" he breathed. "They were laying for you. Costigan leaked the scheme, sure as perdition. How'd you get out?"

I told him of the apparition. "Is that place haunted?"

"Wasn't till now." He regarded me from hooded eyes. "I'd be some worked up in your shoes, too."

"No, I really saw it. So'd the Fenians, believe me."

He nodded, unconvinced, and looked at the street. "This town'll be on its ear in the morning. Anybody see you come?"

"I don't think so. Help me with just a couple of things and I'll be on my way."

We walked Plan B to the Langdon stable at the far end of the grounds. Twain didn't seem much more at home with livery tasks than I, but between us we managed to wipe her down, provide her water and a bit of grain, and transfer her saddle to another horse.

Twain said, "I'll give Robert—he's the one who answered the door—a princely amount to fetch the nags back here. He'll let on he found yours in the hills south of here. Robert'll keep his lips tight." We shook hands. "You're cut from different cloth, Sam."

"That's what I tried to tell you," I said, mounting.

"See you in California," he called softly as I started off, Plan B in tow.

Riding through the darkness I occupied my mind with visions of the uniformed figure. I couldn't help thinking that it had intervened deliberately, to spare my life.

The station in Chemung, a hamlet fifteen miles north, was little more than a shack. I cinched the horses behind it according to Twain's instructions and used the money sacks as pillows to bed down in an old wagon. I slept until wakened by sunlight on my face and the chuffing of an approaching locomotive. I edged cautiously around the building. Nobody was in sight. I hoisted the bags and stepped onto the platform. Moments later I was aboard.

Waverly . . . Barton . . . Smithboro . . . Tioga . . . Owego . . . Campville . . . Union . . .

We stopped at every woodpile and water tank. I gazed dully out my window and tried to stay awake. My shoes and pants were caked with mud. The canvas bags clinked provocatively with the car's movements. A few passengers' gazes burned into me. My crotch burned too; I was horrendously saddle sore.

We pulled into Binghamton, the area's main junction, around ten. Past this point I'd be reasonably safe. With the derringer in my pocket I moved through the station. I remembered the circling bird that had appeared here; I could almost feel again the whistling strafing rush and see the arrowlike flight through the door. It had seemed to lead me to the encounter with Twain. Then there was the horrible-voiced bird in the graveyard, and the other bird at the Mansfield station just before my first vision of the soldier figure. Maybe they worked in tandem to guide me. Or maybe I was just totally fucking crazy.

I bought a Penn Central ticket. Two hours to kill. Nobody seemed to be watching me. I ate breakfast, got shaved and trimmed, and had a bootblack work on my shoes. I purchased a stylish four-dollar Stetson and pulled it low over my eyes. Then I bought a leather gladstone to stow the money sacks in. My right arm felt six inches longer by the time I'd lugged it on board.

It was dark when we pulled into Philadelphia. In a hotel room near the station I bolted my door and counted the loot, a labor of love. A few wads of greenbacks had rotted—moisture in the jars—but who cared? I counted $8,665 in bills and a whopping $14,578 in gold and silver—a total of $23,243. I was still gazing at the lovely piles when I dropped off to sleep.

Philadelphia was baseball crazy. Recent papers lovingly described the Stockings' 27–18 win over the powerful Athletics, hailing the visitors, especially Allison, for fielding "like Chinese magicians." A mammoth crowd of twenty thousand had turned out in hundred-degree heat to see it. George Wright's four hits had included two triples and a homer.

The papers also reprinted several bitter New York columns in which we were denounced as "eclectic." Only because of Cincinnati's "imported" eastern ballists, the argument went, was the West coming to "monopolize" the sporting scene. I was happy to read Chadwick's answer that we were no more eclectic than other clubs—we were just beating the daylights out of them.

I was also glad to see that the Haymakers had been upset by the Eckfords, 22–14. The *New York Tribune* pointed out: "The large party of blacklegs who accompany the Haymakers for the sole purpose of betting laid their money on the favorites and lost." Couldn't happen to a nicer bunch. I wondered if McDermott had been among them.

In an adjacent column was an editorial reprinted from the *New York Times* entitled "Baseball in Danger." It deplored the "enormous sums" changing hands during games between "a western nine and the champion clubs of New York." If baseball were subject to the "plunging" of professional gamblers, the "great charm" of the game would be lost and it would sink to the status of "prizefighting, faro saloons, rat killing, cockfighting, and the like," no longer attracting its "youthful and ardent admirers" to commence "a sporting career."

It was clear that we were shaking things up. I still had trouble accepting the idea that baseball's fate was undetermined. But that seemed to be the reality. More than before I appreciated Champion's concerns regarding his fledgling pros. And Andy's regarding his own career.

The morning heat was so sticky that occasional tepid showers offered the only relief. My high collar chafed my sweaty neck; my shirt was plastered to my chest. I bought a wooden fan from a street peddler and tried to stir the miasmal air. Such fans were mass-produced like book matches in later times—as much for advertising as practical use.

I toted the gladstone to a bank on Market Street and began what proved to be a lengthy procedure. "My goodness," said an official, waving his hands over the wads of greenbacks. "We haven't seen some of these since the war."

"Finally broke into my cookie jar," I said, eliciting a glassy stare. Never joke with nineteenth-century bankers. They're not in it for fun.

At length I received two drafts for $11,620 each. I sent Twain's to

Elmira—I liked the idea of his getting it as he put the finishing touches on *Innocents*—and mine to a Cincinnati bank. Outside, the gladstone felt wonderfully light. So did I.

Another shower began. I bought an umbrella. Since I hadn't figured out how to approach Harry and Champion, I didn't. Instead I strolled down to see the Liberty Bell and visit Independence Hall. I fed the pigeons in Franklin Square. The morning passed pleasurably.

But by midafternoon I couldn't contain myself. I took a hack to the ballpark at Seventeenth and Columbia, where the Stockings faced the Keystones. The driver pulled in among the carriages and announced that he too would stay for the game. We ate peanuts and looked on from center field. I felt strange watching the action from behind Harry.

My teammates looked weary. That plus the Keystones' slugging and the damp conditions made for a sloppy game. We took an early lead, then hung on, flailing the Keystones and being flailed like ungainly punchers. The crowd, expecting a close, graceful exhibition, booed both clubs.

Allison didn't play at all. Hurley started in left and Andy at catcher, but in the first inning a foul tip caught him over the eye; he traded places with George and played a decent shortstop the rest of the game, but I felt guilty for not being available. The game went seven innings before darkness forced a close with us leading, 45–30. Another victory, albeit ugly.

My reunion with the club went surprisingly smoothly. Harry was glad to have his other sub. Champion swallowed my story of a maiden aunt dying and leaving me everything. At least he seemed to. He questioned points of the litigation involved—which I fuzzed with truly inspired vagueness—and he desisted, no doubt deciding it was as well not to know too much. As for the cash box, I claimed I'd been so excited on receiving the telegram that I'd forgotten everything— including telling anybody good-bye or even remembering that I held the team's receipts—until I'd jumped on a train for Syracuse. When I could finally get back, of course, they'd departed.

Well, it was pathetically thin—but better than confessing that Le Caron had tried to murder me again, and then I'd gone grave-robbing. I said I was sorry for inconveniencing everybody and offered to pay cash on the spot to cover my travel and hotel expenses during the tour. Champion lit up at that. "That's the true idea," he said warmly. "Make one's own way!" As I handed him the money, he extended a telegram.

CHAMPION AND WRIGHT, C.B.B.C.: IMAGINE TWO
THOUSAND PEOPLE AT THE GIBSON HOUSE WAITING FOR
THE SCORE. EVERY MINUTE ROARS AND YELLS GO UP. OH,
HOW IS THIS FOR HIGH?

"That came from home during the Athletic match," said Champion. "We're making history. Thousands are sharing our glory, Fowler. You should consider yourself most fortunate to be with us."

"Oh, I do," I said. "You have no idea."

As for the Stockings, I told them how good I felt to be back with the "Eclectics." George retorted that nobody on the club was half as eclectic as me, and Brainard dubbed me "Gone-Again" Sam. Sweasy glowered; whatever bothered him about me seemed no better. Andy, his eye blackened where the ball had struck, picked at my story skeptically. I didn't like lying to him, but it was preferable to having him think I'd risked my life to help his mother—an intent I kept to myself.

The Maryland club fed us terrapin, crab cakes, and oysters at the Gilmor House on North Calvert. Hurley drank too much wine, and I saw Harry eyeing him.

We played at the Madison Avenue grounds, a grassy expanse near Druid Lake. With Allison's and Gould's hands sore from so many games, Harry told me to be ready. I suited up happily. Things seemed simple now, away from New York. Le Caron was in jail and McDermott's crowd, Millar assured me, never journeyed this far except to follow a top eastern club.

The Marylands' clubhouse was festooned with evergreen branches and a banner: WELCOME RED STOCKINGS. Five thousand people—a record crowd here—came out to see the conquerors of the East. Among them were a number of Baltimore's famed belles—the nation's comeliest women, Brainard asserted. Leaving the hotel, we saw several coyly lift their hems as they stepped from curbs, revealing shapely ankles encased in red stockings. The players whistled and shouted.

"I'd fancy 'em all, one after t'other," Sweasy said, keeping his voice low so Harry wouldn't hear.

"They ain't cheap waiter girls," Waterman said. "You wouldn't stand a chance."

As we took the field I reflected that my teammates were changing as their fame grew. Only Harry seemed unaffected. The others were taking on the arrogant assurance of proven winners, stars even. Well, I thought, what the hell, they were kids, barely in their twenties. They had the rest of their lives to be sober and mature.

The diamond was superb, the Marylands jaunty in new uniforms with blue-and-white checked caps and jerseys. But the game wasn't much. Our bats boomed from the start: George and Gould rapped seven hits each; Andy and Harry followed with six, and Brainard baffled the Maryland hitters.

In the eighth, Waterman's shin was spiked and Allison's head slashed by a foul. In what I considered a strange series of moves, Harry stationed George behind the plate, took shortstop himself, and, with us leading 40–7, ignored Hurley and waved me out to center.

"Don't run me down!" Andy cried from left.

"Fine," I yelled back. "You just take everything out this way!"

As luck had it, the second hitter lofted a fly directly to me. Andy sprinted over. "Mine!" I called, reaching for it. In a replay of my first day at practice, the ball bounced out of my hands. Andy dove under me and with a great sliding belly flop snagged it before it touched the grass. Red-faced, I helped him up.

"Thanks for keepin' that ball alive," he said, grinning wickedly. "I might not've got it otherwise."

To a few cries of "Muffin!" I came to bat in the ninth. I hushed my hecklers by driving a low inside pitch that screamed over third and kicked up chalk; I pulled into second with a stand-up double and scored moments later on Harry's single.

"That's the goods!" Andy said.

A sequence, I thought, for my personal '69 highlights film.

It ended 47–7. The belles promenaded as we packed our gear, manipulating fans and parasols with the artfulness of geishas, shooting coquettish glances at us, to the discomfiture of their escorts. It was all a little silly, and yet they *were* gorgeous and still a bit mysterious to me in their panniered dresses, picture hats, and veils. I felt a pang of horniness remembering my night with Charlotte. Could these Scarlett O'Haras compete in her amatory league? I doubted it.

We left for Washington on the 8:20 train. The journey's only memorable feature was a discussion of Harry's batting order, which I'd never understood.

"Why, it's easy," said Andy. "He's got the swift runners striking between the slow, to save force-outs and double plays."

"So George leads off," I said, "and with his speed and base-running ability isn't likely to be forced by Gould, who's slow, is that it?"

Andy nodded.

"Not slow," Gould rumbled. "Sure to bring George home with his run."

I finally had a handle on Harry's unvarying lineup:

G. *Wright*   *Leonard*
Gould   *Brainard*
Waterman   *Sweasy*
Allison   *McVey*
H. Wright

The team's leadfoots—Gould, Allison, Brainard, and Mac—were sandwiched between fast, canny runners. On a modern-day team Allison would never hit cleanup, nor Mac ninth. On a piece of paper I wrote their names in the order I'd have them hit and showed it to them.

Leonard   *McVey*
Sweasy   *Allison*
G. *Wright*   H. *Wright*
Waterman   *Brainard*
Gould

I explained that Andy was the perfect leadoff man, Sweasy a push-along spray hitter, George a rare mix of power and consistency ideal for the third slot; Waterman, while not capable of the towering shots powered by George or Gould or occasionally Mac, hit for extra bases consistently and was undaunted by pressure. The bottom three names were virtually interchangeable.

I thought it was pretty convincing, but they didn't. Sweasy pointedly said nothing. Brainard was offended that I'd slotted him ninth, in rookie McVey's place. George argued that he wouldn't score nearly as many runs batting third.

"But," I countered, "you'd drive in more."

"It's *making* your run that counts," he said with a grin. "It's the whole object."

"Okay, but isn't maximizing the team's run production more important?"

I had a sudden and unexpected ally. "George ain't changed a whit since we were on the Nationals," Brainard said. "He sulked whenever he didn't lead the scoring then—and he'd do it now."

George stared at him, his grin fading. Brainard met his gaze and added, "Course, there's little chance of that, long as his brother's captain."

That produced an uneasy silence. As they looked at each other a moment longer, something seemed to be crystallizing between them.

Oh, shit, I thought, what now?

[163]

◇ 12 ◇

Considering its historic qualities and the fact that I'd spent several weeks there the previous year—a century in the future—I thought I would enjoy Washington.

I did not.

We piled out of a four-horse omnibus in front of Willard's Hotel, around the corner from the White House, at Fourteenth and Pennsylvania. I stared at the unfinished Treasury Building across the way, then dragged Andy out for a walk around the Ellipse—and found nothing but dark outlines of trees and a truncated, half-built Washington Monument. In the far distance, dimly illuminated, was the dome of the Capitol Building. Andy thought he remembered hearing about its completion during the war.

I had a bad moment: a sense of being wrenchingly dislocated, cut off, abandoned. This was the first place I'd come back to that I'd known at all well. While writing a feature on Vietnam vets I'd become familiar with the capital and could picture the way it had looked. That picture was jarringly out of sync with what I saw that night: I scarcely recognized the White House without its wings. The Old Executive Office Building wasn't yet built. Nor the Lincoln or Jefferson memorials. No reflecting pools, no shimmering lights. The broad streets were dirty, the buildings shabby. If ever I felt culture shock, it was then.

"What're you fretting so hard over?" said Andy.

"Even if I told you, it wouldn't make sense."

"You rile me saying things like that," he said hotly. "Go ahead, try me!"

"All right," I snapped. "I'm thinking that the Vietnam Veterans Memorial isn't here. And that it's crazy for me to know about that."

There was silence.

"You're right," he said at length. "I don't make sense of it. It *is* crazy."

He sounded hurt. I felt bad about that. But I was too low just then to do anything about it.

We spent four days in the so-called City of Magnificent Distances. My spirits did not rise very far. It seemed that I was adjusting all over again. Road weariness didn't help. We'd all had enough touring. It would end soon—this was the last major city—but for me, unlike the others, reaching Cincinnati would only pose a new set of problems.

We were celebrities here, as in Baltimore. The *Washington Republican* called our eastern swing the greatest baseball tour ever. At all hours the staff of Willard's shooed rubberneckers from the lobby. People massed outside for autographs.

The players sat for another picture, at Mathew Brady's studio a few blocks up Pennsylvania. The walls there were covered with photos of corpse-strewn battlefields and steely-eyed Civil War officers. A Brady assistant made the portrait. The only notable changes in the Stockings since Newark were tonsorial: Andy had a two-week-old mustache; Sweasy and Mac showed the beginnings of brushes; Gould had shaved his goatee off so that he too wore only a mustache. With so many models around, I'd decided to raise my own crop of whiskers and had not shaved for several days. Once again I declined being in the portrait.

Waterman and Sweasy hid Brainard's baseball shoes so well that in desperation he borrowed mine for the picture. In it he sits on the floor, one oversized shoe pointing upward with spikes attached—I had misplaced the key to unscrew them—while Waterman and Sweasy barely repress smirks.

We were scheduled for two games. On a ninety-degree Friday we faced the Nationals at their new grounds on upper Fourteenth. A crush of traffic made surrounding streets impassable. Trees and rooftops, including that of the State Department across the street—it was situated temporarily in the Orphan Asylum—were crawling with spectators. We waited. And waited. Tempers grew short. People collapsed on the baking turf. Politicians droned floridly. Secretary of State Hamilton Fish was mercifully brief—he must have been a wretched orator—in his enthusiasm for the national game. The entire British legation was introduced. By then nearly ten thousand had assembled—another record smasher—and Champion was all smiles; no more complaints about gate receipts.

While we waited I asked Millar if baseball went back as far here as

[165]

in New York and Philadelphia. He said that teams of clerks had faced off on the "White Lot" behind the White House before the war. Lincoln himself had reputedly played, once stalling reporters with, "Wait until I make another hit." But with the proliferation of teams after the war, Andy Johnson had chased everybody off—hence these new grounds. In '67, having recruited George and Brainard among other stars, the Nationals were easily the nation's best team. Touring westward they crushed the Stockings 53–10, a "Waterloo defeat," Millar said, that had inspired Champion's dream of assembling a western powerhouse.

By four we were ready to play. The contest boiled down to our hitting against the Nats' fielding. They contained us fairly well but mounted no offensive threat. Not a single Nat reached second base until the fifth inning, and by then we were up 13–0.

It was about then that we began showboating.

Told that a slugger had plunked an omnibus in the street outside the ballpark the previous year, George said that wasn't so much. He promptly smashed a drive over the fence in left center. That set the tone for the rest of the afternoon, everybody but Andy and Harry muscling up. As a consequence the Nats' left fielder, one Sy "War-horse" Studley, hauled in fly after fly. But George powered another homer, and we won easily, 24–8.

Saturday dawned cloudy and threatening. The Nats showed up with a coach drawn by six horses draped in robelike ornamental skirts called caparisons, which made them look as if they'd clopped out of a medieval pageant. Our escorts looked a bit smug and secretive as we pulled up at the White House. I assumed we were in for a long-winded tour as a clerk ushered us into a large office. There, to my surprise, behind an oversized desk, smoking a cigar nearly as dark as his wrinkled black suit, sat President Ulysses S. Grant.

He was smaller and grayer than I expected. The hero of Vicksburg and bludgeoner of Lee's armies, sworn in as President only three months ago, he was destined to become one of the worst in history—epic achievements all. His washed-out gray-blue eyes regarded us blandly, betraying nothing but a fleeting hint of humor when he said, "I believe you warmed the Washington boys somewhat yesterday." His thin voice had a heavy smoker's rasp. All in all, I thought, he'd make a fine wax figure.

Champion introduced us. Grant's fingers brushed mine and his pale eyes flicked on to Andy, no sign in them that I had registered. It felt strange to tower over a war hero. I noticed that Grant's movements were awkward and tentative. When Champion invited him to our game, Grant mumbled, "Schedule . . . time." Still puffing his cigar, he moved vaguely toward the door and nodded as we filed out. I realized that he was enormously popular, like Eisenhower after World War II. But this guy had zero charisma. TV would have stopped him cold.

In the Capitol Building we listened to a Congressman from Indiana argue for more western roads. The Library of Congress, lacking a building of its own, was currently housed there also. We visited the Patent Office, located in the Interior Department even though that too was unfinished—a condition that characterized much of the city. There George led the rest in gaping at marvels of steel and steam: engines and boilers and mechanized loaders; telegraphs and steamboats. They were all so *hungry* for progress, so certain it would come. Had I described electric light and power, radio and TV, phones, cars, jets, and all the rest, they'd probably just nod sagely and tell me *their* futuristic visions—including space shots. Hadn't Jules Verne published *A Trip to the Moon* four years earlier?

Grant did not show up that afternoon, when we led the Olympics only 4–0 after four innings. Their pitcher teased grounders from us which their five-foot-four shortstop, Davy Force, ate up. In the fifth a steady downpour began. To our disgust Champion and Harry agreed to a replay on Monday. That meant two more days before heading home.

On Sunday we took a trip down the Potomac. I was surprised to see Mt. Vernon badly in need of paint and portions of Alexandria still war-damaged. Virginia was technically outside the Union, not yet readmitted under the Radicals' reconstruction plan. The home state of Jefferson and Washington was subjugated territory, under military rule.

As we powered back upriver I came across Harry, standing alone near the stern, holding several envelopes and looking subdued. "Bad news?" I said.

"No, just reading Carrie's old letters. Haven't gotten another since Philadelphia. Touring is hard on a family, and Sabbaths are the worst."

I nodded, aware that baseball was not played anywhere in America on Sundays. Harry had several children by a previous marriage. I presumed that his first wife had died, but I wasn't sure; nobody spoke of her. When he'd remarried at the end of the previous season, the Stockings presented him with a hundred-dollar bond wrapped around a gold watch and a medal bearing all their names. According to Allison, Captain Harry had actually been teary-eyed—a dramatic break from his usual stoic persona.

"What's she like?" I asked.

"Carrie?" He sounded surprised, then spoke slowly. "Why, she's the truest wife a man could have, a servant in my home and queen in my heart." His voice throbbed. "To my mind she embodies the noblest elements of the human spirit. She promises the highest I can hope. She purges what is dark within me, strengthens what is failing."

He meant every syllable. I looked away, embarrassed, thinking that it might have been Twain carrying on about his Livy. Willingly or not, women in this time perched on incredible pedestals.

"And your people, Sam? I understand from Andy that you have family in Frisco."

"Had," I said. "I'm on my own now."

"You didn't desert them?" he said sharply.

"No, circumstances forced a . . . separation."

It must have sounded forlorn. His brown eyes warmed with sympathy. "You're welcome to visit our home, Sam. As often as you like. My daughters love to see the nine." *Daughters.* The word sliced into me. "I'd like that, Harry, very much."

He put his hand on my shoulder. The river sparkled around us, radiant and poignant.

Monday, June 28, marked exactly four weeks since I'd come back in time. The Stockings toured Arlington that morning. I didn't go. I'd heard enough about the glorious military dead. And I didn't want to be reminded of coming attractions: JFK's eternal flame, the Tomb of the Unknown Soldier, fields of white crosses from future slaughters.

That afternoon, again swinging for the fences, we scored sixteen runs on twenty-three hits. George belted another homer and a double. Brainard limited the Olympics to five runs on five hits. But we were victims of the game's outstanding play. Their left fielder caught Gould's deep drive going away, then his bullet peg nailed Mac loafing to the plate. George, trying to distract the Olympics by taking off from first, was then gunned down at third. Triple play! Harry looked ready to puke.

The B & O run to Wheeling took nearly twenty-four hours. Hurley and I lost forty dollars playing whist—this time real, not imaginary dollars—to Brainard and Waterman. Worse yet, Hurley was broke; I had to cover our losses.

At the Pittsburgh depot Champion bought a stack of the latest *Harper's Weekly*. Inside was a full-page engraving of the team, made from the Newark portrait. We debated who'd come out worst. Waterman looked like he'd discovered a turd in his pocket; Hurley was a glowering psychopath, George a propped-up dummy, and Allison, Mac, Andy, and Sweasy a row of moronic moon faces.

We stopped long enough in West Virginia to demolish Wheeling's hapless Baltics, 44–0. George went eight for eight with two doubles, two triples, and seven steals. Allison, swinging from his heels, smacked two home runs and Andy one. We were on a power binge.

The Ohio was turgid and yellow, a silt-choked current that disappointed my romantic visions. We ferried across and boarded another train at Bellaire for the final run to Cincinnati.

"What's Sam's averages?" Andy asked Millar, who was preparing Harry's stat totals for press distribution.

"Easy to figure," I said. "I only had the one double in Baltimore. Course, that bunt against the Haymakers *should* have boosted my batting average to six sixty-seven."

"Whoa," said George. "Boosted your *what* average to *what?*"

I elaborated the obvious: one hit in three turns, .333.

"Where'd you get that notion?" George demanded.

"That's not the right way," Andy said, and explained that a player's run total was divided by the number of games he played. The result was expressed in terms of "average and over." "For example," he said, turning to Millar, "what're my striking averages?"

The reporter thumbed through the sheets. "Three and forty-five," he said. "Against two and thirty-three. Third highest on the regulars."

"What's this against business?" I asked.

"You compare your runs average against your outs, or 'hands lost' average," Andy replied. "I'm averaging three runs and forty-five over —that is, three point forty-five runs against two outs and thirty-three over. Let's take you; how many times'd you make your run?"

"Just once."

"So in three games you're averaging oh and thirty-three runs against oh and sixty-seven outs. Not good, but you ain't had much chance."

"That's the dumbest thing I've ever heard!"

"Tell him who leads the nine," said George, grinning.

"You tell him," Brainard snapped, several seats away. "You puff your figures in your head before a match is even done."

George looked grim but said nothing. I began to wonder if the club was still big enough for two stars.

Millar said, "George leads the strikers with five and one against two and five. He also leads in making his base at four and twenty."

"How many times up?" I said, getting out a pencil. "How many hits?"

"One hundred twenty-seven striking opportunities," Millar said. "Eighty-six safe blows."

I figured George's batting average. Jesus, .677. "How many homers?"

Millar counted. "Five on tour, twelve in all."

Twelve homers in twenty-four games. Against top competition. No other Stocking had half that many. George was a Babe Ruth in his own era, no doubt about it.

"This runs-against-outs business," I argued, "doesn't allow for all the times you hit but don't score, or drive in runs, or score on errors. All it reflects is whether you stepped on the plate."

"That's the object," said Andy. "How many outs it takes to score how many runs. All the rest is trimmings. A ballist's freezin' to make his run every time up. Harry's averages tell how often he did it. But accordin' to your way, all that's required is gettin' to first. Why go any farther?"

Well, he had a point. Sort of. "Another crazy thing," I said. "You guys count an out against a forced runner instead of the hitter who forced him."

"But it's the runner who's *out*," said George. "Got to show in his averages."

"Even when it's not his fault?"

"Able runners don't get forced so often—for one thing they'll steal the base to prevent it. So that shows up in the averages too."

Stymied, I decided to let it drop.

Later Millar proudly showed me his homecoming article for the *Commercial*. It began:

> God's noblest work is a perfectly developed man of
> refinement and education. . . . To demonstrate this was
> one of the designs of the tour.

What tripe, I thought, and scanned the rest. Millar lavished praise on our "wholesomeness"—either he was blind or a hypocrite if he hadn't noticed behavior incongruous with "wholesomeness" on the part of certain Stockings—and he gushed about the record crowds in the East, the turnout of respectable ladies and gentlemen, the audience with Grant, and finally trumpeted, "A new era has dawned upon baseballdom. . . ."

"Nice work," I told him. "Very laudatory."

Glasses glinting in the lamplight, Millar looked quite pleased.

I didn't sleep much that night. Partly it was the train's jouncing; partly the knowledge that a new phase of my life would begin the next day. I lay in my berth watching the curtains sway, trying to think about what I wanted to do. Gradually a plan took shape. I decided to broach it to Harry and Champion in hopes of extending what little continuity I knew in this strange existence. As I lay there it seemed that the railway car was like my life—being rushed through the darkness by an engine of fate toward whatever waited ahead.

The hoopla began at Loveland, twenty miles outside the city. A delegation flushed with our victories and their own liquor swarmed aboard. I was ignored until Harry introduced me as the savior of the Haymaker match, then was welcomed as a companion in arms. Cincinnati awaited us in a state of frenzy, they said. One rotund backslapper confided to me that although he didn't know much about baseball, "Glory, but you've advertised the city—advertised us, sir, and helped our business, sir." I assured him that it was my pleasure.

We curved into the city along the muddy swell of the Ohio, on which increasing numbers of vessels trailed black plumes of smoke. The air grew thick as we passed through an industrial area. Very thick. I glimpsed people holding handkerchiefs over their noses. Eyes stinging, I felt like I used to when I drove into Los Angeles.

Gesturing with sweeping flourishes at a scow carrying iron scraps below us on the river, Hurley recited sarcastically:

> *"The barge she sat in, like a burnish'd throne,*
> *Burnt on the water. The poop was beaten gold,*
> *Purple the sails, and so perfumed that*
> *The winds were love-sick with them. . . ."*

Then he pretended to choke, gagging and clutching at his mouth. Champion was not amused.

"What's that about?" I asked Andy, who explained that Cincinnati was notorious for burning a soft coal that permeated the air with soot. An hour of walking outside soiled your clothes and lined your eyes, nose, and mouth with grime; people breathed through fabric when winds didn't ventilate the city.

When we pulled into the Little Miami Station I got a fuller picture. The city filled a bowl-shaped delta cradled between a wide bend in the river and steep encircling hills. Over it rose towers of smoke to a dark ceiling that obscured the sky.

"I didn't imagine so many factories," I said. "This is how I'd picture Pittsburgh or Chicago."

"Oh, we lay all over them," Andy said cheerfully. "Got more foundries than Pittsburgh, more hog packin' than Chicago. They're on the rise, but this is still Queen City, the biggest in the West."

"I see." I was less than thrilled by my new home.

The depot was bedlam. Thousands jammed the streets. Signs and banners waved everywhere. Currie's Zouave Band, in bright red baggy pants, played "Hail to the Chief" as we squeezed into open carriages behind the bandwagon. I rode with Andy and Hurley. We set off through the streets. Men and boys cheered us, women and girls waved red scarves. We turned up Fourth, the city's fashionable promenade, where crowds were even thicker in front of the expensive stores. The color red flowered everywhere. One store had fashioned an enormous C entirely of scarlet stockings. Crimson streamers floated down on us from upper stories. I'd wondered how ticker-tape parades felt to astronauts or World Series heroes. Now I had a pretty good idea.

" 'Is it not passing brave to be a king,' " Hurley quoted ironically, " 'and ride in triumph through Porkopolis?' "

"Who wrote that?" I said, thinking his tone odd.

"Marlowe," he answered. "After a fashion."

"You two can lay off," Andy said. "It's plain you're educated."

"Aw now, me foine lad." Hurley's abrupt brogue was thick as porridge. "It's ye who're the best of us, Andy, make no mistake." A melancholy out of keeping with the occasion edged his voice, puzzling me.

We were deposited at the Gibson House, a newly refurbished six-story luxury hotel on Walnut, where dignitaries awaited us on a second-floor balcony. The street below was a noisy carpet of people. Windy speeches ensued, one boiler-lunged politician bellowing that our march to the sea would have made Sherman proud. Harry, George, and Brainard stepped forward to speak—only George seemed to enjoy it—and then Gould, a popular hometown figure, managed a few words. Finally Champion, at Harry's urging, told the throng that we needed to rest before the Grand Complimentary Game that afternoon.

Since the contest was only hours away, Harry insisted that we remain at the Gibson. Brainard complained, and others echoed. I wasn't happy either; I wanted to look around my new city. But Harry held fast, saying he wouldn't see his own family until after the exhibition match. Then he surprised me by announcing that Hurley and I would captain the "picked nine" against the first nine that afternoon.

He made it sound like an honor. To me, facing the Stocking starters seemed more an ordeal.

We climbed down from a pennant-bedecked omnibus. The double gates of the Union Grounds closed behind us. The crowd's clamor was punctuated by a cannon that boomed in the outfield, lifting me six inches off the grass. We marched onto the field in a line, Caesar's legions returning in triumph. I was coming to like this hero business.

The field was green as malachite in dazzling eighty-five-degree sunshine. It was a gorgeous ballpark, rivaled in my experience only by the Capitoline Grounds in Brooklyn. The grass was thick, the infield a pebble-free mix of dirt and clay, its drainage so good that no trace remained of earlier showers.

A wooden clubhouse rose behind the third-base stands adjoining a ladies' pavilion known as the Grand Duchess, the two structures forming a high *L* behind home plate. Carriages moved on a track inside the fence. From a high platform beside the Grand Duchess's cupola, the Zouave Band floated festive airs over the diamond. Spectator areas were awash in red: scarves and handkerchiefs fluttered; parasols waved; hats flew in the air. At fifty cents a head—not to mention the five-dollar tickets to tonight's Grand Reception Banquet selling fast—I knew the club's coffers must be swelling.

At three-thirty, Hurley and I joined Harry at home plate for the toss. Hearing a commotion, we turned to see a flatbed wagon carrying a bat as big as a tree. A gift of the Cincinnati Lumber Company, it proved to be twenty-seven feet long. The names of the starting nine were inscribed on it in red letters—and then: "Substitutes—Hurley and Fowler."

"You did that?" I said to Harry, who just smiled. After that he could have asked me to climb the flagpole naked and I'd have tried my damnedest.

We set about the business of playing. My teammates included Stockings from previous years, when pros and amateurs had played together. A few were youngsters on the way up. One of them, a strapping lad named Oak Taylor, had considered himself next in line for a substitute spot. He wasn't ecstatic over my presence.

I started at catcher, then played the outfield and first base. Except for a couple of passed balls, I handled my chances without mishap. Our main problem was at short, where a nervous kid named Brookshaw kicked so many balls that Hurley finally took the position himself.

I faced Brainard five times. My first trip up he returned my grin in a friendly way—then put a ball under my chin. It came so fast I barely could twist away. I picked myself up slowly. He was still grinning. Very funny. I dug in and twitched my bat menacingly—and fanned air on three pitches.

"Thanks, Acey," I said dryly. "I realize this is for the whip pennant and all."

"I'll lay one where you can plank it next time," he promised.

He did. I planked it sharply into the left-center gap for a double.

"Charity's done!" he called.

He popped me up twice on rising balls, but I felt my timing improving. My last time up, he hummed in another riser. I adjusted slightly, leveling my swing, whipping the bat fluidly. *Crack!* The ball rocketed to the center-field fence almost before Harry or Andy could react. It bounced high off the boards and back over Harry's head as he sprinted to the track. The crowd laughed and applauded as I pulled into third standing up. Brainard shot me a look under the brim of his cap. I shrugged, grinning happily. I hadn't hit a triple since high school.

It was a rare moment for our side. The nine won handily, 53–11. George and Sweasy smacked homers, and Andy led a swarm of base runners that drove our catchers crazy. I was glad when it ended.

Finally we were free to disperse—for several hours—before returning for the banquet. Andy accompanied me back to the Gibson House. He boarded with Sweasy, Allison, and Mac a block away, at 421 Main. He said he'd ask if his landlady had space for me. I wasn't sure I cared to live under the same roof as Sweasy, but I told him to go ahead. Meanwhile, I booked into the Gibson, where the proprietors let me know they were proud to have a Red Stocking stay.

That night 150 people assembled to honor us. They included, for reasons I never understood, practically every judge in Hamilton County and flocks of grandly dressed matrons who swept back and forth in lavender and lace and taffeta skirts that rustled like dry-leaf forests. It looked like an opera opening night.

We sat at the head table. Beside me, Hurley, tipsy from the beginning, reeked of bay rum. Andy claimed he'd been drinking the stuff—it was 60 percent alcohol—and refused to sit with him. We imbibed local wines and ate succulent dishes I could identify only by the ornate bill of fare: breaded mountain oysters; sweetbreads glacé; buffalo tongue en gelée; Westphalian ham à la Richelieu, and so on. By the time the desserts arrived I was almost "en gelée" myself.

Champion brought an emotional speech to a thumping climax by displaying our twenty-one trophy balls from the tour and exclaiming, hand clasped to heart, that as Stockings president he wouldn't trade places with Grant himself. The place went wild—except for Brainard, who snorted and gave me a knowing look; he figured Champion was on the make in the city's Republican establishment.

There were countless toasts: "To the fair ladies—God bless 'em!" "To the judiciary—always impartial in the game of life!" They elicited flowery responses from whiskered orators. By midnight it was hard to sit through any more. I had to brace Hurley to keep him upright.

We were introduced one by one. We stood and mumbled our thanks, no one attempting a speech—though George stood grinning so long he seemed about to give it a try.

Only a few members of the Stockings' families were on hand: Gould's father, a local wholesaler, and mother and strapping blond brothers; Allison's younger brother, down from Cleveland where he played ball; Carrie Wright, small and plump, with warm eyes that matched her husband's—I liked her at once.

I scanned the faces in the audience carefully, trying to match one with the haunting image I carried in my mind. But no, Andy's sister was not there. When I mentioned it, he said curtly that she did not approve of baseball.

The affair concluded with the Stockings' song, each player's verse sung by somebody else, all of us booming the choruses. When the others had had their turns, Andy stood, pointed at me, and sang.

> *"Our newest man is some for tricks—*
> *It passes all belief.*
> *He tries to snare so many fouls*
> *We've dubbed him 'chicken thief.'*
> *And when he marches to the plate*
> *To strike one foul 'r fair,*
> *Opponents learn his name with haste—*
> *Sam Fowler makes 'em care!"*

I sat there dumbfounded. The others grinned at me like monkeys. When they broke into the final chorus, I swallowed hard, trying not to look like a complete simp.

> *"Hurrah, hurrah,*
> *For the noble game hurrah!*
> *Red Stockings all will toss the ball*
> *And shout our loud hurrah!"*

The street outside was noisy with departing carriages. I'd managed to get Hurley safely into a hack. Gaslit globes burned above the sidewalks. The night air was mild.

"I'm umping a junior match tomorrow," Andy said. "Want to come watch?"

"Sure."

"As for roomin' at our place . . ."

"I can guess," I said. "Sweasy vetoed it."

He nodded. "Sweaze got riled when I brought it up."

"That's okay," I said. "I need to—"

"Andy!" an urgent voice interrupted behind me; a woman's voice, low and throbbing.

As I turned, a figure brushed past and clutched at Andy. I caught a glimpse of pale cheek and jade eyes. *The eyes, the eyes in the picture!*

"Cait!" He wrapped his arms around her. "What is it? Why are you crying?"

"Oh, Andy," she sobbed. "T'wasn't in me to spoil your celebrating."

"What's the matter?" His face tightened. "Is something wrong with Timmy?"

"No, it's Mother." The words were muffled against his chest.

"Mother . . . ?"

"Oh, Andy, she died this morning."

PART TWO

CITY ON A RIVER

———◇———

I was in Cincinnati, and I set to work to map out a new career.

MARK TWAIN, *Life on the Mississippi*

The dove descending breaks the air
With flame of incandescent terror
Of which the tongues declare
The one discharge from sin and error.
The only hope, or else despair
   Lies in the choice of pyre or pyre—
   To be redeemed from fire by fire.

T. S. ELIOT, Four Quartets

—◇ 13 ◇—

A violent storm woke me late the next morning. I sat up sweating as thunder crashed like artillery and heat lightning shredded the room's dimness. The air was heavy and stifling. I pulled the drapes open, and only then heard the knocking at my door.

It was a message. Champion and Harry were waiting downstairs, as I'd requested. Hell, I'd overslept! I splashed water on my hair, hurriedly shaved around the beard filling in nicely over my gashed cheek, and pulled my clothes on, cursing as I rummaged for my collar buttons.

They were drinking coffee in the dining room, Harry looking relaxed, Champion uptight. I soon learned why: the security man hired to keep unwanted banquet guests away had offended reporters and several late-arriving VIPs. Champion had been busy smoothing ruffled feathers.

I nodded sympathetically and plunged in. "Maybe I could handle problems like that, once I knew the city."

Champion raised one eyebrow.

"What I have in mind is serving as a sort of general aide, continuing as second substitute, acting as PR man now that Millar is—"

"Acting as *what?*" said Champion.

"Sorry, public relations. You know, press releases, personal appearances, like that."

The eyebrow lifted again. He glanced at Harry. "We're giving thought to the substitute situation."

A response less than wonderful.

"Look, what I really have to offer," I went on quickly, "are new marketing ideas."

"Yes?"

I took a deep breath and shifted to supersalesman, laying out a half-dozen projects, monitoring Champion's reactions. The more he frowned, the faster I talked. By the time he started shaking his head I was practically jabbering.

"Whoa, Fowler," he interrupted. "Your schemes—"

"The club's taking in money now," I said. "But you told me yourself how serious the debt is. What happens if we lose a game or two? Will the same crowds come out? What if baseball stops being all the rage?"

Seeing that I'd hit a nerve, I played my final cards. "We've got to *keep* people coming out. I'm so sure my ideas will work, I'll put up the money myself."

Both of his eyebrows rose. "Yes?"

"Yes, I'll repay myself from the proceeds."

"What about salary?"

"I'll work on commission. For, say, thirty percent of whatever revenues I'm able to generate."

Champion smiled knowingly. "If all goes as you foresee, that would be most lucrative for you."

"And for the club. But all right, then, I'm willing to work for what Andy makes—twenty-five a week—or thirty percent of what I bring in, whichever is less."

"*Less?*"

"Yes, less. That way, the *most* I'd cost you would be a hundred bucks a month. And then only if I've brought in a lot more."

It was a hell of a deal, and he knew it. In effect they'd get my services free.

"And you would still substitute?" Harry said. "Practice regularly?"

Which meant, I knew from Andy, hard workouts from two to six every day except Sunday. We had today off only because we'd played yesterday and faced the visiting Washington Olympics tomorrow.

"Yes," I said. "I want to be a Red Stocking." Which was bedrock truth. I didn't need the salary. I didn't relish a nineteenth-century career in journalism. Working with the club would provide variety and challenge—and enough structure to keep me from going crazy. I would stay close to Andy and the rest. Actually, if push came to shove, I'd probably pay *them* to keep me.

"You'll require a contract?" said Champion.

"I'll work a month on probation. Then if you want to keep me, I'll sign for the rest of the season."

I think that removed the last obstacle. They exchanged a significant glance. "You'll have our answer tomorrow," said Champion.

"Fine," I said, thinking, ALL RIGHT!

I explored downtown for a few hours. The Gibson House stood on streetcar lines stretching to every part of the city; the post office was close, as were government offices, theaters, and music halls. Directly opposite were the Mercantile Library and Merchants' Exchange. On nearby Fourth were department stores, on Fifth the business centers, on Third the city's Wall Street, on Pearl its wholesale quarter. Open-air markets stood nearby, with their profusions of flowers and fruits. I began to feel quite well situated. In the wake of the storm even the air felt fresher. Spirits lifting, I startled an organ-grinder when I tossed his monkey fifty cents.

"*Danke,* kind man!" he exclaimed.

"My pleasure."

I took a hack to the Iron Slag Grounds, the Buckeyes' West End field near the Union Grounds. The diamond was laid out inside a racetrack—a sodden mass of mud and puddles from the storm. Nonetheless, teams were on hand—the local Buckeye Juniors and Louisville's visiting Eagle Juniors—and not about to miss their turns on the field.

Andy tossed the coin between the captains, his face looking drawn. Guessing that he hadn't slept, I offered to take his place. He said no, Harry expected them all to do stints in the community; he would serve his turn today. Then I offered to help by umping the bases. Andy and the two captains stared at me like I was crazy. So I watched from the sidelines and kept Andy company between innings.

The juniors played good 1869-caliber ball—about to this era what well-drilled legion teams had been to mine. They were high-school age, but it was unlikely many of them attended. They wore uniforms identical to those of their parent clubs, who followed their accomplishments and looked to them for future talent, not unlike farm clubs. The Stockings had their own juniors, who had modeled themselves after the famous first nine even to the point of being undefeated so far.

The visiting Eagles pushed across two runs to win in the tenth, 21–19. The teams cheered each other, then cheered Andy. Two more squads, the Athletes and the Invincibles, scrambled on the field. I'd heard that diamonds everywhere in the city were in use nonstop through the summer; now I saw for myself: baseball was king. Andy stayed to offer coaching tips ("give points") and sign autographs for another half hour. When we finally left, he said, "I'm feelin' better now, but last night was awful."

"I could tell your mom thought the world of you," I said.

He shook his head, whether in sadness or disagreement I couldn't tell. "We talked way into the night. Argued, to put it more plain."

"You and Cait?"

He nodded. "She wants to send Mother back to be buried. Wants Brighid to go along to see it's done right."

"But you disagreed?"

"That I did." He sounded sad. "Sam, please tell me what Mother said to you before we left that day."

I hesitated. "You won't like it."

"I suspect not, but tell."

"She said she knew her time was coming. There would be problems if she didn't go home, as she put it. She thought I might help her."

"You?" There was pain in the word. "How so?"

"I wasn't sure then, but the fact is, I *can* help."

He was silent.

"Look, Andy, is the real problem her being buried over there—or the money it would take?"

"They're wrapped up."

"Think about them separately."

"What for?"

"Because I asked, damn it!"

He looked at me strangely. "If we had money to throw away," he said at length, "the rest of it might be more tolerable."

"So it comes down to the cost?"

"Yes," he said softly.

"What does Cait propose? Can she help?"

He shook his head resentfully. "She can barely even raise her boy. Yet she claims Brighid an' her an' me each have to cover a third. Says for me to borrow the money. She'll pay her part if it takes the rest of her days."

Thick curly dark hair, pale face glistening with tears, muted green eyes . . . I tried to dredge more from the brief moments before I had departed the previous night—but could picture only Cait's photograph. I said, "So where do things stand?"

"Same as they've always stood—it's up to me." The words faded into a groan. "I'm the son, the man."

And finally I understood his dilemma: to confess unwillingness or inability to meet his mother's dying wish—or to burden the family for years to come.

"Listen to me, Andy," I said urgently. "I'll supply the money."

His mouth twisted. "You gonna tell me it's what your dear rich auntie wanted?"

"If that's what you'll listen to."

"You never had no rich aunt, and the answer's no."

"I wasn't too proud to ask *you* for money, remember?"

"No."

"Andy, forget the damn rich aunt. I *went* to get this money because I promised your mom I'd try to help. And because you're my best friend ever. Who else ever stood up and sang for me, for God's sake? The money means nothing. I won't even miss it!"

"Sam, I can't let you—"

"I was sent here for this!" I beat the air with my hands. "Remember when you said it seemed right for us to come together? Like brothers? Well, I think I got left at that train station so this could happen! It's all part of it—and somehow she knew!"

He stared downward. "I can't take your money."

"Put it this way, then: Will you accept a loan?"

He drew a long, shuddering breath and turned away. I put my hand on his shoulder, felt him trembling.

"C'mon, little brother, you shouldn't have to carry this all by yourself. What am I for?"

When he finally spoke, the single whispered word came so softly I could scarcely hear it.

"Okay."

The $2,500 draft was payable to Andrew J. Leonard, transferable to the eastern bank of his choosing. I tucked it in my pocket and walked away from the banks that roosted like fat stone hens along Third Street. Ann Leonard had come to America in steerage. She would go home in style.

Champion's message arrived that evening. I had a job on the terms I'd suggested, starting immediately. An hour later I met him at the new depot at Plum and Pearl to greet the Washington Olympics arriving on the B & O "Fast Line." Millar was there too. He said he was pleased about my new role with the team and that he'd be happy to help me with press connections. The pudgy reporter didn't seem so officious now; we were comrades of the fabled tour.

I escorted the Olympics to the Gibson House, where I'd arranged supper and quiet rooms. The next morning I took voluminous notes on Champion's spiel as we toured the city.

It was a booster's tour. Emphasis on growth, on industry, on bigness. We began at the river, where, before the coming of the war and the railroads, hundreds of craft, from keelboats to floating palaces, had crowded Cincinnati's six miles of curved levee. Now, fewer than twenty paddle wheelers floated lazily at dock.

The Ohio was low in its bed that morning, exposing wide shoulders of shiny ocher mud. On the Kentucky side lay the dark, low shape of Covington, a mass of blackened brick factories. Champion ignored the lung-scratching smoke they emitted until several Olympics asked about it.

Resignedly he explained that the cause was the universal use of bituminous coal costing only seventeen cents a bushel—cheap, but it coated the city with grime. Only Cincinnati's rich could afford to wear light-colored clothing, houses were never truly clean, and even letters mailed from the city carried with them the reek of coal smoke. He deftly changed the subject by pointing to the new thousand-foot suspension bridge connecting Cincinnati and Covington. It soared a hundred feet over the river and could support, he claimed, the total weight of Cincinnati's 250,000 people.

We proceeded up from the river through a commercial gridwork. From plain wholesale outlets—I glimpsed Proctor and Gamble's soap factory on Second—we moved upward to showier retail establishments like Shillito's, where the Olympics bought dress shirts on sale at $1.25 apiece. Champion, meanwhile, kept talking: Cincinnati now boasted sixty-four millionaires; it ranked third in the nation in manufacturing and fourth in the production of books—due largely to McGuffey's famous readers.

Longworth's Wine House on East Sixth was a stop popular with the Olympics. Flickering candles illuminated cellars holding two hundred thousand bottles. Ohio's wines rivaled those of California, Champion claimed, but only Germans seemed able to run vineyards profitably. I noticed that prices ranged from a dollar for local Catawba to three-fifty for Longworth's special Golden Wedding Champagne—certainly not the cheapest drink in town.

Above Fifth, about half a mile up from the river, the buildings grew shabbier. We crossed the Miami Canal, a sluggish channel as wide as a street bisecting the city at sharp angles. A string of barges moved slowly on the viscid surface, powered by polemen. On the other side lay Over the Rhine, the huge, thriving German section constituting roughly a third of the city's population. I looked in wonder at red brick houses with wooden gingerbread trim, charming clock towers, window boxes bursting with geraniums, narrow alleys, busy beer gardens. I promised myself the treat of exploring this city within the larger city.

The foothills were dotted with slaughterhouses and breweries. We stopped before a huge new building. Its sign read: BANNER SLAUGHTER-AND PORK-PACKING HOUSE.

Christ, I thought, does he really mean to take us in there?

He did. It was vivid.

What Andy had said was true: Cincinnati still reigned as the country's primary meat packer. Here a system had originated of packing fifteen bushels of corn into a pig, packing the pig into a barrel, and sending it across the mountains to feed others.

Accompanied by a hellish, deafening squealing, we watched as hogs weighing up to six hundred pounds were killed, scraped, dressed, cut up, salted, and packed. This miracle of efficiency went on ten hours a day and six days a week during the four-month packing season. Only the strictest division of labor made it possible, each worker repeatedly performing the same specific task. The gutter, for example, a highly paid specialist earning six-fifty a day (no other worker topped four dollars), removed each hog's entire respiratory and digestive systems in less than twenty seconds with several rapid cuts. He performed this task, which would take an ordinary butcher ten minutes, some 1,500 times daily. Should the gutter be replaced by a substitute who could do the job only, say, one-fifth as fast, then the whole production process would slow to a fifth of normal output.

The others were visibly impressed by the man's wage. The Olympics received no salary but shared gate receipts. Among the Stockings, only the Wrights and Brainard earned as much as the gutter. But he could have made millions, for all I cared. I stared at the pools of blood and intestines and steaming water, at flabby, naked, quivering hogs, at men in oilskin suits shiny with wetness and grease.

Outside, I breathed the sooty air as if it were elixir, still noting information on my pad: hams went to the smoking department, salting pieces to the cellar, tongue and feet elsewhere; bristles brought seventeen cents, the tongue a nickel; the fat of the intestines alone paid nearly the entire cost of packing.

A triumph of the industrial revolution. A showcase of the assembly line. In this four-month season 180,000 hogs would be slaughtered by this house alone, and nearly half a million altogether in Cincinnati.

Hail, Porkopolis!

We went up into the hills that rose like ocean swells around the city. Above the pall of smoke were Clifton and the other elegant wooded districts, where the wealthy built their mansions. It was clear that Champion expected to take his place among them someday.

He showed us the stone house of Henry Probasco, a local magnate who had begun as an errand boy in the business he eventually headed. Into this house Probasco had poured limitless money, decorating each square inch to the limits of human ingenuity. Champion's voice quavered with moral fervor as he described it all, his subtext obvious: Labor hard to elevate yourself and look at what might happen. . . .

At the Mount Auburn Young Ladies School we ascended to a high cupola overlooking woodlands dotted with villas encircled by groves and gardens. Far below sprawled the city, broiling in its overhanging haze. I gazed in wonder around me, enchanted by sylvan vistas. The hilly suburbs were indeed Cincinnati's glory.

Descending again, we passed the austere Lane Theological Seminary, where Henry Ward Beecher had studied in a bare, forlorn room. The city possessed remarkable religious diversity, according to Champion. Protestants and Catholics actively cooperated. Rabbis—some twelve thousand Jews lived in the city—and Christian clergy actually exchanged pulpits to deliver sermons.

We passed the entrance to the newly finished Garden of Eden Park. I imagined myself strolling over the green expanses inside, Cait at my side. It made a pretty picture.

The news shook me, although most of the others didn't seem too surprised. Just before we took the field that afternoon, Harry informed us that he'd removed Hurley from the team for breaking rules. He didn't elaborate, but Brainard later told us the full story. Hurley had gotten roaring drunk the previous night in a Vine Street saloon—Brainard termed it a doggery—and broken three fingers in a brawl. Harry bailed him out of jail and kept it quiet—even Millar didn't know—but Hurley was definitely finished. I had the sobering realization that, for now anyway, I was the Stockings' only substitute.

I sat beneath a red canopy and manned the score book. On this humid Saturday nearly five thousand at the Union Grounds exulted in the knowledge that Cincinnati was fast becoming a capital on the sporting map. The West End park swarmed with kids trying to sneak over or under or through the fences. In the Grand Duchess dandified swells and lavishly dressed ladies created what Millar called an "Arabian Nights aspect" of vibrant color. The red-trousered Zouaves were on hand, and when they played "My Johnny Is a Soldier," women sang along and some wept.

The crowd was astonishingly polite, applauding in the first inning when the Olympics held us to one run and scored four themselves. Harry seemed proud of their sportsmanship. Not so Brainard, whose fastballs had been hammered.

We broke it open with sixteen runs in the fourth and fifth, coasting to a 25–14 win. Harry had his best day so far with six hits. Andy got an ovation in the third when he drove a shot between the outfielders, tore around the bases, and dove under the tag for the game's only homer.

"Fast little cuss," a Washington reporter commented.

"He was loafing," I told him. "Wait'll you see him *really* turn it on."

Andy drew me aside in the clubhouse to say he'd sent the money to

Newark. Brighid had wired back saying the grieving household was lifted to know that Mother and Father would be reunited forever in the homeland.

"Being the youngest," Andy said ruefully, "I didn't credit how much it meant to the others. I'm obliged to you, Sam."

"Good," I said, "buy me supper."

"I sent Cait word too," he said. "She wants to talk."

"To me?"

"No, to the wall there."

My breathing seemed jumpy. "Well, that's fine. Just fine. When?"

"She asked if I'd bring you by the boardinghouse she keeps. How about tomorrow after I'm done with church?"

"Well, that's a pretty busy time, but I guess just this once I could clear a space in my appointment book."

He rolled his eyes. "Ain't that a dinger?"

We found Hurley packing in his room, disconsolate and drunk. One hand was encased in plaster and his face bore bruises. He resisted our attempts to cheer him.

"I'm done here." he said. "Harry caught me out more times that I can count. He gave me every chance."

"Why couldn't you stay square, Dick?" said Andy.

"I don't know." His words were slurred. "Maybe I'm just not one to prosper. God knows, I scarcely think about anything else—but I have no answer. The drink's taken hold."

"You know," I began, my heart going out to him, "I've had some problems with the stuff too, and—"

"Let it be, Sam," he interrupted. "It's all done."

He left that night, a solitary figure on the late train. We accompanied him to the depot. He said he'd scout around his hometown in Pennsylvania, maybe get a teaching job, play local ball till he could hook up with a top club again. We wished him well and told him he'd be missed on the Stockings.

"Beware the hold of those bright leggings on you," he said.

> "Horses are tied by the head; dogs and bears, by th' neck; monkeys by th' loins, and men by th' legs . . ."

He waited for me to guess.

I cleared my throat and played his game one final time. "*Macbeth?*"

"The Fool," he said, "in *Lear*."

He waved once from the train. I waved back, hoping I would see him again. As things turned out, I would not.

Sunday was the Fourth of July, but in these God-fearing times no celebrating would occur until the following day. I slept late, dozing over a copy of Dickens's *Dombey and Son* I had borrowed from the Mercantile Library.

I dreamed of Andy's two sisters. I kept trying to see them close up, but each time I did their features were those of Stephanie, my ex-wife.

Enough, I told myself, and got up.

It was a large two-story frame house with wisteria climbing over a jigsaw-piece veranda. It sat in the middle of a block not far from the Sixth Street marketplace in the West End. Andy and I took a horsecar out Eighth and walked the remaining blocks. He led me through the front door and sat me down in a small parlor. There I waited with growing nervousness as he went upstairs to get Cait.

Around me were houseplants, a small reed organ, horsehair chairs. Framed on the wall opposite was a large scroll decorated with an Irish harp, sunburst, and wreath of shamrocks. Inscribed in the center was an inscription I took to be Gaelic.

A cutting voice behind me said, " 'They shall never retreat from the charge of lances!' "

I wheeled around to find a dark-suited, mustached man with penetrating blue eyes standing in the parlor doorway. The eyes seemed to pierce me. I was vaguely aware of a woman and a boy behind him.

"What?" I said.

"You were trying to read it," he said, jabbing a finger impatiently at the scroll. The gesture matched his aggressive tone; his voice was knife-edged, a weapon. " 'They shall never retreat from the charge of lances!' " His fixed stare challenged me.

I felt myself bristling. "How quaint of them."

As if I'd physically threatened him, he recoiled into an even more rigid stance, the ice-blue eyes flashing. I met his stare with my own.

Andy edged into the parlor and shot me a look that said he didn't like the guy either. "I didn't introduce you proper the other night," he said, drawing the woman in. "Sam, this is my sister Cait." He nodded toward me and said, "Sam Fowler."

She wore a dark dress and a hat with a veil. Through it I saw gray-green eyes and a pale face. She stood very still, nearly as tall as Andy and the other man.

"Mr. Fowler," she murmured.

"Nice to see you again," I said. My brain was doing odd blippy little things. "Call me Sam."

"She certainly will *not!*" snapped the man.

Andy looked pained. "Sam, this is Mr. O'Donovan."

"*Captain* Fearghus O'Donovan, sir!"

So *this* was O'Donovan. My pulse danced faster, more irregularly. "Right," I said, and turned to the boy. He was about seven or eight, a good-looking kid with alert gray eyes and his mother's black curly hair. He wore short pants, a jacket and tie. His Sunday best, I thought. All three of them, in fact, looked spruced up. For what? I wondered, and said to the boy, "*You* call me Sam, okay? What's your name?"

"Tim O'Neill," he said forthrightly. "Are you a ballist, like Andy?"

"Not like Andy," I told him. "Andy's the best—an ace. Are you coming out to see us?"

I saw I'd dropped a conversational bomb. The boy looked beseechingly at his mother, who said nothing. Andy shifted his feet uncomfortably. O'Donovan, whose face had darkened when I snubbed him, looked grimmer yet.

"I want to," the boy said. "At school they talk of nothing else but the Red Stock—"

"Timothy, mind yourself!" said O'Donovan, glaring at him. "You know your mother's wishes. We're not here to talk of a game."

Why *are* we here? I wondered.

"Fearghus," she said, "would you wait with Tim a bit?"

"Caitlin," he said heatedly, his pronunciation echoing Mrs. Leonard's "Cat-LEEN." "It's not proper that you be left alone with this . . . gentleman." The word sounded wrenched from him.

"It's not alone I'll be," she replied, and for the first time I heard a touch of brogue. "Andy will stay. It's a family matter, Fearghus, please."

He turned reluctantly, reaching for the boy's hand. Timmy ignored him and walked ahead toward the door.

"Cait, why not let the lad come out to the grounds?" Andy said. "It's all in fun."

"I'll not have it discussed," she said. The words were severe, but her voice held a timbre that intrigued me, a low, throbbing, restrained urgency that I found inexplicably familiar, holding some tonal quality that resonated deep within me.

She reached up and removed her hat, revealing a dark curling mass of hair held by several green ribbons. I saw her features clearly for the first time. Where Andy's eyes were emerald, hers were jade, long-lashed, far less open to the world than his. Her nose was straight and small, her lips full. Her skin was very white, with a faint splash of freckles over her nose and cheeks. Tiny stress lines converged at the corners of her eyes and mouth. Maybe she wasn't the most beautiful woman I'd ever seen. Maybe. But no other had exerted such force on me.

"Please do not regard me so," she said abruptly.

"I . . . excuse me," I said. "I saw a photograph of you, and now I realize . . . well . . ."

Her lips tightened. "I told Andy that I wanted to thank you. For a certainty, 'tis a great service you have done."

I looked into her eyes. "You're welcome."

"But I wonder just why it is you've become the benefactor of our family."

"There has to be a reason?"

"I believe so," she said, frowning slightly as she studied me. "Shouldn't there be?"

"Well, okay, Andy's like a brother to me," I said, resenting the feeling that I was being grilled. "When I met your family in Newark, I liked them. Very much. Your mother especially spoke to me in a way that touched me—perhaps because I can't remember my own mother—and so I was very happy to help make her last wish possible."

She paused as if considering it all. "And you are with the sporting club?" The unspoken message seemed to be, "Where did *you* get so much money?"

"Yes, the sporting club."

"There's no need for anger, Mr. Fowler." The green eyes regarded me. "I believe my curiosity to be natural."

"I'm not angry," I lied. "Look, I never had a brother either. Does any of that make sense? Cait, there's no ulterior motive. Would you rather I hadn't done it?"

"I am to be called Mrs. O'Neill."

I sighed, at the same time remembering that Timmy had used that surname. "Fine, you still just call me Sam."

"You are familiar, sir!"

"And you are cold."

There was an intense moment as our eyes locked.

"What the dickens's got you two so peevish?" Andy demanded.

She put her hat back on and adjusted the veil. "I appreciate what you've done, Mr. Fowler, and I intend to repay you," she said. "You may count on it."

"Fine, I'll start counting. Let's go, Andy." I walked outside, shook Timmy's hand, exchanged a brusque nod with O'Donovan, and set off up the dirt sidewalk. Andy caught up with me half a block later.

"Whew! You two didn't 'zactly hit it off."

"Brilliant, Sherlock."

"Sherlock? Slow down, you're walkin' faster'n I can keep up. I tried to tell you, Sam. She's been like that since Colm died."

"Well, I didn't kill him," I said. "And if that O'Donovan jerk is the one we were talking about, then he and McDermott deserve each other."

"He's the one," Andy said. "Colm's friend. Made sure Cait got pension money and helped her get set in the boardinghouse."

For an instant I thought the milkiness was hovering, ready to descend. I shook my head, clearing it.

"Wonderful warm guy."

"My hunch is that for Cait," he said thoughtfully, "it's not so much O'Donovan himself as the connection with Colm. And someone for Timmy."

We walked another block in silence.

"Could be she's jealous of you coming up with the money instead of one of us in the family."

"It doesn't matter."

"Sam," he said gently, "I wouldn't think too much about her, if I was you."

Jesus, was it that obvious?

"Don't worry," I told him. "I won't."

14

On Monday, July 5, I woke to pistol shots and sounds of processions. Half the city was on parade, the other half heading for picnic spots in the hills. The day was mild and beautiful.

That afternoon the Union Grounds held a festive throng of seven thousand who came out to see us take on the Olympics again. City officials made grand entrances in festooned carriages and made patriotic pregame speeches. The Zouaves complemented their red pantaloons with blue sashes and white blouses for this occasion. The crowd sang as they played "Mabel Waltz" and "Tommy Dodd" and "Champagne Charley." The last was Brainard's favorite.

> *"Champagne Charlie is my name,*
> *Good for any game at night, my boys,*
> *Good for any game at night. . . ."*

A group of ragged boys broke into a cancan on the sidelines. The crowd roared—and roared more when we banged out a series of ringing blows that swept us to an early lead, 14–4. Our fielding lacked its usual crispness, but everyone in the lineup had at least three hits—Andy's five included two triples—and we won easily, 32–10.

Afterward we sat in the clubhouse drinking lemonade and bantering. Our record was 26–0. No contests were scheduled for a while, a chance for the starters to rest. And for me to get going on my ideas.

"I saw in the papers where we can sit on our laurels, now that the tour's over," said George, flashing his grin. "But since our sticks ain't laurel, what'll we do—sit on our ashes?"

We cheered as Allison dumped his lemonade over George's head.

At dusk we stood in a tight group—Andy, Sweasy, Mac, Allison, and I—near the Fifth Street Market. Suddenly rockets streaked up over the river like brilliant snakes. We yelled and clapped with twenty-five thousand others jamming the downtown streets from Main to Elm, a sea of heads bobbing as far as I could see. The rockets exploded into fire balls, then showered golden rain overhead. Oohs sounded from the crowd. I loved all of it. Without TV and movies, without neon signs, without vivid twentieth-century colors, it was as if my eyes had been washed and rejuvenated.

At the players' rooms we drank a tub of foaming, locally brewed German lager that Allison ordered from a nearby saloon. While we played whist, Mac strummed on his guitar. I tried to teach them "Yellow Submarine." Mac handled the chords easily enough, and they seemed to understand what a submarine was. But they thought the lyrics were stupid.

Next morning I met with Champion and a saturnine man named Townley, an insurance executive, the club's treasurer. Townley said he appreciated the nine's new glory as much as the next man—but not its finances. When we finished going over his books, I saw why.

In March, when the players had assembled and begun drawing their pay, the club was already $16,000 in debt. A $15,000 note due this November hung over the organization like one of the city's smoke clouds. By leaning on a few wealthy members Champion had managed to raise a subscription of $500 for the eastern tour. We'd returned with $1,700, a net gain of $1,200. But player salaries—$300 weekly—were a constant drain. Good-sized crowds at the two Olympic contests had helped, but we needed more. Lots more.

As I stared at the formidable columns of figures, several things became clear. The Stockings, for all Champion's brave talk of being among the nation's soundest sporting clubs, were hanging by their toenails. Some members might be flush, but that didn't mean they'd pour money into the baseball team. The Stockings needed to be self-supporting. Even now, with all the hoopla, Champion was finding it difficult to meet costs.

It was also evident why Harry hadn't brought up Oak Taylor to replace Hurley: it would mean one more salary. Since I was already on the payroll and committed to funding myself, I would serve. I wondered how Harry privately felt about that.

What if we raised admission to fifty cents every game? Champion admitted that Harry wanted the higher figure. But he himself was opposed, except for top matches, unwilling to see baseball revert to a game only for the affluent. Poor laborers needed diversion too, and deserved to share in the excitement. His egalitarian views surprised me. Champion had a sense of community stewardship that was genuine. Some things about him I was grudgingly coming to admire.

Well, then, how about selling beer? Cincinnati's lager was the finest I'd tasted anywhere. No, absolutely not; spirits attracted the worst sorts, engendered gambling, sparked violence.

Okay, let's start by installing turnstiles at the gates; that would give us accurate attendance figures.

They looked at me in puzzlement. What were turnstiles? Good grief, I thought. Square one. I suggested posting uniformed members of the juniors at all entrances, to count paid and unpaid admissions, and to discourage the gatekeepers from letting people slip in. They both liked this hard-line approach.

And what, I inquired, was the deal on concessions? Not much, they admitted. Vendors, mostly from local restaurants, operated freely on the Union Grounds during public events. But, I argued, we were a red-hot property now. We ought to get a cut. Who else was regularly putting seven thousand hungry and thirsty customers out there for them? Furthermore, I wanted to introduce some things of our own. Things tried and tested the American way, like hamburgers and hot dogs.

What exactly were those?

Trust me, I told them.

Looking for a permanent place to live, I checked out the Henrie House on Third, between Main and Sycamore. Recently it had been refurbished and charged only two dollars a day—a buck less than the Gibson. Third-floor rooms offered a nice view: to the east the shipyards at the foot of Deer Creek Basin; to the north the Miami Canal and Over the Rhine; to the west the Mill Creek Hills behind Lincoln Park and the Union Grounds. But the Henrie's gilt wallpaper and frescoes of cherubs entwined with grape leaves put me off. Not to mention two large parlors "exclusively at the disposal of ladies" from which rococo piano strains floated incessantly.

In the end I settled for my room at the comfortable Gibson, with its spittoon-littered, high-ceilinged lobby redolent of cigar smoke, its floors of black-and-white Italian marble, its saloon with the long, elegant mahogany bar, and a fully equipped billiard room with six tables. The ladies' parlor and washroom were shunted upstairs near the reception and banquet rooms. The Gibson was primarily a man's environment. It lodged visiting teams, convenient for me in my new role. It cost more, but what the hell. I had money, and not much to spend it on.

Harry worked our asses off that week. We spent mornings at the YMCA on West Fourth, hefting Indian Clubs and a variety of free weights, and practiced at the Iron Slag Grounds in the afternoons.

He drilled us endlessly at "headwork": cutoffs, relays, defensive shifts, hidden-ball tricks—George had already pulled one in a game— and pickoffs. I showed them one pickoff play in which I flashed a sign from behind the plate to initiate a silent count. On three, Brainard whirled and threw to George breaking behind a runner leading off second. Harry promptly included it in his tactical weaponry.

Augmented by Oak Taylor and several of the juniors, we played intrasquad games pitting "Fats" against "Slims." Harry assigned me to the Fats with Mac, George, Gould, and Waterman, our power hitting a counterpoint to the others' fielding and quickness.

It was hard, systematic work. We knew it kept us ahead of competitors, but that made it no less grueling. Tempers flared: Sweasy and Allison would have traded punches if we hadn't separated them; Waterman threw a ball at one of the juniors after being upended by a hard slide; George and Brainard, their animosity growing, exchanged verbal cuts almost daily. Even Gould, the most stolid of workers, muttered about Harry's unrelenting pace. After missing a session, Brainard showed up complaining that the practices were sapping his strength and straining his pitching arm.

Harry confronted him. "Asa, is that your brand of ginger?"

"You're working us too hard."

"Then take more time away."

As Brainard walked off, Harry added, "Your pay will suit your new hours." Brainard turned back, scowling. Harry put him in the outfield and ran him to the verge of exhaustion.

My muscles had hardened from the daily workouts. Above the whiskers that hid my gash and made me look like a House of David player, my face was deeply tanned. I drank nothing stronger than beer now, and was in by far my best shape since college.

One morning Andy said, "Cait told me she didn't mean to stir you. She's a mite sorry, I'd guess."

"Tell her I'd like to see her." It came out before I could edit it.

"I don't guess she's *that* sorry."

His idea of humor didn't always send me into laughing fits. "Tell her anyway, okay?"

He shrugged. "If you say so."

◇

[195]

My off-hours—what few there were—I spent exploring. I rose early and climbed Mount Adams to see the city before foundries began pumping out smoke and was entranced by sunlight glowing on church steeples and glimmering on the river. I poked around the riverfront and stood gazing at the huge side-wheelers' twin stacks and curved decks, imagining what the glory times must have been like, back when Twain was a Mississippi pilot. I walked through slums spreading above the river enbankment: Rat Row, Sausage Row, Blacktown, Helltown; through alleys where anything could be bought, where honky-tonks and whiskey groceries abounded, and where derelict blacks and whites mingled without distinction.

I also made forays to Over the Rhine, into teeming German neighborhoods. None of the Stockings could tell me where to find what I needed—though Brainard and Waterman knew all the leading beer palaces. Since little English was spoken in the district, I made next to no progress—until the morning a most improbable individual nearly ran me over.

I had just stepped from the plank curb onto Mulberry when he careened downhill around the corner on a battered velocipede that bounced crazily on the cobblestones straight for me. I froze for an instant, then tried to leap back to the curb. He skidded and swerved, grazing my hip as he bucked wildly past, his feet splaying off the pedals. The velocipede toppled sideways. Through some quicksilver shift of weight he stepped away just as it crashed. Ignoring it, he lifted green goggles and looked at me calmly.

"Johann Sebastian Bruhn," he said in a high-pitched voice, "at your service."

I forgot about my hip as I stared at him. He was skinny and angular, a mulatto with light-coffee skin, yellow mud-colored eyes, and a lopsided grin. His hair was orange-red and kinky where it poked out from under his jockey cap, and his ears stuck out from his narrow head like enormous pressed flowers. He wore a patchwork jacket of reds, yellows, and blues; baggy pants were wrapped at his ankles; long square-toed shoes made his feet look like paddles. All in all, probably the silliest-looking character I'd ever seen—which is saying something, considering I went to school in Berkeley. I couldn't help returning his grin.

"Getting in trim for the county heats," he explained. "Sometimes I forget myself coming down Mount Auburn. You hurt?"

I rubbed my hip. "Not really."

"Everybody around here knows Johnny." He gestured at the storefronts. "I'm good for any damage I do, just ask."

"You know people here?"

"Sure as beans."

"Okay if I ask you a few questions?"

"Least I can do."

He picked up his bike—it was wooden, with iron-rimmed wheels—and wheeled it to the top of a steep street where he opened a gate below a sign, GASTHAUS ZUR ROSE, and led me inside a tiny courtyard. We sat at a table in the shade of a grape arbor. I could see a slice of the city below.

"*Helga!*" he shouted. "*Kommen Sie bitte heraus, wir haben Besuch!*"

It couldn't have astounded me more if he'd burst out singing like Marlene Dietrich. His German was convincing—but he *looked* like he should be spouting pure Stepin Fetchit. Within seconds a plump woman bustled from a doorway, apron flapping. Her cheeks were red, her graying hair pulled into a bun. Something in his tone, and in her familiar deference to him, suggested they were intimate. Did he live here with her? She went off and reappeared with mugs of steaming chocolate.

"Helga keeps the best lodge in Over the Rhine," he said. "Ever need a place, you can't do better'n Gasthaus zur Rose."

"What does it mean?"

"Inn of the Rose," he said, pointing at trellises where tree roses were covered with blossoms. Banks of primroses and geraniums spilled over planters and window boxes. I looked around, aware of his scrutiny. "Not many non-Dutch come up here, except to the beer gardens on Sundays. What brings you?"

After ascertaining that by "Dutch" he meant German—I would come to find that it was a commonly used derivative of Deutsch—I gave him a general idea what I was looking for. He said it was no problem at all, he could arrange everything in a matter of hours. When I told him it involved the Stockings, he grew excited.

"Brother athletes!" he said, gripping my arm. "Keepers of our bodies!"

"You're a bicycle racer?"

"Velocipedist," he said proudly.

"You make a living at it?"

"Haven't made a dime—yet." He grinned. "Been a mainstay with old John Robinson's till lately."

"With who?"

"You don't *know?*" He took a breath and launched into a frenetic barker's spiel. "John Robinson's Leviathan World Exposition! Mastodon Menagerie! Cosmographic Caravan! Monster Musical Brigade! The Animal, Arenic, Antiquarian, Aquarium, Aviary, and Amusement Aggregation of the Age! Acrobats, Funambulists, and Olympiads! Worlds of Wonder under a Continent of Gaslit Canvas! Carloads of Curiosities! The Albino Moor! The Living Skeleton! No Humbug! No Ventriloquial Frauds! A STRICTLY MORAL CIRCUS!!!"

He had me laughing by the end. He said he'd worked for years as a clown and tumbler in Robinson's Circus, which wintered in Cincinnati. This spring when it departed he'd stayed behind, intending to become a racing champion.

"Velocipede matches are nearly as big as baseball," he said. "Right up there with billiards, horse racing, and pedestrianism." The latter, it turned out, meant track events. "I'm saving for a racing wheel now," he said enthusiastically.

"But how do you live since you've left the circus?"

"Oh, there's lots of jobs in Over the Rhine."

"What sort of jobs?"

"Connecting, you might say." He explained that his language fluency enabled him to operate as a sort of agent, putting people in touch with whatever they sought. "You, for instance," he said, grinning. "I'm just the one you need."

I eyed his ragtag coat. "You really named Johann Sebastian Bruhn?"

"The Dutch called me it in fun, and I liked it," he said, shrugging. "I was born John Brown, but that got touchy back before the war. Heap of Secesh here, you know. In the circus I was always Jughandle Johnny"—he flapped his ears with his fingers—"on account of these. Want more chocolate?"

Over another mug I learned that his mother was black, his father a white dry-goods peddler. Growing up in the riverfront slums, Johnny had recognized early what life might hold for him. Finding he had an innate ability to make people laugh, he'd begun as a street dancer and graduated to the circus.

"How'd you happen to learn German?" I asked.

"Hid up here during the riverboat troubles." He saw my blank look and explained. "After the war some of the niggers hereabouts tried out the new freedom by riding the boats first class. They got themselves chopped up and tossed in the river by gangs of roughs. For a while it looked like things might spread over the whole city."

"Jesus Christ."

"I hid out up here. The Dutch people, most of 'em, haven't been over here so long. They'd had their own miseries with the Know-Nothings. They gave me work, taught me Dutch."

As he favored me with the lopsided grin, I made my decision. "Tell you what, let's tackle this first project together and see how it works out."

He grinned again. "Yassuh, Boss."

"One thing, Johnny."

"What?"

"Call me Sam, okay?"

Champion's message was urgent: get as many players as possible on the night train. The Olympics had failed to show up to play the Illinois state champs, Rockford's Forest City club. People were journeying from as far as St. Louis. To save the day Champion had agreed—for a share of the gate—that the Stockings would replace the Olympics. All we had to do was get there. Fast.

I hired a hack and managed to track down everybody except Gould, Brainard, and Waterman. I left messages for them, tipped the hackster a small fortune, and reached the depot barely in time.

We filled the next twenty-four hours with cards and newspapers. I read that Queen Victoria had just turned fifty—a fact I found impossible to assimilate. General O'Neill was urging the Fenian Senate of Pittsburgh to initiate a policy of "active operations," whatever that meant. *O'Neill.* I stared at the name. Cait used it. Did she consider herself married?

In baseball news, the Brooklyn Atlantics had beaten the Philadelphia Athletics by the whopping score of 51–48, the largest ever posted by two professional clubs. Attendance was noted as over fifteen thousand.

"We're the ones who stirred 'em back there," George said, "but it's the eastern clubs cashing in."

Talk turned to our opponents, the Forest Citys. My ears pricked up at mention of a pitcher named Spalding.

"They'll be burning to steal our glory," George said. "Folks a hundred miles around will be on hand, too."

He probably underestimated. We had trouble even claiming our reserved rooms at the Holland House, a four-story brick hotel beside the Rock River. The city's population of twelve thousand was swollen with thousands more. Bob Addy, the Forest Citys' catcher, who boarded at the Holland House, told us he'd never seen the like.

"Course we're just farmboy amachoors," he said slyly, spitting tobacco. "But we'll show up on the grounds anyway."

Technically the Forest Citys were unpaid, but the town was so ball-crazy that numerous groups, including churches, had subscribed

to compensate them for every minute lost from their jobs while practicing. A fine line, I thought. The reality was that all of America so
loved its new sporting heroes that it eagerly showered them with
rewards. In Cincinnati it took the form not only of salary but increasing numbers of gifts—meals, clothes, jewelry, livery service—
representing a substantial income boost. George claimed he now
banked almost all of his pay. Andy figured he received as much value
in free services as he earned each month. Even I was deluged with
offers of drinks each time I set foot in the bar of the Gibson.

Brainard and the others arrived the next morning, only hours before
the game. Ten thousand people jammed the fairgrounds at the end of
Peach Street, buffeted by near-gale winds swirling dirt in high spouts.
The diamond was chalked inside an oval racetrack. On it the Forest
Cities warmed up, most of them small and wiry, very quick in their
drills. Harry cautioned us not to take them lightly.

Odds favored us up to four to one, but there were few takers after
the first inning. Spalding—he had to be the future sporting-goods
magnate, I decided, studying him—looked nervous. About nineteen, a
six-footer, he was dark-haired, unsmiling, a budding Chamber-of-
Commerce type. His pitches had excellent velocity but little variation.
George watched a couple go by, then, taking advantage of the wind
blowing out, teed off and slammed a ball far beyond the distant tree
row in left for a homer. Gould followed with a stinging double to
center; Andy later cleared the bases with a triple, and we led 13–1
after one.

"They'll come back at us," Harry cautioned. And they did, but not
until the final two innings, when they struck for ten runs while holding
us to two. Though the rally came too late—we won handily, 34–14—
it set the crowd bellowing to see that the big-city pros weren't invincible after all. Rockford's captain insisted on a rematch in Cincinnati,
and Harry agreed.

"They'll learn from their mistakes and work on the points of their
game," he told us on the train on the way home. "They'll come
gunning for us."

We didn't worry. We were 27–0. And riding high.

We got home on Sunday morning, July 11, and learned that the
Washington Olympics had arrived just ahead of us after careening
around in a large circle, winning in Louisville and Mansfield, losing in
Cleveland. Now they would play the Buckeyes on Monday and face us
for the fourth and final time on Tuesday.

I spent the balance of Sunday in Over the Rhine, haggling and finalizing our arrangements with Johnny interpreting. Everything, he assured me, was going to work out splendidly.

Good, I thought. Let's hope there's a big crowd.

It turned out to be respectable. My newly stationed observers counted 4,563. We found that receipts were over a hundred dollars short. Either four hundred people—almost ten percent—had gotten in free, or gate money had been pocketed. The juniors suspected the former, reporting that a ticket taker at the main gate had let friends slip past, and that a number of boys had sneaked through the east-side carriage gate during the heaviest influx of vehicles. Champion, pleased, said he would fix the gate problem at once. I pointed out that that alone would more than cover my salary the rest of the season.

"Yes," he said shortly. "That's why we're paying you."

The day's big news involved our concessions. At a booth beside the clubhouse, the smells of hamburgers and hot dogs wafted over the grounds for the first time. A world premier, so far as I knew. Johnny and I had brought in a small wagonload of supplies early that morning. While Helga unpacked our custom-baked round and long buns, we set up a grill and went to work.

"Vy you call dem Hamburgers and Frankfurters?" Johnny translated for her, affecting a thick accent. "I yam from Wiesbaden!"

The sausages' skins were a bit too tough, but they tasted right. We'd had the beef ground that morning. Ketchup didn't exist, but we had some of the finest German mustard I'd ever tasted, lots of pickle relish, and chopped sweet onions. The lack of tin foil or other insulation stumped me at first, when I'd envisioned selling our sandwiches in the stands, but then I'd hit on the booth idea.

To test our products, Johnny and I delivered samples to the clubhouse when the Stockings arrived.

"What's the nigger doing here?" Sweasy demanded. Blacks showed up at the Union Grounds only when one of the local colored teams played. Slavery had not rooted this far up the Ohio, but Jim Crow had laid down its iron divisions. Blacks rode on the outer platforms of omnibuses, lived in colored neighborhoods, attended colored schools, were nursed at the colored hospital, were even buried in colored cemeteries. A comprehensive system of segregation, cradle to grave.

"He's Dutch," I said, extending a hot dog. "Here, try this."

He took a bite. "That's damn good. The nigger's gotta go."

I moved closer. "He's my partner," I said. "Don't say any more, okay?"

Sweasy stared up at me. Behind his eyes a calculation went on.

We both knew that I could beat the shit out of him if it came to that.

The Stockings went for our food like sharks. Three burgers disappeared into Mac before the others had finished one. Harry commanded Gould to stop after half a dozen hot dogs, fearing his limited fielding range would shrink to nothing.

"What'll you do next?" Waterman demanded, wiping mustard from his mustache. "Make our bats?"

"Never can tell. Here, have the last burger."

From my post at the scorer's table I watched lines form outside the booth and heard people exclaiming. Johnny and Helga worked frantically. By the fifth inning all six hundred sandwiches were gone. Their ingredients averaged four cents, and we sold them for twenty. After paying Johnny and Helga five bucks each—top-scale wages; I felt extravagant on this landmark day—we netted eighty-five dollars for the club, an amount equal to nearly a tenth of gross paid admissions split between the two teams that day. My trial balloon had soared.

The Olympics left after seven innings to catch the six-thirty boat to Portsmouth. Home runs by Andy and George, plus sharp fielding that limited the O's to eleven hits, gave us the win, 19–7. Davy Force tripled twice, once after faking a bunt down the third-base line, which angered Waterman and drew a protest from Harry.

"He heard about *you* doing that," Waterman said accusingly to me between innings. "Every baby hitter'll be trying it before long."

"So stop crying and work on your defense," I retorted, thinking that the Stockings, like everybody else, preferred their own "head-work" to an opponent's.

As we were about to leave the clubhouse, Andy approached with a perplexed expression. "They're here."

"Who's here?"

"Cait, with Timmy."

A tingle of excitement moved up my spine. "I thought she didn't like baseball."

"They've never come before. But she and Timmy were in the Grand Duchess. O'Donovan, too."

"Oh." The excitement quieted.

"You said you wanted to see her."

I nodded, unsure now.

"So, you coming with me?"

I paid Harry for a new ball and followed Andy through the main gate, where he was promptly surrounded by autograph seekers.

"Sam?" He stood to one side, small and shy, a curly-haired figure in short pants.

"Hi, Timmy." I held out the ball.

His eyes widened. "For me?"

"Sure is, just like the one Andy knocked for a homer. Wasn't that something to see?"

He examined the ball as if it were the rarest treasure.

"Bring it back next game," I said. "I'll have everybody sign it."

He nodded gravely, took a pencil from his pocket and held the ball up. "Would you, Sam, now?"

I loved him for that. When I finished, he touched his fingertips to the signature and then dashed off, yelling, "Andy!"

They were in a small open carriage beneath overhanging elms. As I drew close my vision suddenly and frighteningly was flooded with the milky half-light. I sensed the presence of a bird—the great bird in the graveyard—and the trees around me swayed and shimmered as though underwater. But all that was peripheral. What my eyes fixed on was her dress: it was pale and flowery, yellow with tiny pink buds and leaf clusters, the dress of the picture and quilt.

"Are you well, Mr. Fowler?" The words came from somewhere beneath her broad-brimmed hat. I tried to focus. I saw her eyes. Cloudy jade.

"Mr. Fowler?"

"The heat . . ." I blurted. "Hello, Mrs. O'Neill."

"It must be wearing to wield a pencil as your striking stick." O'Donovan clipped his words with military precision; his tone dripped sarcasm.

I looked at him, still seeing through a thin milky haze. His tunic, sash, and epaulets were forest green. Covered with phoenixes, sunbursts, shamrocks. Buttons and braid glittered. Icy blue eyes. Firm jaw. Waxed mustache. Portrait of the hero.

Footsteps behind me ended the long silent moment.

"Andrew," barked O'Donovan. "We saw you strike your blow and make your run!" He touched Cait's arm with maddening familiarity. "Your sister stood and cheered lustily with the others, she did."

She smiled, the first time I'd seen her do so. Her eyes crinkled and her lips parted, revealing white, straight teeth. For a moment she looked younger, as she must have been as a girl. I longed to know that younger Cait.

"I was proud, Andy," she said. "Thousands screaming your name, and so many of them ladies."

As Andy blushed deep red, Timmy appeared. He held his ball aloft. "See what Sam gave me?"

O'Donovan turned to me. "They truly *pay* you to sit beneath a sunshade?"

"Sam's first substitute," Andy said. "He only keeps the score book when he's not playing."

"Ah, the score book," O'Donovan repeated acidly.

"Sam's important," Andy insisted. "Did you see his new booth?"

"Making sandwiches while you make runs," O'Donovan said. "Poor work, I'd say."

Cait murmured something.

I felt myself heating up dangerously. Who did this asshole think he was? "So far I've only seen a few of the costumes worn by hick clubs in the boondocks," I said. "But I'll bet they don't come any sillier than the one you're in."

A faint gasp came from Cait. Timmy giggled and Andy nearly choked. O'Donovan blanched and stood erect in the carriage. His words came through clenched teeth. "This is the uniform of the Irish Revolutionary Brotherhood. I'll consider your insolence dark ignorance for the moment, only because a lady is present." He snatched up the reins. "We'll be leaving now, Caitlin."

I lifted Timmy to the seat. Meeting Cait's eyes I said, "I'm glad the lady is present." Color spread across her cheeks. Her mouth tightened as she looked away.

We watched the carriage move down the lane. Timmy waved the ball at us. Andy waved back. My eyes were fixed on Cait. I sent her silent commands to turn and look back at me.

She didn't.

15

Harry and I lugged everything into the clubhouse. We'd spent the morning at Ellard's Sporting Goods Emporium on Main; it claimed to have the largest stock of baseball equipment in the West. George Ellard, a regular on the club's cricket squad, gave us wholesale rates, which was fortunate since lately we'd had a rash of broken bats. We bought a dozen of the finest: six willow, five ash, one elm—Brainard claimed he could only hit with elm—with handles prewrapped and sleek barrels ready to be branded with players' initials. I'd already burned *SF* on the heaviest ash model.

We also bought a box of balls, six bases, a half dozen sets of brass spikes, a copy of *Beadle's Dime Book* with current rules—Sweasy had torn up Harry's old copy when an ump's ruling went against him in the last Olympic game. Also a supply of elastic bands for our stockings—Harry had considered garter belts, but I talked him out of it—and several cane-handled cricket bats.

"Congratulations on your booth," he said, and went on to confess that he'd failed as a concessionaire himself. The previous winter, after the club had flooded the Union Grounds to form its annual skating pond, Harry had sold coffee, canned peaches, New Orleans oysters, and even—surprisingly—hot whiskey drinks. Despite offering baseball on ice and other attractions, the club hadn't made a dime. "You, though," he said, "seem to know what people want. Such bold ideas!"

I smiled modestly, as if bold ideas were my forte. "More coming," I said, and hoped it was true; Johnny was scouting future projects that day.

"I've tried the new fungo bat," Harry said. "I'm improving."

I'd had the lumber company turn a slender hardwood fungo. With it I could put a ball inside a twenty-foot radius anywhere on the field. I used it to give Andy the extra work he wanted on deep drives. Harry had seen its applications immediately and put me to work drilling all the outfielders.

Otherwise he treated me like everybody else, working me each day till I dragged. At night my muscles jerked as I heard him yell, "Runner on second, one out!" In part his purpose was to keep us from getting big heads. Not an easy task, given the mounting hoopla. Repeatedly he advised caution in accepting merchants' favors, restraint in drinking—the specter of Hurley hung over us, though Harry never referred to him—and avoidance of gamblers.

Heat descended on the city. Blistering, sweltering, lung-searing heat. Pavement and brick sidewalks burned through shoe leather. Dung in the streets flaked into particles and was swept up by sultry air currents off the river to mix with soot and form a toxic, eye-stinging dust; people walked outside with their heads completely covered. Horses collapsed on the cobblestones, unable to pull streetcars or buses up the steep hills even in double and triple teams. Each day the papers carried lists of people who'd succumbed to sunstroke. *Air-conditioning,* I fantasized, sweating from morning to night. *Cold showers . . .*

Ice was in tremendous demand. Floated down canals in great blocks from Lake Erie each winter, it was packed in sawdust and stored in underground icehouses. Now its price shot to unprecedented heights. Johnny and I had been trying to add sodas to our Union Grounds fare. The soda-water business, a fairly new industry, was booming. Inexplicably, nobody had yet come up with ice-cream sodas. At first Johnny thought I was crazy mixing the two, but after a few tentative sips, followed by deep pulls and considerable lip-smacking, he pronounced me a genius. Our trouble was that rocketing ice costs boosted our selling price to thirty-five cents each. We decided to try it as a luxury item, figuring that the swells accompanying satin-bedecked women with silk parasols could well afford it.

In the middle of one of the very hottest days, in a burst of inspired bravado, I had Johnny deliver two ice-cream sodas—packed in a frosty ice bucket and topped with fresh cherries—to Cait and Timmy. I told him to wait while they tasted it and say, "With Mr. Fowler's compliments."

When he returned he said, "Miz O'Neill didn't exactly brighten up, but she took a sip, then called the boy in, and the boy gulped his down and said it was the bulliest thing he'd ever tasted. Then Miz O'Neill sipped some more, and they both agreed it was real cooling."

"That's all?"

"Well, then she washed everything. Then she sat down brisk-like and wrote this." He reached inside his patchwork coat—Johnny's unchanging costume made no concession to heat or cold—and handed me a slip of paper.

Written in a rounded, flowing hand, it said:

> *Mr. Fowler,*
> *Andy tells me that you give in a spirit of honest friendship.*
> *We take your offering in that spirit and we are grateful.*
> *Caitlin O'Neill*

I read it a dozen times, my eyes lingering on "we are grateful."

"I think she fancies you," Johnny said.

I was flabbergasted. "You do?"

"But she don't know it yet."

Thursday, July 22, was one of those mornings when information pours in and for days afterward sifts and settles into place. I woke up sweating—for the eighth straight day the heat showed no sign of breaking—and stiff from Harry's sadistic workout the previous evening. At least we were now practicing after the hottest part of the day.

I tugged the bell rope to have coffee and the morning papers sent up. On the third page of the *Enquirer* I was astonished by a small item.

A TRIAL OF THE "AERIAL STEAMER"

> Several citizens to-day witnessed a private trial in the open air of the aerial steam-carriage *Avitor*. The steamer rose in the air about seventy-five feet, the machinery operating successfully, buoying up and driving the vessel forward at a considerable rate of speed. A public trial of the *Avitor* will be had on Sunday next.

It was reprinted from the *San Francisco Chronicle*—what a strange rush I felt seeing *that*—and datelined a few days earlier.

I searched the other papers for corroborating items and found one in the *Gazette*, reprinted this time from the *San Francisco Times*, whatever that was, which added that the *Avitor* was a 40-foot working *model;* its inventor, Mr. Frederick Marriott, fully expected to complete a 150-foot passenger version soon. He now stood "where Fulton did when he made his first steamboat."

Sure, I thought.

And yet part of me wanted it to be true. With my grandparents I had watched the astronauts set foot on the moon. Grandpa hadn't seemed impressed; Grandma wanted to watch "Lassie" on another channel. I understood better now. Given what they'd seen—autos, airplanes, radio, TV, the Bomb—the space program must have seemed tame. Space-suited NASA employees were distant. Thundering over a field in a crate of wood and wire and fabric—that could be *you!* I suddenly wanted to see Marriott's flyer. Maybe he *would* scoop the Wright brothers this time around.

Downstairs a letter from Twain awaited me. It was postmarked Hartford and addressed only to Sam'l Fowler, c/o World-Beating Red Leggers. It had duly been routed to Cincinnati, delivered to Champion, and forwarded to me.

> *Dear Sam,*
>
> *Abundant & fulsome considerations have prevented my writing sooner. To put it plainer, I've been in a humor to lie low. Even plainer, I've been scared eight points out of my wits. I jump like a cat at every sudden noise. You'll reckon me a saphead for such carrying on. Livy's family is at the heart of it—no, rather, her sweet unquestioning trust in me. If the slightest shadow fell now, with our engagement booming forward like it is, I'd blow my head off. Ten thousand times I've cursed myself for telling you that story. But then I think of our money & feel all secret & smug like a boy after stealing the pie from the window. But then I start brooding on the consequences all over again & I dive into a perfect swamp of gloom & imagine the Langdons finding out and falling on me like a thunderbolt. Oh, I am a raw specimen of desperado!*
>
> *You can't imagine the upheaval you stirred here. For days nothing could hold up one-tenth to events at the cemetery. Rumors had the Rebs coming back for vengeance, Quantrill's Raiders or their ilk starting in with graves & next would come the banks & then homes . . . well, it went on & on. The local rag printed "clues": dug-up earth around the grave & the splintered coffin top & horses racing down outlying roads & banshee screams & corpses lit up like lamps—oh it was a booming tide, a torrent. Then this ad appears:*
>
> > Sizable cash award offered for information concerning whereabouts of missing war revenue rightfully ours.
>
> *Elmira's Fenian Circle was given as the place to contact. Well, as you can imagine, that started everything up again at full paddle, & THEN it reached a PERFECT HOWL two days later when Costigan was found in his office with his throat slashed.*

I put the letter down, stunned, picturing Costigan in the sweltering office; he'd played me cleverly, taking the money, knowing all along he would set me up. When I escaped they must have figured he'd crossed them too. Or maybe they'd just wanted to silence him. His throat cut. I shuddered. Jesus, for somebody trying not to meddle with history I was doing one hell of a job. I read on numbly.

> You can't imagine the fuss that kicked up. Folks talking the downfall of civilization, pent-up Christians looking to the imminent appearance of Satan in Elmira Township. Nor can you picture the sweat I was in, fearing every minute that Robert was witnessed bringing back the nags & that he'd be forced to spill everything. I paid Solomon's treasure to button his mouth, but the Fenians could surely unbutton it.
>
> Naturally you were the object of considerable speculation. (I mightily appreciated you passing yourself as a duke, by the way.) The constable got quite an itch to find you once he'd traced the livery wagon. Lately some others showed up asking about you too. From what you told me, I reckon I guessed their identity—one a large-sized hard-smiling Irish sport with red hair and washed-out eyes; the other a poison-mean breed who raises your neck-hair just to glance on him. I don't have to tell you to watch your step with those two. They tried not to show it—I observed them from Elmira's billiard palace, where I am wont to demonstrate my modest skills to neophytes—but I could tell they want you the worst way.

Again I lowered the letter. How had Le Caron been sprung so fast? What the hell kind of network had I gotten myself tangled in? I prayed it didn't extend this far.

Twain finished by congratulating me on pulling the whole thing off. He swore that for security purposes he planned not to touch any of his share "for years & years."

In August he still intended to visit California. Meanwhile he was looking for a newspaper to buy controlling interest in. The first four hundred copies of *Innocents Abroad* were finally off the press. It was a handsome, big volume, he said, and he was mortally sick of the whole thing.

> I will follow your progress in the National Game. (How could I not? The exalted feats of your red-hosed mates are trumpeted over the continent like installments of Homer's epic!) Some day, when our venture is no longer fearsome & merely the stuff of old men's lies, we'll drink champagne and chuckle. Meanwhile, fasten all latches & burn this to powder!

It was signed "SLC"

I didn't burn it, of course. Wondering if he'd read about the *Avitor,* I tucked the letter into the drawer that held my important possessions: the note from Cait, the tiny red stocking emblem I'd received at the reception banquet, and my gun.

We played the Buckeyes that afternoon. Allison's mother was seriously ill, and he'd left that morning for Philadelphia. Harry asked me to catch.

With security tightened at the gates, we collected virtually a hundred percent on admissions that afternoon. The booth ran out of wares midway through the contest. Several hundred satisfied customers were introduced to our new delights: big German pretzels and ice-cream sodas. We netted over two hundred bucks—but I nearly had to take Johnny to a hospital afterward. Physically exhausted, he said he'd swallowed the smoke from three hundred frying hamburger patties.

The game was hardly artistic. Using our new bats, we hammered fifty-three hits including ten homers. I went only three for ten—fewest hits among the Stockings—but I made them count, lining a double over short, banging a homer off the top of the fence, and later clearing it with a towering shot down the left-field line. I have a wonderful sense-memory of it—the shivering impact up my arms, the recoil of the heavy bat, the deep *THOCK!*

In the final inning a pitch got by me and rolled back to the foot of the Grand Duchess. As I chased it down, a boy's voice yelled, "Quick, Sam!" I threw to Brainard, covering the plate, then turned and saw Timmy looking down. I gave him the thumbs-up sign, then found myself staring beyond him into Cait's eyes. It couldn't have lasted long—a second, two seconds—but in that interval some kind of throbbing, eerily familiar energy pulsed between us. I forced myself to turn away, realizing afterward that I hadn't noticed whether O'Donovan was there.

The next pitch produced a foul tip that tore the nail halfway from my left index finger, effectively capturing my attention. At game's end, when I finally looked again, they were gone. I felt let down.

Stockings 71, Buckeyes 15.

The Forest Citys arrived at one in the morning. Champion had let me know he didn't want to be disturbed, so I met them at the Indianapolis & Lafayette depot. The Rockford players greeted me pleasantly, except for Spalding, who gave me a fish-eyed glance.

"Say," said Bob Addy, "we hear Allison ain't gonna catch agin' us."

"That's how it looks."

"You kept the score book before, so you're the first substitute?"

"That's right."

He looked significantly at my bandaged finger. "Why, that's good for us, then." He laid a country-boy shit-eating grin on me. "Real good."

Even with the heat wave finally breaking, we should have known better than to expect an off day between games. To Harry, if baseball was your profession, that's what you *did*, six days a week, like any other job. So with juniors filling some positions, we played a long intrasquad game Friday afternoon. Allison was definitely gone till next week. Brainard and Sweasy were AWOL from practice. Harry looked more than a little pissed off.

I was starting to worry about Brainard. While it was true that everybody but Andy and Mac tried to beg off practicing occasionally—even George, to Harry's consternation—Brainard was becoming chronic at it. His jealousy of George verged on the obsessive, and his sizzling of us, always barbed, was becoming cynical and deadly. I'd noticed too that his eyes were bloodshot a number of afternoons. Where, I wondered, did he spend his nights?

Because of my damaged finger Harry spared me from playing catcher or first. I spent the afternoon shagging flies in center, unsure whether Harry's reminders to Andy and Mac not to leave me unguarded ultimately boosted or undercut my confidence. But I did know I was finally hitting with authority. Getting my weight into them, I unloaded a series of shots during my turns at the plate. Too bad there weren't pinch hitters or DHs. I'd've been awesome. I think Harry wished something similar after I'd belted the second homer against the Bucks. True, it had come on fat pitching, not Spalding's, but still . . .

That night, after making sure the Forest Citys' needs were met at the Gibson—they had skipped Champion's city tour to work out on the Iron Slag Grounds—and stopping by Gasthaus zur Rose to see that Johnny and Helga had the next day's concessions ready, I directed my hack driver to the West End. He looked at me questioningly as we stopped in front of Cait's boardinghouse. Staring at the wisteria-laced veranda, I made up my mind and told him to wait.

Timmy answered my knock. "It's Sam!"

Inside, feet shuffled and chairs scraped. Timmy dashed away, leaving me in the foyer. At length Cait appeared, her hair in a scarf. She wore a plain pleated gray dress. When she spoke she sounded tired.

"It's not a proper hour for visiting, Mr. Fowler."

Flustered by the green-eyed gaze, feeling bulky as a moose this near her, I blanked out what I'd rehearsed.

"I wanted to talk," I blurted.

She said nothing.

"Look, I don't really know how to visit properly," I said hopelessly. "What I mean is, I don't have visiting cards to send, there's no phone—"

"Phone?" She tilted her head.

"I'm sorry, I just mean—"

Timmy rescued me by appearing and declaring urgently, "They don't believe it's the real article, Sam!"

"What article? Who doesn't?"

He held up his ball. "My pals won't believe it's truly from one of the Stockings."

"Well, that's one reason I dropped by," I said, glancing at Cait. "Come to the game tomorrow and we'll get it signed."

"That'd be grand!"

"Timothy, enough for you now," Cait said. "Go inside, please."

"But, Mother—"

"Away with you."

"Bye, Sam."

"He talks of nothing else," she said. "It'll be the death of me."

"Yet you brought him out yesterday."

She sighed and said, "It's not in me to deny all that a boy loves. Andy's long been his hero."

"Is that the only reason you came?"

She looked away. "I mustn't neglect my boarders."

"Cait—Mrs. O'Neill—I'm not sure how to express it, but since I first saw your picture I've had this strange—"

"Caitlin!" said a peremptory voice within.

O'Donovan. Sonofabitch!

She stiffened. "I must go."

"Boarders?"

"He *is* a boarder. I'm thinking I needn't explain myself to—"

"Cait!" boomed O'Donovan. "What's keeping you?"

The parlor door swung open. O'Donovan's eyes narrowed as he recognized me. Before he yanked the door shut I glimpsed three or four men sitting inside.

"What in hell are *you* doing here?" he demanded.

I smiled into his glare.

"Come in," he told Cait. "I'll handle this."

She turned to face him. "It's not quite finished I am." Her tone offered no compromise.

He frowned and said, "I'll be just inside." He looked at me darkly. "Call if you need me."

"Thank you, Fearghus," she said. She swung back toward me when he had gone. "Do you see the strain you put me to?"

"That's not my intention."

"What *is* it, then?"

I hesitated, sure that O'Donovan was listening. Then again, did it really matter? "When I first saw your picture I felt this funny pull, as if I were supposed to meet you, or had known you before, or—" I stopped, aware of some quality in her eyes changing.

"Known me before?" She tucked a wisp of hair beneath her scarf. On her ring finger I saw a thin silver band bearing a heart design.

"Yes, well, not exactly. I mean, there's this feeling of unfinished business. Yesterday I thought maybe you felt it too." I groped for amplifying words, found none. "I guess that's really all I wanted to ask. Whether you've felt the same, or if it's just me."

She regarded me silently.

"Look, I don't mean to mess up your arrangement with O'Don—"

"I have no *arrangements,*" she said hotly. "And I think it's time you leave now, sir."

"All right, but answer me."

She shook her head, small quick movements.

"You felt something, didn't you?"

She raised her face defiantly. "Mr. Fowler, what you are trying to do is not welcome." Her voice was shaking. "You have no right to do this to me!"

I knew it would have been disastrous to try to touch her. But I also knew that I'd never wanted anything more than I wanted to take her in my arms just then.

"Whatever's happening, it's not just me doing something to you," I told her. "It's happening to both of us."

She brushed the air with her fingers, as if to say what did it matter. I could hear her breathing in the ensuing silence.

"Please, bring Timmy tomorrow and have dinner with Andy and me afterward."

A sound escaped her, a combination of sigh and sob. "I've just now said to you—"

"Just do it," I urged. "Don't be afraid."

I left before she could answer. From inside the hack I looked back and saw her standing in the dim hallway, slender and rigid.

I ran newspaper ads touting the Forest Citys as "Crack Champions of the Northwest" and told Johnny to increase booth supplies a third in expectation of a sellout crowd. Champion, following my design, had had carpenters install the nation's first scoreboard atop our right-field fence: a wooden billboard with a walkway on which boys waited to hang the green metal plaques bearing white numerals on the hooks for innings. No longer would spectators strain to hear the scorer's megaphoned shouts. Dubbed the "telegraph board," it proved to be instantaneously popular.

The trouble was that only three thousand came out. A top-level opponent should have drawn more. I concluded that the small-town Illinois squad simply couldn't match the pull of a top eastern club. Several times during the contest I saw Champion gazing dolefully at me. I could guess his thoughts: Would we lose our shirts on all this new stuff? He looked positively funereal when Johnny ended up donating our unsold sausages and beef patties and buns to the Home for the Friendless. On the positive side, our latest innovation, a primitive version of Cracker Jack, was a budding success, though we hadn't gotten the blend of caramel, molasses, and corn syrup quite right yet.

During the game itself I was too busy to give off-diamond developments much thought. The Forest Citys showed up in new uniforms—again I was struck by this amateur club's affluence—with gray checked pants and ice-white shirts. From their grim demeanor it was clear they wanted to take us. And that with Allison gone, they thought they could do it.

Harry won the toss and sent them up. Barnes stepped to the plate and checked our defense. Harry had pulled a switch: he was pitching, Brainard catching, I manning center. It was risky, but it made sense. Brainard didn't possess a particularly strong throwing arm behind the plate, but he had quick hands and was savvy—and Harry's slow twisters wouldn't tax him. With Andy, George, or Mac catching, we'd sacrifice a great deal in the field.

The crowd buzzed and applauded Harry in his old position in the box. Shouts came for the "Old Vet" to show his pluck. Anticipating Brainard's speedballs, the Forest Citys overswung on Harry's dewdrops and went one-two-three in the first.

"So much for the Sucker State!" somebody yelled.

But we started off no better against Spalding, who worked smoothly, mixing speeds and brushing the corners. He obviously had a "book" on us after being knocked around in Rockford. George and Gould popped up; Waterman did likewise, but his dropped safely behind second. That brought me up in Allison's place.

There was no on-deck circle. Strikers generally took a few swings in front of their bench—as much to demonstrate stylish form as to loosen up. Our bench, painted bright red, of course, was situated in the shade of the Grand Duchess on the first-base side. I'd been swinging vigorously, trying to spot Cait and Timmy among a profusion of red parasols and handkerchiefs and hats.

"Sam!" said Harry. "Spalding's in form. Legs!"

Which meant that since runs might be hard to come by, we'd be aggressive on the bases. I stepped in and looked for the sign. Harry touched only the white parts of his uniform: take. I watched Spalding's first pitch blur past, scarcely able to pick up its spin. Waterman sprinted for second. The ump yelled, "Warning, striker!" Addy, fumbling in his haste to nail Waterman, dropped the ball. He swore and took his place again. I missed Spalding's next blazer by half a foot. Addy was up and throwing as Waterman scrambled for third. The peg had him cold, but he bamboozled the third baseman with a gorgeous hook slide. Just bring him home, I thought, waving the bat and digging in. I fouled off a low inside pitch and barely held back on a shoulder-high hummer. Then Spalding laid one down the pipe. With visions of sending it into space I strode forward—and realized too late he'd taken something off it. I tried to correct, swung awkwardly, and missed badly. Strike three. Shit!

"Don't get rattled," Harry told me. "Bear down in the field. We'll be fine."

Bats warmed up in the second. Forest City pushed across a run on slashing hits to right center, which I was glad to let Mac play. Harry singled in our half, stole second, and scored on Andy's liner to right. Andy swiped second and was doubled in by Sweasy, who scored on Mac's sacrifice fly.

Forest City came back in the third on Spalding's double, tallying three runs and regaining the lead. They whitewashed us again—twice in three innings they'd done it, an ominous trend. I fouled out to Addy my second time up. I wasn't the only one having trouble solving Spalding. The Stockings popped his rising fastballs up repeatedly, and the few grounders we managed all seemed to go straight to Barnes at short.

In the fourth, Brainard, playing agilely behind the plate, ran down a foul bound, and Mac speared a sinking liner to snuff a rally. We laid a goose egg on them in turn, and finally touched Spalding in our half, scoring four runs; with two out I stepped to the plate with Waterman again on third. Spalding, working me inside and out, finally got too cute. Timing an outside change-up, I drilled it up the right-center alley. The ball slammed off the fence and caromed among the carriages. By the time the outfielders retrieved it I'd slid into third. We led 8–4. Andy led cheers on the bench. The crowd roared. It was one hell of a moment. Standing there tingling and grinning, I wanted them all to be up there in the stands: Cait impressed, Timmy yelling his head off, O'Donovan seething.

Refusing to be blown out, the Rockfords came back stubbornly with three runs in the fifth. They were aided considerably by me. I went deep for Barnes's long fly, couldn't hold it, then overthrew the cutoff, allowing Barnes to circle the bases. The next Forest City crushed one off the fence, a mile beyond Andy. When a hard-hitting lefty moved to the plate, Harry waved us over in a shift as severe as any ever put on for Ted Williams. Sure enough, the batter lined to Sweasy in what normally would have been the hole between first and second. We came in to take our licks—and got whitewashed again, on sensational fielding by Barnes.

"He's getting on my nerves," George complained, having a rare bad day at the plate.

Barnes was getting on all of our nerves. So was Spalding. The Rockfords trailed us like grim shadows.

Stockings 8, Forest Citys 7.

In the sixth, Harry and Brainard changed places. Brainard, tentative in the box without Allison's reassuring presence, walked the first Forest City. The second punched a hit-and-run single past Sweasy. Two infield outs produced a run. Only an acrobatic stop and snap throw by Waterman saved another. In the bottom half we regained our bare lead on Mac's double and a seeing-eye single by Gould—who then brought Harry as close to cursing as I'd seen him by getting himself picked off first. My usually imperturbable mates showed signs of cracking.

In the next moment a foul off George's bat caught Addy full in the face. Blood spurted from his nose as he sagged to the turf. I thought he'd been brained. We ran to him; his nose was smashed, his cheek already swelling. I brought ice from the booth. At length he staggered to his feet and insisted on playing. It was plucky, everybody agreed. In my estimation it was also fairly stupid. Nobody asked me.

When Addy led off the seventh, Harry pulled us in a bit, figuring the injury had sapped his strength. But the stocky hitter connected on a high pitch and drove it far over my head. Again they had knotted the score, 9–9.

I led off in our half. Spalding glowered, mindful of my triple last time. Brush-back fastball, I guessed. As he strode into his motion I adjusted my stance. The ball blurred toward me, rising slightly and spinning inside—but not as far as Spalding intended. I swiveled into it and whipped the bat. *CRACK!* The ball rocketed into the blue summer sky. It hung for a long moment above the left-field fence before dropping lazily into Kenner Street.

[216]

I wish I had videotape of it. I wish shutters and film had been fast enough to capture any of the lovely sequence that followed as I rounded the bases and was mobbed at the plate. The *Commercial*—bless Millar's florid soul—would term it "a grand old hit," one of the "longest ever made on the grounds," and the *Gazette* would say that "Fowler, a new hand, filled Allison's place admirably." I stashed the clippings in my special drawer.

A grown man hitting a ball over a fence. Silly, probably, but for an instant of existential joy, a moment of pristine *sensation,* it was hard to beat. Andy was all over me. Mac and George and Gould bobbed around me like toys on a string. Harry nodded as if it had been no more than he'd expected. Brainard, Waterman, even Sweasy, pumped my hand. Heady stuff. No wonder old-timers don't want to quit.

The crowd stayed frenetic as Harry followed with a ringing double. Andy grounded out, but Brainard drove a ball into the corner and circled the bases when it skipped past the right fielder. They shut us down then, but we'd scored three.

Stockings 12, Forest Citys 9.

If there were any justice it would have ended there, with me the day's hero. But it didn't. The Forest Citys jumped all over Brainard in the eighth. The first hitter smashed a liner that I botched trying to play on the hop; he took second and scored on Spalding's grounder that George fielded cleanly but slipped setting himself to throw. The next batter doubled, sending Spalding home. Addy followed with a slow bouncer that George charged, picked up beautifully, and whipped to first. But Gould was astride the bag. Addy lowered his head, broken nose and all, and plowed into the big first baseman, knocking him flat. The ball whizzed past. Addy scrambled all the way to third while the other Forest City scored. Four runs in. We were behind now, and getting clobbered.

Harry changed places with Brainard again. He got his first man to pop to Sweasy. As the second stepped in, he motioned me toward right. Sure enough, a lazy fly came directly at me.

"Got it?" yelled Mac, running toward me.

"Yeah, mine!" I caught the ball and saw Addy tagging up at third. Bypassing the cutoff, I threw to the plate with all my strength. Addy, trotting in leisurely, was astonished as the ball whistled to Brainard on one bounce. Again he put his head down and crashed into a defender. Brainard made the tag and held the ball. But the umpire ruled that Addy—sprawling supine, out cold—had touched the plate first. Brainard stalked off furiously. Sweasy rushed in, foaming with rage, threatening to punch the official. Harry wrestled him away.

"Throw was a dinger, Sam!" yelled Andy from left.

[217]

The next hitter fouled out to end the inning. They'd scored five runs and led by two. Then, rubbing it in, they whitewashed us in the bottom of the eighth. Another zero went up on the new telegraph board.

Stockings 12, Forest Citys 14.

An ominous stillness settled over the stands. The next minutes held the fate of our 29–0 win streak, the longest ever. Not to mention Cincinnati's position in the sporting world.

Sweasy cursed loudly as we started toward the field. Harry told him to be quiet and gathered us together.

"What's required," he said, looking each of us in the eye, "is that we try our best. Play hard and fairly. Every moment. This inning is no different from any other."

If so, I reflected, why was he saying it now?

"God willing," Harry concluded, "we will prevail."

"Let's dose 'em with our ginger!" Andy yelled, thrusting out his hand. We clasped ours over his and yelled as we burst away toward our positions. I bellowed with the rest, energized. The Forest Citys looked at us sardonically.

I'd seen each Stocking carry the club at one time or another with clutch fielding, hitting, running. But I'd never seen us enter a ninth inning trailing. Now that the chips were truly down, would one of us be able to rise to the occasion?

I soon found out.

Pitching brilliantly, Harry treated the Forest Citys to an amazing assortment of floaters. They cocked their bats, crouched, poised, lunged, swung ferociously—and went down in order.

"Now," he said, when we reached the bench, a smile playing on his lips, "it's our turn to test *their* mettle."

I then had to face a central fact I'd tried to keep out of my mind until that moment: I would lead off the bottom of the ninth. I hefted my bat as the crowd's clamor built into a chant.

"Home RUN! Do it AGAIN! *HOME RUN!*"

God, wouldn't it be sweet? No, don't think about it. Meet the ball. Get on base. Two to tie. Three to win. I stepped in and swung in level grooves, concentrating.

Spalding didn't give me a thing I could handle. I looked at off-speed teasers on the corners, then misjudged a rising fastball and popped it straight back to Addy. So much for storybook. Three fucking pitches. I walked back to the bench, staring at the ground. The stands were eerily silent. I almost wished they'd booed.

"Lift your head, Sam," said Harry on his way to the plate. "You're a Red Stocking!"

God bless you, Harry Wright.

"START IT, HARRY!" bellowed George. I'd never heard either of the Wrights exhort the other on the diamond. But this was no time for sibling restraint.

I forgot my own failure in the drama of this new confrontation: thirty-four-year-old Captain Harry battling the nineteen-year-old phenom. Spalding worked the edges cautiously. Harry waited, poised gracefully, no sign of tension; the man should have been an Olympic athlete. He stepped, swung, and met a low fastball smoothly. We jumped to our feet at the crack of the bat.

"I knew it!" George exulted.

The ball slashed over Barnes's straining fingers into left. My voice was lost among the others. Mac pounded my back as Andy strode purposefully to the batter's box.

"Come on!" I yelled. "You can do it!"

The crowd was up now, imploring. Spalding, abandoning finesse, came at Andy with nothing but heat, bent on overpowering the smallest Stocking. Andy took a ball, watched a strike, fouled off four consecutive fastballs—timing the big pitcher and wearing him down. Harry took off from first as Spalding came in with another fastball. Choking up on the bat, Andy spanked the ball into right. Again we leaped up as Harry made third easily, and now the tying runs were on the corners, our fastest man on first. I felt myself beginning to hope.

Brainard stepped to the plate, toothpick waggling. If he was nervous he didn't show it. Noise erupted from the crowd. From third Harry flashed a sign to Andy and Brainard, but I couldn't believe I'd seen correctly: STEAL!

Spalding looked in, concentrating on Brainard. Harry got an enormous jump and broke for the plate at the instant Spalding moved into his windup. Andy simultaneously sprinted for second. Brainard leaned forward, masking Harry's approach until the last possible instant. Then he stepped back as Harry dove headlong for the plate, his body stretched in the air, one arm reaching beneath Addy, who had caught the rising pitch and plunged to make the tag. There was a pileup and a curtain of dust.

The umpire spread his arms. "Safe!"

I nearly peed my pants. I'd never seen anybody try a stunt like that under those circumstances. Maybe Jackie Robinson did it, I don't know. But nobody—NOBODY—could have beaten Harry that afternoon. The play galvanized us. I could almost feel energy draining from the Rockford players as a big white 1 appeared on our peg on the telegraph board.

Stockings 13, Forest Citys 14.

[219]

Brainard shook Harry's hand matter-of-factly and stepped back in. With the crowd still vibrating over the double steal, he poked Spalding's first pitch safely into left center. Andy sprinted home well ahead of the throw. The game was tied.

"It's curious," said George on the bench. "Brainard's not big, fast, or strong. He's certainly not dependable—yet he beats you. Last year when I was on the Morrisanias and the Stockings upset our cart here, it was Brainard made the winning run. Same thing against the Mutes on the tour, remember? I'll wager he does it again."

Just as he said it, Sweasy sent a looper that fell short of the charging left fielder and just beyond Barnes's clutching fingers. Brainard, running hard, slid across the plate to pull out the victory, 15–14.

Instead of 29–1 we were 30–0.

After the final outs, the crowd spilled onto the field, mobbing us. We dispensed with songs and cheers and ran for the clubhouse. The glum visitors challenged us to games in Chicago and Rockford the following week. After wrangling free lodging and a fat slice of gate receipts, Champion accepted.

Timmy waited at the gate. "We got here in time to see you make your run, Andy!" he yelled.

Great, I thought. It meant he had missed my homer and seen me pop up in the clutch.

I looked up the lane and saw Cait. She seemed to float toward us in a pale green dress that set off her jet hair and jewel eyes.

"I couldn't keep Tim home," she said. "He'd have burst."

"You oughtn't be here alone," Andy said.

"You struck well," she replied, ignoring what he'd said. "The ladies cheered you again."

"Sam knocked a homer," Andy said. "Clean over the fence."

"You DID?" Timmy said.

"It's a worthy thing to do?" Cait asked.

Timmy explained a home run.

"I saw you perform that, did I not?" Her tone suggested that since I'd shown myself capable of it, why make further fuss?

"Yes," I said. "Are you accepting my invitation?"

She shook her head. "I must go straight back."

"I see." I tried to hide my disappointment. "Maybe there's time to take Timmy in the clubhouse. Most of the team's still there."

"Could I?" he implored. "Please, Mother?"

Her answer nearly caused my mouth to fall open.

"Would you take him, Andy? I want a word with Mr. Fowler."

Andy said he'd be delighted. As they moved off, we stood silently.

Birds sang in the nearby elms. Dusk was coming on. I tried to imprint in my memory the freckles sprinkled on her nose and cheeks.

"I believe I owe you an answer," she said gravely.

"You do?"

"I thought about little else last night," she said. "I wanted to deny what you said about something happening to both of us. But I cannot keep denying what I know inside to be true." Her tone softened. "Even should I not want it so." She paused. "This must sound quite the mystery."

"I'm not sure," I said.

" 'Tis strangest of all that it was going on well before you arrived. Although I didn't know for a *certainty* till the night you first appeared with Andy."

"Know what, Cait?"

The green eyes held depths into which I could have plunged and lost myself forever.

"That someone very like you, Mr. Fowler, would be coming to me."

$$\diamond \ 16 \ \diamond$$

I saw her only once before we left for Chicago. It was a mild and sleepy Sunday when I called for her and Timmy in a rented carriage. We stopped at the Downtown Fifth Street Market—where vendors were talking violent opposition to a plan to raze the market and erect a fountain—and at Findlay's, housed in a huge iron structure. Fully provisioned, we went up to Garden of Eden Park and spread our picnic beneath an oak on the edge of a hillside meadow.

Timmy alone seemed free of self-consciousness. He steered conversation, insisting that I tell him everything I knew about baseball and the Stockings. He was ecstatic when I presented him with a bat I'd repaired with brads and glue, a light one that Hurley had cracked. I'd brought another ball, too, and we played catch while Cait made sandwiches.

"I fancy being a pitcher," he said. "Is Mr. Brainard truly bigger on his throwing side, like Andy says?"

"Acey *does* look a little lopsided without a shirt on," I said. "His right arm's definitely longer, too."

"Honor bright?"

I laughed. "Honor bright."

He examined his own skinny arm. "You think someday . . .?"

"*That's a strong arm you've got, Samuel.*"

"*Like Christy Mathewson's?*"

"*Could be.*"

"Let's make a pitcher's box," I said, tracing a rectangle on the ground with the bat. "We'll use the tree as a backstop. You pitch and I'll knock 'em back."

"For a certainty, he's taken to you," Cait said later as we sat beneath the tree watching Timmy explore the meadow. "He's often jealous if another takes my attention."

"O'Donovan?" I said, and mentally kicked myself.

"Timothy doesn't care for him, it's true," she said. "And Fearghus isn't one for children. But he's been good to us."

"I see." So far we'd stuck to safe topics like Timmy and Andy and childhood recollections of Ireland. Suddenly the terrain was uncertain.

"Yes, truly, we're obligated to Fearghus," she said. "It's troublesome to know he'd not accept my being here like this."

"But here you are."

"Yes, here I am."

I stole a long look at her as she brushed an insect away. Her face, framed by the dark curls, looked almost fragile in its soft paleness. The silver ring glinted for an instant in the sun. There was so much we didn't know about each other. But it was all right; I was where I was supposed to be. I rested my head on my coat and drowsed pleasurably beside her in the warm shade; not even inadvertently did we touch.

"Cait," I breathed, not aware I'd said it out loud.

"Hmm?" she murmured.

"Oh, I . . . just said your name."

She said tentatively, "Samuel."

It whispered among the rustlings of the grasses.

Later, walking back to the carriage, she said, "When I was a girl I would go each day to sit in a lovely green dell. It was my secret place." She shook her head slowly. "It's been so long since I've thought of that."

I looked at her silently, in love beyond my depths.

"Thank you so much for bringing us, Samuel."

The St. Louis Empires, "Champions of Missouri," blew in early in the week, boasting of how their heavy strikers would beat new tunes on us. I doubted it, especially now that Allison was back. After practice Andy and I saw the end of their game against the Bucks. The visitors won, 27–14, but we knew they didn't have a prayer against us.

The Empires were saved by rain, as it turned out. No longer boasting, they trailed 23–0 when a deluge ended matters in the top of the fourth. There would be no makeup, since we had to leave the next day.

Another train trip. We arrived in Milwaukee at suppertime, twenty-two hours after leaving Cincinnati. Missing no opportunity, Champion had scheduled a game the next day against the local Cream Citys. We stayed at the Lake House, a picturesque inn opposite Union Depot and the steamboat docks. The evening was warm, the sky streaked with vermilion and orange. Andy and I sat on our second-story veranda and gazed out at Lake Michigan.

"You ever miss bein' back home?" he asked.

"Yeah, I guess." At this point "home" seemed an abstraction.

"Your friends and kin," he persisted. "You still don't recall much about 'em?"

"It sort of seems like they're all dead."

"You must feel some cut off."

"At times."

"I guess you don't want to go into it."

"There just isn't much to say, Andy."

"Okay," he said, unconvinced. We sat in silence as the last sunlight disappeared and the lake turned vibrant blue and then purple.

In the morning we got the obligatory city tour. The featured highlight was the National Military Asylum, a forbidding edifice filled with semicomatose patients and equipment so primitive I couldn't understand how anybody survived hospitalization. The others seemed impressed by the facility. God help them. Anyway, the grounds were beautiful.

Everywhere in Milwaukee people stared at us and exclaimed, "The Red Stockings! The champion ballists!" Shortly before three we were escorted to Cream City Park, where we found the grounds crowded with some three thousand spectators. The field was rough and pebbly, making every ground ball dangerous.

The "CC's" were Wisconsin champs, but they hadn't faced anybody like us. I got a kick out of watching them gape at the shots from our bats and contort themselves trying to connect with Brainard's tosses. By the end of seven innings, when an end was mercifully called, we had hammered seventy-seven hits for a hundred and forty-seven bases. George went ten for ten, including two long homers, three doubles, a triple, and six steals. Harry, true to form, refused to let us ease up. The poor CC's managed only nine hits. The final score was 85–7.

When we left for Chicago on the overnight steamer *Manitowoe*, a number of the CC's were on board. "Wanna see you face the Rockfords," one explained. "Everybody within five hundred miles'll be there."

He was hardly exaggerating. The atmosphere in Chicago rivaled Troy before the Haymaker game or Brooklyn before we met the Mutes. The Forest Citys, touring triumphantly after the narrow loss to us, had defeated the Buckeyes, 40–1; Mansfield, 83–14; Detroit, 32–10. They were riding high again.

Champion and no fewer than two hundred Cincinnati club members met us at Chicago's steamer dock and took us to the Revere House, where we banqueted with the Forest Citys. We learned that huge delegations were on hand from Detroit, St. Louis, and Cleveland—

plus virtually the whole town of Rockford—and that betting was incredible. Chicago's gamblers were backing the Forest Citys.

"Don't they know I'm here?" Allison demanded.

"They know it," said one of the Forest Citys. "They figure we'll warm you anyhow."

"Not by a long chalk," said Allison.

I'd never seen Champion happier. The raucous crowds swelling the foot of Ontario Street near the lake shore and trying to enter Ogden's Skating Park numbered at least ten thousand. Admission was pegged at fifty cents. Champion had negotiated half for us, a fourth for the Forest Citys, the remaining fourth for a sponsoring Chicago club. No carriages were allowed; Ogden's was literally packed with bodies. We watched in amazement as men stormed the fences like besieging invaders, many with tickets clamped in their teeth. An overloaded bleacher toppled, trapping several persons beneath it. Then dozens of brawling young roughnecks burst through the foul ropes and surged over the field. It was the most chaotic ballpark scene I'd witnessed.

As if inspired by it, we and the Forest Citys put on a truly horrendous performance—"first-class muffinism," Harry said disgustedly—once the diamond was cleared. It wasn't wholly our fault. The field was terrible: bumpy, pitted, and splashed with white sand in right; worse, the fences were so close that the captains decided that balls hit over them—or over the high sand bank in left—were automatic doubles. The afternoon saw far too many of them.

Scoring nine runs in both the third and fourth, we burst to a 19–5 lead. To loud boos, the Forest Citys crumpled as we tallied a whopping twenty runs in the sixth. Harry pitched the final innings, allowing ten runs, but by then it didn't matter. George sealed things with a blistering homer in the eighth, and we wrapped it up, 53–32.

We got off the field in a hurry. Harry sent me around the clubhouse to show each player his fielding column in the score book. We'd committed eight outright errors and any number of bonehead mistakes.

"I know," Andy groaned when I approached. "Muffed two balls, slow handling on that caulker down the line, caught out four times striking."

In an afternoon of general slugging Andy had scored five times and been put out four—seemingly not too bad, yet only Mac had done worse on the Stockings.

We shared a train car to Rockford with the Forest Citys. Addy wasn't his usual wisecracking self. Barnes had disappeared. Spalding maintained an aloof silence. They'd had visions, I guessed, of defeating us in front of record crowds and seeing *their* pictures in national magazines. Instead, they'd been clouted around the lot and now faced the possibility that even on their home diamond they could not beat us in a fourth and final game.

There was talk of rumored plans in Chicago to field a top-notch pro club next season, the White Stockings. Businessmen were reportedly raising large sums to recruit ace players at no less than two thousand apiece—an unheard-of salary base. Brainard allowed as how he would play for them at that price; Sweasy and Allison said pretty much the same. George was noncommittal, though I suspect he was tempted. I admired Andy, Mac, and Gould, who said flatly that they would stay with Harry. It seemed to me that more than money was involved: Harry had molded them into the best team ever and gotten them the first guaranteed salaries. They owed somebody something, in my opinion. Waterman said nothing on the subject, but I figured he'd go with Brainard. Nobody asked what I'd do.

Banners flapped over the streets of Rockford. A brass band greeted the Forest Citys at the station. Local pride was untouched by the debacle in Chicago. After all, weren't their home-grown boys putting the town on the map?

We waited out a sleepy—boring, to be more precise—Sunday. I hiked along the Rock River thinking of Cait and wondering if she thought of me. I wished I could take her boating on the river. And Timmy, too. It was strange to find myself thinking of him instead of Hope and Susy on a day like this. But I felt little guilt or sadness. They seemed of another age, distant now.

That evening I read Twain's new piece, "Personal Habits of the Siamese Twins," in the current *Packard's Monthly*. I remembered his fondness for Barnum's Museum, where the twins, Chang and Eng— still alive and connected at the chest—had once been employed. Predictably, Twain's humor was of the tall-tale sort. He had the twins fighting on opposite sides in the war and taking each other captive. I was moderately amused. But when Andy picked it up he chuckled, snorted, guffawed—and soon was reading it to the others.

> "They filled Chang full of warm water and sugar and
> Eng full of whisky, and in twenty-five minutes it was
> not possible to tell which was the drunkest. Both were
> as drunk as loons—and on hot whisky punches. . . ."

They all howled. I realized I was still considerably out of synch in certain areas of taste.

The *Chicago Tribune* reported that the Brooklyn Eckfords had taken two of three from the Mutuals and now held the whip pennant. The item also noted that their '63 championship team would play the new '69 champs. A sort of old-timers game. Something like that might make a good promotional at the Union Grounds, I thought. And how about some kind of giveaway day? Hmm, not bad.

In other reprinted items, the New York Tribune branded as "monstrous" a scheme to revive the Chinese coolie trade to alleviate the South's current labor shortage. In Philadelphia, Elise Holt's troupe was wowing packed houses with shows "to which Miss Holt lends all the fascination of her shapeliness and the indecorousness of her posturings." I closed my eyes and got fragmentary pictures of blond hair and high-kicking legs.

That night I made the mistake of testing Brainard's skill on a pool table. Spotting me points and shooting left-handed, he won twenty bucks in less than two hours.

"Can you pitch lefty too?" I joked.

"Depends how much cash is at stake," he said tersely, lining up a shot.

Which was typical of him lately. Brainard dressed as fashionably as ever but wasted little personal charm—of which he had plenty—on any of us but Waterman. I would like to have been friends, but Brainard's demeanor said clearly that he'd go his own way, thanks.

We played at the fairgrounds again. This time there was no gusting wind. Partly to conserve Allison's hands and partly to keep the Forest Citys guessing, Harry started Allison in right and Mac at pitcher; he brought George in to hurl in the second and finished with Brainard.

Angry and doubtless feeling they were being toyed with, the Forest Citys jumped out in front, 5–2. Then Brainard went to work in earnest, allowing only two runs while shutting them out in four of the last six innings. Behind Sweasy's solid hitting and Andy's baserunning, we notched seven runs in the fourth, four in the fifth, and went on to win convincingly, 28–7.

Nobody had held them to so few runs all season. In thumping our foremost western rivals, we'd extended our streak and given critics the scientific baseball display they wanted. And now we were heading home.

"Listen to this," Andy read later from the Winnebago County Chief. " 'When the boys of the F.C.B.B.C. meet any other than the nine red-legged giants gathered from the four quarters of the Union and rendezvoused at Cincinnati, they can gobble them up; but when they run against these nine scarlet runners they come in contact with nine gentlemen whom they cannot handle.' "

"About time a country paper admitted we were the best," said Allison. "They can say we're from the moon, so long's they admit we warmed their butts."

" 'Nine red-legged giants,' " Andy repeated. "That's good writing, ain't it, Sam?"

"What if it had been 'red-legged midgets'?" I countered.

He grinned. "That'd narrow it to our *top* aces!"

We reached the Pearl Street depot on Tuesday just before dark. Champion was waiting to tell us he'd scheduled a game with the touring Syracuse club the next afternoon.

"I'm not playing!" Brainard exclaimed as soon as Champion was out of hearing. "They're wringing us dry. I didn't sign on to sweat my life away!"

Harry stepped in front of him. "Asa, calm down."

"They're making money and puffing themselves off us," Brainard said angrily. "Are we getting a fair slice? Hell, no! They think we'll settle for banquets and parades!"

"You signed your contract," Harry said. "No one forced you." His tone was flat. "Be on the grounds tomorrow or catch a train home."

We drifted away. Hearing Waterman trying to pacify Brainard, I turned and walked back to them.

"Best leave him be when he's riled," Waterman said.

"Asa, we're all tired," I said. "I don't like the schedule lately either, but you can't blame Champion for trying to—"

"What the hell do you know?" He swung around and faced me, his voice an angry buzz. "I've pitched for this club till my arm's dead. I gave up my life to come out to this damned place. I've got financial obligations. In New York we'd be in the clover. But Holy Harry expects us to fall over dead to glorify him and his pet brother!"

"Oh, bullshit," I retorted. "Harry's just running his ball club, and you can't deny he does a hell of a job. Champion's trying to pay off the club's debts. Simple as that. There's no conspiracy against you."

" 'Simple as that,' " he repeated, jaw muscles working. "Well, I say some things ain't simple at all. Take what's happened with you, say. You used to be readier'n most to bend rules to suit yourself."

"I haven't forgotten how you helped me."

"You weren't no damn company man then," he said. "You hadn't hired on as Champion's flunky."

"Asa, you're well-known here," I said, trying not to let him provoke me. "You've got business sense. This concession thing at the ballpark just might take off. If we expand I could use another partner—"

"I ain't no huckster," he said, and spat on the platform. End of discussion.

It was dark at Cait's. The hack waited while I deposited the gifts from Chicago on the porch: for Cait a silver chain and pendant bearing two doves; for Timmy a pine toolbox and set of kid-sized carpentry tools. I left a note saying I'd see them soon and walked down the steps. Something caught my ear. I moved to the corner of the house. Muffled scraping and thumping seemed to come from directly below. Somebody working in the basement, I thought, and turned back to the hack.

In the morning I sent Johnny to ask if Cait and Timmy were coming to the game. And if I could visit that evening. He returned and said that nobody had answered his knock. The packages were not in evidence.

"Could you handle the pickups?" I said. "I want to find out what's going on." Seeing his reproachful look, I added, "Time and a half pay."

"Hell, Sam," he said, wiggling his ears comically, "for *that*, Helga and me'll do the works every time!"

Traffic was bad that morning. It took the better part of an hour to flag a hack and get across town. I arrived to find the boardinghouse as quiet as it had been the previous night. I banged on the door and shouted.

It opened suddenly, and there she stood, unsmiling, heartbreakingly beautiful.

"Cait, are you all right? I was worried."

"You needn't."

"What's the matter?"

"Nothing."

I tried to read her expression. "Did you get the presents?"

"We did, thank you. Tim was very excited and wants you to show him the use of the tools."

"I will. Where is he?"

"Away for several days."

I waited in vain for her to elaborate. "Cait, last night the place seemed deserted except for weird noises in the basement. You didn't answer for Johnny earlier. What's going on?"

"There's no mystery." I thought I saw apprehension flicker in her eyes. "The boarders are away just now. Fearghus has taken Tim on a trip with him."

"A trip? What about the basement?"

"I don't know what you heard, perhaps Fearghus packing."

"I see." I felt like I was running in place. "Did you like the necklace?"

She gazed at me for a long moment. "Why did you buy it?"

"Why . . .?" I blinked. "I guess I was thinking about you and—"

"No, Samuel, why did you buy *it?*"

"I thought you'd like it. I don't understand. Is anything wrong with it?"

She shook her head.

"For God's sake, I bring it for you and you act like I've done something wrong."

"Maybe you have."

I felt a surge of anger. "Are you going to explain that?"

She hesitated, then said, "I don't think I can bear to."

"That's great," I snapped, stomping down the steps. "Just great." If she said anything behind me, I didn't hear it.

◇ 17 ◇

By the time the game got under way, several things were obvious. One was that we hadn't overestimated the crowd—roughly two thousand were on hand—and therefore wouldn't have to deal with unsold food. Another was that Syracuse's Central Citys, youthful amateurs all, had no chance of winning against us. A third was that Harry, for the first time in my experience, was openly having trouble with some of the players.

Brainard showed up but sulked, complaining of a weary arm. Sweasy groused that we never got comp days for Sundays on the road. Allison griped that playing so often gave his hands no chance to heal. He had a point, but it was also true that since coming back and learning we'd nearly lost without him, he'd been acting quite the ace; his head was as swollen as his hands.

Exasperated, Harry pitched the whole game himself, stuck Brainard in right, and moved Mac to center. Later he brought Brainard in behind the plate and switched Allison to right. Keeping score, I noticed things that must have been eating at Harry's guts: Waterman loafing to first on a pop-up; Sweasy failing to back up George on Andy's high throw; Gould forgetting how many were out.

With lackadaisical play came mix-ups that first amused the crowd but eventually brought boos: George dropping a pop-up after ostentatiously calling Harry off in the pitcher's box; George again, trying to score from first, failing to hear us yelling "Get back!" when Gould's liner was ruled foul, and being put out; Allison's halfhearted catching that encouraged the Central Citys to take liberties on the bases. Perhaps worst of all, in Harry's view, was almost everybody trying to knock the ball over the fence. Sweasy pounded three homers, George and Gould two each. But a lot of flies settled harmlessly in outfielders' hands. Harry observed it all with commendable stoicism, putting up with the sort of unscientific baseball he detested. We won easily—too easily—by a score of 37–9. Then we discovered he had been biding his time.

"Light practice at ten A.M.," he announced curtly in the clubhouse. "The Central Citys want to play again tomorrow. I've decided to accept that challenge. The day after that we'll play the Clevelands here. Starting this moment, anybody who complains or shirks will be fined immediately."

I glanced involuntarily at Brainard, whose dark eyes glittered with resentment.

"We carried Jimmy to his folks' house on Henry Street. His face was whiter than lime. I could feel him dying, the best feller I ever knew." Brainard pulled at his whiskey. His eyes were red-rimmed. "We were both twenty-one back then. Jimmy was the first ace, could've done anything in his life, but it ended in awful agony."

Brainard stared into his glass. Andy fidgeted; he'd heard it before. Across the table, Waterman arranged toothpicks in geometric patterns, his whiskey untouched. Andy and I nursed beers. The four of us were hunched over a table in a private room at Leininger's, an oyster bar on Fourth.

"Jimmy Creighton," mused Brainard. "Flung balls past the best strikers in the land. Nobody could touch us on the Excelsiors. We toured up and down New York—first time any club did—everybody making a fuss over us. Then we won matches in Philly and Baltimore. People couldn't thank us enough for our exhibitions. They took us into their homes, let us know we were *respected and wanted!*" He refilled his glass and downed the liquid in one swallow. "It wasn't all so goddamned organized then. We played for the sport of it and made out fine. Jimmy was the only one got a regular salary. He was the first true professional, you know. Some claim Al Reach of the Athletics, but I know better. The rest of the Excelsiors shared the gate receipts, all of us in it together. Not like now, when those paying ain't the ones playing. They take all our profits and use 'em however they care to!" He looked at me sharply. "Now they're proposing to sell stock. They treat us like factory hands already. You watch, next they'll try to auction us like niggers."

"How did Creighton die?" I asked.

"Busted his gut open, the doc said. Jimmy was thin, didn't carry much meat. Struck a ball so hard that something snapped inside him. Ran the bases to make his run, then collapsed crossing home. All us Brooklyn ballists went in on a marble headstone with a bat and ball. It's up on Tulip Hill, in Greenwood."

Brainard wiped his eyes. "I miss old Jimmy," he said thickly. "Miss

[232]

them old times. Ask Harry, he knows how it was before he turned himself over to Champion and the sucking politicians."

I looked at Waterman. His face wore its usual bland mask. Our eyes met. I thought I saw a hint of something in his glance. Amusement? Concern?

"We played like gents and were treated like gents." Brainard's voice rose aggressively. "Lots of times we'd banquet with the other club—spread the table right there on the grounds after. We didn't play for riffraff, neither. One time, against the Atlantics, when toughs kept yelling insults, we walked off the field cool as could be, even though we were leading eight to six, with piles of money riding on the outcome. That was in 'sixty." He sighed noisily. "Jimmy passed on in 'sixty-two, and that's when it all started to go sour. Now it's all for cash, ballists revolving from club to club, jumping like beetles around the country."

Nobody bothered to point out that Brainard himself was playing in a strange city, for cash.

"C'mon, Acey," said Waterman. "Let's go, match tomorrow."

"Match every damned day!" Brainard snapped. "They think we're machines, use us however it suits 'em—which means scramble for every dime in sight—and we're supposed to turn out and bow and grin. And never lose. All so Champion can make speeches and ride in parades. Well, I ain't playing tomorrow, that's it."

"C'mon, Acey." Waterman practically lifted him from his chair.

"Harry knows better." Brainard waggled his finger at us as Waterman pulled him to the door. "His brother skips practice or shows late for a train, what happens? Nothing! But you heard him today. He'll keep my money if I so much as *say* something he don't care to hear. Is that how gents go about their sport? Harry knows—" The closing door cut him off.

Andy and I looked at each other. "What do you make of it?" I said.

"Jealous, mainly. Acey figures it should be his time on top."

I nodded. "But something else is bugging him, too."

"I think the same," said Andy. "But I don't know what it could be."

This time she opened the door readily. "Hello, Samuel," she said matter-of-factly, as if I dropped by every night at ten. "I'm missing Tim and feeling alone in this big house. I'm glad for your company."

"Are your boarders still away?"

"Yes, it happens sometimes. They'll be back tomorrow night, I believe."

"And Timmy?"

"Tim also. Would you like tea?"

[233]

She took me to her kitchen, where I sat next to an iron wood stove. Pans were suspended overhead. I watched as she prescalded a teapot and added three spoonfuls of black tea to water.

"One for the pot," she said. "The Irish always make it the same—strong enough to trot a mouse on, Father said."

While it steeped, she showed me her tea cozy; it was white with blue embroidered flowers and had come over with the family, one of the few possessions she had from that distant life.

I watched her graceful movements. The oil lamp in the room made her skin almost amber. As she pushed strands of hair back from her cheek I realized I didn't even know what her bare arms looked like; I had never seen them. God, what a repressed age.

"You're lovely," I said.

She did not reply, her head bent as she poured milk into cups and then added the tea. My vision was caught by her thick, luxuriant black hair, then by the flash of metal on her hand.

"Let me see your ring," I said, taking her hand. I bent and looked closely at the design. Worked into the worn silver, a heart was framed by two hands and topped by a crown. Her fingers trembled feather light in my hand; she withdrew them.

"It was from Colm," she said softly. "I'm sorry for this morning. Your gift touched me, for a certainty, but . . ."

"Yes?"

"Samuel, there are two doves on it."

"And?"

She lowered her head. "Oh, this is so hard. Colm means 'dove' in Gaelic, Samuel."

"I see." I felt as if something had hit me. "Well, I'm sorry about that. Unfortunate coincidence."

"There's more to be told," she said, "but I never thought I would."

"Do you want to?"

"I think I *must* tell you." Her eyes rose to mine, unfathomable as whorls of serpentine. "Some weeks after Colm died, there came a pale gray mourning dove. . . ."

It appeared on her windowsill each day and looked in at her, its shadings muted and delicate. She put crumbs out; they were not taken. She tried to coax it inside, but it stayed calmly where it was. The idea that it wanted something from her, or wanted ..er to understand something, began to haunt her.

"Then one day it was gone. It never came back. Another light in my life had gone out. I felt I'd failed the poor creature, as I'd failed Colm."

"Wait," I said. "Didn't Colm die in the war?"

"Yes, but I didn't stop him from going, don't you see? I couldn't

[234]

hold him, even when I gave him my body—for which I believed God would surely punish me."

"But if you loved him, and you did everything you could—"

"I know that now, Samuel, but then everything was so confused. Colm had been the whole of my world. For him to leave me forever, and then the dove, his namesake, to leave too. . . . Do you understand?"

"I think so."

"It devastated me again. Tim was still several months away. I was big as a cow, and hysterical. Mother took me to a spiritualist—"

"Was her name Clara Antonia?"

She looked at me quizzically. "How did you know?"

I tried to gather my thoughts. Somewhere a composite picture must exist. All I had were fragments. "Andy mentioned her," I said.

"Oh, Andy. He and Brighid, always the practical ones. 'Twas Mother and me respected the Old Knowledge—we'd have burned as witches in other times."

"What did Clara Antonia say?"

"That the dove was truly Colm, and that my suffering had brought him great distances. She said it was hard to believe he stayed as long as he had. The message he brought must have driven him through unimaginable hardship."

"And could she tell you his message?"

She shook her head. "But he'd delivered it, she said, and I should search my heart, for it was there."

"Did you?"

"Ah, God, I tried." A tremor edged her voice. "Everything I seemed to receive involved Colm's perishing, his being dead. It was too painful."

The ghost figure of the soldier appeared in my mind, arm beckoning or pointing.

"I became frantic, thinking I'd failed yet again. I was desperate to try anything. So that when Fearghus and John O'Neill wanted to bring me here to start a new life, I insisted on journeying first to the ground where Colm fell."

"To the battlefield?"

"In Maryland, yes. Fearghus flatly said no, he'd never go back there. Doing so was terribly sad for John, I know, but he went with me. And he had men brought who could answer my every question."

"Can you tell me?"

"You truly want to hear?"

"Yes," I said, the ghost soldier still in mind, "I do."

She talked for a long while, a rush of words spilling softly. She did not cry, though she came close. Colm O'Neill joined Meagher's Irish Brigade in 1862 and marched off under summer skies to rousing music and cheers. Two months later, one September afternoon, he sprawled into oblivion at Antietam. It was, Cait had learned, one of the war's bloodiest—and stupidest—military engagements. The Irish boys were ordered to attack Longstreet's rebels dug in along a sunken road soon to be called Bloody Lane. In front of it the Confederates had laid fence rails. These positions, lying just beyond the crest of a hill, could not be hit effectively by rifle fire or even cannon. More rebels were concealed in a cornfield behind the forward lines, with artillery trained for maximum devastation. It was a death trap.

The brigade moved toward the crest. Flags with the golden harp of Eire fluttered beside the Stars and Stripes in the autumn sunlight. So many of those green banners were shot to tatters that boys set leafy sprigs in their caps so that they could fight and die beneath the green. They launched themselves into an inferno. The hill exploded in fire and smoke, eruptions of earth, deafening noise. Musket fire raked them. Cannon volleys decimated them. In the first minutes, half the Sixty-third New York lay slaughtered. The brigade ran out of ammunition only a hundred yards from Bloody Lane, held its position in the maelstrom, was reinforced, charged blindly again. And again. Of the first twelve hundred, less than five hundred still lived. They fought on. Colm was in the final advance which cleared the last of the enemy from Bloody Lane, by then so filled with corpses it no longer served as a trench. They had done the superhuman, but the Union commander, cautious McClellan, failed to commit reserves for the decisive blow. Lee's army limped away, still intact. All the valiant Irish lads, some would claim, had died for nothing. Among the corpses in the woods near Bloody Lane was that of Colm O'Neill.

"I have his medal for bravery," said Cait. "I keep it with his letters. But there was nothing brave about that place. The wind sighed in the trees. There was desolation. And death. And I stood there with Colm's son inside me."

And finally she lowered her head and wept. She did not resist when I took her hand. I felt the work-roughened pads of her fingers and the soft skin on top and tried to think of some comfort to offer.

"I'm sorry," she said, wiping at tears. "I scarcely do this now."

"It's okay."

She looked up at me. "You're a kindly man, Samuel."

I squeezed her hand. "Since you're not cooking for boarders, how about coming to tomorrow's game? Harry's wife and little girls will be there. We could eat afterward."

"Perhaps," she said, rising. "But only after you have answered a question."

"Anything."

"Wait," she said, and left the kitchen. She returned and handed me a tintype. I held its cardboard frame carefully, aware of sensations building and weaving within me, a thin piping fugue. I saw the handsome features of a dark-haired boy about twenty. She didn't tell me who he was. She didn't need to. I stared into the laughing eyes, half expecting to feel the inexplicable force Cait's portrait had exerted on me. But there were only the piping sensations.

"What's your question?" I said, glancing up to find her eyes fixed on me.

"I have to know." Her voice was controlled. "Are you him?"

It stunned me. And yet I think I'd almost anticipated it. *Was* I Colm? So simple. A confusion of possibilities whirled in my brain. Why did she think I might be? What about her yellow dress?

"If I answer without knowing everything involved," I said slowly, "will you accept it without explanation?"

"Yes," she said. "For now."

"Then, for now, as best I can honestly tell, no, I'm not Colm O'Neill."

She swallowed and looked away.

"And if I'd said yes?" I asked.

She turned back, and, very gradually, the corners of her mouth curved upward. Some of the heaviness in the room dissolved.

"I suppose I would still attend your match tomorrow," she said. "But it would be vastly different, would it not?"

She sat beside Carrie Wright in the first row of the Grand Duchess. With only several hundred spectators on hand, Cait was easy to spot. And I was not alone in appreciating her ebony hair, pale features, and striking eyes.

"Who's the dark beauty next to Harry's missus?" Allison asked.

"Andy's sister," said Sweasy. "Prettiest lass ever in Newark. Us kids looked up to her like a queen. Ain't seen her in years."

"Remember, Sweaze, how she'd tell me, 'Don't let Charles stray into trouble'?" Andy said, laughing.

"Hell, I didn't *stray*," Sweasy said. "I went looking!"

"She's the true goods," said George, eyeing Cait in a way I didn't like at all. "Whyn't you introduce me after the match, Andy?"

"Sam's ahead of you," he replied. "Cait's never come here just to see *me* play."

"Sam?" George, sounding startled, appraised me curiously. Sweasy shot me a malevolent stare before turning abruptly toward the field. I gathered he wasn't overjoyed with Cait's taste either.

One of our problems on the diamond that afternoon was that the Central Citys weren't yet convinced of our superiority.

The other was that Brainard never showed up.

The game, which the *Enquirer* would call the "poorest ever played in the West," was long and frustrating. With Allison again begging off catching, Harry started Waterman behind the plate, Allison in right, Mac in center, and me at third. Early on, after a liner shot between my legs, Harry switched me with Allison. The Central Citys teed off on Harry's floaters. He tried George and Mac in the box. Nobody was particularly effective. At the end of seven we were tied, 22–22.

In the field we stunk. I had only one chance in right—a foul fly I couldn't reach to take on the bounce—but the others had plenty, and they botched far too many. Several of George's throws sailed ten feet over Gould's head. The usually sure-handed first sacker dropped others. Allison and Sweasy looked like they were asleep. The Central Citys, hardly defensive whizzes themselves, played with growing confidence. We were making them look good.

We didn't get to the Syracuse hurler until the top of the eighth. By then it was nearly eight o'clock, and the game had run well over three hours. The sun was settling behind the Mill Creek hills, darkening the smoke-laden sky. Venting our frustrations with hit after hit, we tallied thirteen runs before making a single out.

The Central Citys began to stall. If darkness ended play, the score would revert to the end of the previous inning—giving them a tie and spoiling our record. Their pitcher went through increasingly complicated windups, threw wildly, took his warnings, and issued walks. The catcher retrieved balls leisurely after letting them bounce past him. Knowledgeable spectators began to protest. On the bench we muttered curses as we watched the hurler study the ball, the batter, the defensive alignment, adjust his uniform, wind up, throw. Another wide called. The catcher jogged for the ball. Only when the ump threatened to call a forfeit did they clean up their act a bit.

Harry went down swinging on three pitches for our first out. Andy legged a shallow shot to left into a double. I slammed my first pitch over second for a single, scoring him. Sweasy rapped a ball to shortstop, who threw it suspiciously wide of first. Sweasy tripped and fell—deliberately, I was sure—on the baseline. The first baseman retrieved the ball and had no choice but to tag him. Two out.

And at that point it ended.

The Central Citys' president, having risen from the scorers' table to talk to the ump after Harry's strikeout, now rose again. In a voice that carried over the diamond, he announced that Harry and Sweasy had deliberately made outs, and that darkness made further play too dangerous. At his command the Syracuse players trooped off the field.

We were aghast at the flagrancy of it. There was plenty of light— we'd all played when it was far darker. Harry instructed Mac, due up next, to stay at the plate. He remained there a good five minutes while Harry argued our case. I found myself wondering about Harry's strikeout. I didn't think he'd deliberately lie or deceive. But he wanted fiercely to win. Had he subconsciously pulled a fast one?

The ump awarded us the game by the existing score of 36–22. Since Syracuse refused to continue, it seemed the only choice. I'd heard of clubs quitting the field after disputes, and I remembered Champion wanting to pull us out in Troy—where we most certainly would have taken a forfeit loss. The problem was that no standing body existed to settle disputes. The association met only in winter. We had our victory, but it left a bad taste.

We went to Andy's favorite eatery, the Main Street Dining Saloon, a noisy, crowded restaurant near the Gibson that offered tasty food at moderate prices. We apologized for the sloppy game, but Cait said that she had enjoyed Carrie Wright's company and found the game's disputes interesting. Later at the boardinghouse she fixed tea for me again. This time we talked of nothing very serious. I felt comfortable with her. When I asked about Timmy's return, she said sometime that night, she expected. I kept from asking any of the questions that occurred to me.

It was as though mentioning Brainard would jinx us—or maybe him. In the clubhouse we'd made no reference to his absence. But the next morning he got plenty of mention in the press.

I read Millar's *Commercial* piece with growing surprise. After recounting the Syracuse walkout, he mentioned that a "very self-important member" of the Stockings had been missing. Not content with that, he wrote, "Mr. Brainard, a very clever gentleman, whose opinion of himself has been considerably elevated by the praise of flatterers, was absent, and, as a consequence, his club found it pretty hard to pull through. . . ."

Whew, I thought, what's he doing?

Farther on, Millar wrote, "Allison, who has not yet revived from the large share of flattery lately bestowed upon him, refused to occupy his accustomed place. . . .

I had an uneasy feeling there was more to this than sportswriter carping. Millar usually mirrored Champion's views.

I heard my name and looked up. Waterman was striding toward my table in the Gibson dining room.

"Gotta talk," he said. "Private." His tone was forceful, his expression a degree less bland. For Waterman this was a highly emotional state.

"Sure." I finished my coffee.

Up in my room he said, "It's about Acey."

"I figured. Where's he been?"

"That's only part of it. Also *who* he's been there *with*."

"Okay, who?"

"First, you got to know Acey's hit the spirits hard lately. It's always a sign he's feeling sorry for himself. And booze ain't all. He likes to have people around who'll play up to him, make him feel important— and he's always been one to run with the champagne set."

"Let me guess," I said. "He's in over his head with gamblers."

"Partly that."

"Partly?"

"There's this woman named Maud," he said. "Acey's pet blonde, a fast one. He's been piling fancy clothes and jewelry on her. Got accounts at the big downtown stores. More than he can cover. Then he lost playing the trotters over at Buckeye track a couple days ago. He borrowed to cover that, and now they're squeezing him."

"Who is?"

"Don't know exactly, but I can tell Acey's scared of 'em."

I had a sudden suspicion. "Did he skip out on us so somebody could clean up betting long odds?"

He looked at me shrewdly. "You got a quick mind for larceny, Fowler."

"Well, did he?"

"No, but it'll look that way. What happened was, after you saw us at Leininger's I went home, but Acey kept drinking. He came up against the crowd he owes money to, and they wanted to collect. He couldn't pay 'em, being as how he didn't have the cash. They laid hands on him, saying they'd break his pitching arm. Acey fought loose and ran and hid at Maud's, where he filled her ear all night with how bad Harry treats him and how nobody truly appreciates him."

"Horseshit."

"Well, you and I might think so. But that's Acey. Anyhow, next thing he knew it was afternoon, past game time, and he was on the floor with the ugliest head of his life. He won't say it, but I think Maud doped his whiskey."

"I think I'm getting it," I said. "After the Central Citys lose nearly four to one in the first game, she tips somebody that Brainard will miss the second one. So they bet on Syracuse to lose no worse than, say, two to one, and they clean up when it ends thirty-six to twenty-two."

He nodded. "A whole lot of cash changed hands last night down on Vine. But I haven't come to the worst yet."

"You've got to be kidding."

"Nope," he said glumly. "Acey was in such a miserable state that he took it into his head he was washed up on the Stockings. He went over the bridge to Covington, still some drunk, and tried to sign on with the Live Oaks. First thing they did, naturally, was send word to Champion."

"Oh, shit," I said. "How's Champion taking it?"

"He wants to fire Acey."

"He wouldn't do that."

"No? Last year he sure as hell put Jack Hatfield on public trial, then made sure it got printed in every sporting paper in the country. And poor Jack was only going back to the Mutes, where me 'n' him revolved from in the first place; it was the Stockings who made raids on other clubs. Anyhow, Acey's in a tight spot, and he's only got one thing working for him."

"Harry needs him."

"Even that might not be enough. No, it's the win streak. The whole damn country is following us. You can be sure Champion doesn't want *that* to end."

"You think he'll let Asa stay, then?"

"I reckon he'll let him stew a bit, then allow Harry to talk him into giving Acey one more chance." He took a cigar out and rolled it in his fingers without lighting it. "It's the other part I'm hoping you'll help with."

"Jesus, Fred, don't you think I've butted in enough with gamblers?"

"If Acey could just get some cash, there'd be no trouble."

"How deep is he in?"

"Almost a thousand."

I thought it over. Maybe the Elmira money was mine only as some sort of trust.

"This afternoon be okay?"

"You'll lend it?" He looked surprised. "Sam, that's a hell of a thing. Not many'd do it. Acey'll stand good, sooner or later. You're the cash article in my book."

"A sucker is what I am."

"Maybe a little of that, too," he said wryly. "Acey brings it out in his pals."

I expected a harangue from Champion, at least a pep talk from Harry, but instead it was business as usual in the clubhouse that afternoon. Brainard suited up, red-eyed and sheepish. The others were curious, but nobody asked what had transpired.

"I guess Fred told you this counts a lot with me," Brainard said as we went out to the field.

"You were going to cover for me in Troy," I said.

"I owe you."

"Damn right."

The Clevelands, termed by Millar the "second best team in the state," looked snappy in white knickers and blue stockings patterned after ours. Allison's younger brother Art played first for them. I was pleased to hear him ask Allison about all the crap he'd been reading. Allison looked chastened. He was back behind the plate today, catching Brainard.

The Clevelands were wound so tightly that they took themselves out of things in the first inning. Their errors plus our relentless hitting—capped by Gould's drive over the fence—gave us a 9–0 get-away lead. The rest of the afternoon was a slugfest. Clouting seven more roundtrippers, we trounced them 43–27.

In the booth Johnny worked to exhaustion again, even though we had added another employee, Helga's cousin Anna. We'd abandoned Cracker Jack as too much trouble, but now had french fries—Saratoga potatoes—bubbling in a pot of hot oil. We sold everything by the seventh inning, netting 212 dollars. Champion informed me I was an innovative genius.

That night Cait, Timmy, and I went to a concert in Lincoln Park. I didn't see O'Donovan when I picked them up, and Timmy made no mention of their trip together. At first subdued, he brightened when I showed him the miniature sloop I'd bought for him in a toy store on Fourth.

"You'll spoil him," said Cait, watching him launch the little craft on the sailing pond.

"Good."

Lincoln Park was a wonder. Although the Union Grounds lay just behind, I'd spent little time in the park itself; usually I bustled through one corner of it after taking the Seventh Street cars to Freeman. This night the trees were lit magically with oriental lanterns. A blaze of lamps framed the central gazebo, where the Zouave band played.

We rented a rowboat and circled the little island where in daylight children played with squirrels and rabbits, fawns and peacocks. Timmy fell asleep under a blanket in the bow. I stopped rowing and we drifted silently on the dark water.

"I've been thinking," I said, "about everything you told me of Colm."

"Yes?" She faced me on the boat's other seat, shadows playing over her.

"Did you ever think that he came back as another kind of bird?"

"Another?"

"A redwing blackbird, say, or something larger—an owl or hawk?"

"No, why?"

"Just asking."

"I didn't tell you all that Clara Antonia said."

The throb I had heard before was in her voice. It was remarkably sexy, I decided. "What else?"

"She said that no matter how it might seem, death is not final, and that I should never despair. There is more than bare existence and the snuffing of that existence."

"Did she say what more there is?"

"Are you laughing, Samuel? Do you think my mind unbalanced?"

"No, I think you found what solace you could."

"It was more than solace. It was instruction. And in part it involved you."

"Me?"

"She said that a man would come to me through the family somehow. He would want to help. And I would want to love him, but would fight against doing so."

"And did she advise on *that?*"

"She said I should not fight, were it a true thing, for love is the means of transcendence, the bridge."

"To what?"

"That I'm not sure. It was vague and dreamlike to me. I believed that Fearghus was the man she meant. He was Colm's closest comrade. He visited our home—coming through the family, you see?—but it was all so soon. I knew he wanted me, but he was so different from Colm. Colm had been lighthearted, flowing with music and laughter. There was never music in Fearghus. And then they hurt him like an animal in a British jail, and he came back burning with a mad anger."

She hesitated before going on.

"The years passed, and I put the prophecy out of mind. It was part of back then, the horrible sadness. When Andy told me of your gift to Mother, I felt my soul being torn open. I struggled against the sad memories, against feeling so badly again."

"And then you got a good look at my mug."

"I was terrified of you. Of myself, to say it truly."

"But you relaxed when you saw I was too big and hairy to be Prince Charming."

A trace of a smile appeared. "Sometimes you're a stranger to yourself, Samuel. You frightened me, but I also saw a man who was exciting and alive. I saw that you loved Andy, and that you were kind. Most of all, I saw how you looked at me."

The band was playing a waltz. Cait's face was a pale oval in the moonlight. I moved close and put my arm around her. She leaned in, her hair brushing my shoulder, her weight precious against me.

"I'm not sure how to kiss a Victorian lady," I mumbled.

"And what might be one of those?"

"You're one."

"A *lady* would never be seen here unescorted." She smiled up at me, her eyes gray with moonglow. "I'm a woman, nothing more."

Our lips met, and her arm slowly encircled my neck. My fingers rested on her cinched waist, and I could feel the soft fullness of her breasts against my chest. She tasted of warm mint. The night burst into energy, brilliant, pulsing, intoxicating, glorious. The universe smiled.

◇ 18 ◇

On Saturday, August 7, Harry dismissed practice an hour early. I had rushed to pick up Cait and Timmy. By then the city was coming to a standstill. All week the papers had bristled with ads for railway excursions to Louisville, the area's best vantage point, and for boats to river locations beyond the city's smoke. The *Enquirer* ran long-winded installments by James Fenimore Cooper describing the eclipse of 1806. Today's, billed the "astronomical event of the century," had brought anticipation to a peak. Those unable to get out of Cincinnati, like us, headed for the cleaner air of the surrounding hills. Now we sat gazing upward, like millions of others.

As the sky took on a greenish hue, birds vanished to nests and mothers called their children. Cait shivered and pulled Timmy close to her. Through a piece of smoked glass I'd bought for the occasion, we watched the final sliver of sun disappear. Sitting in untimely darkness in our Eden Park meadow, we laughed at how strange it was to picnic during a solar eclipse.

I eyed Cait suggestively in the gloom and said, "Maybe you should go back to wearing hoopskirts."

"That's wanton and terrible!" she said, half-shocked and half-laughing. We'd seen a woman in one of the huge round things, fashionable a decade ago, step from a curb in front of the post office. Her foot went into in a pothole and she toppled to the pavement. Trapped and unable to rise in the hoopskirt, she kicked petticoated legs in the air and screamed bloody murder.

"Aw, let's not talk about that," said Timmy, bored.

"What shall we talk about?" said Cait.

"Baseball! When I grow up, I'll strike the ball heavy like Sam and run fast like Andy!"

"Okay," I said, "so long as you don't run like me."

"Can I try for the juniors, Mother?"

"We'll see." The laughter was gone from her voice.

"Fearghus says I'm to be a soldier, that's all he talked of when we went—" He halted abruptly and looked guiltily at me. "A soldier like my dad was," he went on. "Fearghus got mad when I said I'd rather be a hero at ball like Andy."

"Heroes fight for their country," said Cait.

"This is my country!"

"Tim, that's enough now!"

When the sky began to lighten he took his tool chest and worked on dead branches with the saw I'd showed him how to use. It was very possible, I realized, that Timmy was suffering from too many would-be father figures.

"I don't mean to cause you problems with him," I said.

"It's not you alone," she said. "He hears baseball everywhere. I can understand its attraction. I'm swept up in excitement myself at the grounds. But I'll not have him believe it's more important than the brotherhood."

"The Fenians?"

"Yes, of course."

"Why are they so important to you?"

"Isn't that equal to asking why a free Ireland is important?"

"Fair enough," I said. "But why do you feel it so much stronger than Andy does?"

"He's too young to remember Father's head bloodied by Orangemen in the pay of the damned English," she said. "He thinks Father died only of drink. The truth is he was first beaten down by those bastards. Finally, to save his family, he let them swindle us out of the land. Steal our land!" Her eyes flashed and her voice rose. "Andy's a pup, pampered from the first by Mother and Brighid and me. Now he'll play his game and be damned while others die for his country."

"He says this is his country," I said, and realized I had echoed Timmy.

"He's wrong, for a certainty." Her eyes locked with mine. "None of us has a true home here. They call us Micks and Paddys and Bridgets and worse, and deny us decent lodging and work."

"But isn't it getting better?"

She waved a hand, dismissing the idea.

"Do you want to return to Ireland?"

"To a free Ireland," she said emphatically. "And I shall do that very thing before I'm too much older."

I looked at her in silence, thinking how different we were, how problematic it was for me to love her.

"It was not my intent to carry on so, Samuel."

"I asked," I said. "To find out how you felt."

"Indeed you did," she said.

When I carried Timmy inside around nine, I thought I heard faint thumps below. Cait heard nothing. I was convinced it wasn't my imagination. Outside I stopped and listened again. Dead silence.

I slept fitfully. At six I was up and on the first horsecar. I approached Cait's from the rear, looking for a door to the basement. I found one secured with a heavy padlock and noticed that it was hinged from the outside—a fact I mentally filed—and that the sod in front was tramped down. Something or someone had been down there.

Rounding the corner of the house, I stopped abruptly. In the street stood a wagon and three-horse team. Two sweating workers were cinching a tarpaulin over its empty bed. A black-whiskered man I recognized as one of Cait's boarders stood watching them. He spotted me, said something, and pointed. From the other side of the wagon Fearghus O'Donovan appeared. He too was sweating, and his long overcoat was streaked with dirt and grease. He ran toward me, followed by the others.

"What's the meaning of this?" His blue eyes raked me.

"He's been around here lately," Black Whiskers said.

O'Donovan moved within inches of me. "I asked you a question."

I nodded toward the wagon. "What's the meaning of that?"

"None of your affair." His eyes flicked up at Cait's window and something in his face changed. "Ah, I see." He wheeled toward Black Whiskers. "Why the devil didn't you tell me he was sniffing around here?"

I didn't appreciate his choice of verb.

" 'Twas an oversight, Captain O'Donovan, with all the work—"

"Enough!" O'Donovan swung back to me. "So, you're preying on a poor widow's weakness, is that it?"

"I'm not preying on anybody," I said. "But I'm curious as hell about what's going on around Cait."

" 'Cait,' " he repeated mockingly. "And curious, are you? I'll soon know what *your* game is. I've begun asking questions."

"I'll try to think up some answers," I said, "when I've got time to waste."

The icy eyes narrowed. "Your circumstances are graver than you imagine. I'd advise you to stay away from Mrs. O'Neill."

"I appreciate that," I told him. "It's splendid advice." I brushed past him, feeling him go tense. "Keep up the good work," I told Black Whiskers, jabbing a thumb at the wagon.

I strode along the sidewalk, feeling their eyes bore into my back.

"Samuel, I cannot tell you more."

"But you haven't told me anything."

"I'm not allowed to," she said stubbornly.

"Who gives permission? O'Donovan?"

She said nothing.

"Great."

"Samuel, don't, please."

I let out the mainsheet to catch a languid puff of wind. We'd been in irons, hovering off the Covington shore to keep the current from carrying us miles downriver. My fantasy afternoon was failing on all levels. Having sailed often in my other life, I'd scouted the riverfront till I found a sloop advertised for rent in the East End, where boat builders were slowly giving way to the slums of Rat Row.

It turned out to be more of a skiff and steered like a raft. A far cry from sleek fiberglass craft I had known. And the Ohio was hardly San Francisco Bay. We floated dully on yellow, silt-choked water beneath a hot, cloudless sky. Where were the tricky currents and tides, the exhilarating, unpredictable winds? No wonder pleasure boating on this stretch of the Ohio was limited to excursion steamers. The only good thing I'd seen all afternoon was giant side-wheelers, their whistles blasting and black smoke belching from their twin stacks, hoving into view around the bend above Cincinnati, already as doomed as dinosaurs with railway and telegraph networks enveloping the country.

It had taken some effort to get Cait to go on this outing. Timmy was ill, and she hadn't wanted to leave. I'd brought Johnny over to stay with him. He promptly entranced Timmy by doing handstands, conjuring coins from the air, and balancing a burning sheet of paper on his nose—tricks he'd perfected in the circus. Cait, though less impressed than Timmy, agreed to come. But she insisted on wearing layers of clothing and shading herself beneath a bonnet that enfolded her head like a tent. I was boating with the most beautiful woman I could imagine—and I couldn't see her features.

The sail filled slightly and I felt us pick up speed. "Did you talk to O'Donovan this morning?"

"Why, no." She sounded surprised. "He's been gone for days. After he brought Timmy home he immediately joined General O'Neill in the South. He'll be away for some weeks."

"You're sure?"

"For a certainty, why?"

Was O'Donovan concealing his activities from her? I wondered. Or was she lying?

"Cait, tell me about your secret society."

"It's not secret," she said. "Although the Church tries to say it is. That was true at first, in Ireland, but no longer."

"Then what is it?"

"An army, Samuel."

"Whose army?"

"Ireland's army."

"You're telling me that the army of a nation not yet in existence is operating inside this country?"

"Ireland exists," she argued. "It exists in subjugation, at the mercy of English tyranny. It exists to be plundered by landlords and to be exploited in the name of religion. It exists to be stripped of its people." Her hand clenched into fists. "Oh, it exists!"

"You're a Fenian, then?"

"Oh, Samuel, if I say yes, you'll ask ten thousand questions. If I say no, you won't believe me." She sighed beneath her bonnet. "I am not at liberty to tell you."

The river lapped at the boat's hull. In the distance a factory whistle shrilled and a bird's cry answered starkly overhead.

"Not at liberty," I muttered, looking at this woman from a different era, seeing her old-fashioned clothes and button shoes. As we floated along a sunlit stretch of shoreline, clear images of my daughters came to me: laughing, calling "Daddy," running to me in the sunlight of another century; I saw their faces, heard their voices.

"Samuel . . . ?"

I looked up. She was leaning forward, peering at me with troubled eyes.

"Are you ill?"

I shook my head. "Daydreaming."

"You were so far away, you frightened me."

"Sorry."

"Samuel, try to be patient. Please?"

I managed a grin. "It's not my strong suit."

"Remember," she said, "there is a great deal I do not know about you."

"I guess that's true." My understatement of the century.

As I steered back to the dock we exchanged wistful smiles that seemed to acknowledge the complexity of it all.

◇

I ransacked every paper I could find covering the past month. Sitting with stacks of them in the Mercantile Library, I learned that five hundred delegates from all over the United States had assembled at Fenian Headquarters in Manhattan. General O'Neill had been present and "the veil of secrecy" was drawn "with unusual care" over the session.

A recent *New York Times* article asserted that the Fenians contemplated an immediate move on Canada and were also plotting to abduct Prince Arthur should he visit there or this country. I leaned back and rubbed my eyes. Unless the *Times* had fabricated the whole thing, the Fenian leaders were either insane or blowing smoke clouds. But why? Were they not yet ready, but hoping to build momentum? Were they covering up what they *really* hoped to pull?

No less confused than when I'd started, I focused on the most immediate question in my mind: What exactly was in Cait's basement?

I was truly gorgeous in my best dark suit. My collar was starched and snowy, my beard and hair trimmed. I managed the block and a half from the Gibson to the photographer's without wilting in the noonday heat. They were waiting for me, Timmy in short pants, Cait looking sensational in a green satin dress.

"You're beautiful, Miz O'Neill," I said.

"And you, Mr. Fowler," she said, smiling and taking my arm, "are most noble to the eye."

I think she felt a bit guilty about our boating afternoon. When I'd said I wanted to have a portrait made of her and Timmy, she surprised me by insisting that I be included. In terms of our relationship, she was hard to read. Not only were her moods unpredictable when we were alone together—so far we hadn't repeated our one transcendent kiss—but I couldn't really tell if she saw me as gentleman friend, admirer, potential lover, or a brotherly sort of extension of Andy. Perhaps in her mind we were engaging in heavy courtship. I had no idea. I was trying hard to learn the rules as I played. And trying equally hard not to push things.

"All is ready!" The photographer, a tall, nervous man named Daviscourt, his fingers stained brown from chemicals, led us to a backdrop painted with an idyllic woodland stream in front of which were imitation flowers, shrubbery, and a bark canoe. He posed me with Timmy inside the canoe and settled Cait on a stool between us—which made her look, I thought, as if she were sitting in the water. He handed her a parasol and me a rustic walking stick. Props at the ready, we waited. He ducked beneath his black cloth, emerged to inform us that light conditions were posing unusual problems, and eventually made half a dozen exposures of us gazing frozenly at each other or into his lens. Timmy had trouble staying still so long.

"Uncommonly difficult," Daviscourt grumbled. "The skylight seemed to give off unusual radiance, but not uniformly. I hope another sitting won't be required."

We said we hoped the same.

"Sam, can we toss the ball?" Timmy said at home. "My throwing's stronger!"

I pulled out my watch. "Sure, for a couple minutes, then I have to get to practice."

"Who do you play next?"

"We leave for Portsmouth tomorrow."

Cait looked up. "When will you return, Samuel?"

"Friday morning," I lied, wondering if her interest were only casual. We were actually scheduled back Thursday evening. I had a bit of sleuthing in mind.

She nodded gravely, her eyes holding mine for a moment.

I felt like a shit.

The pennant-holding Eckfords were coming to play us next week. A sure sellout. Deciding the occasion called for new products, I visited Bertha Bertram, a seamstress, in her millinery shop on Elm. Harry employed her each year to make the club's uniforms. She looked at my designs for silk rosettes and ribbon badges bearing red-stocking insignias and said she could make them for six cents apiece. I agreed readily, thinking I could sell them for at least a dime, and ordered as many as she could have ready.

Next I went to a print shop on Vine. Sheet music for "The Red Stocking Scottische," which was "dedicated to the ladies of Cincinnati," had recently been published. On its cover were the players' likenesses, pirated poorly from the engraving in *Leslie's*. I lent them my print of the original photograph and ordered five thousand small posters to be made along the same format: oval head shots of the starters, with Harry in the center. I figured I'd easily clear a dime on each. Champion would go nuts.

The house lay dark and silent in the half-light. No wagon stood in front this time. I crept to the basement door and took a screwdriver from my pocket. The hinges were not rusted, and the screws came out easily. I lifted the door free. A ladder led to a dirt floor some eight feet below. I descended warily and lit the stub candle I'd brought. Eyes adjusting to the dimness, I saw long wooden crates stacked to the ceiling. Stenciled in block letters on the side of each was ELASTIC JOINT IRON ROOFING, Thewlis & Company, 130 West Second Street, Cincinnati. It seemed unlikely that O'Donovan had stockpiled roofing materials. With the screwdriver I pried the lid from one of the crates and removed a canvas tarp underneath. A dozen rifles lay packed inside, their long greased barrels gleaming like sharks. ENFIELD was stamped on their stocks. Replacing the lid carefully, I set about counting the crates. I was about half-finished at over a hundred when I thought I heard something. I snuffed the candle, edged up the ladder, and peeked over the top. Nothing stirred in the morning quiet. I refastened the door and moved quickly away.

Two thousand new weapons, I calculated. Did Cait know about them? In my heart I didn't think so. I was half-tempted to go back and show her. Watch her reaction. But what then? For now it seemed better to find out all I could about the plans of Mr. Fearghus O'Donovan.

We took the *Bostona* southeast along the Ohio to Portsmouth, covering the hundred or so miles in six hours. The hometown Riverside team didn't figure to be much competition; Cleveland had recently demolished them, 48–12.

Everybody except Brainard and Sweasy seemed in good spirits. Allison gave Gould a hotfoot. George fashioned what he called a "Yankee contraption," a sort of wire spider, and dangled it in our faces while we dozed. He even tried it on Brainard, who challenged him to fight. George—big, muscular, unintimidated—merely grinned.

The mood shifted when Harry told us that Champion, not along on this trip, wanted all of us to sign a temperance pledge. There was an ominous silence. I sneaked a glance at Brainard, whose face showed nothing. I could understand Champion's viewpoint: first Hurley and now Brainard had come close to disgracing the club.

"Hell no!" said Waterman. "Is this a damn milk-and-water club? I'd go back to the Mutes first."

"If they'd take you," George needled.

"Poke it up your ass!" Waterman snapped.

Harry looked somberly at Waterman during the exchange. I could roughly guess his thoughts: he couldn't risk losing his star third baseman and splitting the team at this point. But I sensed that Waterman wouldn't last forever with Harry. Nor Brainard.

"The true problem here," he said, interrupting a rambling commentary by Allison on the rights of individual freedom, "is that Mr. Champion would wish it *announced* that the nine had taken such a pledge." Harry looked at us, his eyes deceptively gentle. "I see that it would embarrass some of you."

"That's right," said Waterman.

"He wants to stifle rumors," Harry went on. "Rumors of drunkenness and gambling—the worst threats to our business, gentlemen."

There was silence. Again I glanced at Brainard, who remained impassive, as if the topic were only of abstract interest.

"Anticipating your reaction, I tried to convince him that a signed pledge is unnecessary. He finally agreed, but only with the understanding that further transgressions will bring drastic measures."

That night, when Andy and I talked about prevailing currents on the team, we drew a blank on Brainard. I suggested that maybe he'd cleaned up his act. Andy doubted it. I asked what was with Sweasy.

"He's meaner than ever," Andy said. "Nearly mixed with Mac over some fool thing at our place. Called Allison a fool to his face. Those two are fixing to find new lodging. Sweaze is hardly even civil to me anymore."

"Any idea what's eating him?"

"No, but one of his worst spells was after he found you were sparking Cait. I thought he'd explode!"

"What's that to him?"

"Don't know exactly. I mean, he knows he wouldn't stand a Chinaman's chance with her himself. I guess he thinks your standing's shot up with me 'n' Cait, while his own has dropped."

"What should I do about it, Andy?"

"Nothin' to do."

Brainard was sensational, striking out four—one for each hit he allowed—and whitewashing the unlucky Riversides in all nine innings. Although we had only one homer—a line shot by George in the ninth—our thirty-six hits were good for forty runs. The Riversides were actually pretty good fielders, but nobody could have held us that afternoon.

Our record was now 37–0.

All the way home on the train I pictured all those wooden cases with their deadly contents. Back in Cincinnati Thursday evening, I took a long soak in my room and got a shave in the barber shop. In the papers I read that Clara Barton, the famous war nurse, was sailing for Europe as things worsened between France and Prussia.

I took my time over supper. Around ten, wearing dark clothes, I cautiously approached the boardinghouse. Streetlamps were fortunately sparse in this part of town. I edged along the wall outside the brightly lit parlor and heard voices arguing inside.

"—won't keep till next spring!" O'Donovan's brittle, urgent tones.

An older man's voice responded, "We have no alternative but the St. Patrick's Day Circular."

Wedging myself into thick shrubbery beside a window, I raised up by slow degrees until I could see inside with my right eye. O'Donovan's buttocks were inches away. He faced a man with bags under his eyes who looked to be in his midforties and wore a green uniform resembling O'Donovan's. He sat erect, pulling at his goatee, his gaze fixed on O'Donovan. I dropped down and listened.

"But everything's set," O'Donovan said. "In Chicago, St. Louis, here, we've got stores for nearly twelve thousand. Add Troy and Buffalo, Nashville and Louisville—my God, man, we're ready across the nation!"

"Mind yourself, Captain!"

"Sorry, sir." O'Donovan sounded anything but apologetic. "It's that I fear we'll lose momentum if we don't act soon. We have twenty thousand lads at the ready, two-thirds veterans. We have at least that many stands of arms, two million rounds of ammunition, thousands of breech loaders—"

"You've briefed me exhaustively on our military stores," the older man cut in. "Can you tell me the amount in our treasury at this moment?"

"Well, not precisely, sir, but I would think—"

"Less than seventeen hundred dollars, and bills are coming so fast—largely for those weapons dear to your heart—that it all will soon be gone. Then how are we to feed the fearsomely armed fighters we've launched on an invasion?"

There was a pause.

"Fearghus, I'm as sick as you of picnics and speeches and bond sales. I've traveled the country without respite. I'd like nothing so much as to fight tomorrow. Remember, it was I who pushed earlier operations when others wavered."

"I remember, sir," said O'Donovan. "The courage of John O'Neill is beyond question."

Ah, Colm's uncle, I thought, the big Fenian cheese.

"We cannot fall short again," said O'Neill. "Even another close thing like Ridgway, where we'd have won if reinforced, would finish us with Canada. We must pick our time and targets carefully, strike with coordinated effort, and smash our way to a sure and final victory."

His voice was rising to an oratorical pitch. I risked a glance. O'Neill was standing now, his booted feet widespread. He was as crazy as O'Donovan, I thought, and pulled back from the window.

"And there's the South," O'Neill continued. "You know, Captain, that I'm involved in delicate negotiations with no fewer than eight Confederacy officers?"

"Yes, sir."

"Since the defeat of their last hope, Seymour, and Grant's ascendancy, they're finally swinging to us. With Longstreet and others taking up our cause, lured by prospects of resettling in Canada, we'll be immeasurably strengthened. To act prematurely now, when we are so close, would be fatal." Another pause. "Caitlin, you've never been lovelier, there's a bloom to you."

"Thank you, Uncle." Cait's voice sounded to the left of O'Donovan. She'd been sitting there all along. I burned with jealousy, wanting to crash through the window.

"Isn't she the picture of a colleen, Captain?" O'Neill's voice was suffused with pride.

Tell him to fuck off, Cait.

Her light laughter mingled with O'Donovan's mumble.

"Isn't she?" O'Neill insisted, and now there was no mistaking his role: matchmaker.

"Aye, she is," said O'Donovan, his voice tight.

"Colm and his Caitlin were always quite the display," O'Neill said expansively, a pronouncement that evoked heavy silence. "Well, Captain, there's another matter we must discuss. Cait, if you don't mind . . ."

"Of course, Uncle."

Why does she call him that? I thought nastily. He wasn't *her* uncle and she'd never really married his nephew.

A chair scraped, footsteps, a door closed.

"They're not made finer than Cait on this earth," said O'Neill.

"Indeed," O'Donovan said, and again his voice sounded constricted.

"I understand some fellow has been paying her calls."

"Yes, damn his soul," said O'Donovan. "One of those ballists they're all falling over here. A big cheeky bastard named Fowler, friend of her brother. Caitlin's silly fancy will pass once this sporting craze ends."

"Nothing at fault with the game," said O'Neill. "I encouraged it during the war. Good for the lads. But there's more to Fowler than a ballist—if our countryman McDermott has his facts straight."

"It'd be the first thing straight about that one," O'Donovan said contemptuously. "Why is filth like McDermott allowed to contaminate us?"

"You didn't sing that song when he delivered the arms at half price," O'Neill said mildly. "It's true his morals aren't the keenest. But he's proven useful at times. And this may be one. McDermott claims Fowler took our money from Elmira."

"*What?*"

I leaned against the wall and listened numbly to O'Neill recite McDermott's description of me.

"Scar on his cheek!" O'Donovan said with growing excitement. "That's the giveaway! Wearing a beard now, of course! And he has money. Caitlin said he paid to bury her mother in Ireland. So the rumored treasure *does* exist! Oh, to steal it from us is a profanity!"

"We'd surely put it to grand use," O'Neill said. "There's more on this: He also swears Fowler stole our weapons payment in New York."

"'Tis more likely McDermott lost at wagering, as our reports had it," said O'Donovan. "But it's all one. What I don't understand is how Fowler still walks the earth."

"Through no want of effort by Red Jim, I'm thinking," said O'Neill.

"He's protected, then?"

"That we don't know."

"The man's surely an agent," O'Donovan said grimly. "A paid Pinkerton informer. Or in the employ of the bastard English!"

"The matter is grave," O'Neill agreed. "I thought it too serious even to risk using the wire. When I learned that Fowler'd been in this very house, I came straight down from Detroit."

"Playing up to Caitlin to get information," O'Donovan added. "I'll kill him."

"You'll obey orders," O'Neill said. "We have a fine chance to discover useful information and at the same time confuse our enemies."

"Through Caitlin?" O'Donovan did not echo the other's enthusiasm. "Does she know about him?"

"No," said O'Neill. "And for now that's best. We don't want her to act differently and alert him. We'll start her on the money; that is our first need."

Well, I thought darkly, if our relationship hadn't been complicated enough, it now promised to bristle with intrigue.

"I suspected something was up with him one morning when we unloaded the guns and suddenly he was standing there looking at us," said O'Donovan.

"Have you checked the stores?"

"No, he's out of town; there's no problem. Still, it might not be a bad idea."

My mind froze with the abrupt realization that I'd left the candle down there. It would confirm all their suspicions. I pushed through the shrubbery and ran toward the street. At the corner I looked back and saw O'Donovan emerge with a lantern. He moved purposefully toward the basement door. Shit!

We'd trounced the "champion" Brooklyn Eckfords, 24–5, on their home grounds. But they'd found a way to pooh-pooh it, claiming that the earlier game had not been a *match* contest since several of their top players had been absent. It rankled us. If we beat them again, we would still need to go East for a third victory to claim the coveted pennant. It made us so mad, in fact, that we drubbed them mercilessly, 45–18, behind George's six hits and four stolen bases.

More than eight thousand paid fifty cents apiece to crowd the Union Grounds. The new posters and ribbons and rosettes sold like crazy; the concession booth was mobbed, and our vendors—we'd rigged a few kids with baskets—did a brisk trade in hot dogs and pretzels among the carriages. Champion, glowing, promised to raise my salary ten dollars a week. Mr. Generous.

"Gentlemen," Champion announced after the game. He was standing on a chair in the clubhouse waving a piece of paper. "Yet another opponent, not convinced by previous defeat, has challenged us. They propose to come here and expose us as frauds before the entire nation!"

Champion smiled benignly as we hooted, until Waterman said crisply, "Horseshit."

"Who?" George yelled.

"None other than our old friends," Champion replied, "the Troy Haymakers!"

While the others roared, my stomach bounced on the floor.

"I gather," Champion said, milking the moment, "we accept?"

"Bring 'em on!"

I stood there thinking. Thinking quite hard. In my guts I knew beyond doubt who would show up with the Haymakers: McDermott and Le Caron.

Cait waited at the Laurel Street gate. I moved forward eagerly, thinking she had come to the game after all, despite Timmy being ill. Then I saw her expression.

"What's the matter?"

Biting her lip, she held out a flat packet stamped Daviscourt Photography Studio.

"The shots of us?"

She nodded, her eyes wild.

"Hey, they can't be *that* bad."

"Look at them," she said.

There were five five-by-seven-inch prints. In each one, hovering over the painted stream, was a face. A muted face, not nearly as defined as our three, but quite distinct. An aquiline nose, dark hair, dark, softly staring eyes, lips pressed together. Below the strong jaw was what appeared to be a uniform collar.

I knew who I was looking at. I had seen him before, although in the other photograph he was infinitely younger and unburdened. It was Colm's face.

— ◇ 19 ◇ —

Dear Sam'l,

As the man said, it was ever so different before it all changed. Tiring of me moping about in mortal dread of the lecture circuit, Mr. Langdon finally took pity & sent me shopping for a newspaper with about as much care as he'd give to Livy's purchasing new gloves. Well, a hat, maybe. I had a good-sized nibble in Cleveland & if it had stayed on my line you & I would be Ohio neighbors.

I found a sweeter deal in Buffalo, however, well inside Mr. Langdon's coal kingdom & close enough to Elmira to be less uprooting for Livy after the wedding—which is in February, by the way, & which you must attend. Anyhow, Saturday week (the 21st) I take one-third possession of the Buffalo Courier and commence work as chief editor of my own sheet. I wish you, my ever-silent partner, could have seen Mr. Langdon's face when I said that instead of him covering the entire $15,000 I'd pick up half—in cash! My stock in the futures market soared tolerably with him.

It's a tame prospect partly—like coming off the river to open a dry-goods store—but I've navigated alone for too long & I'm eager now to settle with the dearest woman on this planet. No trip to California now, & I confess to a certain amount of relief on that score. But I'll miss witnessing Freddy's Avitor, of which I am sure you have read, & no longer hold doubts. I saw where the English established an Aeronautical Society three years back & already have exhibited likely models at the Crystal Palace. We should be in on the

[259]

"ground floor" of this, don't you think? Since our first venture was so lucrative, why not pursue another?

Enjoyed your letter of last month. Porkopolis must be nigh delirious over your club. I can't visit anywhere now without having my head pounded by talk of Brown Stockings, Green Stockings, Ivory Socks, Maroon Hose, & on & on through rainbows of leggings till my ears sag. Couldn't you boys lose, just once, so the National Game could go back to being a game & stop being pure bunkum religion?

Must post this now. Regards.
Cordially,
SLC

P.S. The Fenian uproar has died down & a high fence now circles the military cemetery. Your work has spawned a whole generation of ghost tales, however, and I suspect folks hereby are privately thankful for your livening their drab lives. You've taken on a sort of immortality.

Immortality. I liked that. I thought about Twain on the verge of the emotional security and social respectability he wanted so badly. Soon he would enjoy the stable pleasures of family life. I envied him that. But I also remembered that Jervis Langdon, after buying the newlyweds a mansion in Buffalo, would die within the year. Livy's sister would also die during their Buffalo residence, and they would lose their own firstborn, an infant son. Stunned with grief, Twain would sell his share in the paper at a loss, sell the house as well, depart from Buffalo.

He was blissfully unaware. My foreknowledge made me feel old and weary. I wondered about my own life. I'd been thinking of my daughters again, and, by extension, of the world I had left. I missed the oddest things: the taste of pizza, the sounds of aircraft, late-night TV movies, driving a car, paperbacks, electric lights, and innumerable other things that blipped unexpectedly into sense-memory. Pizza was the most nagging.

I'd been back in time for two and a half months. What must my daughters be feeling? Was it that long for them too? If so, they'd think I deserted them. Shades of my father. Maybe it was possible, on the other hand, that I was still there, living simultaneously in two dimensions. Maybe it had always been that way, my consciousness simply shifting from there to here. But I didn't like the idea. And I couldn't see what to do about it anyway.

◇

[260]

Daviscourt had tried to comfort Cait—she nearly fainted when she'd first seen the prints—with vigorous assurances that there was simply no explaining the extra face, or why one print had been ruined by overexposure; he'd never experienced anything similar. None of which, of course, spoke to what she was feeling.

We went back to see him together. I grilled him for nearly an hour. He walked us through each stage of his developing and printing process, showing how he had prepared the glass plates in solutions of collodion and silver nitrate only minutes before our sitting, explaining that the exposures had to be made while the plates were still wet.

"So no previous image could exist on the glass?" I asked.

"Absolutely impossible," Daviscourt said.

"So something had to be there with us when you took the pictures?"

"I would conclude so," he said reluctantly.

"Have you heard of this sort of thing before?"

"Not among recognized photographic artists," he said archly. "Of course one reads of it among spiritualist flummers and fakers."

"Enough, Samuel," said Cait, sounding distraught and tired. "There's no explanation here. I think we knew that before we came. You're not at fault, sir."

"Madam, if you wish it . . . removed," he said tentatively, "I believe it is within my means."

Which raised an interesting question: *Could* he remove the intrusive image? But Cait would have none of it. She shook her head violently and tugged me through the front door.

Outside, she looked me in the eye and said, "Will you help me with something?"

"If I can."

"You can," she said. "We'll talk to someone."

I knew before she told me. I'd seen the advertisements. Clara Antonia was in town. Scheduled to speak Friday evening at Greenwood Hall.

"After her lecture we'll find our answers," Cait said firmly, "if any are to be obtained."

"Why after?"

"Because that's when her seances are."

It was not a wonderful week. I dropped by Cait's evenings after practice—all her boarders seemed to have vanished—to deliver little gifts and to chat. I worried about both of them. Cait looked drawn and tense. Timmy seemed tired and weak all the time.

The specter of the photographs haunted us, though we pretended otherwise. I developed an eerie and pervasive sense that we were not alone. Colm filled my thoughts. Why had he appeared to us, seven years after his demise? Was he jealous? In the pictures he hadn't *looked* jealous. Just intent.

The Fenian question also lay between us like a bog. I didn't want to spoil our time together by raising the subject. For her part, Cait didn't bring up the money issue. We were probably trying to nurture our feelings for each other. Not easy, under the circumstances. Love surely feeds on mystery—but only to a point.

Tensions also continued on the team. Gould accused Allison of loafing during practice, and the two nearly came to blows. George was absent one day, provoking dark mutterings from Sweasy and Waterman.

Trying to capitalize on the Stockings' cresting fame, Waterman and Brainard had each lent his name to a local cigar store. These were not the tiny magazine-and-smoke stands I had known in San Francisco, but were spacious halls with pool tables and chairs and spittoons, hangouts for the sporting life. Kimball's, on Fourth, became Brainard's and Kimball's, while Schipper's Cigars, on Vine, became Fred A. Waterman & Company's Red Stocking Headquarters, and there business reportedly boomed even more than at Brainard's.

At practice, however, Waterman still groused over Champion's threatened temperance pledge. Brainard, on the other hand, went about his chores like a model citizen.

"Settle up with you before long, Sam," he told me one afternoon.

"Oh?" I said, surprised. "Things going that well at the store?"

"Could be," he said. "Could be."

I thought I heard a note of smugness.

Greenwood Hall was narrow, gloomy, and jammed. With four hundred others we sat on creaking, straight-backed chairs and waited for Madame Clara Antonia to appear on a small stage heaped with flowers. The gathering's size surprised me. I recognized several professional men, affluent members of the club. A cross section of the city's population seemed to be there, including boys making predictably rude noises. With no preamble, a short and very fat woman appeared from the wings. Applause swept the hall, undercut by the boys' guffaws. She moved calmly to the lectern.

I'm not sure what I expected—a nun in exotic habit, a flamboyant gypsy in headdress and gold bangles—but whatever it was, I felt disappointed. Clara Antonia wore a plain dun-colored dress trimmed in dark velvet topped with a lace collar. It hung on her like a grocery sack. The boys' observations grew creative. But it no longer mattered what she wore when she lifted her eyes to us; the irises—pale gray or blue, it was impossible to tell—were opaque, almost luminous. They scanned us like unfocused cat orbs, seemingly oblivious to what lay immediately before them. Was she blind?

"The spirit world is not entirely alien," she began, her voice girlish and piping, almost comically incongruous with her bulk, yet carrying distinctly through the hall. "We catch inklings of forces at work in the spirit world—electricity is one—in our daily lives, and certainly in our dreams."

A deep-voiced man behind us scraped his chair and said, "Least she don't grope all over the landscape for words, like most female elocutionists."

Cait turned and glared at him.

"Spirits exist in an atmosphere etherealized around our tangible world," Clara Antonia said. "The forces in this spiritual ether are unnamed because they are largely uncomprehended. And yet, as with electricity, they can be used, though they are not fully comprehended."

She explained that clairvoyants received certain emanations from the spirit world. She had realized early on that she herself had such capacity. It had come unbidden and, until she learned to help and comfort others with it, she had thought herself cursed.

Snickers came from the rude-boy contingent.

Clara Antonia's eyes tracked slowly to them. "Your twenty-five cents does not buy you the right of disrespect," she said matter-of-factly. "It's also inappropriate since one of you—that boy in the sweater—grieves over a dear companion recently arrived among the spirits."

"Cripes, Willy," one of them blurted. "Yer brother, how'd she know?"

It sent a ripple through the crowd. Too pat, I thought. Prearranged.

"My task here is not to communicate with spirits, although I sense a number about us." She paused as another hum passed through the hall. "Rather, I will tell you something of their nature and dwelling conditions. Those of you who might wish me to communicate with a particular spirit may so arrange with my agent at the conclusion of this lecture."

I leaned toward Cait and whispered, "What does she charge?"

"Shh, I've paid."

Clara Antonia spoke for ninety minutes. In no-nonsense phrases she asserted that the spirit world was a better world than this, that guests in that world were of a higher order than in this material life. Just as geology showed the original mass at the center of the earth to improve in high qualities as it approached the surface, she argued, so too was humankind elevated and refined through a process of decomposition. That part got a little hazy, but my interest rose when she described her work with dying soldiers in Union hospitals.

Time after time she had witnessed the departure of spirits from their corporeal bodies. First a dark, leaden vapor arose over the chest. Lights shone from the brain, dim as gas jets seen through a glass. As the patient grew feebler, emanations from his body made the vapor denser, while the brain light stretched upward to it, as if trying to extract nourishment. In two to three hours the vapor gradually assumed human form. If interrupted during that time—for example, if the body was about to be carted off to the dead room—then other similar forms looking on came down and took the emergent form tenderly and bore it away.

Toward the end she answered questions. Yes, she had seen manifestations of dogs and cats and birds and flowers in the spirit world. No, the spirits of former humans didn't run around naked, but gathered a shadowy sort of raiment about themselves, according to taste and character. The clairvoyant could generally tell from this what they had been in life; indeed, she thought it very possible that spirits appeared in that way so as to be recognized. Those with unfinished business were those, obviously, who went to greatest lengths to be recognized.

Cait sat very still beside me. I knew she was fixated on the photos. What was Colm's unfinished business? I wondered.

I was startled when somebody asked, "Can a spirit be photographed?"

"Only if it so desires," Clara Antonia replied, drawing a laugh, and added that she had heard of it, but it lay outside her direct experience. It would require enormous effort for a spirit to make itself visible to a camera.

"Are spirit photographers charlatans, in your opinion?" the questioner persisted.

"There are those in every human activity," she replied calmly. "Just as there are those guided by the truth. To test what is true, you must listen to your heart, your inner voice, for that is where the spiritual world is usually manifested."

She bowed and walked from the stage to enthusiastic applause. When the hall emptied, Cait and I were ushered backstage by a sallow-skinned youth who turned out to be Clara Antonia's son. We entered a plain dressing room, where she sat facing us. Up close she looked much older, her face creased with wrinkles and her hair streaked with gray. The strange pale eyes fixed on Cait as she beckoned us to sit.

"Hello, child," she said gently. "Your mother's spirit is reunited with your father's. Her crossing over was eased by returning to her homeland."

"She knew, then," Cait said. "You've talked with her?"

"You might phrase it so," she replied. "She is most thankful."

"Samuel made it possible."

Clara Antonia's eyes found me. Seconds passed. I experienced a queer vibrating sensation.

"Are you all right?" Cait said anxiously.

"I . . . I think so."

There was a puzzled expression on Clara Antonia's face. Her eyes bored into me. She brought her hand up to where the beard covered my wound, not quite touching me. I felt a pleasant warmth there. She closed her eyes finally, and it was as if I had been released.

"You've come a very long distance, haven't you?"

I did not answer.

"God in Heaven!" said Cait. "What are you saying?"

Clara Antonia seemed to be formulating a complicated question in her mind. She looked at Cait and appeared to reach a decision. "Child, you are afflicted by painful questions," she said. "What is their nature?"

"You remember, Colm . . . returned . . ." Cait said.

"When you first came to me," she said with a nod. "The dove spirit departed, assured that you were safe."

"Yes, but now he's returned." Cait described our portrait sitting and produced the prints.

Clara Antonia gazed at them for a long moment, passing her hand over Colm's image in one of the prints. "So," she mused, "that is why that photography question was asked tonight."

"Someone had the same experience?" I said.

She shook her head. "Sometimes when no questions arise my assistants provide them. Often what come to them are emanations from audience members."

There was a pause while we digested that. I was quickly losing the last shreds of skepticism. I was willing to believe—hell, I *wanted* to believe—that she could provide some answers.

"You wish to communicate with Colm?" she asked. "I sense his presence strongly."

Cait's hands twisted nervously. "I . . . don't know," she said, surprising me.

"Yes, we do," I said.

"Yes," she echoed.

"Very well." Clara Antonia nodded to her son standing quietly in one corner. He dimmed the gas jets until the room was nearly dark. I thought I saw a subtle luminosity around Cait.

"He is here," Clara Antonia said softly.

A chill ascended my back, and goose bumps stippled my skin. I couldn't make out Clara Antonia's face. She sat very still, a black bulk in the dimness. Beside me Cait was trembling. I reached for her, then hesitated with Colm on the scene.

"Yes, take his hand," said Clara Antonia, her voice strange and even higher pitched than before. For an instant I thought she was talking to me. Then I felt Cait's cold fingers slip into mine and realized that Clara Antonia must have been picking up on Cait's thoughts.

"What do you wish of him?" her high voice said.

"Is he all right?" Cait's voice held a tenderness that opened a vein of jealousy in me.

There was a pause.

"He lives now in a happier world. His spirit longs to be free of this one. But it is not. He hopes that what he has done is right."

What has he done? I wondered.

"His uncle . . . there is much . . ." She paused. "I think he does not want his uncle to take Caitlin."

Cait's hand stiffened.

"There is another . . . he hates and fears . . . who wants her."

It was my turn to stiffen.

"Ask him why he was in our picture," Cait said. "Did he mean to frighten me?"

The longest pause yet followed.

"It is not clear. He was . . . happy. . . ."

He hadn't looked it, I thought.

"He departs now," she said in more her usual speaking tone. "The effort has been beyond our imagining. He returns to the spirit world."

"I've got to know," I blurted. "Did he bring me here?"

The words reverberated in the small room.

"He's gone," said Clara Antonia.

The gas jets illuminated the room. Her opaque eyes fixed on me. "The answer to that question does not lie within you?"

"If so, I don't know how to find it. Do you know the answer?"

She looked put off by my bluntness. "What comes to me," she said, "is that he did not bring you here. Not in the sense that you mean."

I didn't know whether to feel relieved or disappointed.

"But," she said, "I think it likely that he made it *possible* for you to come. If you so chose. As of course you did."

[266]

Cait turned and stared at me.

"I believe making that choice possible to you," Clara Antonia said, "is what Colm wonders whether it was right for him to have done."

"Samuel, hold me."

I put my arms around her. We stood in the darkened foyer of her boardinghouse. She clutched my shoulders and pulled herself tightly against me. I stroked her hair, tried to ease her trembling.

"I know that you love me," she said. "I feel it from you."

I said nothing, waiting.

"I don't know if I can love again. Not the way I loved Colm. When he died, I felt he took all within me that had loved him so completely."

It hurt to hear, but at the same time I felt a lessening of responsibility, a small relief.

"I think I understand," I said. "It's all right."

She pressed her face into my neck for a moment and then tilted her head back. "You're good to me, Samuel," she whispered.

She leaned upward. I brought my mouth down on hers. She kissed me with an urgency I hadn't felt before. Her arms wrapped around my neck. I wanted her. But first I wanted her to stop trembling.

After a long moment she drew back. "Will you tell me where you have come from? When it is right to tell?"

"Yes," I told her. "When it is right."

"Aw, you fellers didn't need to do this," Gould said, blushing with pleasure. We could scarcely hear him over the cackling and clucking of twenty-two chickens. They were our present to him, one for each of his years.

"Here's to Charlie Gobble-Gould!" proposed George, raising his beer stein.

We drank, then gave him three cheers. He wiped foam from his blond mustache and looked ridiculously happy. He said it was the best celebration he'd ever had.

" 'Happy birthday to you,' " I began singing. None of them had heard it before. What was with this era? To their credit, they did think it a catchy little tune.

The New Orleans Southerns came in to test us two days before the Haymakers would arrive. Attending to the Louisiana players was a relief for me. I was already jittery as the vanguard of the eastern sporting crowd began to trickle into Cincinnati. I imagined eyes on me, even in downtown streets. I didn't tarry in the Gibson's lobby now. And I carried my gun.

The Southerns, a solid amateur team, were the first Dixie organization ever to tour northward. They had won all six of their road games in Memphis, St. Louis, and Louisville. On the diamond we eyed each other curiously. The notion of salaried ball players evidently jarred their sensibilities. In thick accents almost incomprehensible to us, they asked about our contracts, pay, and practice schedule.

"So, y'all make a business of pleasure," one drawled skeptically, doubtless thinking, How like Yankees.

From them we learned that the national game was relatively new to the South, introduced by returning soldiers and prisoners. But it already enjoyed huge popularity; everybody down there, they assured us, knew of the famous Red Stockings.

We played in choking ninety-eight-degree heat. Instead of spikes the Southerns wore light moccasins and consequently had trouble with their footing all afternoon. We kept them hopping, too, with wicked liners and daisy cutters.

The Dixie batters touched Brainard for only eleven hits and three runs. We pounded thirty hits and scored thirty-five runs. George and Sweasy homered. Andy produced the day's defensive gem by snagging a drive down the left-field line, then turning and uncorking a powerful throw to double up a runner and earn a standing ovation.

"Anybody read about the Haymakers?" George said in the clubhouse.

"Saw they're in Ohio," said Allison. "They warmed the Mansfields real good."

"Warmed Cleveland, too," said Mac.

We were their next stop. I felt like Rome awaiting the barbarians.

The notices were side by side in the afternoon *Gazette*. One was headed:

FENIAN BROTHERHOOD

The members of the Cincinnati Circle are requested to attend a meeting at the Armory on Fifth Street on THIS (Tuesday) night at nine o'clock. Business of utmost importance from Headquarters and other important matters will be heard. All Fenians attend, by order of the Center.

The other was in bold type.

A LECTURE
MOZART HALL
Tuesday, August 24, 1869
Half Past Seven O'Clock
CAPT. F. J. O'DONOVAN
Subject: "American Citizens in English Bastilles."
Admission: 50 Cents
Proceeds to aid needy Irish-American citizens

I had cynical thoughts about what sort of "aid" would go to which "needy" citizens. It might be instructive, I told myself, to venture out that night to hear what O'Donovan had to say.

It turned out to be quite a lot. Delivered at white heat, in bombastic, inflammatory style. I sat near the door, a slouch cap pulled low over my eyes. The half-filled hall was fairly dim; I didn't fear being recognized.

O'Donovan, martial in his green uniform, told hair-raising tales of patriotic Irish-American lads who'd tried to bring supplies to their homeland. Imprisoned unjustly, ignored by their American ambassador, tormented by bestial jail keepers, they still languished in British dungeons.

At the end he reached a booming crescendo: "Release our citizens or we will war to the knife! The Saxon foe will never relax except by the persuasion of cold lead and steel. *Will you echo me with WORDS OF STEEL?*"

The assemblage roared. When they subsided, O'Donovan called for hands to show how many favored immediate war with England. That did it. Time to get out.

In a hansom outside, I considered the issue. The United States was hardly likely to make war on England, particularly after the recent devastation here. But the degree of anti-English sentiment I'd picked up suggested there might be widespread support for letting the Fenians do their thing, even for helping overtly. Maybe I had underestimated them.

O'Donovan emerged with another man from a stage door. I closed the hansom's curtain until they climbed into a vehicle. "Follow that carriage," I said. I'd always wanted to utter those words.

The Fifth Street Armory, a forbidding stone structure, was less than a mile away. O'Donovan's carriage bypassed the front entrance and vanished around the side. I paid my driver and moved in darkness beside the armory. Hearing singing, I pressed my ear to the wall.

> *"Many battles we have won,*
> *Along with the boys in blue.*

[269]

Now we'll go and capture Canada,
For we've nothing else to do."

They certainly weren't shy about making their intentions known, I thought, peeking around the rear corner. The carriage pulled away. O'Donovan, alone now, moved toward a doorway. When he entered it, I sprinted after him.

". . . is dark," I heard a voice say inside the door.

"As black as heresy!" said O'Donovan. "That's fine, man! Never let up on the password!"

"Aye, sir!"

"Are they ready?"

"Not yet, sir. And a man is waiting here to see you first."

"Oh? Who's that?"

I heard a door open. A familiar voice said, "Your old pal Red Jim, that's who."

I hugged the wall hard. McDermott!

"What do you want?" O'Donovan said coldly.

"You know what," said McDermott. "We're going through with it."

There was silence.

"We'll talk in the office down the hall," O'Donovan said.

"May I be excused, sir?" said the guard. "There's nothing back here. I'm missing everything."

"Hold your post!" O'Donovan snapped.

Footsteps receded. After a minute I rapped the door smartly. It swung open and a pudgy boy holding a rifle frowned at me suspiciously.

"Lefty O'Doul," I told him. "Civilian aide to Captain O'Donovan. I have urgent information before he enters the meeting."

"The night is dark," said the boy, the rifle braced across his chest.

"Black as heresy," I said. "Where is he?"

To my astonishment he put his rifle down and brought his right index finger to the tip of his nose while touching his ear with his left index finger.

"Yes, yes," I said impatiently, doing the same and hoping I hadn't botched it. "Now direct me. It's urgent."

He pointed to a door and said, "End of the walkway."

The door clicked behind me. A sliver of light shone down the corridor. I took out my gun and tiptoed forward.

". . . I tell you, *'twill* work!" said McDermott's voice emphatically.

"But if it didn't . . . or did but came to light afterward," O'Donovan retorted, "we'd have the whole city around our ears. They're the darlings just now."

"How'd it come to light?" McDermott countered. "When he vanishes, it'll naturally be taken as the work of Haymaker backers—no connection with the brotherhood."

Vanishes? I thought. Who?

"And that's only if the worst happens—that is, the operation takes longer and word leaks out," said McDermott. "Most likely Fowler'll cave in right away from the pressure on him, see? That way the brotherhood gets its money, I clean up on the match, and both of us settle our scores with the son of a bitch."

That last part didn't sound like fun. I kept the derringer trained on the door.

"So what's the fault in it?" McDermott demanded.

"None that I see," O'Donovan said reluctantly. "But if Caitlin learned I was party to it, or if he came to harm . . ." His voice trailed off.

That puzzled me. Since when was O'Donovan solicitous of my well-being? Wasn't harm precisely their intent?

"She's the colleen you've chased since before the war?" McDermott laughed his braying laugh. "Look, I tell you, he won't be hurt. It'll go off just like I laid it out: Soon's we get the money, I send a message saying where and how much it is. Your boys recover it, rescue the grateful prisoner, and come away heroes. Bully for Captain O'Donovan!"

There was a long silence.

"There's worse things for her to find out," McDermott said finally.

"What does that mean?" O'Donovan snapped.

"Have you forgotten I'm the one who knows what happened to your precious Colm?"

Something in the way he said it chilled me.

O'Donovan muttered something too softly for me to make out. A chair scraped. I edged backward.

"So, we have our wee understanding," McDermott said jovially. "It's my thought we'll prosper."

I left the corridor rapidly. "I informed the captain you're doing a hell of a job," I told the guard, who beamed and squared his shoulders. We repeated the nose-and-ear salute, and I was through the door and into the sheltering darkness.

Walking north to Over the Rhine, I mentally replayed what I had heard. They obviously planned to kidnap me and extort the treasure. Once the Fenians had the money, they'd hand me over to McDermott.

What that had to do with him winning his bets remained a mystery. As did what he knew about Colm.

I gave serious consideration to leaving the city until the Haymakers had gone. But if McDermott and O'Donovan were as determined as I thought, they'd simply wait for me to return. I couldn't stay away from Cait and the Stockings forever.

So running away was out. But not hiding.

The Haymakers trooped into the Gibson the next morning. Millar was there with a dozen other reporters. Throngs of well-dressed visitors, many of them gamblers, milled inside the lobby arguing with desk clerks in futile efforts to book rooms. Special trains would bring thousands more in the next twenty-four hours.

With unfortunate timing I arrived at practically the same moment from Gasthaus zur Rose, where I'd slept in a snug attic room and wakened to sunlight filtering through red geraniums in a window box. I glimpsed Bull Craver's sullen bulk, the burly King brothers, Clipper Flynn's hatchet features. I felt my muscles tensing.

All it took was seeing them again.

Practice was light and easy, mostly BP and muscle stretching. In the clubhouse afterward Brainard paid me five hundred dollars in crisp new bills.

"Hope you didn't expect it all at once," he said.

"Hell, I didn't expect *any* of it this fast."

"Got my cart hitched to a swifter nag now."

I was still wondering what that meant when I stopped to buy Timmy a toy steam locomotive. Arriving at Cait's, I checked to make certain the derringer was loaded. My sense of foreboding was soon justified. Sitting as though waiting for me—which on reflection I supposed he was—I found Fearghus O'Donovan in the parlor.

"Where's Cait?" I said.

"To your credit, Mr. Fowler," he said, calm and contained, "you assisted a good Irish family. I have no quarrel with that."

"Oh, thank you."

He studied me like a cat sizing up a large and delectable but potentially formidable bird. "However, I have the responsibility of recovering certain long-missing funds."

"How exciting," I said, and started to step around him.

"You don't seem to realize your situation," he said crisply, blocking the way. "Grave-robbing is a heinous crime, Mr. Fowler. If necessary we can transport you to Elmira, remove those convenient whiskers, and see if a certain stable boy can identify you to the police."

"My finances are none of your business," I said. "And even if you could prove what you say—which you can't—the authorities would confiscate everything; you'd never get it."

"Ownership would be difficult to establish," he agreed. "That is why I am trying to reason with you. Our lads' blood darkened the ground of that camp. You could be excused for not knowing that when you took the money. But now there is no excuse."

I felt like saying the money had been nothing more than a catalyst for cheating and murder. But I wasn't about to acknowledge anything.

"Return it," he said, "to serve the cause of Erin."

"So you can buy guns and shoot Canadians? Spare me the bullshit." His face was flushed as I pushed past him to the foot of the stairs and called for Cait.

"Up here, Samuel."

I started upward and felt his hand clutch my sleeve. I shook free and whirled, poised to hit him. His fists were clenched and his breath whistled in through his teeth, but he made no move; I think he knew I'd flatten him.

I entered their room for the first time. It was spare and light, with two small beds. Timmy lay in one. He rose on one elbow when he saw me, then sank back.

"You still sick, Timmy?"

He nodded and said hoarsely, "Throat hurts."

His forehead felt hot to my touch.

"Fearghus went for quinine earlier," said Cait.

"Oh," I said. "Good."

I filled the locomotive's tiny boiler with water, stoked the burner, and after getting a head of steam, ran it across the floor as Timmy watched.

"It's tip-top, Sam!"

"We'll find cars to go with it," I told him.

After a racking fit of coughing, he sank into sleep. I looked at Cait. "Shouldn't he see a doctor?"

"Tomorrow, if he's not better," she replied. "Samuel, I have to ask something."

"Yes?"

"Fearghus swears that you took money belonging to the brotherhood." Her voice was tense. "He claims you're a spy."

"Do you believe it?"

"I don't want to."

I took a deep breath, weary of the whole thing. "Okay, sit down, then, and listen. I've got a lot to tell you." I started with McDermott and Le Caron at the Rochester game and told her of the shooting in

Albany and my third brush with Le Caron in Jersey City. I spoke of meeting Twain and learning of the treasure; of being touched by her mother's plea; of going to recover the gold and what transpired in the cemetery.

"Not even Andy knows all of it," I finished.

"McDermott sounds a monster!" she exclaimed. "Fearghus speaks scornfully of him, but I had no idea! The buried money was no more than gambling winnings, then?"

I nodded. "O'Donovan seems to think that since most of the guards and prisoners were Irish, it belongs to him."

Timmy's labored breathing sounded in the ensuing silence.

"Do you still think I'm a spy?"

"I never truly did," she said.

"Cait, what do you do with the Fenians?"

"Not *with* them, Samuel. I *am* one. I've tried to keep my work separate from you, all the time fearing I couldn't."

"What *is* your work?"

"I maintain this Circle House," she said. "Beyond that I can't say, Samuel. I'm sworn to secrecy. We all are."

"The papers are full of invasion rumors, your basement is full of guns—"

"Which you took upon yourself to discover."

"Only because I care about you."

She reached out and touched my chest. "Oh, Samuel, what's to happen?"

Pool sellers favored us two to one. That seemed a bit heavy, considering we'd barely pulled off the 37–31 win in Troy. But the Haymakers, though winning eleven of fifteen since then, had been spotty, beating the Mutuals decisively, getting blown out twice by the Eckfords, and splitting a pair with the Atlantics. Their run totals against weak teams had been suspiciously low. We figured that they'd been up to their old tricks of shaving scores, perhaps even losing deliberately to the Brooklyn clubs to establish themselves as underdogs against us. Given that scenario, they would now bet heavily on themselves and play their damnedest, using every trick at their command to contain us. Not that they needed more incentive, I reflected darkly, than avenging their loss in Troy, breaking our win streak, and drawing national attention to themselves.

While the Haymakers themselves were shunted back and forth to the practice field and sequestered tightly at the Gibson, their supporters were boasting how they were going to knock us off.

The downtown streets were a mess, clogged with thousands of

visitors. The Gibson's lobby and saloon were virtually impassable around the clock. Rival luxury hotels, the Burnet and Spencer, were overflowing. Smaller establishments had quadrupled their rates—and were booked solid. Contingents still poured in, trains from surrounding cities carrying dozens of excursion cars. Champion had ordered two thousand additional seats erected. We advertised "Plenty of space for ladies." Johnny and I had doubled the size of our booth, tripled our foodstuff orders, hired yet another woman, and added five more vendors. The streetcar companies were offering half-fare rates to the ballpark, and a special line had been installed from Western Union's downtown office to transmit scores in the showdown contest to cities everywhere.

The national game indeed, and we were at its hub. In spite of my preoccupation with McDermott, I lay in bed at Gasthaus zur Rose the morning of the game and found myself dreaming that I had to go in for Allison again; punching out Craver once more; smashing a colossal home run over the fence with two out in the ninth to pull out a deathless victory, my name shouted through the city, wired across the nation. . . .

Well, it was a nice fantasy. In reality, my services would doubtless be confined to the score book, Craver was unlikely to provoke another fight, we probably wouldn't need last-ditch heroics to win at home, and even if I did come to the plate in that spot, more likely than not Cherokee Fisher's fastballs would make short work of me.

Restless and fairly certain I'd foiled McDermott by hiding in Over the Rhine, I decided to go out to the park early—it was a little after ten—and help set up the booth.

I had barely reached the corner and was waiting for an omnibus when I heard a voice calling me. I spun around and saw Sweasy running toward me. His clothes were rumpled, his hair disheveled.

"Jesus, where you been?" he cried, his voice edged with hysteria. "I've looked all night! Your nigger at the grounds sent me up here."

"What's the matter?"

"It's Andy—they've got Andy!"

I stared at him, dumbfounded.

"It's all your fault, you son of a bitch!" He snatched a crumpled paper from his pocket and thrust it at me. "When I came in last night, Andy was gone and I found this."

It was scrawled in pencil:

Fowler—
If you want Leonard in against the Haymakers bring the money you stole to public landing at noon. Put it in a satchel

by the water post at the foot of Broadway. We will watch. Just drop it and leave. If you don't or try to bring police, the Leonard boy won't be fit for games again.

I crumpled it, thinking how stupid I'd been. McDermott had intended to take Andy all along, then trade him for me after the game. No wonder O'Donovan feared Cait finding out.

"Where's the money they're talkin' about?" Sweasy said. "You got to get it before noon."

"You don't understand," I said. "They won't let Andy go before the game, money or no money. Who've you told about this?"

"Nobody. I was going to Champion if you weren't here."

"Come on," I said. "We don't have much time."

"Where we going?"

"Harry's." I waved at a passing hack. "But first we have to round up the others."

◇ 20 ◇

Cincinnati's public landing seethed in the midday heat. It was far less crowded than it would be later, when fleets of packets would depart after the Haymaker game. Now a dozen steamers along the dock moved with the river's undulations. Heat shimmered on the vast paved loading area. Across the river in Newport I made out the United States barracks and esplanade. To my left, wagons stood partially loaded with barrels from the hold of a freighter, the job put off until cooler hours. To my right, a street vendor pushed his cart along Front Street. He'd find few customers in these unshaded areas.

My footsteps echoed on the concrete landing. I made my way toward the embankment. Along the levee stretched a line of massive posts, three feet thick and twenty feet high, to which the steamers were moored. At high water the swelling current brought the vessels to the very top of the posts, most of which were marked in footage to gauge the river's rise and fall. One of the posts stood squarely at the foot of Broadway. I headed for it, forcing my eyes straight ahead. I put the valise down at the foot of the post, arm muscles cramped from the heavy burden. I turned and walked back the way I had come. Sweat glued my shirt to my skin.

Before I had gone thirty feet somebody yelled, "Mister, you left this here!"

The voice was Johnny's. I kept walking.

"Mister!"

I was nearly to the corner of River Street before I heard another voice. Glancing back, I saw a man approaching Johnny.

"No, it's his," said Johnny loudly. "HEY MISTER!"

A hack pulled up nearby, and Charlie Gould stepped down, looming huge and blond. I nodded pleasantly and climbed into the hack as Gould ambled toward Johnny and the other.

"What's the trouble?" I heard Gould say.

And that was all, for as the hack entered River Street I yelled, "Hit it!" and the driver whipped the horse into a gallop. We clattered wildly for a half block and careened onto Walnut, scattering a group of boys playing marbles. Another lurching turn onto Front, and we raced to the rear of the Spencer House. I jumped out and sprinted down the landing. A small animated group had formed around the valise. Gould and Johnny were arguing with two men, one of whom was trying to wrest the valise from Gould.

Johnny spotted me and, on cue, began screaming "POLICE!" His shouts carried along the riverfront. Somebody yelled in the distance. One of the men grabbed at Johnny, but he ducked easily behind Gould, who still gripped the valise. The yells were drawing a few onlookers from nearby streets. One was Sweasy, who walked rapidly toward the scene.

Then I saw what I feared I would see. A dark figure emerged from a warehouse behind Gould. He took in the scene—including me running—and moved quickly into the struggling knot. Something glinted in his hand. I didn't need to see his face clearly to recognize him: Le Caron.

"Look out!" I yelled. "He's the one!"

Johnny tumbled out of the way as Le Caron's knife flashed at him. Gould dropped the valise and stepped back quickly. The man wrestling for it went over backward. Le Caron snatched the valise from him.

"Stop!" I yelled, fifteen feet away.

He ignored me. I fired the derringer over his head. Its small *pop!* froze everything for a moment. Le Caron's black eyes drilled into mine. I sighted on him, holding the gun at arm's length with both hands, like in police movies.

The shot had been in part a signal. In response, a wagon swung onto the landing from East Front. Le Caron looked at it nervously. I knew what he was seeing: Harry, George, Allison, and Mac—good-sized men, all brandishing baseball bats—coming straight for him. His eyes flickered at me; then, tucking the valise under his arm as if it weighed nothing, wheeled and broke into a crouching run along the embankment, moving with surprising speed. I fired another shot over him; he did not slow. As the coach pursued him and the others spread out to cut him off, I bent over the man on the ground and dug my gun into his neck. Its two chambers were empty, but he didn't know it. His eyes widened and his Adam's apple bobbed convulsively.

"Where's Andy Leonard?" I demanded.

Wet sounds came from his throat. "Boat."

"Which fucking boat?"

"The *Mary Rae.*"

I jabbed the barrel deeper. "Where do you have him?"

"Starboard cabin," he gasped. "Stern."

"Does it have a number?"

His eyes rolled. "Don't remember, honest."

"Where's it docked?"

"Other end, by the gasworks."

I turned and chased the others. Le Caron, already a hundred yards down the landing, dropped the valise as the four Stockings jumped out of the wagon behind him. Had he known it held scrap iron and newspaper, he might not have carried it so far. For a moment, as they closed in on him with bats poised, it looked as if he were trapped. But Le Caron turned and bounded goatlike up the steep embankment. He poised and dove. I heard a faint splash.

"In the wagon!" I yelled.

With Mac and Gould, I clung to the outside. Harry, handling the reins deftly, took us thundering along the docks. I scanned the names of boats as we passed. *Melody Lady . . . Cheyenne . . . Silver Spray . . . Clifton . . .* Moored at the foot of John Street sat the *Mary Rae,* a weather-beaten, medium-sized stern-wheeler. A rugged-looking deck-hand stood in the shade of the pilothouse overhang.

"Where you headed?" he growled, blocking the gangway as we swarmed up.

Without a word Mac and Gould threw him in the river. It was a mistake not to muzzle him. He shouted a warning even as he plunged toward the surface. We scrambled up a runged ladder to the passenger deck and moved sternward like grim commandos, wrenching compartment doors open.

There were few signs of life on deck, but that was hardly true in the cabins. Curses and shrieks echoed in our wake. Glimpses of gaudy clothing and hastily covered bodies told us what sort of passengers these were. I wondered if McDermott was aboard.

Everything we'd counted on in our hurried strategy meeting at Harry's had so far worked out: the kidnappers hadn't expected a trap to be sprung from so many directions, particularly since I'd done nothing suspicious at the outset; Le Caron had been flushed, as I thought he or McDermott would be; and Andy was near the riverfront, where the kidnappers could escape far easier than by railway or road—which would be closely watched had I gone to the police.

Harry and I burst into the last compartment and saw Andy bound and gagged in the far corner. His eyes bugged at us and his head shook violently. In the instant I realized he was trying to warn us, Harry yelled, "Watch out!"

I twisted sideways as something exploded on my right shoulder. Staggering back against the bulkhead, I saw a man stalking me with something that looked like a rolling pin. Behind him, others crowded through the doorway. The rolling pin flashed at me. Sick with the certainty that I couldn't move fast enough, I tried to duck. There was a splintering impact over my head. For an instant I thought I had been brained. I tumbled to the deck as fragments of wood showered on me. I looked up and saw Harry drop the handle of his shattered bat. Swearing, the deckhand lifted his club. Harry stepped inside the up-raised arm and crashed a textbook right hook to his jaw. The deck-hand's knees buckled and he sagged to the deck beside me.

Then they were on us. A boot kicked at me. I grabbed it and pulled myself upward.

"Help!" Harry was yelling. "In here!"

They pressed us back against the bulkhead. It looked bad. Only the cramped space worked in our favor as the half dozen men trying to get at us were practically jumping over each other. I sent one down with a hard left but took several flailing hits in exchange. Harry, fighting desperately, suddenly crumpled as a plank thudded against his head. I grabbed him before he fell and tried to shelter him. I was rocked by a blow to my neck.

God, I thought, this is it.

THWAAAAACKKK!

A burly man in front of me screamed and nearly folded over backward. A cloud of dust rose from him. Behind him, George cocked his bat and looked for a new target. I saw Mac and Allison, too. As our attackers turned to meet the new threat, I jumped one from behind. The next minutes were a jumble of straining bodies and brutal sounds. I pried a deckhand off Sweasy and slammed him against the bulkhead. Harry, back on his feet, threw a timely rolling block to save Allison from being blindsided. Gould snatched away a knife that had stabbed him in the shoulder and snapped its owner's arm over his knee like kindling. I was having trouble landing clean punches. Mostly it was a matter of wrestling and gouging in the too-narrow space.

Then, suddenly, straddling several inert bodies on the deck, only Stockings were upright in the cabin. Panting, we looked at each other. Sweasy bent over Andy and worked to free him, intoning, "I'm sorry, pal, I'm sorry, Andy, I'm sorry," a litany which struck me as oddly uncharacteristic.

"We gotta move," said Allison, peering through the doorway.

"Folks're comin' out everywhere. I think the roughs went to the texas deck."

"Where's that?" I said.

"Above, by the pilothouse," Harry said.

"Pleased to see you fellers," said Andy, standing unsteadily. The gag had left raw marks by his mouth. "All I've been hearing is how these sharps on board'll clean up today."

"Let's get to the grounds," Harry said. "Before anything else happens."

We were almost to the gangplank when George sniffed noisily and said, "Where's that coming from?"

We stopped as the acrid smell of burning wood and paint reached us.

"FIRE!" somebody bellowed above.

A crush of people began to swarm around us. The narrow passageways jammed within seconds. Half-dressed men shoved furiously. Near us a woman cried out in pain and fear. I saw some of the deckhands we'd just fought forcing their way through, no longer concerned about us. A contagion of terror was about to erupt.

"WAIT!" boomed Harry, brandishing his bat. "FIRST THE LADIES!"

It was a generous use of the term, considering the women in question. To my amazement, it worked. He jangled their Victorian conditioning enough to halt the rush—and our cocked bats doubtless helped. Harry guided the disheveled woman to the gangplank himself and made sure others were allowed to pass to the front. "There's time for all!" he cried repeatedly.

He was nearly wrong. By the time we stepped on the gangway ourselves, tongues of flame licked high in the black clouds billowing from below. "Hurry, get off before the boilers go!" Sweasy yelled, voicing what we all feared.

My feet no sooner touched the dock than there came an enormous *CRUMP!* The boat lurched violently, then a booming explosion hurled me forward. A fiery column erupted between the tall stacks, bending them outward; they toppled into the pall of smoke. The decks were buckling, the entire bow section a roaring inferno. Through the smoke I saw dim shapes plunging overboard.

Along the landing a chorus of bells and whistles sounded. One horse-drawn fire pump arrived, then another. A neighboring steamer was hosed down to protect it from the searing heat. That was about all that could be done. The *Mary Rae* was doomed.

"Say," exclaimed an onlooker, "ain't you the Red Stockings?"

"We're the Haymakers," George told him.

"Come on," Harry said, pulling us away. "We face them in less than an hour."

We moved toward our wagon.

"Singular how that fire broke out just when it did," Andy said grimly.

"Sure is," I said. I had no idea how Le Caron had reached the *Mary Rae* so quickly or how he had managed to ignite the fire. But I hadn't the slightest doubt he was responsible.

"How'd you find me?" Andy asked as we rumbled away from the landing.

I explained how we'd gotten the threatening note, lured Le Caron into the open but failed to capture him, and forced Andy's whereabouts from the accomplice. I started to get the shakes as I thought about how close we'd come to catastrophe.

"Thought I'd be stuck in there forever," he said. "They seemed to figure that with me out of the match, we didn't stand a sucker's chance."

"Probably true."

"Naw, Harry'd've let you lick 'em again."

"I'll be content letting you do it."

He grinned. "How're the odds running?"

"They dropped this morning," I said. "Now it's us to win by ten runs."

He whistled. "The ones I heard on that boat were plungin' heavy on the Haymakers. Talkin' tens of thousands. No wonder the odds fell some—but they're still good for them." He leaned close. "Sam, I think they're playin' other angles. I heard 'em say, 'It's in the bag, they took the money.' "

" 'They'? Meaning Stockings?"

He nodded slowly. Possibly it was my imagination, but it seemed that Sweasy, sitting nearby, was being studiously casual. I had a feeling he was straining to hear. "Any names?" I said.

Andy shook his head and whispered, "But I heard one say, 'It cost a pretty penny, but he'll deliver the game to us like on a tray.' "

"Who'd they mean?"

He hesitated, then, "They said the signal'd be for the first two tosses to go wild."

That left little doubt. Now I knew where Brainard had gotten his money.

"We can't tell Harry," he whispered. "Acey'd be finished."

Sweasy shifted position, glanced our way. My mind raced. I tried to put aside shock and just deal with the logistics of the situation.

"I may have an idea," I whispered. "Don't say anything yet, okay?"

He looked relieved. "You bet."

It took us half an hour to crawl the last quarter mile west on Seventh. If we hadn't been so banged up we'd have gotten out and walked—except that it wouldn't have been any faster. Crowds swarmed every thoroughfare, jammed all sidewalks. The city seemed to have shut down completely, everybody surging to the Union Grounds. We tried to shield ourselves in the wagon but were soon recognized. Hiding our scrapes, we waved back to throngs clapping and cheering, yelling encouragement, reaching up to touch us, tugging at our clothes. We were their team, their champions, projections of themselves. I wondered if medieval knights had felt like this on their way to the tilting grounds.

In the clubhouse a near-apoplectic Champion could barely speak when he saw us. Harry told him we'd gotten banged around a bit in traffic. Which was true enough.

Brainard and Waterman had not accompanied us, for the simple reason that we couldn't find them. I tried to read their faces as they listened to what had happened. I wondered if Waterman was in on the deal too. As usual, neither of them showed much. Deciding to tackle the toughest first, I approached Brainard, who worked his toothpick in irritation when I said I wanted to talk privately.

"Ain't the time, so close to the match."

"That's exactly what we need to discuss. The match. And your future."

He eyed me warily and stood. We moved down the long room to a bench near the equipment closet.

"Word has it you'll sell us out today," I said with brutal directness. "To show the deal is on, you'll start with two wild pitches."

The toothpick stopped moving. "Where'd you hear that?"

"Does it matter? Harry doesn't know. Yet."

"Throwing off a match is a serious charge."

"*Very* serious."

He stared at me, trying to determine, I imagined, what I wanted.

"Asa, I'm not gonna make you tell me whether it's true—"

"Goddamn right you're not!"

"—but if you've got a deal with McDermott, it had better be good for life. You'll be through with baseball."

"Horseshit."

"You think Harry will just forgive and forget? You think Champion won't crucify you?"

He worked at a piece of tape on the floor with his spikes.

"Whatever the arrangement is," I said, "we're not losing today."

He glanced up, his eyes ironic, world-weary. "No?"

"That's right. I know the stakes are high. And I know better than you that McDermott plays rough and wouldn't look kindly on a double cross. So here's what you're going to do."

"Look, Fowler, I've listened to—"

"Quiet, we don't have much time. You're going to make those two wild pitches to open the game. Meanwhile I'll tell Millar you were approached by gamblers and offered a bribe."

His eyes widened. "You *what?*"

"We'll start it circulating as a rumor. Maybe I can get him to print something. You'll be vague, shrug it off as one of those things. I'll line up police protection during the game and after. Look, Asa, if you *did* take money from them, for God's sake give it back. You can forget what you owe me—I'll even give the five hundred back if you need it."

The toothpick began waggling as Harry called us. Brainard rose and said, "Who else you talked to?"

"Nobody. Just throw your two pitches and I'll take care of the rest. After we kick the Haymakers' butts, I'm going to be scarce the next few days. You might do the same."

He gestured casually, brushing me away. But I sensed that he was calculating like mad.

"Who's the other?" I asked.

He looked at me. "What?"

"The other Stocking. Is it Waterman?"

"Don't you say that," he snapped. "Fred's on the square."

"Sweasy, then?"

"I ain't saying nothing to you about any of this," he said flatly. "And I won't."

Looking us over, his own face bandaged, Harry shook his head. We didn't inspire confidence. Sweasy was hobbling, Gould was practically one-armed, and the rest of us bore marks from the fight. My shoulder felt leaden. I might be able to bat, but throwing was out of the question. Andy, ironically, had come out in the best shape among us.

But we must have made a brave picture as we emerged in the sunlight. An earsplitting sound swelled from the crowd. Spectators clustered on the roof of the Grand Duchess, overflowed the new stand, clung to the fences, covered carriages and drays circling the outfield, and were packed outside the foul lines so densely it would have been impossible to sit had they wanted. Police worked to clear the diamond, a slow process.

We warmed up methodically, no sleight-of-hand exhibitions today.

I stood next to Sweasy while we waited for the Haymakers to appear.

"Remember the guy on the landing?" I said. "The one who told me where Andy was?"

"What about him?" Sweasy said.

"He told me a few other things."

Sweasy fumbled an easy throw from George and looked at me with stricken eyes. "What'd he say?"

I knew I had him then; how much easier he was than Brainard to crack. "He mentioned Acey," I said casually. "And you."

"I didn't go back on us!"

"How much did you get?"

"God Almighty." His voice quavered. "I told 'em I wouldn't throw off. They said they'd pay me just to listen to their proposition. No fault in hearing them out, was there? I turned 'em down!"

The last piece clicked in place in my mind. "You stupid asshole, where'd you meet them?"

"I can't tell," he protested. "I promised."

"What happened while you were gone?"

He stood as if frozen. George yelled at him.

"Throw the damn ball," I said. "They set you up, didn't they? They knew Andy'd be alone, and that's when they took him. You couldn't go to the cops because you'd compromised yourself. So you tried to put it all on me, sweet guy that you are."

"I didn't know." It was almost a whisper.

"That's right," I said. "You didn't know shit, so you ended up selling Andy out."

His eyes stabbed into mine, imploring. "You ain't gonna tell him."

A gathering murmur came from the crowd, punctuated by loud cheers from the visitors' area behind third, as a pennant-festooned omnibus rumbled through the carriage gate in right field and moved around the track.

"It depends," I said. "If we lose I'm gonna beat you to a pulp and go public with the whole shoddy story. How does that sound?"

"We won't lose," he said nervously. "Not on account of me."

"Well, that's all you have to worry about. Just yourself. I'll be watching. Everything. Understand?"

He nodded.

The omnibus halted near the visitors' bench. The Haymakers emerged in jaunty new uniforms, no longer their old-fashioned brown cords but now a splash of patriotic colors: red caps with white peaks, white pants and shirts, red belts, blue stockings, tan canvas shoes. They looked confident. And mean as ever.

I studied them: Clipper Flynn tossing his blond locks and posturing before the Troy rooters; the King brothers already swaggering and shooting us hard looks; agile Bellan moving with lithe grace; Cherokee Fisher smiling sardonically at jibes from the crowd, many of whom had cheered him last season when he pitched for the Bucks; and Bull Craver, whose eyes sought mine before he turned away to take Fisher's warm-ups. I had the same feeling I remembered in Troy: we'd need everything we had to beat them.

As cops finished clearing the field, I informed Millar that Brainard had been offered a bribe.

"Jupiter!" he said. "How'd you know? He tell you?"

"Not exactly, but it's no secret by now. Ask him yourself. Others may have been approached too. Haven't you heard the rumors?"

"There've been nothing *but* rumors for days now. Morrissey's supposed to have twenty thousand dollars on the Haymakers."

"He's here?" I asked quickly.

"No, but our friend McDermott is."

I followed his gesture and saw the red-haired gambler standing behind the Haymaker bench staring darkly at Andy. That was good. It meant he hadn't been in touch with Le Caron—although I wasn't optimistic enough to think that the latter had been trapped in the fire. Andy's your first surprise, Red Jim, you bastard, I thought. Not getting the ransom is your second. And with any luck your third will come when we win big and you lose even bigger.

"Who's next to him?" I asked, eyeing a short dapper man in a white summer suit.

"McKeon, Haymaker president."

Christ, another Irishman. It seemed they ran everything.

"Given the situation, a cop or two near the benches might be good," I said. "But I'd rather not bother Champion with it."

Millar gave me his owlish look. "Chief Mercil's here. You think there'll be trouble?"

"The odds still with us?"

He nodded. "Latest I heard from Vine was that eastern money was pouring in on the Haymakers to finish no more than nine runs behind."

Almost a cinch bet, even with Andy on hand and Brainard—I hoped—playing to win. We'd barely taken them in Troy—and we hadn't started out with a pregame brawl. With all the angles he thought he had going, McDermott must have bet every dime he could find.

"There'll be some real anxious bettors, then," I said. "And a lot of sore losers."

"Understood," Millar said, and went off to find the police chief.

Ten minutes later uniformed cops stood conspicuously behind the players' benches and scorer's table. I felt about as secure as I was likely to that afternoon.

"What were you doing at that big steamboat fire?" Millar asked. "People swear they saw the nine there—carrying bats, even—just about the time the boilers blew."

"Just passing by," I said. "On our way here."

"By way of the landing?" When I didn't elaborate he sighed. "Well, that's more than I got from Harry and the rest."

"How so?"

"They all said, 'What fire?' "

The umpire Harry proposed was Joe Brockway of the Great Westerns. I'd seen him play and ump; he was accurate, fair, and respected locally. Surprisingly, the Haymakers accepted him with no quarrel. Brockway, a tall man with thinning sandy hair and sunburned skin, flipped a coin, which landed in Troy's favor. Craver waved us to the plate first with a peremptory gesture. Harry came away looking sour.

"Those fellows require another lesson," he told us.

The Haymakers surprised us by starting Fisher at second and pitching Charlie Bearman, a player we hadn't seen in Troy. His slow warm-ups looked easy to hit. As if to confirm it, George pounded his first pitch through the infield for a single and promptly stole second. But Gould and Waterman popped up, and Allison's liner was snared by Bellan at third. We'd been whitewashed in the first. Not a good beginning.

As the Haymakers came in, McDermott stood clapping beside McKeon, his eyes on Brainard.

Now was the pitcher's moment. I'd seen him note the cops and glance at me. Now I studied him in the box. His motion looked jerkier than usual. His warm-ups came high and low. Allison went out to talk to him.

The leadoff Haymaker stepped in—and took a pitch ten feet over his head. The crowd groaned. Twelve thousand pairs of eyes fastened on Brainard. His next pitch went completely behind the hitter. McDermott, grinning broadly, leaned close to McKeon. Was the whole Troy club in on the fix?

Brainard worked the hitter to a full count, then gave up a sharp single to center. Mart King, up next, did not lift the bat from his shoulder. He walked on four pitches. Enough, Acey, I thought. The runners advanced on a ground out. Another grounder scored a run. Then the roof caved in. Flynn swatted a curving drive down the line that Andy misjudged. Craver smashed one in almost exactly the same place. Andy, breaking late, couldn't reach it in time. Steve King's blow to the right-center gap scored the runners. Bellan lofted an easy fly to left. Andy, completely rattled by then, dropped it. The disease spread as Mac muffed a routine fly and Waterman, usually the most reliable of infielders, let a pop-up slip off his hands. By the time we got the third out, I felt sick. For the first time I regretted my new scoreboard as a white 6 appeared beneath our 0.

"You okay?" I asked Andy. The Haymakers would have scored only once had his errors not opened the gates.

He shook his head, his cheeks burning. "I feel queer and I'm not seeing right. I didn't eat and I—"

"You didn't *what?*"

"They didn't feed me on the boat. I haven't had anything since yesterday. I think it's making me dizzy."

"Jesus, why didn't you say something?"

"Forgot. Besides, there's been no time."

"I'll be back," I said, and dashed off to the booth. There, things were a mess. Helga and the other women had lagged far behind, with Johnny off on the steamboat rescue. Now the four were frantically trying to catch up and serve hundreds of customers standing in line.

"How're we doing out there?" Johnny asked. He was drenched with sweat. A lump swelled his forehead where he'd taken a hit during the fight.

I wrapped up some fries (square-bottomed paper bags hadn't been invented, so we, like everybody, twisted paper to form cone-shaped containers, much the way flowers are wrapped) and a hamburger and poured an ice-cream soda into a glass (disposable cups didn't exist either) and said, "So far it couldn't be much worse."

I got back in time to see Andy thrown out by a step on an infield bouncer. Harry, breaking from first on Bearman's floater, sprinted all the way to third. To my surprise he didn't stop there. A roar erupted from the crowd. Too late the Haymaker first baseman realized what was happening and threw to the plate. Harry slid past Craver's lunging tag. Only one run—but it was a start.

Andy wolfed the food down. I settled back at the scorer's table. Brainard was due up next, then Sweasy. To me they'd looked as energized as the rest when Harry scored. If either intended to sell us out, he was putting on a good show. It got better: Brainard worked Bearman for a walk and Sweasy singled up the middle. Mac then drilled the ball past a diving Bellan to score Brainard, and George's low shot over third base scored two more. Then Gould topped a roller down the line that Bellan, playing deep, couldn't get to in time. Snakebit, he slammed the ball to the turf in frustration. Waterman walked to load the bases, then Allison stroked a single that, coupled with a wild throw, scored all three runners. We yelled with the exultant crowd. And it wasn't ended yet. Harry, playing with the brilliant intensity he'd shown in the Forest City squeaker, singled Allison home and dove into second on the throw.

"I see good now," Andy told me, heading for the plate. He quickly proved it by slamming an inside pitch to left that scored Harry for our ninth run of the inning. McDermott's grin had long since vanished.

The Haymakers moved Fisher to the box. Andy went to work on old Cherokee with dancing leads off first. To the crowd's delight he stole second and third on consecutive pitches—and when Craver threw wildly over Bellan, he trotted home.

Something about the way Craver stood with hands on hips triggered in my mind his spiking of Andy. Not again! I thought. I jumped up and ran toward the plate, yelling, "Watch out! Watch their catcher!"

Brockway glanced curiously at me, then at Craver as Andy tagged the plate. Craver's face turned purple. He pointed at me and snarled, "Get that nancy boy away!"

I pointed back. "Next time you want to step on somebody, try me!"

Andy grabbed me, and suddenly I was hemmed in by Stockings.

"Calm down," Harry said. "He hasn't done anything."

"He intended to," I said, and looked at Brockway. "Watch that ape—he likes to hurt people."

"I'll run this, not you," Brockway snapped.

"Enough, Sam!" Harry pushed me back. "Haven't you had your fill today?"

"Meet me after!" Craver yelled. "I got a score to settle, nancy boy!"

"Anywhere!" I yelled.

Harry and the rest practically dragged me back to the table. Only later, after the Haymakers had argued in vain that my interference invalidated Andy's run—Brockway ruled there was no possible play at the plate, and in any case I hadn't actually stepped within the diamond—did I consider how monumentally stupid it would be for me to stick around to fight Craver instead of leaving the ballpark as soon as we'd won.

Assuming we did, that is, by enough runs. The Haymakers came at us again in the bottom of the second. After diving spectacularly to snag a sinking liner, Andy, playing more erratically than I'd ever seen, turned an easier drive into a two-base muff. A sequence of scratch hits preceded Mart King's towering triple, on which Haymakers circled the bases like windup toys. Only Waterman's ballsy knockdown of a blistering smash saved more Haymaker runs. As it was, they tallied seven and moved back in front, 13–10.

We got two back in the third on errors, then blanked them in their half when Andy snared a foul bound in the corner and Harry leaped high to rob Craver.

The next half inning belonged to Andy. Taking first on a fielder's choice, he stole second and third again, outrunning Craver's bullet throws with flashing speed that amazed even me. The burly catcher looked homicidal.

Then Brainard lofted a fly to short right. Andy tagged and set himself to sprint home. Flynn caught the ball on the dead run and launched a low whizzing peg. Andy's legs drove him toward the plate. Craver straddled the base path several feet up the line. The ball arrived on a perfect bounce.

"Watch him," I yelled at Brockway, jumping up again. "WATCH CRAVER!"

The throw had Andy by six feet. Craver wheeled for the tag, a murderous obstacle. I wanted to look away as Andy bunched his shoulders and ducked his head. No, I thought, not headfirst! Craver dropped to one knee and held the ball with both hands, ready to rip upward with it. But Andy had decoyed. Instead of diving he straightened abruptly and vaulted into the air. The suddenness of it was startling, as if he had exploded upward from the sod. For an instant— an indelible instant in the minds of the thousands watching—Andy seemed to air-walk over Craver. Realizing he'd been fooled, the catcher bellowed and reared, thrusting the ball upward with maiming force.

And Andy kicked it from his hand.

He landed on the plate with the tying run. In itself the vertical leap was astounding. In these circumstances it was the stuff of legend. The crowd shrieked and roared for minutes afterward. We pounded Andy nearly to the ground. The Haymakers, led by McKeon, formed a shouting, gesticulating circle around Brockway, arguing vehemently that Andy should be out.

When he finally ordered them to resume playing, they managed only one ball out of the infield in the bottom of the fourth. The game's momentum was all with us now. McDermott, I saw with mixed feelings, had disappeared.

Haymakers 13, Stockings 13.

"I checked with Western Union," Millar said. "When the first inning's score went out, every sharp in the East tried to get money down on the Haymakers."

"And now?"

"Now the wire's jammed with messages for McKeon."

"What sort of messages?"

"They can't tell me, but I'll bet we see the Haymakers pull some curious stunts, now that we're settling to our business."

Millar's words proved to be prophetic.

In the top of the fifth, Brainard's double scored two and sent Andy to third. Andy then scared the daylights out of me—and rubbed salt in Craver's wounds—by stealing home, belly-sliding to touch the plate before Craver drove the ball hard into his thigh. Andy bounced up as if he'd felt nothing. We led by four runs.

"Don't try him again," I warned. "He'll kill you."

"I've gone over and under him," Andy said, laughing. "Next time maybe I'll go through him. Wouldn't that be a dinger?"

"No, it'd be suicide."

Fighting back, the Haymakers kept the game what Millar called, "Dick pull, Devil pull." Brainard's late start for first on a grounder to Gould allowed a runner. I scrutinized Brainard, wondering if the miscue had been deliberate. So far he'd been nearly as up-and-down as Andy. Then he walked Flynn—Brockway's calls had favored hitters all afternoon—and Craver stalked to the plate. Uh-oh, I thought. Sure enough, Craver smashed a belt-high fastball into the left-field corner for a triple. Brainard grooved another to Mart King, who went for it like a shark after blood, ramming the ball clear out of the Union Grounds. So much for our lead. It was now 17–17.

"What the hell're you doing?" I demanded of Brainard when he came off.

"Not showing the white, if that's what you're saying." He massaged his pitching shoulder. "My wing's nearly used up, and they're heavy strikers."

"We gotta win," I said. "By at least ten runs."

He shrugged, as if it were out of his domain. The crowd's noise rose around us. We turned toward the plate, where Craver was talking animatedly with Brockway. Mac looked on in the striker's box. Harry strode past us.

"What now?" I asked.

"Can't tell," Harry said. "A wide called on Fisher, I think."

But it was more than that. Mac had fouled a pitch straight back that Craver bobbled. Brockway ruled that it touched the ground before he'd secured a hold on it. The catcher now turned away and looked questioningly at McKeon. He did so again after the next pitch, a called ball. Brainard and I exchanged looks. Something strange was going on.

Fisher delivered again. Mac swung late, barely making contact. The ball flew back on a low trajectory, striking the gravelly dirt between Craver's feet. He bent quickly, rose, and held it up. "How's that?" he demanded.

We couldn't tell from the Stockings' bench whether Craver had taken the ball cleanly on the first bound. Brockway, however, stood only several feet from the action.

"Two bounces!" he announced promptly. "No out! That's two against the striker!"

Craver didn't say a word, but looked at McKeon, now walking toward him. They exchanged a nod. McKeon said something to Brockway. Then, before our disbelieving eyes and those of the buzzing crowd, Craver waved the Haymakers off the field. They began packing up their bats.

"What the hell?" I said.

"They figured there's too much chance of losing," Brainard said. "Or their backers did."

We watched the carriage gates swing open and their omnibus come on the track. A rising murmur of discontent issued from the stands.

"Gonna get stirred up here," Brainard said.

"But what happens to all the bets?" I said.

"Don't you see? We've finished five innings, so they'll claim a tie. They were hoping for this or better."

"McDermott will collect, then?"

"He'll try, depending on what else happens. But he sure can't lose now."

As I tried to digest what that might mean for me, the Haymakers boarded their bus. A band of boys broke through the ropes, dodging cops and flinging rocks at the departing vehicle. Behind them the crowd flooded over the police line. Around us suddenly scrambled men yelling and running and hurling things.

"Let's go," I said, and was simultaneously aware of a subtle, almost subliminal whizzing sound. I heard it again, then a thud in the sod exploded dirt upward in a tiny eruption before me. I stared at it stupidly, then felt a tug at my pants. I saw a neat hole in the baggy white material just above my knee. Only then did I realize that somebody was shooting at me.

21

I grabbed Brainard's arm and we wedged through the crowd toward the clubhouse. Inside, I breathed easier. As the others came in, we pieced together what was happening. Mac held his place at home plate while Harry talked to Brockway, who at length climbed atop his chair and announced he was awarding us the game. To leave no doubt, Harry had him write his decision in the score book:

> McVey at the bat. The Haymakers refuse to proceed. I decide in favor of the Cincinnati club. J. R. Brockway, Great Western B.B.C.

While I changed and waited for the others—no way I was venturing out alone—I saw Millar approach Brainard with pencil and pad. "Asa," he said briskly, "I need your comment on rumors that you were offered money to throw off this match."

Brainard gave me a probing look. "You can say that I'd swear to it under oath."

"Jupiter!" said Millar. "That's some—"

"What I'm saying," Brainard interrupted, "is that's how the *rumor* has it."

"But I want your firsthand statement."

"You asked about a rumor," Brainard said. "That's what I'm commenting on. According to the *rumor,* I'd testify I was approached to throw off this game."

"That's all?"

"That's it."

"What if I say you don't want to comment?"

"Print that," said Brainard, "and you'll never get anything from me again."

"That's hard on me, Asa."

"Too damn bad."

For the next four days I laid low at Gasthaus zur Rose. When Johnny wasn't around to talk to, I read, stared at the geraniums in the window, and wondered morosely what new plans McDermott and O'Donovan were cooking up. The notion of Le Caron stalking me in Cincinnati was terrifying. I'd rather face the whole Fenian army.

Stories of the disputed game filled all the papers. The consensus was that if the Haymakers had not quit the field to protect gamblers, we'd have gone on to win convincingly. But I wasn't so sure. The Haymakers were fighters. Now we wouldn't know, unless we played them again in the East.

Which, according to the papers, was increasingly likely. The leading New York clubs, practically begging for return matches, were practicing hard, particularly the Mutuals and the Atlantics. Prospects of capturing the pennant, plus receipts from eager crowds, I reflected, must be a powerful lure for Harry and Champion.

The Haymaker game had been on Thursday, August 26. They left town on Sunday. I didn't emerge from my refuge until Monday the thirtieth, and had it not been for Andy's message I might have hidden longer. Johnny brought the note to me. It was brutally simple: Timmy's sickness had been diagnosed: typhoid fever.

Typhoid . . . I didn't even know what it was. Something that killed people. Like diphtheria, whooping cough, scarlet fever—things people used to get before new vaccines and preventatives eradicated them.

With Johnny I raced to the West End, fearing what I would find. Andy answered Cait's door, his face haggard.

"How bad is he?" I asked.

"Can't get much worse."

Timmy lay motionless, thin and wasted, burning with fever. His eyes were half-shut. Cait, bending over him, looked ravaged. She hadn't slept, Andy said, for three days.

"Samuel," she said softly, her eyes lifting to meet mine. I saw frightening depths of resignation in them.

"When did a doctor see him?"

She shook her head.

"He was here day before yesterday," Andy replied. "Said there's nothing for it but to wait."

"Wait?" I exclaimed. "What the hell kind of doctor is that? Let's get him over right now, for as long as we need him."

Cait said nothing. Andy looked uneasy. "Irish don't always rate that kind of crack attention," he said.

I stared at him. "You mean to tell me—"

"Wait," Johnny interrupted. "There's a wizard doctor in Over the

Rhine, a Dutchman, came here in the 'forty-eight revolutions. Looks after Helga and me sometimes. Charges top dollar, though."

"Go get him," I said.

"He speaks mostly Dutch," added Johnny, heading for the door.

"Then you can translate."

Two hours elapsed. Andy left for practice. I sat beside Cait, watching Timmy and listening to his choked breathing. Occasional groans emerged through his parched lips. Cait squeezed drops from a drenched cloth, but he could barely swallow. I held him, his body fearfully light, over a bedpan four times in those first hours; a foul-smelling, pea-soup diarrhea spilled from him, and each time he cried and clutched his stomach.

Cait's weary passivity irked me. We can't just sit here, I thought, we've got to *do* something. Questioning her, I learned that there had been a gradation of head and joint aches, coughs and sore throats, nosebleeds, chills, and suddenly the relentless high fever with alternating spells of constipation and diarrhea, vomiting, and terrible abdominal pain. The prescribed quinine had been too harsh on the boy's weakened system, so Cait had stopped it.

How often is this fatal? I wondered, and then wondered if I really wanted to know.

The doctor arrived, a balding man named Unzelman whose aristocratic bearing and superior German tones put me off, but he treated Johnny with surprising deference.

"That's 'cause he knows I'm a performer, an *artiste*," Johnny said later. "They're serious about the circus where he came from."

Unzelman put a hand on Timmy's brow and muttered. He checked his pulse and lifted his nightshirt. A welter of rash marks dotted the boy's swollen abdomen. The doctor pressed gently on one, watched it go pale.

"What are those?" I asked.

"Rose spots," replied Johnny, after an exchange with Unzelman. "A prime sign of typhoid."

Translating carefully, Johnny gave us Unzelman's instructions: withhold quinine until Timmy was stronger; keep him on a high-protein, nonfibrous diet of milk and eggs; apply cold compresses to his head and warm gum-spirit compresses to his abdomen.

The fever, Unzelman said, rose in staircase escalations. Timmy was approaching the peak, the crisis point. If he survived it, his chances would be fair.

"Doesn't mince words, does he?" I said. "What caused it in the first place?"

"Bad air," said Johnny. "You know, the ether."

At that word Unzelman's head jerked and he rattled off something with harsh quickness.

Johnny looked abashed. "He says I'm an idiot, no such thing as evil air."

Unzelman insisted that Timmy's compresses, bedding, and all waste material be carefully disposed of, or the disease would spread. The house would have to be quarantined, its occupants restricted in their movements. I saw a shadow of a worried frown cross Cait's face. A quarantine, I thought, might not fit Fenian plans.

"I'll try to sterilize everything in here," I said.

"Do what?" said Johnny.

"Boil stuff," I said. "Kill germs."

He spoke to Unzelman, who regarded me approvingly.

"He says that's one of the most intelligent things he's ever heard in Cincinnati. Wants to know if you're familiar with the new work of somebody named Pasteur."

"Sort of."

"He's impressed," said Johnny, adding that Unzelman was willing to return daily. His visitation fee was five dollars.

Cait looked despairingly at me.

"Let's make it twice a day," I said, taking her hand. Money was least among our concerns.

The days and nights that followed contained long sleepless vigils punctuated by fits of intense activity. I boiled rags for compresses, soaked them in the gum spirits—the odor of turpentine permeated the house—wrung them out, changed them periodically. During the rare intervals when Cait dozed, I followed Unzelman's instructions carefully in preparing Timmy's milk. It had to be heated to approximately 150 degrees, maintained there for half an hour, then cooled rapidly and kept cold to kill remaining bacteria. Andy and Johnny, though visibly skeptical, kept us supplied with ice; and I was learning to regulate the wood stove in the kitchen with some facility.

During my second night Timmy sank horribly. His skin burned with fever, his breathing was irregular, his pulse barely discernible. We thought for one terrible moment that he had died.

"If he goes," said Cait, "I'm going with him."

The finality of it chilled and angered me. "Don't say that," I blurted, slamming my fist against the wall. "We're not losing anybody!"

She looked at me wordlessly, her expression unreadable.

The world shrank and was encompassed by the walls of that room, a world in which our resources consisted of each other. It was an emotional cauldron. We forged bonds there that linked us, in my mind, forever.

Timmy moaned, body writhing, intestines locked in agony, Cait crying with him in the worst times.

With daylight it seemed a bit easier.

We went on.

It was hard to pinpoint the crisis. Only days later were we sure that the fever was subsiding and that the worst had passed. The danger of relapse, Unzelman warned, would be extremely high for at least another week.

It was about then that the ghost came.

Cait and I were drowsing, around three or four in the morning. An oil lamp gleamed dimly above Timmy, the only light in the room. I woke with a start at the sound of a branch striking the side of the house. Strange, I thought, for a storm to rise so quickly.

A high, thin wail escaped Timmy. Later I wondered if it were a cry of recognition, of welcome. But at the time, thinking the noise had frightened him, I rose and stepped toward the bed. At that point several things happened.

The lamplight dimmed to a tiny glowing point and disappeared.

I heard Cait say, distinctly and wonderingly, "A bird."

"What?" I fumbled in my pockets for matches, wondering where to find more lamp oil.

"That sound," she said. "It was a bird."

Hell of a big bird, I thought; and then my mind flooded with recollections of ghostly winged apparitions. I said cautiously, "You see it?"

"I suppose I dreamed it," she said. "But I think it was . . ."

Colm.

I became aware of loamy odors; tangible, heavy fragrances of green leaves and tree bark and earth. It was in the room, a presence emerging in the gum-spirit atmosphere.

"Tim!" Fear strained Cait's voice.

I reached out to be sure he was still there. To my surprise he was sitting halfway up. I kept my hand on him and drew Cait close with my other arm.

He was there with us.

I didn't think the room brightened, but I wasn't sure. I saw a shape limned in light, a dark, familiar shape in a long military coat, one arm stretched to us, as if in greeting. Or beckoning. I couldn't *be* more frightened than I was then. Cait sagged against me.

God, I thought crazily, if it *is* Colm, how must this look, the three of us, me with his family?

Timmy suddenly squeezed my hand with surprising force. Sitting erect, looking straight at the apparition, he mumbled something.

As goose bumps rippled over me the apparition turned slightly toward him, or perhaps it was just the outstretched arm that moved.

"NO!" Cait shrieked.

"Wait," I breathed, holding her as she struggled toward Timmy.

We watched its other arm rise slowly, as if in benediction. Then the figure began to recede, slowly at first and building to a great rush. Just before it vanished I glimpsed tiny figures, humans, standing across a distant stream beyond him.

I found a match and lit the lamp. It held plenty of oil. Timmy lay supine, eyes closed, asleep. Cait and I looked at each other.

"Did you see the others?" I said. "At the end?"

She nodded, swallowing hard. "It was the Other Side we were seeing."

"My God," I said.

"I feared he wanted to take Tim."

"Could you make out what Timmy said?"

"No, but I know it was Colm standing there for a certainty."

She sounded more sad than anything. I wondered if she were still in love with him.

"Cait, I had this strong feeling he was trying to help."

"Yes," she said.

Several days later, when Timmy felt up to talking, I asked if he remembered any unusual dreams. Cait leaned forward tensely.

"Like what?" Timmy asked.

"Like, say, someone was here with us, a soldier maybe."

"A soldier?" he said, eyes widening. "Here?"

"Yes," I said, "like he suddenly came through the window or the wall, and—"

"Like the bird did," said Timmy.

"What bird?" said Cait.

"There was this big soft-looking bird, all friendly, like he was my pal. He came to be with me 'cause I was sick. Least that's what he said."

"He *said?*"

Timmy laughed weakly. "Sounds wrong now, but it wasn't then. It was real as life."

I sketched on a piece of paper. "Did he look like this? A dove?"

"That's it," said Timmy. "The chest was puffed out like that, and the eyes were all warm, like they were lit up."

Cait began to cry.

The quarantine imposed by the city consisted of a red warning sign posted on the front door. Nothing else. Andy and Johnny came and went freely, bringing supplies. Several times I asked Cait where her boarders were. Her answers were vague.

I began taking afternoon walks. One day I returned to find the illustrious Fenian hero himself, Captain Fearghus O'Donovan, emerging from the parlor. In the street, regarding me coolly from a carriage, were half a dozen other men. I recognized several from Cait's.

O'Donovan faced me on the porch.

"Back from the wars?" I said.

"Wars?"

"The ones you're trying to start?"

He gave me a long, cold stare. "Caitlin tells me you rescued her brother."

"Yes," I said. "Worse luck for you that Le Caron screwed up."

"I'm not familiar with that person."

"McDermott's cutthroat. The one who did the kidnapping and tried to kill Andy and the rest of us by firing the boat. Ring any bells?"

"No."

"I suppose you deny knowing McDermott, too."

He took a deep breath. "Blackguards may serve causes nobler than themselves."

"Like gambling, you mean?"

"You'd be well paid to contain your insolence, sir."

I laughed, wondering if I could provoke him into admitting his complicity. I had the impression he was feeling his way, deciding how to play me.

"Until now I've shown forbearance on Caitlin's account."

"Bullshit," I said. "You haven't come at me only because you thought I might disappear. Then you'd never learn who I worked for. You're so paranoid that—"

"I'm *what?*"

"—you assume I'm a spy. But most of all, you'd never get your hands on the precious money."

"Ah, there!" he exclaimed. "You've as much as admitted robbing us!"

"How can you be robbed of something you never had?"

"General O'Neill has ordered me to recover it."

"I see." I grinned maliciously. "While he's off recruiting the KKK, you get the fun stuff—like sucking up to McDermott."

His fists clenched, knuckles whitening; his eyes glittered with malice.

"You ought to give up extortion," I said. "Even with McDermott's expertise, you're not very good at it."

"Why do you talk of him?" he hissed.

I saw no point in revealing my eavesdropping adventure. On the other hand, I enjoyed watching him wriggle on my hook.

"Maybe because his name goes so well with yours. 'McDermott and O'Donovan.' Like a partnership, no?"

"You have a fortnight, sir," he stated.

"For what?" Was he challenging me to a duel?

"To deliver the money."

"Oh, for Chrissake, can't you drop that?"

"I don't make idle threats. Have it together when I return in mid-September."

"How generous to give me that long."

"Another matter, more personal. I intend for Mrs. O'Neill to become my wife. You have no right to see her."

"She's the one to decide that."

"Not necessarily."

I lost it then. The words whooshed out in an explosive gust. "I'm tired of threats. I'm tired of being told what to do. If something happens to me, you can be damn sure Cait will find out your precise role in her brother's kidnapping. I've already arranged for it. Not only that," I added, swept on by my own lies and my anger, "she'll get the full story on Colm!"

I suppose I'd meant it as a probe, a shot in the dark. The instant the words left my mouth I realized I'd hit ground zero. He staggered back as if I'd socked him. His face went pale, and he stared at me with narrowed eyes. In the street the cab doors opened abruptly and men began to climb out. O'Donovan waved them back.

"Who are you?" he breathed.

I said nothing, intrigued by the dramatic reaction.

His voice rose above a whisper. "Now it's plain why you brought up that bastard McDermott!"

"Is it?" This was proving interesting.

"You dare link his name with mine, when *you're* the one conspiring!"

"Conspiring?" I wanted to snatch his shirtfront and shake him. "O'Donovan, you dimwit! *Bullets* were flying around me at our last game! Le Caron blew up an entire boat! You're trying to force me to give you huge amounts of money and to stay away from Cait and Timmy. Now *you're* bent out of shape because you got a threat back? What the hell's wrong with you?"

"A fortnight," he said, staring into my eyes. "Honor will be satisfied, should I have to pursue you to earth's end."

Later I would have cause to remember his phrase.

I returned to the team to find that Champion had also given me notice. As soon as he hired a new substitute, my playing tenure would end. I'd keep my other roles, but at half salary. Thanks a lot.

Actually, I wasn't surprised. Harry was sympathetic, but I'd missed far too much practice. I knew that he could use somebody younger, with more speed and versatility. And who wouldn't suddenly disappear or get shot. I was welcome to work out with the team, he assured me, even keep the score book during games, if I wanted. On balance I wouldn't be losing all that much.

Champion's decision, I suspected, stemmed only in part from my most recent absence. Somehow he'd gotten word of the steamboat escapade. Though our presence there had not made the papers— coverage of the fire was eclipsed by the disputed game—to Champion it must have represented exactly the sort of reckless adventuring he dreaded.

I got back in time to suit up for a game to benefit the Buckeyes. Their resources were currently at a low ebb, so we were helping out.

"Typhoid Fowler's back," Allison greeted me in the clubhouse.

"Quarantine's lifted," I announced. "Your hero is here!"

They hooted me.

"Curious how you and Acey laid off," Waterman said, "when Harry was grinding our butts into the dirt."

"Acey?" I looked over at Brainard, who was pulling on his cotton undershirt.

"Been sicker'n a pup," he said soberly.

"Everything clear?" I asked him on the diamond. "McDermott gone?"

" 'Pears so," he replied. "You mind if I hang on to that other five hundred a mite longer?"

"No problem," I said. "Were you going to throw that game?"

He said nothing.

Probably just as well. I might not have liked his answer.

Before a fair-sized crowd, we set about battering the Buckeyes. It was pathetic. George, Sweasy, and Mac had thirteen hits *each*, and every starter scored at least ten runs. We hit eleven homers. We won 103–8.

In the final inning Harry let me bat for Allison. I went to the plate thinking it would probably be my last time up as a Stocking. I wanted to make it count.

The Buck hurler came in with a low medium-speed spinner. I strode into it and whipped the bat. Solid contact. The ball flamed on a line to the fence. "Hold!" yelled Harry as I rounded first. The left fielder played the carom perfectly. I sprinted for second, not about to stop. The throw came in strong. I hooked away from the baseman, outside the bag, catching it with my bent left leg. He lunged to make the tag, lost his balance, sprawled over me.

"Safe!" hollered the ump.

I hadn't ignored a base coach since Little League. I brushed myself off, feeling elated and guilty.

"Sorry," I said later to Harry. "I just didn't want it to end so fast."

"I noticed." He smiled faintly. "Perhaps there'll be chances for you on the nine again, once things settle." The warm eyes regarded me shrewdly. "But don't *ever* run through my directions!"

We stopped by Cait's, finding her and Timmy in good spirits. Andy displayed the small Stocking uniform he'd had specially made. I thought Timmy's eyes would pop.

"The fellas say you can be our mascot," Andy told him.

"Oh boy!"

"We'll see," Cait said quickly.

"MOTHER!"

That night, before a special meeting of the club, most of the nine and a number of Buckeyes gathered to eat at Leininger's. George read aloud from a *New York Sun* story on the Haymaker game, reprinted in the *Enquirer:* "The Umpire very properly gave the game to the Cincinnati Club. . . . The Haymakers have always had a bad reputation. No club ever visited Troy and returned satisfied with their treatment. . . ." Last season, the article continued, before a contest with the Atlantics, the Haymaker president had tipped Mute players to back Troy because "a job had been put up." If such was true, the writer concluded, the Haymakers should be expelled from the association.

We toasted the *Sun* reporter, grateful for eastern support.

Allison got laughs saying he'd heard that Lansingburghers were now so broke that housewives bought fish with flatirons and got change in matches and soft soap. In saloons drinks averaged two shirt collars.

"You fellers headin' East again?" said one of the Bucks.
"Tonight will likely decide that," George answered.

Three hundred club members applauded us in Mozart Hall. From the podium a smiling Champion orchestrated with grand gestures. We were in for a surprise.

"Gentlemen," he announced, "the repute of our invincible first nine [more applause] has spread across the bosom [sly chuckles] of this continent. An invitation has arrived from the Pacific Slope, from the assembled baseball clubs of San Francisco and Sacramento, challenging us to a series of matches [shouts, laughter]. What's more [dramatic pause and triumphant crescendo] they want us so badly they'll pay our entire fare on the Pacific Railroad, lodge us at their expense, and give us half the receipts from all matches!"

The resulting roar reverberated in the large room. Not all of it signified support. Gould and Mac were on their feet yelling, "Let's go!" George and Waterman shouted, "No! The whip pennant!"

Debate lasted two hours. Go East or go West? Either choice would reward the club and add to its fame. There wasn't time to do both; contracts expired November 15, and September was already upon us.

I sat numbly as voices droned, one arguing for storming baseball's traditional strongholds again, another dwelling on the glory of being the first to play on both coasts. Harry said nothing. I suspected that he and Andy and the other eastern players preferred going for the pennant, playing again before their families and friends. But the lure of crossing the continent was strong. The gold rush had happened only twenty years before. The West was wild and exotic, still inhabited by untamed Indians.

"I'm for Frisco," I heard Brainard remark to Waterman. It occurred to me he might have his own reasons for not wanting to visit New York just then. But Allison also liked the idea, as did Sweasy.

In the end the chance to ride the four-month-old transcontinental railroad—already it was the rage among the fashionable—won out, especially since it would be free. An experience roughly equivalent, I thought, to a passenger shuttle to the moon. Except that reaching the moon wouldn't take two weeks.

By a narrow margin the club voted to send us to California.

Tangled emotions played in me. I had no defense against bittersweet memories. San Francisco. Where I had left my little girls, my identity, my life.

"Sam!"

Andy was grinning at me.

"Ain't it dandy for you!"

"What's that?"

"Why," he said, looking at me expectantly, "you're goin' home!"

PART THREE
THE PACIFIC

———◇———

. . . and I will remark here, in passing, that all scenery in California requires distance *to give it its highest charm.*

MARK TWAIN, Roughing It

Go, go, go said the bird: human kind
Cannot bear very much reality.

T. S. ELIOT, Four Quartets

Fowler . . . continued his discoveries, with the result that I came out safe and sound, at the end. . . .

MARK TWAIN, Autobiography

22

"ood grief, Cait, what's wrong?"

She looked at me silently, took a deep breath. "I'm not sure."

It struck me as an honest assessment. She had been distant and fretful for several days. When I'd told her about the nine going West, she said, "How nice for Andy," and asked how long the trip would be. I said it would take the better part of a month. Would I be going? she asked. I said I didn't know yet. What I didn't say was that it depended partly on her. Her matter-of-factness upset me. I wanted more from her. I wanted to talk about the jangling inside me that the prospect of going to San Francisco set off. Of the hauntingly strange pull I felt, almost like what had drawn me to her. But I couldn't. Why was she being so distant? Didn't she care?

"Whatever is wrong with me, as you put it," she said a moment later, "you are likely the cause."

I felt stung, as if she'd slapped me.

"Your coming to help truly was a miracle," she added quickly, "but you must know that it brings pressure."

"From O'Donovan, you mean?"

She looked troubled but said nothing. The silence stretched between us.

"Is it something else?"

Her answer was barely audible. "Knowing that you desire me . . . as a woman . . . it's . . ."

"It's what?" I said. "Pressure?"

She nodded, looking down.

"You think I might want you"—a blush crept up her face at that—"and so you feel pressure? That's all?"

"Samuel, I—"

"Don't you have desires of your own?" Anger was rising quickly, dangerously, in me. "Or maybe it's that yours don't involve me."

[307]

"Samuel, please, I cannot—"

"Just how did Timmy come about?" I demanded, overriding her. "Did Colm force himself on you?"

I regretted it the instant it left my mouth. Christ, we'd never even alluded to sex and now I say something like that.

"I *gave* myself to Colm," she said, her eyes flashing.

"Because you loved and wanted him," I replied. "Was that pressure?"

"That's not your concern."

"Fine."

We sat through another silence.

"I can't see you for a few days," she said finally.

I kept from asking what difference it made. "Why not?"

"I can't tell you."

I stood up. "It was okay when I was a visiting nurse, but now I guess it's back to real life: Fenian war games."

"Samuel, I didn't mean to upset you, but you will NOT speak slightingly to me of the society!"

"I'm going," I said. "Good-bye."

Helga didn't want to charge me for the room, but I paid two weeks in advance at Gasthaus zur Rose. I took to sleeping there most nights and rising early to stop at the nearby *Backerei* for sweet rolls and coffee. Then I sauntered along the river—following any breeze that carried its pungent smells away—and through the jumble of narrow streets. I loved the old-world brick houses with clean-swept sidewalks and garden plots and gingerbread windows swelling with flowers. I loved the early-morning bells in tall churches with clock towers. I tested my pidgin German on old women wearing wooden shoes who sat knitting in the sunshine, and on their husbands smoking long pipes nearby, figures out of Brothers Grimm.

I also kept my room at the Gibson, where I dropped by the aromatic barbershop more to hear the latest sporting talk than to have my beard trimmed. I liked the downtown bustle: cries of bootblacks and vendors; rumbling carriages and drays, their drivers shouting furiously; clanging bells of streetcars and omnibuses; organ-grinders and oom-pah bands in squares and parks; the busy squalor of the riverfront; the cool green hills ringing the city basin. I'd fallen in love with Cincinnati, I realized. Why had that feeling—and everything else, lately—taken on such urgency?

Afternoons I worked out with the Stockings, mostly because I had little else to do. Johnny and Helga had the concessions running smoothly. I'd doubled their pay as they took complete charge. Johnny had used his earnings to buy a gleaming top-of-the-line velocipede to race in the county finals at the upcoming annual fair. Several mornings I watched him train on the track at the Union Grounds. His spindly legs generated impressive power on the new machine. I hoped he had a real chance to win, suspecting that losing would devastate him.

Meanwhile, with the western trip looming, there was no reason to work harder or dream up new promotions. My job, already marginal, would soon end. With the passing of baseball season I'd have to confront the issue of purpose in my life. Sports offered a cozy refuge from reality. On the other hand, what was real? Some mind-numbing job to keep me from wondering what to do with myself? I had enough money—over six thousand dollars remained from Elmira—not to worry for a while.

I tried to stay calm about Cait. But not seeing her made me realize how large a void she and Timmy had filled. Insofar as I could remove them from my thoughts, memories of my old life seeped in. My job at the *Chronicle* didn't seem so inconsequential now. Working at one's craft—wasn't that essential? And the idea of raising my daughters, even part-time, brought back old aches. Ah, the biological imperatives. Had I deluded myself in thinking I could satisfy them with Cait and Timmy?

We met the visiting Rochester Alerts two days after my fight with Cait. I sat at the scorer's table in street clothes for the first time, feeling decidedly less glamorous. Harry had already hired Oak Taylor, the star of the juniors; he would make the western trip. I toyed with the thought of disabling him.

My own status cleared up a bit when Champion assured me that sufficient space existed and that he had no objection to my going. That was how Mr. Warmth put it. But I'd have to pay my own way. Did I want to do that? I told him I'd let him know before final ticket arrangements had to be made. *Did I want to go?* God, yes, I wanted to go—in some inexplicable way I *had* to. And yet was unaccountably afraid of it. I didn't know what I wanted.

Seeing the Alerts in their crisp white jerseys took me back to the first game I had witnessed, on that distant rainy day—was it really only three months ago?—when I'd awakened in Rochester. They were a good-looking club, second only to the Rockford Forest Citys among all-amateur clubs we'd faced. But in the fourth, sparked by Mac's gargantuan homer and Andy's steal of home, we broke things open.

The Alerts matched us afterward but couldn't gain, and it ended 32–19.

Images of San Francisco haunted me. At night, my sleep torn by exhausting dreams, the city beckoned me like a lover, calling me to come back, whispering that my destiny waited there. But the city in my dreams was the one I had known. Not whatever existed there now.

After vacillating for nearly a week I went to Champion and asked if the club would consider paying half my train fare if I covered all food and lodging. No, he said. How about a fourth? I'd help with security, run errands, and provide Harry a second substitute. I reminded him of the Troy game, when two regulars were injured, and said I'd hate to see the perfect season ruined for the sake of saving a few dollars. My salesmanship was never better. With some reluctance he agreed.

Next I visited the *Enquirer* and *Gazette* and made each an identical offer: pick up half my travel costs, and I'd wire them exclusive reports. I pointed out that if only Millar went, readers would buy the *Commercial* to follow their beloved Stockings through the exciting West. The *Gazette* was lukewarm, but not so the *Enquirer*. Tired of being scooped by their Republican competitor, they hired me on the spot and handed me an advance check.

Having taken care of half my living and ¾ my transportation costs, I told Champion to book me on. I felt relieved. That night the dreams stopped.

I found the note in my box at the Gibson:

> *Samuel,*
> *We miss you. Will you visit tonight?*
> *Caitlin*

My heart nearly catapulted from my chest. I let out a yell that lifted the feet of lobby dwellers from the gleaming parquet floor.

I arrived with a 150-piece Noah's Ark set fashioned in Bavaria that I'd found in Over the Rhine. We covered the floor with intricately carved animals and birds. Timmy fell asleep with the lions in his hand.

"This is for you," I said, handing Cait a small box.

She smiled. While I played with Timmy she'd watched quietly. She wore her green dress, the one that made her eyes even more jewellike and at once concealed and suggested the contours of her body. I could scarcely look at her. Or keep from it. She was too beautiful.

"Samuel," she breathed, holding the heart-shaped silver locket by its chain. It gleamed in the lamplight.

"Like it?"

She cradled it in her hand and gazed at it. "When I was a girl," she said, "I hoped . . ."

She didn't finish.

"I missed you, Cait."

"I couldn't follow the Circle leaders' talk," she said, smiling, "even when they spoke of the most serious military matters."

"Why was that?"

"Thinking of you."

I moved toward her. "Are you marching off to war?"

"Not just now, for a certainty."

I took her in my arms, pressed her to me as our mouths met. She held me so tightly that I could feel the trembling of her body.

"I do want you," I breathed into her hair.

She kissed me again, then leaned back and looked into my eyes. She fastened the chain around her neck and lifted my hand to cover hers holding the locket. Around its edges I felt the soft swell of her breasts. "Can you be patient, Samuel?" she said softly. "I care for you, very much."

Although attention was focused on the trip, the local baseball scene was not entirely quiet. A letter appeared in the *Gazette* arguing that the game was fast becoming, like boxing and horse racing, "a sport for gamblers and blacklegs to make money on." It should not be played for pay, but solely "for the exciting and health-giving exercise it affords," and employers should give their "best young men" time off to form amateur teams.

It was a popular argument. The country as a whole seemed obsessed with the subject of youth's corruptibility. The Stockings weren't impressed. "They'd grab for the cash fast enough if it came *their* way," Waterman said bluntly of critics. "But who'd pay to see raggedy-ass muffins?"

The Pittsburgh Olympics came in to try their luck against us. Since Johnny now spent all his time training, with the fair about to open, I turned the score book over to Oak Taylor and busied myself feeding the multitudes. When the last of the hot dogs and hamburgers sold, I was more wrung out than after one of Harry's workouts.

The game was a blowout. The Stockings took a 10–0 lead in the first and never slackened. In the face of Brainard's two-hitter, George's eight hits and six steals, and Andy's two homers, Pittsburgh fell, 54–2, in only two hours. A most efficient drubbing.

That night Johnny and I packed our supplies and equipment. The Stockings would not play here again for at least a month, until after California.

Departure was five days away.

Next morning I brought Cait and Timmy to the Hamilton & Dayton depot, where Johnny waited with his sparkling three-hundred-dollar Demarest with its gleaming steel rails, ivory handlebars, silver-plated wheels, and hard rubber tires.

"Take me for a ride!" Timmy pleaded, eyes riveted on the mechanical wonder.

"I dunno, Tim," said Johnny.

"For a certainty *not!*" Cait said.

"Tell you what," I said to Johnny. "You save your legs. I'll give him a spin around the platform."

"*You* can ride?" said Timmy wonderingly, as if it were a wild bull.

"I'm an expert."

"Sam, I don't think . . ." Johnny began nervously.

"Real slow and easy." I straddled the bike and lifted Timmy onto the handlebars. "No problem." We set off over the planks of the platform.

"Samuel!"

"Jeez, Sam!"

I wobbled a bit, giving Timmy several unintended thrills. Then I got the feel of it and we rolled smoothly. At the far end I set him on my shoulders for the return trip.

"Wheeeeee!" He clutched my hair, his knees pressing the sides of my neck, his elation fusing into me, making me young again.

"Look, Ma!" I said, lifting my hands from the bars as we coasted back.

"Samuel!"

"Where'd you learn?" Johnny said as we dismounted.

I waved at the bike and started to say it was something you knew as a kid and never forgot—then remembered that few people had mastered the new two-wheelers. "Guess I must be a natural," I said.

"Wow, Sam!" said Timmy.

"Just jump on and ride my Demarest!" Johnny said incredulously.

"Ain't Sam a dinger?" Timmy demanded, sounding for all the world like Andy.

"Samuel's fond of his surprises," Cait said, hugging him and looking at me over his shoulder. "For a certainty."

I saw the locket hanging at her throat.

When the train arrived we lifted the velocipede aboard. Johnny was already edgy.

"You'll make a fine showing," Cait told him as we pulled out of the city.

"Fine ain't enough," said Johnny.

Cait smiled uncertainly, not sure if he was serious. To her it was a marginal pastime. To him it was a new identity, the launching of his future.

Carthage lay ten miles north. We arrived at noon and shuttled by coach to the fairgrounds. Clouds of dust rose from the road. We passed beneath a banner.

FIFTEENTH ANNUAL FAIR
HAMILTON COUNTY AGRICULTURAL SOCIETY

At the gate Johnny let it be known that he was a racer and we were his guests. The ticket taker gave him and the velocipede long looks, then let us pass. The prize and concession booths were just opening. A sad-faced clown stood nearby holding balloons.

"Yo," he called, "Jughandle John!"

"Yo, Fish," said Johnny. "How's business?"

"Poor of late," he said.

I bought a balloon for Timmy. Johnny had worked with Fish at Robinson's Circus. When Fish could no longer do the strenuous routines, he'd gone into balloons. Even without his makeup, Johnny said, Fish was a sad case. "Could go like that for me." He patted the velocipede seat. "If not for my new career."

We ambled past hog pens. The prizewinner, a 935-pound leviathan, inhabited what a sign called "the most spacious apartment in swine-dom." Farther on was an amphitheater in which young bulls were being shown. Attendants led them by rings in their noses, jerking upward to force their heads high. People in the stands watched atten-tively. Judges examined each bull in turn, prodding and measuring, feeling the tightness of skin, having the attendant jerk the nose ring or walk the animal once more.

"I'll not witness this," said Cait. "It's torture for the poor crea-tures."

We bypassed an enclosure where horses were judged and entered, at Cait's urging, Floral Hall, where we walked among fragrant lantana, heliotrope, begonia, achyranthes, moss fuchsia, myrtle, and countless rose varieties. Johnny and his velocipede drew curious stares. Every five minutes he asked me to pull out my watch. Finally he said he'd go out to the track; he was too nervous.

"We'll go too," I told him. "Here, we brought something for you."

Cait squeezed my arm. The gift was my doing. I handed him the package I'd been carrying. He opened it and pulled out a maroon cyclist's suit and a pair of canvas shoes.

"It's silk," I said. "Remember Mrs. Bertram, does the uniforms? She made it from your measurements. Here's the cap, underneath. Those are the new light sporting shoes Harry's ordering for the team."

"Hell, Sam," he said, swallowing as he fingered the silks.

"Come on, let's sign you up and find the dressing tent, see how you look."

We walked to an oval track behind the exhibit halls where contestants already wheeled around the circuit. We followed Johnny to the judges' stand.

"Bruhn," said Johnny. "Sent in my deposit a month back."

The official, a pleasant-looking man with ruddy cheeks and yellow hair that matched his straw hat, ran his finger down a list, found the name, glanced at Johnny, then stared.

"You funning me?"

Johnny stood silently, very still.

"What's the problem?" I moved forward. "Don't you have his entrance money?"

"This isn't for coloreds."

I stood dumbfounded for an instant, then wondered how we'd been so naive not to think of it. Hadn't Johnny known? I glanced at him. Kinky red hair, flat nose, coffee skin—features suddenly overwhelmingly dominant. Had he hoped to brazen his way through? I couldn't read his frozen expression. Christ!

"Look," I said placatingly, "if it's a question of compensation, maybe we can reach some sort of—"

"Niggers don't race here," the man said flatly, pleasantness draining from his face. "Here's your fee." He held out two greenbacks.

Johnny did not move.

He shrugged and laid the bills on his table. "I'm sorry, I didn't make the rules."

"You can't turn him away," I said. "He's practiced for weeks."

"Don't beg, Sam," said Johnny quietly. He turned his velocipede and started back the way we had come.

"What is it?" I heard Timmy say. "Is Johnny a nigger?"

"Hush," Cait said.

With the helpless feeling that something enticingly close was slipping away, I yelled, "Wait!" I caught Johnny and wrapped my arm around his shoulders. "Come on, we've got to think of something."

"I'll never get used to it." There was a faint quaver in his voice. "In the circus it didn't matter, 'cause in makeup nobody noticed, least-ways you could pretend they didn't."

"We'll work something out," I told him, without a glimmer of an idea.

". . . no dignity in it, Sam." His voice shook more perceptibly. "All's I want is the chance to be something on my own."

"Makeup!" Cait suddenly said behind us.

I turned. "What?"

"If Johnny borrowed clothes from his friend," she said, "and wore makeup . . . you see?"

I saw. It was brilliant. Or at least an answer. "Let's go!" I practically knocked Johnny down trying to turn him around.

"No, no, NO!" He dug his heels in, anchoring himself. "Miss Cait, I appreciate you trying to help me." He held the racing suit up; the fabric shimmered. "I want to wear these colors you got me, like a racer's supposed to." He turned toward me. "Sam, I don't want to be no damn *clown* no more."

Cait and I looked at each other. Timmy held her hand. We stood there. In the distance we heard the official's megaphoned announcement that the race would begin in five minutes. People were moving past us toward the track.

"This isn't right," I said. "Walking away, giving in."

"That's 'cause of who you are," Johnny said, sounding calmer. "Tell you what, we'll watch 'em race. Find out about the competition."

I suspected he was doing it more on my account than his own. We made our way back to the official.

"No problem with us going in to *watch,* is there?" I said dryly.

"Matter of fact," he said, looking less than pleased, "there is, but I won't push it. 'Less there's trouble."

"Thanks," I said. "Thanks a hell of a lot."

"Samuel, don't," Cait warned.

We sat in the grandstand. Johnny secured his velocipede below us, where he could watch it. It attracted a lot of attention.

Over two dozen entrants gathered at the starting line. The winner's prize would be fifty dollars, the distance two miles—four times around the long oval. Johnny scrutinized the racers disdainfully. Only two wore racing gear. All of the machines were wood. Closely bunched, the cyclists pedaled furiously through the first lap. The pace slackened noticeably as the pack stretched into a thin line during the second and third laps, and fell off dramatically in the stretch run.

"Nothing," Johnny muttered.

One burly farmboy looked like something, though, his thick legs still pumping tirelessly as he flashed across the finish line a quarter lap ahead of the second finisher.

The straw-haired official stepped forward and droned through his megaphone, "THE WINNER . . . SILAS ALSTON OF SYCAMORE TOWNSHIP!" Scattered applause sounded in the stands. We sat silently. A small-time, dismal affair, I thought. It was hard to see how winning this could take Johnny or anybody else very far.

"THE WINNING TIME . . . A TWO-MILE RECORD FOR HAMILTON COUNTY . . . SEVEN MINUTES, THIRTY SECONDS!"

"I'd've beat that," Johnny said.

"You sure?" I said, thinking it would take half a dozen of his spindly shanks to form one of the winner's tree-trunk legs.

"He would've!" Timmy said loyally.

"For a certainty," added Cait.

I had an inspiration. "Johnny, why not race him in a special heat?"

"They won't do it." His mouth bent downward. "You're wasting your time, Sam."

I got up. "Well, let's see."

"You again," the official said. "What now?"

"How about he takes on the winner in a special race?"

He shook his head wearily.

"Nothing officially connected with the county," I persisted. "Just an exhibition."

He took off his hat and wiped his forehead with his shirtsleeve. The sweatband had flattened his pale hair in a wet oval. He put his megaphone down. "Look," he said, "it's done. The winner don't *need* to race, he already *won*. 'Sides that, he'd be a mite tired to do it again." He regarded me sourly. "And 'sides *that,* you don't seem to understand the nature of things here. Suppose the nigger raced—presuming a white man'd go on the same track with him, which he wouldn't—and he happened to win. You think it'd do him good? You think folks wouldn't resent one of theirs shown up by a nigger? You don't picture trouble?"

"Stop calling him a nigger," I said. "His name's John."

A grimace of irritation passed over his face. "Suppose your . . . boy loses. Well, that's what everybody figures should happen anyway, see? Either way no good can come out of it."

"Nice of you to consider everybody's feelings," I said. "Well, then, how about a special exhibition, just him against the clock?"

"He's welcome to use the track. After hours. But you're touched if you think folks'd come out to watch a nigger wheel around in circles by himself."

I'd had my limit. I shot a hand out and clutched his shirt, yanking him so close that I felt his gasp of tobacco breath on my face. "Next time you call him a nigger, I'm going to slap your fucking head."

Eyes large, he gulped and managed, "All right."

I released my hold. "Now, let's go on considering possibilities."

He smoothed his crumpled shirt. When he looked up again, something in his face had changed; a hint of calculation leavened his wariness.

"Why is it you think your nig—think the boy's so hot? He don't look like any great shakes."

"Tell you the truth, I don't know how good he is. I just want him to get his chance to ride today. Here. In front of people. With you announcing it." I paused. "I've got money to argue he *is* pretty damn good, though, if that's what's called for."

"Wouldn't hurt none," he said carefully. "Tell you what. I'm willing to match my trotter again' him, five miles to his three. Full harness rig. Hundred dollars each to make a purse. Oughta draw a fair crowd."

"I'll check," I said. "We might have a deal."

"In fairness I should mention that my mare's never lost. Nobody hereabouts'll go against her anymore."

"Right."

I put the proposition to Johnny.

"No!" exclaimed Cait. "Samuel, how could you even think of it? Compete with an animal!"

Somewhere in my mind a memory was sparked: a reproduction of a slave-auction poster advertising the raffle of a horse and a woman, each to become the chattel of some lucky winner. "It's the best I could do." Suddenly I didn't feel so good about it.

"I want to," said Johnny.

"You sure?"

"Wow!" said Timmy.

Johnny said, "But I'll go two miles 'stead of three, same distance as the county race. Show them I'd've won, see?"

"That's a point."

"Tell him I'll do two miles against anything over that for his rig."

"You may end up with worse than he's already offered."

"I'll ride." He gripped my arm, and his yellow eyes burned into mine. "I'll beat anything on legs or wheels today, Sam. You could bet the sky on it!"

Probably what I'll have to do, I thought.

The official licked his lips and looked thoughtful when I proposed that Johnny ride two miles against his horse's three and a half. "Short-

[317]

er distance could work against me," he said cautiously. "Three and a quarter?"

"Three-eighths."

"How about a third?"

"Okay, I guess."

"You got yourself a match."

I thought I detected a trace of smugness. "But," I went on, "I want to raise the bet to five hundred—"

"That," he said, grinning pleasantly, "strikes me as a sporting—"

"—against your thousand."

His grin slackened. "That's a stiff amount."

"Your mare's never lost, remember?"

Considering it, he said, "You got it with you?"

I nodded.

"It'll take a spell to get mine in cash," he said. "But I think I can raise it from friends right here. Race in two hours?"

"Fine."

"*Nigger's gonna race Brad Hoge's prize mare!*"

We heard it spread over the fairgrounds. People gravitated toward the track. Cait and Timmy and I walked the other way, killing time. We viewed turbine waterwheels in Mechanics' Hall, eyed prize food displays—Mohawk potatoes, firestone peaches, canned white cherries—and Jersey cattle and black Spanish chickens.

Cait led us into Fine Arts Hall. There, despite Timmy's overt disinterest, we saw prizewinners in an astonishing range of categories: best "fancy" painting, best decorated cake, best collection of insects, best woolen mittens. At the ladies' exhibit we chatted with an exuberant seventy-six-year-old whose rag rugs had clobbered the competition. We viewed the latest sewing machines. I carried Timmy on my shoulders.

We returned to the track as Johnny finished his warm-ups. There was scattered talk of betting, but nobody seemed willing to back Johnny at any odds. Maybe Hoge had gotten a bargain at two to one. Given Cait's disapproval of gambling and dim view of this race, I didn't tell her of my bet. In a privy I slit the lining of my coat and pulled out the five one-hundred-dollar bank notes I'd sewn inside for emergencies. They, along with a shower of coins and bills from Hoge, went into a hat held by a man introduced as Constable Williams. I kept a close eye on him.

The harness rig appeared, guided by a boy handling the reins with casual arrogance. The mare's roan coat glistened, rich with highlights in the hot sun. Muscles rippling, radiating nervous energy, she pranced and tossed her head like equine royalty. We'd been suckered, I thought. Poor Johnny.

The stands were packed. A few admiring oohs mixed with the laughter that followed Johnny and the shining Demarest to the starting line. It was obvious that the crowd had never seen anything like the velocipede. Or exactly like Johnny either. The maroon trunks bagged above his skinny, knotted legs. The new shoes looked enormous. The jockey cap perched on a cushion of orange-red wool.

". . . RACING IN A PRIZE MATCH AGAINST THE CHAMPION TROTTER, SARAH JANE . . . JOHANN SEBASTIAN BRUHN!"

I'd dictated the form, but I couldn't control Hoge's intonation. "Johann" came out comically, with hard "J" and flattened "a," the three names drawn out to ridiculous length. The spectators, their numbers by then swelled to nearly a thousand, roared with laughter.

"The nigger fancies hisself Dutch," somebody behind me chortled.

I tensed and started to turn. Cait gripped my arm. "You wanted him to have this," she said, "so let it be."

Hoge raised a heavy cane and slammed it on the judge's stand. *THWACK!* On the far side of the track the mare surged forward, energizing the harness rig smoothly and instantaneously. Johnny started slowly, wobbling as he built up speed. Before he was halfway through his first circuit, Sarah Jane pounded past him on the outside, enveloping him in swirls of dust.

"Oh God," murmured Cait.

"She has to go six-plus laps to Johnny's four," I said. "It's not over."

Not reassured by my own words, I tried to reconcile myself to having thrown away a hell of a lot of money.

"ONE FIFTY-EIGHT!" Hoge boomed through his megaphone as Johnny swept below us, completing his first lap. I made a calculation and groaned mentally. To post his record time, the earlier winner had *averaged* 1:52 per lap. Johnny was well off that pace, and was bound to slow from fatigue. Meanwhile, the damned mare was burning up the track as if her life depended on it.

In the second half mile Johnny appeared to get his stroke, though Sarah Jane came on very fast and was about to lap him again.

"THREE THIRTY-EIGHT!"

He had done his second circuit in a minute and forty seconds, nearly twenty seconds faster than the first. My gloom brightened a tiny bit. He was closing in on the earlier winner's pace. It would be something if he could at least beat the record.

The third lap was brutal. Johnny labored in dust stirred by the rig.

In the searing heat it streaked to mud on his face. His drenched silks drooped on his straining body. He bent low over the handlebars and drove his legs in churning, pistonlike rhythm.

"The poor man," Cait said.

"He's still in it," I said.

"FIVE MINUTES, TEN SECONDS!" droned Hoge as Johnny flashed past the line below us.

A minute thirty-two. Somehow Johnny was getting faster with each lap. Incredible pace. If he could only sustain it, maybe . . .

The rig passed before us to enter its final circuit, scarcely a third of a lap behind Johnny. The winner would be the first one across the line. Sarah Jane's driver used his whip to lash her heaving flanks. The rig sped around the oval, gaining inexorably.

"He's losing ground too fast," I said. "Come on!"

"It's a cruel thing," said Cait grimly, her hands clenched, "to man and beast."

"Johnny, Johnny, Johnny!" yelled Timmy, waving his arms.

Johnny leaned into the final curve, chest heaving, strokes no longer smoothly rhythmical but frantic and flailing. Strain knotted his arms and swelled his back as he began the homestretch. His eyes were nearly closed, his mouth gasping, lips stretched in a sneer of agony.

Behind him, like a thundering storm, Sarah Jane rolled on, closing the distance. Johnny took a desperate glance over his shoulder and forced his legs faster.

"God in Heaven," breathed Cait, hands on her face, "he'll burst his heart!"

Sarah Jane gained steadily. The driver worked the whip furiously over her ribs. Streamers of foam trailed from her mouth. Her hooves drummed a dull thudding beat on the track.

A roar around us seemed to lift us to our feet.

"Yes, Johnny!" I yelled.

"COME ON, JOHNNY!" we screamed.

He swept toward the finish line. Sarah Jane came up on the outside, nose almost even with his rear wheel. They were in the last twenty yards.

"WIN IT, JOHNNY!"

The mare's straining head reached the velocipede's saddle, Johnny's shoulder . . .

Cait covered her eyes.

They crossed the line.

"HOLY CHRIST!" I shrieked. "HE WON!"

The result was unmistakable. There was no doubt, no argument. The crowd's hubbub subsided to a buzzing.

"Oh, he's hurt!" cried Cait.

The Demarest wobbled violently and toppled sideways, pitching Johnny to the track, where he lay unmoving. I vaulted over the grandstand railing. He was conscious, but his eyes were filmy and his chest heaved as he gasped for air. Must be badly dehydrated, maybe heatstroke, I thought, and carried him to the shade of the stand. Cait found ice somewhere and brought it in her scarf. She swabbed his face and wrists. Johnny stirred and groaned.

I bent over him. "What?"

". . . win?"

"You did it, buddy," I told him. "Looked impossible, but you pulled it off."

He smiled weakly. "Time . . .?"

I looked around. Hoge and the man holding the stakes were talking, frowning, heads close together.

"Hasn't been announced yet," I said. "But I know you broke the record."

"Want to hear," he mumbled.

"I'll check on it. Cait, Timmy, stay with him, okay?"

Hoge saw me coming. He didn't look real happy.

"Announce it," I said.

"Huh?"

"Announce Johnny's time."

"Here's your money." He dumped the contents of the hat on the table between us. "I wouldn't push farther."

I stuffed the money in my pocket. Then I shoved the table aside so that nothing stood between us. "Announce it," I said, giving him my best death stare, "or I'm going to hurt you. Bad enough so you won't forget it for a long time. And fast enough to keep anybody from helping till it's all over."

Neither of us moved. For an instant I thought it wasn't going to work. Then he lifted the megaphone.

"WINNING TIME . . . SIX MINUTES THIRTY-NINE SECONDS."

"He broke the damn record," I snapped. "Say it's the record!"

"Look." He gestured at the grandstand.

I looked. It was two-thirds empty. Those remaining looked on silently, faces slack and staring.

"Say it anyway." I took half a step toward him.

"A NEW HAMILTON COUNTY RECORD." He lowered the

megaphone. "That's all you get, mister. You'd best not stay around here."

It sounded less a threat than a statement of fact. There was something chilling in it. I took his advice, half carrying Johnny.

"My wheel, Sam."

"Timmy's walking it."

"Wait." He struggled to shake free of my arm, failed, and, feet dragging and body twisting, shouted at the grandstand, "DID YOU SEE ME?"

"Come on, Johnny," I urged.

He dug his feet into the dirt. "I'M CHAMPION! I'LL RACE Y'ALL! RIGHT NOW! EVERYBODY!"

His shouts echoed in dusty silence. I glanced at the stands and saw a knot of men beginning to exchange looks in a way I didn't like.

"We're going," I said, and picked him up bodily. I carried him clear out of the fairgrounds, Cait and Timmy moving fast to keep up. Tears formed rivulets in the grime on his face, disappearing into his sopping jersey. The tears didn't stop completely until we were halfway home on the train.

"Look," I said, pulling out the money. "You won more than just the race."

He counted it and looked up. "Fifteen hundred?"

"Five's mine. The rest was the purse. It's yours. Not too bad, your first time!"

He looked at it wonderingly. "You bet that much on me?"

"Johnny, you rode that last lap in a minute twenty-nine. You smashed the record by nearly a minute!" I laughed. "Those guys paid a stiff price for doubting you."

"I want to be a racer!" Timmy said. "Will you show me how?"

"That's right, ain't it so," said Johnny, unheeding. "I made 'em pay, didn't I?"

"You sure as hell did."

Cait looked at me. I knew what she was thinking: They might have paid, but they'd only let him on the track with an animal.

"Nobody's ever believed in me like that, Sam."

It was sad to think it might be true.

23

W hat would you think if I dressed in man's clothing?" Cait said, lowering her newspaper.

"What?" We sat side by side in the parlor, swaying in our rocking chairs like an elderly couple. The gas jet cast a cozy light. It was almost ten o'clock. Timmy was asleep. O'Donovan and the others were still away. We were alone.

"You heard me," she said.

"I suppose," I ventured, wondering if she visualized a Fenian uniform, "it would depend on the man."

"Not a bit funny," she said. "Read this." She handed me that day's *Enquirer* and pointed to an item titled "Women in Men's Clothes," by Elizabeth Cady Stanton.

> The true idea is for the sexes to dress as nearly alike as possible. . . . A young lady on Fifth Avenue dressed in male costume for years, traveled all over Europe and this country. She says it would have been impossible to have seen and known as much of life in woman's attire, and to have felt the same independence and security. . . .
>
> There are many good reasons for adopting male costumes. First, it is the most convenient dress that can be invented; second, in it woman could secure equal wages with man for the same work; third, a concealment of sex would protect our young girls from those terrible outrages from brutal men reported in all our daily papers.

"Well?" she said, when I'd finished.

"I'm not sure just changing clothes will remedy all those things," I said, mindful of jeans-wearing women of the future. "What do you think?"

"I think it's a true argument about women's rights in general," she said. "Mrs. Stanton wore those horrible bloomer costumes enough years to find out."

"Yeah? Bloomers?"

"Samuel, you haven't said what you'd think of *me* in male dress."

"Well . . ." My eyes roamed over her, moving up from the tips of her small shoes peeking beneath the hem of her heavy, pleated, full-length skirt. I wondered whether she was cinched in just then by a corset. A cream-colored blouse—she called it a "waist"—was fronted by a bow that de-emphasized the swell of her breasts. The mass of black hair was pulled high and secured by combs. Her neck looked pale and slender and—had I already adopted the peep-show mentality of Victorians?—very sexy. I tried without success to imagine her slouching around in pants.

"I like the way you look now," I told her, "but everybody should have the right to be comfortable."

She'd blushed a little as I inspected her. Now she looked at me curiously. "It *would* be a blessing to dress differently at times, but it's a rare man who'll hear it."

"If you mean bloomers, I'm not sure—"

"You big gossoon," she said, rising and facing me. "Not bloomers, just . . . " She gestured to indicate her torso with a small movement of her hands. And blushed furiously.

She was achingly provocative in the gaslight.

I stood up too, no fool I.

She moved into my arms and kissed me gently.

"It's my appearance you fancy, then, is it?" She leaned back, green sprites dancing in her eyes.

"That's it," I replied, and kissed her again, not so gently. Her fingers tightened on my neck as our breathing quickened. My tongue touched her lips; they parted slightly, and with a sigh she pressed against me, soft and yielding, tasting like spring herbs. With almost frantic urgency I ran my hands upward over her hips and stiffly encased stomach—a corset, sure enough—and found the soft fullness of her breasts. She writhed against me for a moment and abruptly pulled away.

"Not here," she gasped.

"Huh?" I couldn't believe I'd heard right.

"Not in this place," she said, more controlled.

I looked around. "But you live here."

She nodded, as if we agreed.

[324]

"I don't get it."

"Not in this house, Samuel."

What was wrong? Timmy upstairs? No lovemaking in Fenian hide-aways? None of the above, merely an excuse?

"Cait," I blurted, voice husky, "I love you."

Oh my God, I thought.

She took one of my hands in both of hers and held it tightly. Backlit by the gaslight, I could see tiny reflections of myself in her eyes. Her lips curved in a soft, enigmatic smile.

W. J. Hatton of San Francisco arrived the next Monday. He would escort us West. An Aussie immigrant, he and his brother had bought level ground in the Mission district, built a high wooden fence around it, and named it the Recreation Grounds. A large part of the Hattons' business involved circus shows and athletic events. Probably because he owned the only enclosed ballpark on the Pacific Slope, W. J. Hatton had dreamed up the idea of inviting us to play there.

It was impossible not to like Hatton. He was portly and freckled, with thinning sandy hair and a broad, quick grin. I shook his hand with the rest of our delegation. Within minutes he had Champion, who would be making the trip, laughing as if they were boyhood chums. Champion even decided to show him around Cincinnati himself, relieving me of the honor.

Which left considerably more time to pack. I fell asleep under hot towels at the Gibson barbershop, then wandered around downtown for a while and purchased a state-of-the-art Magic Lantern for eight dollars. It was a primitive slide projector which, by means of a gas lamp and lens, transformed two-inch glass "chromatypes" into four-foot images. Twelve views came with it—"House of Parliament," "Pyramids & Sphinx," "Mosque of Mahomet," and the like. For Timmy I bought another set: "The Little Gymnast," "Yacht Under Full Sail," and "Ah! Ha! Gold!" Catchy stuff.

While I was out, a thin letter from Twain arrived, postmarked Buffalo. His message was short and to the point.

> Sam'l,
>
> When I read that your red-shanked band would be journey-ing to California I regretted changing my plans. I'd trade my back teeth to sit down with you in Frisco's Heaven on the half shell, the Occidental Hotel, over champagne & oysters. You can have my portion this once.
>
> Just before I sat down to write, a dispatch came off the wire to wit: Freddy is offering Avitor stock at a bargain $25 each

thousand shares. Will I chaff this away? I guess not! I'll take a
flyer on Freddy's flyer! Carve out 40,000 shares immediately
on arriving if the price is steady. Wire me first if it's gone
higher. I advise you to plunge also. Hope you're willing to be
my Western agent. Hearty thanks.

Wedding schemes thicken like cement. If it weren't for
sweet Livy, I'd die from the planning. Don't forget—you must
come!

Regards,
SLC

Inside was a thousand-dollar draft. I went to my bank on Fourth, requested my account total, learned that I had $6,347. How, I wondered, would O'Donovan react when he returned to enforce his mid-September ultimatum and discovered I had left? On a morbid impulse I took out a safe-deposit box in Cait's name and placed in it twenty-five hundred dollars in gold, instructing that in the absence of further communication from me she was to receive it in three months' time. Figuring the five hundred I carried plus what Brainard owed me would be plenty for the trip, I obtained a letter of credit payable to Wells Fargo for the balance of my money and Twain's draft.

O'Donovan would have to work like hell to get a cent of it. And if something happened to me, Cait could shape her life as she wished. Feeling a bit silly, I wondered what it was about this trip that made me so spooky.

The afternoon dragged. The Gibson room was expensive to keep while I was away, so I stored my few possessions at Andy's. I packed and repacked my gladstone restlessly.

Cait hosted an elaborate farewell dinner that evening, serving us baked chicken. Andy was there, and, to my surprise, so was Sweasy. Cait wore her yellow dress, the one of the quilt. She was excitedly happy, almost giddy. And coquettish, too, clearly enjoying her role as the only woman among us. Sweasy, on his Sunday-best behavior, called her "Miss Cait" and treated her reverentially. Since the kidnapping he'd been cautiously polite to me; that evening he was almost cordial. They talked about old times in Newark. Timmy and I played catch when we grew bored. With the bottle of Catawba Andy had brought, we toasted each other and the trip West.

"To your brave American game," Cait said gaily, raising her glass. Andy grinned. I sensed a breakthrough in sibling relations.

"To the Irish," proposed Sweasy, adding, with a glance at me, "and their allies."

For dessert I provided ice cream with late-season strawberries packed in ice. When it grew dark we watched lantern slides. Timmy sat on my lap, marveling at the bright-tinted images. Sweasy promised to bring him slides of California. Andy, not to be outdone, hinted broadly that a stereoptican viewer might lie in Timmy's future.

"You'll spoil him, the lot of you," Cait protested, unconvincingly. She was glowing at Timmy's excitement.

When we stood up to get our coats from the foyer, Cait touched my arm and whispered, "Come back—with a cab."

I almost said "What?" but she had turned away.

After the others dropped me at the Gibson, I hired a carriage and directed the driver to the boardinghouse. Cait emerged with wool blankets and a large handbag.

"Top down?" She pulled the blankets around us and moved close.

"What about Timmy?"

"He's being watched." She pressed her cheek to my shoulder.

"O'Donovan's back?"

She squeezed my arm. "Not hardly."

The driver lowered the cab's top and took us through dim streets beneath a full, blood-orange moon. The night was extraordinarily clear following afternoon winds. We gazed up at a canopy of stars.

We passed Pike's Opera House downtown. Cait told me that Junius Booth had been booed from the stage there after his younger brother had killed Lincoln. We crossed the Miami Canal, gleaming like milk in the moonlight, and ascended Mt. Adams to the observatory, where we looked down at the shining river and the boats' lights twinkling along the landing. Then out to Spring Grove Road, a tree-lined thoroughfare where the fast set enjoyed racing their high-wheeled "suicide gigs." Moving at medium speed, trees blurring at the edges of my vision, moon burning overhead, Cait's hair flowing in the night wind—it was romantic beyond anything in my life. And I knew it. Even then.

Her fingers touched my cheek. I crushed her against me, my face buried in her hair. We kissed until we couldn't breathe.

Her lips brushed my ear, the words coming as softly as night shadows. "Yes, Samuel."

I carried her up the winding stairs at Gasthaus zur Rose. Helga's head emerged from a doorway and swiftly withdrew. In the attic room I turned the lamp low.

"It's lovely," Cait said, her voice throaty.

"Come here."

"Put the light out."

I turned the key until only a glow remained. "Okay?"

She came slowly forward. "I want to please you."

I knew then that I had died and was in heaven. There was no other explanation. We melted together.

Long minutes later, stymied by an impenetrable personal security system of hooks and straps and buttons and stays, I leaned back on the bed. "And I thought *bras* were tough."

"What?" Cait reached behind her back.

"Never mind."

"Here, unfasten these . . . and these . . . and this . . . now leave for a moment."

"*Leave?*"

She laughed nervously. "Go outside for a moment," she said, starting to blush. "I'm going to be wicked for you."

Wicked? Was any of this happening?

In the hall, wearing only my pants, I heard faint sounds from the washstand, and finally a creak from the bed. I opened the door. Wearing a silk nightdress, Cait perched on the edge of the bed, bare feet tucked together, hair down over her shoulders. She looked up, green eyes luminous in the scant light.

"May I enter, your ladyship?"

"Do you notice . . . differences?" She sounded self-conscious.

"Cait, I can scarcely *see* you."

"Come closer."

"What's that . . . scent?" I'd almost said smell.

"Hagan's Magnolia Balm," she said. "Is it nice?"

I'd seen the slogan, of course; it was everywhere: "Fresh as a maiden's blush," it would transform a "rustic country girl into a city belle." The fragrance was flowery, faintly cloying.

I sat beside her. "Very nice."

"But that isn't what I meant. Look at me."

I looked.

"My *face,* Samuel, my eyes."

They seemed a bit smudgy. "What have you done?"

"Remember the magazines you brought? Well, according to *Godey's Ladies Book,* mascara is a wicked influence."

So she'd gotten some for this night. I started to tell her she didn't need mascara or anything else, but then let it pass and kissed her. Now my hands encountered no buttons or layers of rigid fabric. Just sheer silk and the soft contours of her.

She responded eagerly to my mouth and hands, but stiffened when I tried to remove the nightdress. It occurred to me later that she'd concealed herself all her life. In society's view only "low" women derived pleasure from sex. Husbands sated their lust—swiftly, presumably, and in missionary position in total darkness—upon nigh-comatose wives.

I wasn't into that at all.

But I went slowly. At first. Until I found the strings securing the nightdress and pulled it away. Over her gasps I said, "I want to please you, too."

"Samuel . . . I . . . oh . . . you mustn't . . . SAMUEL! . . ."

I'm not sure she knew about orgasms. When hers happened it shook her violently. She clung to me, quaking, half sobbing afterward, her hair tangled, mascara smeared, feeling at first, I think, utterly debased. I wrapped the silk around her, held and kissed her, whispered to her.

"I've denied myself for so long." Her voice was low, almost a groan. Then, astonishing me, "Love me again, Samuel."

I pulled her on top of me. In the dimness her body was pale and smooth as a living statue, opalescent, beautiful in its nakedness, her full breasts and hips wonderfully curved, her skin firm and soft wherever I touched. Before long I neither knew nor cared where her body ended and mine began. On the verge of coming, I muttered, "Should we be careful? I'm about to—"

"I *want* you." She braced her hands on my chest and moved her hips fiercely in an age-old rhythm, sucking me into the core of her, yearning for me, straining, demanding me, reaching, taking . . . all. . . .

The explosion blew Cincinnati off the globe.

When the fallout had settled and we lay wrapped around each other, she whispered something that sounded like "time in graw latt."

"Huh?"

"*Táim in grá leat,*" she repeated softly. "In the old language it means, 'I'm in love with you.' "

I stayed silent for a moment. It did for my soul what no amount of Hagan's Magnolia Balm would ever do for anybody.

"Anyone particular in mind?"

She burrowed her nose in my neck. "For a certainty."

"Could you tell me? In the new language?"

"Sure and I could."

Only when I threatened to tickle her did she do it.

"I love you, Samuel."

In the gray light of dawn I cut a small piece of fabric from inside the hem of her yellow dress and put it in the back of my watchcase. I wanted to see it each day on the trip. As I climbed back in bed she reached for me.

"You've made me a wanton already."

"Excellent!" I raised the covers to look at her.

"No, Samuel!"

She gave in reluctantly—and briefly—only when I argued that a lover's body was good, not evil, to look upon. And Cait's was good indeed, though slenderer than the Rubenesque proportions in vogue. A dusting of freckles ran down from her shoulders to splash the tops of her breasts. Long thighs, now pressed firmly together—perhaps her sexiest feature, although the matter would certainly require further research—gave way to molded calves and small, high-arched feet. God, she was a work of art, a treasure.

"You're not ashamed of me?"

I bent and kissed a vaguely heart-shaped freckle near one pelvic bone.

"Cait, you should be bronzed."

That was too much for her, and she tugged the cover up. I lost myself again in her hair and skin, contours and crevices, the textures and tastes of her.

"You're immodest," she murmured, moving her hands and lips over me with increasing urgency.

By the time we were through, light streamed in the window, casting geranium shadows on the floor.

"How can I go away for a whole month now?" I groaned, then raised up on one elbow with an inspiration. "Cait, how about you and Timmy coming?"

"No tickets," she said drowsily.

"I'm serious," I said, excited. "We could follow the team by a couple of days, no problem. Timmy'd love seeing it all. So would you!"

"He's not well enough yet, Samuel. Remember what the doctor said about the danger of a recurrence?" She smiled, a trifle wistfully. "It's sweet to think of such a journey, but I cannot go."

"Your work?"

"That," she said, "and there is you."

"Me?"

She turned to me, the jade eyes probing mine. "I'm frightened by your going, but I've sensed how you need this journey."

"You have?"

"I think it's connected with the purpose you seek, Samuel. Or that you *believe* it's connected. Which is the same."

"What if my purpose is simply to be with you?"

"If so," she said softly, "then we'll discover that very thing." She took my hand. "Won't we?"

◇

[330]

A crowd of club members and well-wishers had jammed the Indianapolis & Lafayette dock by the time we arrived. The nine was there: Harry trying to stop his kids from dodging around piles of luggage; George laughing with reporters; Gould with his family; Brainard and Waterman looking sleepy; Oak Taylor, fresh-scrubbed and eager.

Timmy ran to Andy, and we followed. Heads swiveled as men ogled Cait and women scrutinized her. Mac and Allison, standing with Andy, were as tongue-tied as if meeting a princess.

"I was thinking you'd vanished again," Andy said accusingly.

"No way," I said. "Important business."

"Going off with Mother and leaving me home," said Timmy.

Cait's cheeks turned crimson.

"Ain't that a dinger," Andy said. Mac and Allison gave me disbelieving stares.

The wife of one of the club officers appeared to pin miniature red stockings on our jackets. She had fashioned the emblems herself. "This is to show Western ladies," she announced, "that our nine possesses no shortage of admirers in the Queen City!"

During the applause that followed, Cait drew me near and whispered, "Perhaps I should have sewn for you instead of—"

"Mascara?" I said.

She blushed again.

When the baggage was loaded, the locomotive's bell sounded a heart-wrenching peal.

"Let's board!" Harry shouted.

"Whooooeeee!" Andy yelled, lifting Timmy high. "Here we go West!"

We looked at each other. Cait's eyes were unnaturally bright. My chest felt like it was being squeezed. In the swirl of humanity on the dock, it was as if we stood on an island swiftly washing away.

"I don't care what the others may think," she said, tilting her head. "Please kiss me, Samuel." After I did she took the silver ring from her finger. I thought she meant to hand it to me. Instead she put it to her mouth, kissed it, then slowly turned it and replaced it on her finger. "When you're far from here and thinking of me," she said, "ask Andy the meaning of it."

The train's whistle shrilled and a blast of steam erupted. The cars inched along the platform.

"Go quickly," she said, tears rimming her eyes.

"You'n Andy are my heroes!" Timmy exclaimed as I hugged him.

"I'll bring you Indian stuff," I managed to say.

"Wow, Sam!"

From a window I waved, and they waved back. *I love you, Cait.* I burned into my memory a final image of her standing silently among the cheering people, dark and regal in her long yellow dress, one arm around Timmy, the other lifted to me.

It would remain with me all the days to come.

We discovered that our itinerary had been widely advertised. At Indianapolis and smaller stations all along the route, people gathered and rubbernecked to catch a glimpse of the famous Red Stockings. If any of us had previously doubted, now we could see clearly the power and extent of the sports legend we were fashioning. In my mind we were this era's '27 Yankees—already legendary, utterly invincible. It was heady stuff. I enjoyed it, although my thoughts were filled with Cait.

That night in our sleeping car, I asked Andy about the ring.

"She turned it?" He looked startled. "Colm's Claddaugh ring?"

"Hands holding a crowned heart," I said. "She said you'd explain."

"Well, Claddaugh rings are made in Galway. Irish girls wear 'em on their right hands with the heart pointing out to show their own hearts aren't taken. If the heart's turned in, it signifies a love is being considered."

"But Cait's is on her left."

"She's worn it like a wedding band," he said. "It was about the only thing of Colm's she had—'cept Timmy. You say she turned the crown, heart pointing in?"

"That's right."

"You sure?"

"Positive."

"That means," he said slowly, "two loves have become one and can't be separated."

I was far distant from words.

"Say, maybe we'll end up brothers after all," he said, laughing. "Wouldn't *that* be a dinger?"

We pulled into East St. Louis at eight the next morning. A crowd practically bowled us over in the station. "Where's George Wright?" "Isn't the older one Harry?" "That's Brainard!" With magazines spreading their images across the country, the Stockings were recognized stars.

We coached to the Laclede Hotel, at Fifth and Chestnut, and had crayfish for breakfast. That afternoon, in gorgeous weather, we demolished the Unions at a park crammed to capacity.

"Clockwork fielding and steam-powered batting" was how the

local *Democrat* described our play, and that about said it. We pulled off three double plays. George, Waterman, and Brainard each had eight hits.

Stockings 70, Unions 9.

That night at the Olympia Theater we saw an interminable farce called *Chiron and Chloe in the Back Room.* I left at intermission, anxious to get back to the hotel to write to Cait. Posting the letter early in the morning, I realized it wouldn't reach her for days. So I also sent a telegram: "Samuel loves Caitlin."

We played the Empires on the same grounds. The crowd held considerably more women than the previous day's. Word must have gotten out. The Stockings were young, suntanned, muscular, famous, well paid, and wore sexy uniforms. What else did it take?

Allison's hands were sore again, and he allowed a number of passed balls. The Empires fielded fairly well and their pitcher wasn't bad, holding us to thirty-one runs on an equal number of hits. In the field we made eight muffs, but the outcome was never in doubt. Our record stood at 45–0. We would next play in San Francisco.

After totaling the score-book columns, I worked up my first dispatch lead for the *Enquirer.* "St. Louis fans turned out in brilliant weather to witness an exhibition of less-than-flawless baseball as the Red Stockings coasted to a 31–14 win over the hometown Empires." Mundane but serviceable, I thought.

Millar didn't. When I asked him to critique it, he immediately crossed out "fans"—as yet *fan* or *crank* or *rooter* had not appeared; no single identifying term for a sports fanatic existed. He made "baseball" two words. Then he tossed away the whole thing and wrote, "The match this afternoon on the St. Louis grounds, captured by our stalwart lads with thirty-one runs to the Missourians' fourteen, was viewed by a fair audience, there being probably two thousand people present, including many ladies."

Hopelessly cumbersome. "Why do you make a point of women?" I asked.

"So as to elevate the sport," he said, the pedant in his glory. "You *do* want that, don't you, Fowler?"

"Oh, more than life itself."

Again that night we went to the theater, this time as guests of Edwin Adams, the famed actor, who performed the title role of *Narcisse the Vagrant: The Great Tragedy in Five Parts.* To me the acting, with its posturing and overblown sentiment, was hard to take seriously. Hurley would have enjoyed it, I thought, and wondered how he was doing; he must feel wretched every time he heard of us.

A telegram arrived for me at the hotel.

SAMUEL STOP TERRIBLY ALARMED STOP FEARGHUS RE-
TURNED STOP RAGING SAYING MCDERMOTT PURSUE STOP
BE MOST WATCHFUL STOP YOUR CAIT

My mind flooded with anxious thoughts. Had Cait taken risks to warn me? Had O'Donovan discovered I'd withdrawn the money from the bank? He must think I was running away. I stared at the yellow paper. *Raging saying McDermott pursue.* . . . So they'd be coming after me again. Would they try for me in San Francisco? Or set a trap earlier, along the train route? These two days in St. Louis gave them that much time to gain on me. Shit.

I touched the words *Your Cait* with my fingertips. Then I went up and loaded the derringer. Restlessly I walked out in the dark streets. The air was warm and velvety. When I reached the river I aimed at a spot in the water, looked around briefly—nobody was in view—and squeezed the trigger. There was a brittle *pop!* Concentric circles rippled the black water.

◇ 24 ◇

We razzed Mac hard as we pulled out of town on the Northern Missouri line. The big kid looked sheepish. He and Allison had sneaked out to a beer hall the previous night. Mac had made advances on one of the Pretty Waiter Girls—the generic sisters of dance-hall women, with their plump arms, short boots, and skirts displaying a few prurient inches of pale tights and flesh—and promptly landed in a fight and then in jail. Harry had had to vouch for him. Fortunately the St. Louis cops were ball fans.

The passing countryside began to take on a different look: more grazing land, with fewer farmhouses and haystacks; rolling hills with clouds piled high behind; tree rows stretching in dark lines across paler land; wildflowers—golds and purples and blues—along the embankments, their smells, with those of grasses and nettles, drifting to us at the country stations where we stopped for water and coal.

Sweasy conducted a seminar on Indians in our car, recounting a succession of lurid stories: A Swedish settlement on the Saline River had been overrun only two months ago by marauding Sioux. A soldier had taken the scalp of a live Indian prisoner after witnessing the same done to a white settler. A copper-skinned killer named Red Cloud, who stood taller than Gould, was even now roaming the plains with two thousand bloodthirsty painted horsemen.

"Truly, Sweaze?" said Andy. "I mean, out where we're goin'?"

"Listen to this." Sweasy opened a copy of the *St. Louis Republican.* " 'We have received particulars of the Indian massacre: The tongues and hearts were cut out of the dead bodies; the calves of their legs were slit down and tied under their shoes; pieces of flesh were cut from their back; pieces of telegraph wire were stuck into the bodies; the ears were cut off and heads scalped. The Indians boiled the hearts of their victims for medicine.' "

He looked grimly pleased at the shock it produced.

"Where's the damn army?" said Gould.

" 'Companies A and D of the Seventh Cavalry, under Colonels Weir and Custer,' " Sweasy read, " 'are to be sent after the depredators.' "

"Seems they're a mite late," Waterman said. "Answer what Andy asked, Sweaze—these things happening close by or ain't they?"

"Just down in Kansas," Sweasy said ominously. "Near Hays City, where that Hickok feller shot some men just last month. Not more'n a hundred miles from where we'll pass. Course you gotta keep in mind that Injuns travel all over the countryside. There's trouble up in Montana, too, so it's my hunch we'll pass right through the middle."

"But I saw in the paper," Harry said, "that everything was peaceful along the Pacific Railroad."

"I read that," Sweasy admitted. "But it's likely temporary."

Like the rest, I wanted to see real Indians. Herds of buffalo rolling like thunder over the plains. The Wild West—even now already sensationalized and romanticized.

"On the Washita River, not three hundred miles due south of here," Sweasy went on—he'd obviously done his homework—"is where Sheridan took on Black Kettle last November. Sent Custer to surprise 'em in their winter village. Left a hundred savages dead in the snow."

"No women or children, of course," I said.

"They went in a-shootin'," he said. "At anything that moved—and some as didn't."

It got a laugh.

"Are we supposed to cheer about a massacre?"

He looked at me coolly. "They didn't stay on their reservations like they're supposed to."

"Like *we* say they're supposed to."

This produced a general silence.

"You Quaker?" Sweasy demanded.

"Why?"

"You talk like a John Injun-lover."

At that point Champion, who seldom participated in our conversations, moved down the aisle. "I've studied military tactics," he said. "I'm certain that Sheridan ordered a winter attack because the Indians' lighter ponies could outdistance cavalry mounts in summer, laden as they are with weaponry and equipment."

Thanks, General, I thought. Go back and play with your toy soldiers. "A *tactical* consideration," I said, "but morally—"

I stopped as Harry touched my arm. "They haven't developed the land, Sam." His tone was mollifying, the voice of reason.

I took a breath, realizing I was up against the century's dominant ethos: progress—meaning whatever could be profitably exploited.

"One of the Empires knew California Jack personal," said Allison, changing the subject.

It drew immediate interest. Recently a Pennsylvania bank had been relieved of twenty thousand dollars by a robber of that name.

"Said he lived only a few doors away," said Allison. "Wife and kids, right there in St. Louis."

The notion of a bank robber having a family life stirred discussion. Gould claimed that the country's first train robbery had happened outside Cincinnati in the spring of '65, when a gang of roughs derailed a baggage car and looted its safe.

"Anybody heard of Billy the Kid?" I asked. Nobody had. I tried the Jameses, Youngers, Daltons, Wyatt Earp, Calamity Jane, Joaquin Murietta, Bat Masterson. None got a glimmer of recognition. Either it was too early or the Stockings were abysmally ignorant. "Zorro?" I tried.

"Sam, you're talkin' queer," said Andy.

In northern Missouri we crossed level prairies thatched with wild strawberries and freshened by clear streams. For lunch we had catfish—fried, breaded, served with corn fritters—in Hannibal, the town where Twain had grown up. It had doubtless changed a good deal since he left fifteen years ago. The railroad's arrival had brought a booming lumber business. Sawmills crowded the foot of town, along the river. New buildings stood everywhere.

I walked to the Mississippi. In the distance kids shouted as they jumped from a half-submerged log, splashing into placid water, which looked leaden on this blazing day. It was weird to think that *Tom Sawyer* and *Huckleberry Finn* hadn't yet been written. I looked around, considering the sluggish river, the drab frame structures and dusty trees, the buzzing flies. Maybe it was idyllic to be a boy here, but for me it would be brain-killing, stifling, a long deadly summer of monotony. Small wonder Twain romanticized but seldom revisited his roots.

We swapped our spacious sleeping car for a dilapidated Hannibal & St. Joseph coach that swayed and lurched so crazily we could scarcely stand up. Glasses and books and decks of cards were thrown periodically to the floor. Sweating through the heat-blasted Missouri landscape, we were hardly comforted by the evidence of past wrecks along the tracks. In one place seven smashed cars formed a triangular heap, their locomotive nose-down in a swampy hole.

Our slow pace worried me. The Pacific Railroad began at Omaha, jumping-off point for all transcontinental traffic. It was a likely place for McDermott to intercept me. Was he already there, waiting with Le

Caron? We poked through St. Joseph, crossed into Iowa, dragged westward. Twenty-four hours on that wretched line.

At last the conductor called, "Council Bluffs! All for Omaha change to the stage!"

We changed with a vengeance, stampeding to omnibuses lined before the station. Andy and George got choice seats inside; Brainard, Gould, and I—the lead foots—had to sit on top with the luggage. For one solid bone-rattling hour we were jolted and tossed as a four-horse team moved over muddy ruts—"defects in the road," the driver termed them. We climbed down shakily at the ferry landing on the Missouri River. Before us on the opposite shore, set on a hill and crowned by a white-domed capitol, lay Omaha City.

We crossed Big Muddy's silt-laden current on a flat-bottomed steamer—it was hard to comprehend these boats journeying two thousand miles up the Missouri, farther than we still had to go to San Francisco—and we duly disembarked in Nebraska, proud new thirty-seventh state.

The Union Pacific depot was a scene of vast and boisterous confusion. There were dandified easterners in stovepipe hats, their women richly bonneted and shawled, children cavorting on piles of luggage; haggard miners; loudmouthed agents pitching stocks and myriad get-rich-quick schemes; Jewish pack peddlers; soldiers; hucksters who shilled for saloons and gambling houses; hunters carrying long Sharps rifles; German and Irish and Swedish emigrant families.

That day's Pacific Express to Sacramento was packed to the last inch of space. Worse yet, nearly a thousand would-be passengers waited to pay higher rates for an express with guaranteed Pullman cars—exactly what we wanted. I felt the old tension in my shoulder blades. We would be stuck here for some time. I pressed close to the others and kept a nervous watch. Le Caron could be anywhere.

"Hey, Sweaze!" somebody yelled. "Injuns!"

Sure enough, near some foul-smelling frontier types in greasy animal skins stood a shabby group of Indians in white people's clothing, wearing feathers in their braids and necklaces of beads and talons, the men's black eyes glassy—from whiskey, we learned—as they begged from new arrivals by silently holding out their hands; one woman, more aggressive, offered peeks at her baby for ten cents.

Sweasy, shoved forward by Mac and Gould, forked over fifty cents to actually hold the infant. As he did so, a strange softness came over his face. We watched in amazement as he made cooing sounds and tried to nuzzle the baby. Alarmed, the mother snatched it away. We burst into laughter. From then on she was known as "Sweaze's squaw."

A ragged black huckster emerged from a line of baggage and express wagons and approached us, shouting the merits of the Cozzens House. Brainard finally yelled, "That's enough! We *know* about it!"

The man paused, doffed his hat with comic politeness, and bowed deeply. "Which road does you own, suh, de Union or de Westun?"

Brainard's cheeks burned.

Hatton and Champion decided it would be better to take the next day's express rather than wait around for a mixed train—freight and passenger—which would stop at every station. I felt relieved when we finally shouldered our bags and set out in search of the Cozzens House. I wasn't wild about staying overnight in Omaha, but at least I wouldn't have to feel like a clay pigeon at the station.

We'd anticipated a woolly frontier town. Instead we found a bustling city of twenty-five thousand. The mud in the broad streets looked rich enough to yield crops, but downtown boasted clusters of four-story brick buildings.

The Cozzens House turned out to be owned, like much of Omaha, by an eccentric promoter, George Francis Train, who'd had the foresight to buy hundreds of acres of prime land, including the port area now called "Traintown," at nominal prices. The coming of the transcontinental line made him a multimillionaire. The desk clerk told us that Train expected Omaha to mushroom to one hundred thousand, making it the largest city after New York and a veritable Athens of the West.

Don't hold your breath, I thought.

The local ball clubs quickly found us and took us around in open carriages. We saw dizzying numbers of UP supply yards and storage sheds. I learned more than I ever wanted to know about railroad construction. But I did enjoy seeing the Lincoln Car—the famous coach in which the President's body had been conveyed from Washington to Springfield—reserved now by the UP for ceremonial occasions.

Our hosts showed us new frame dwellings going up by the hundreds. Single lots sold for a thousand dollars and up. Housing was at a premium.

"Shoot," said Allison, eyeing one tract. "Them dinky things're crabbed so close they'd all go together in a fire!"

Champion gave him a sour look.

"I been counting," Waterman informed us. "It's a close thing, but the grog shops lay over the churches."

As though picking up on his cue, our guides deposited us at the Tivoli Gardens, where we hoisted schooners of lager that evening under gaslit locust trees and swatted mosquitoes the size of bees. George purchased pennyroyal leaves to rub on our skin, but it didn't repel them.

"Interestin' out this way," said Andy, examining a bite on his hand. "But I wouldn't fancy it."

"Me neither." I sat against the wall, gun in pocket, keeping watch on the entrance.

A noise at the door. Had I dreamed it? I sat up in a sweat, eyes straining in the early light. It came again, a faint tap. Heart racing, I looked around. The others—Andy, Sweasy, and Mac—were asleep. I moved to the door, gun in hand. Would they really try it here?

Again a tap. I pressed against the jamb and muttered, "Who is it?"

"Sam?" came a whisper. "It's me."

It was Johnny's voice.

Distrusting my ears, I opened the door a crack. He stood in the hallway holding a battered valise. I pulled him inside. He waited silently while I slipped into shirt and pants. We stepped into the hall.

"How'd you find us?"

"Followed you," he said tentatively, as if fearing my reaction. "Got on the next train after yours. Didn't figure to catch you till Frisco."

"Why'd you come? What about Helga?"

"She took it hard, but she understood I had to make a change. I sold my wheel to buy my ticket."

"What about the money you won?"

"Used most of it to settle up with Helga." He smiled faintly. "Still have most of what's left, since they'll only let me ride third class. Said there ain't special colored cars yet—but took my money quick enough. Damn near a freight car, what I been in."

"Johnny, why're you doing this?"

His amber eyes blinked. "Gonna make a new life out West."

I was thinking that the fairgrounds race had hurt him more deeply than I'd thought when his next words startled me.

"And I knew you weren't coming back, Sam."

I stared at him. "That's a hell of a lot more than I know. How can you say that?"

"I only been close to a few people," he said. "They all went away. By now I know when it's set to happen."

It gave me a funny chill. "I'm just taking a trip."

He shrugged and said, "Me too," as if each of us had our little delusions.

"Johnny, what is it you want with me?"

"What if I said when it got down to brass tacks, I didn't want you going off without me?"

"I'd say that was pretty hokey," I told him.

"I could pass as your manservant. Hell, I'd *be* your servant to go first class!"

I considered it. We were already short of space; his presence would hardly be welcome in our car.

"I'd pay the extra fare, wouldn't cost anybody—"

"I don't think you can come with us, Johnny," I said, and felt bad when I saw his expression.

"How about you take a different train, Sam? We go to Frisco together."

"But I've already paid for my ticket with the club."

He looked at me silently.

"Damn it, Johnny, you shouldn't have come all—"

"Okay," he interrupted. "I'll be going on then. See you in Frisco." He started down the hall, then turned. "Oh, one other thing. Remember the dark breed who got away from us, set the boat afire?"

"Le Caron." My blood slowed abruptly.

"I saw him with that red-haired gambler, the one that laughs real loud when nothing's funny."

"Jesus, where?"

"A few stations out of St. Joseph, can't recall which one. Just caught sight of 'em for a second climbing on a different train."

"Oh, shit. Heading this way?"

He nodded and turned away again.

"Wait a second." My thoughts spun in new directions. "You know when the next westbound's scheduled?"

"In an hour, at seven, but it's not an express."

I made up my mind. The club had no chance of departing until much later. "Meet me at the depot in forty-five minutes."

"Okay!"

I dressed and packed, knocked on Champion's door. He looked silly in a nightcap and sleeping gown. I gave him my contrived story.

"That anxious to see your folks, eh?" He didn't look heartbroken at the prospect of my departing. "Well, all right, though you'd probably make swifter time waiting for the express."

"Thanks, sir, but I'm awfully anxious to see 'em—more so every minute."

I woke Andy just before I left.

"You in trouble again, Sam?"

"Naw, just itchy."

"Stay out of hot water this time, hear?"

"I'll try," I told him. "See you on the coast."

The depot was not nearly so crowded; by now only parties reserving entire cars, like the Stockings, still waited. The individual fare was $133 to Sacramento, $76 due then as the UP portion, another $57 to be paid the Central Pacific at Promontory, Utah, where all passengers changed trains. We had no problem converting Johnny's ticket to first class. I broke one of my hundred-dollar bills grudgingly, hoping I could get a partial rebate from the club.

"Maybe I'll strike it rich out West!" Johnny exclaimed as we put our bags on a loading cart.

I breathed the cool air, aromas of leather and hay and coffee. "The gold rush is over."

"Money's lyin' around everywhere, so I hear."

"Good luck picking some up."

"With you familiar out there, Sam, I figure I'll get a start."

Great, I thought.

A shill shouted, "Last chance for train insurance! Spare yourself loss or injury! Reasonable rates!"

I thought about my cash and letter of credit. How dangerous was this trip?

"Just a dodge," said Johnny. "Scare the suckers, then sell 'em your cure. Saw it plenty around the circus."

We boarded a dismal day car that converted to a sleeper by means of hinged benches folding from the walls. Imagining the Pullman awaiting the Stockings—velvet carpets, spacious berths, ventilation, suspension system that removed all but the most severe bounces—I was already envious as we sat on threadbare upholstery, breathed stale air, and were jolted as the cars lurched forward.

"Ah, the real goods," Johnny sighed, envying no one, stretching on the seat beside me. He pointed to an omnibus disgorging some thirty immigrants into third-class cars. "See them? That's how it was for me all the way here."

"In that case you'd better shape up as my darky," I said. "Or I won't keep you on."

"Sam, don't you start *believing* that stuff!"

We left Omaha's bluffs and chugged across a wide plain. Occasional trees or rock outcroppings crawled past. When a rotund black conductor punched our tickets I asked how fast we were going.

"Twenty miles each hour, suh," he said, eyeing Johnny narrowly. "Maybe twenty-five just now. Steady work."

But slow. Faster trains averaged in the forties on level ground, twenty-five to thirty-five on ascents.

"How long will it take us to go on through?"

"Depends on the traffic, but only a few days." He beamed at me. "A revolutionary time, suh! New York to San Francisco in ten days! Down to six when the rivers are bridged. A revolutionary time!"

It took some four weeks, I knew, by the Isthmus route. If nothing went wrong. And just about everything could go wrong, from storms to fatal epidemics. For overland pioneers in ox-drawn wagons it had been worse: crossing from St. Louis to California required three months. The railroad had reduced that journey to less than a week. Revolutionary, indeed.

The passengers in our car didn't resemble the usual first-class crowd. Most looked a bit down on their luck. There were only three women, one with a squalling baby who promised to make our lives miserable. Sheathed in heavy clothing, they already wielded fans as the day's heat began to break upon us.

The first dining stop, at Grand Island, was typical of those to come. Informed that we had thirty minutes, we poured into a rough dining room (the sign simply said R.R. HOUSE) where we gulped beefsteak, eggs, potatoes, and cubes of some sort of mush—all fried in thick grease. As we moved westward the steaks would become antelope and buffalo, though I suspected it was all stringy beef, accompanied by hoecakes, sweet potatoes, and boiled Indian corn soaked liberally in syrup. Any variance from this—chicken stew, for example, which might really be prairie dog—was cause for discussion. Meals were expensive, too, usually at least a dollar.

About a hundred miles out of Omaha trees disappeared entirely. We entered a high barren prairie dotted with bluffs. Squads of antelopes raced the train—and generally won. We saw occasional elk and numerous prairie-dog villages, sights which excited the easterners in the car. But as the miles passed and no buffalo or wild Indians presented themselves, telescopes and opera glasses were put aside.

"Har har!" chortled a leather-faced, Popeye-sounding man several seats ahead. "That's a rich 'un!" He read laboriously from a *Leslie's* supplied for a fee by pain-in-the-ass vendors known as "train butches," who paraded through the cars selling everything from tooth powder to guidebooks.

A plump Chicago dry-goods dealer named Beard bent my ear interminably, claiming that the UP was pulling a gigantic swindle in wrangling ninety-six thousand dollars for each mile in this so-called mountain section, which was actually level. The company was already paying its backers one hundred percent dividends, and the road had barely been open four months.

"Does sound a bit fishy," I said, remembering that Grant's administration was rocked by scandals. Had the transcontinental line been one? I couldn't recall.

"Mark me, sir," said Beard. "When everything comes to light a foulness will rise under heaven!"

Johnny yawned prodigiously and got up to pursue a train butch who'd passed through hawking plums.

Beard quit his polemic as my long looks out the window grew more frequent. Actually there was little to see: tumbleweeds blowing in acres of sun-blasted gray grasses that undulated like flowing water; it was as if we weren't moving at all, but were adrift in a hot, monotonous sea. Not even the Platte, which we'd followed for miles, was now visible.

At length Johnny returned with plums. In a low voice he said, "I went up and down the cars. Looked in every one. There's a passel of card games going on. I checked those especially close."

"And?"

"No sign of them on this train."

So far, so good, I thought.

25

Night was a relief. Not only from the heat, but from the constant selling. As if the train butches weren't enough, local peddlers were out in force at each station pushing food, clothes, handmade goods. Competition made the butches more aggressive. They thrust day-old newspapers at us, magazines, postcards, dime novels, handbooks, guidebooks, maps, joke books; whispered that we might like spicier fare, flashing dog-eared copies of *Police Gazette* and naughty novels, *Velvet Vice* and *Fanny Hill*. They hawked apples, pears, oranges, California grapes, dried figs, fresh bread, country butter, maple sugar, cigars, razors, candy, peanuts—the last salty and followed by noisy campaigns for soda water. Peace came only when we pulled down our shelves at night, crawled into them two by two, and fastened the curtains.

In the night we crossed the north fork of the Platte. Morning found us well on toward Cheyenne. The look of embarking passengers roughened. Open drinking increased and the number of women diminished. Turnover was frequent, and it became clear that few in our car were going all the way to California.

The guidebooks touted Cheyenne as the largest city between Omaha and Sacramento, leading us to expect more than we got. It was a rough, dreary, filthy collection of unpainted board-and-canvas structures. There were the customary card and billiards tents, saloons, railroad sheds, government offices, and crude hotels with signs saying SQUARE MEALS & LODGINGS. I was no longer surprised at seeing a theater. Like small-town movie houses of the future, they were everywhere.

It was a study in brown. Nothing green grew anywhere. Beyond the tracks, stirring dust against an infinity of dun plains, horsemen idled with ridge-spined, long-horned cattle. The town itself numbered about four thousand, almost all men—menacing, slouching types in boots and broad-brimmed hats, conspicuously armed with revolvers, rifles, knives. I bumped into one, a grizzled miner with wiry whiskers and mad staring eyes. " 'Scuse me," I said, provoking a double-take and a curse. Shootings and stabbings were nightly occurrences. When things got too far out of hand—*that* must have been something—the local Vigilance Committee sent the offenders a drawing of a tree with a man dangling from it, and the message "Clear out."

Sweet place. It was one thing to see quaint, rough-hewn towns in movie Westerns. Quite another to be in one of the stinking, depressing places, where every hitching area was a cesspool. I was fast getting my fill of the Old West.

We'd all been hoping for a better-than-average breakfast, but the only attraction in Cheyenne's dining room was a row of stuffed big-game animals staring down at us from the walls. Two Chinese waiters, the first we'd seen, worked frantically to feed everybody.

Just as our turn came to order, the conductor shouted, "Get aboard!"

"Steak looked tough as whipcord anyway," Johnny said.

We bought cheese sandwiches from a butch.

"Smile?" a burly man in buckskins said, taking a seat in front of us.

"What?"

"He's askin' if you want a drink," said Johnny.

"Oh," I said. "No, thanks."

He snorted and spat a fountain of tobacco juice that missed the nearest spittoon by a yard.

"How'd you know what he meant?"

"Circus," Johnny said. "You run into all kinds."

"Here, too."

As we chuffed upward toward Sherman Summit, the man in buckskins began a discourse on buffalo hunting, an art he'd practiced with single-minded dedication.

"We was droppin' 'em so fast the skinners 'n scrapers couldn't keep up. Get upwind of 'em, you know, and they're so thick brained they just stand there with their mates falling all around. Three . . . four thousand. Don't know how many I kilt. The barrel got hot enough some days to set the grass afire just touchin' it. That was when I worked for the Goddard brothers feedin' the Kansas Pacific crews." He took a pull from his bottle and belched. "Hell, I knowed them days was doomed even then. Too sweet a thing to keep others away from. Got so there was a thousand hide-hunters out there a-stalkin' our buffaler. Soon after, weren't nobody makin' money. Price dropped from five dollars a hide to less 'n one. How you gonna kill a animal for one measly buck? Got so's the skinners'd slit the buffalers' bellies and rip their hides off with teams of horses. Left the carcasses to rot." He took another long pull. "Yep, I saw the end a-comin'."

A black-and-white image: bones heaped on the prairie, gathered by scavengers to sell to soap makers; the pathetic remains of the endless herds. I'd seen the photograph somewhere; now, in my imagination, rotting hulks in the prairie grasses were interspersed with the corpses of Indians killed in their villages—the vast West, a killing ground.

"Don't look like my story's settin' too good with you," Buckskin said, spitting.

"I don't like slaughter."

"Eat meat?"

I nodded.

"Wearing shoes, ain't you?" he said, pointing at my feet. "Leather shoes?"

"You're right, I'm part of it."

"You sure as damnation are!" He snorted and looked around triumphantly, laughing. "What's your line?" he asked at length.

"Newspaperman."

His face changed with comical abruptness. "Why'nt you say so? Shoot, I wouldn't've been so ornery. You looking for action yarns?"

"Maybe," I said. "You got some?"

"Listen, I'll feed you stories nobody ever thought of. I've outshot, outdrunk, outlied, and outscrewed the worst of 'em!" He leaned close, his breath reminiscent of a zoo's elephant house. "Just last night," he said significantly, "after I'd taken my medicinal quart of whiskey, me'n this feller went out to shoot the heads off'n rattlers. He wuz pie-eyed 'n' 'most blasted his toes off. But me, I jus' kept knockin' them critters down, thinkin' ahead to the real guzzlin' to come." His laugh turned into a phlegmy hack; he spat and said, "That's the sort of stuff you'd want, ain't it?"

"Uh, maybe."

"Name's Bruce Hobbs," he said. "How's about us teamin' up on one of them dime novels? Call the first one *Nebraska Bruce, Prairie Detective*."

I fought back a smile. "A detective named Bruce?"

"Well, my uncle's Ralph. How about Ralph Hobbs?"

"Doesn't quite make it."

"Earl?"

"Keep coming."

"Ray?"

"*Nebraska Ray Hobbs, Prairie Detective,*" I mused aloud. "Tell you what, look me up in San Francisco in a couple months. Maybe we can work something out."

"Jus' might do that, pardner!"

"But you won't be there," Johnny said to me later.

"No kidding."

At Sherman Summit we stopped longer than usual for water. Johnny and I climbed down stiffly from the car along with the rest. We gazed at snow-crowned mountains rising from dark purple depths to peaks of glistening pearl. Somebody pointed out Pike's Peak, clearly visible some hundred miles distant. Granite slopes nearby held strands of stunted pine and cedar. For the easterners especially, who'd never seen true mountains, this panorama of the Rockies was breathtaking. We stood for long minutes shivering in the thin air. Already we had traveled nearly half of the UP's long stretch between Omaha and Promontory.

Our prairie detective disappeared in Laramie, where we had lunch. We then chugged through miles of high, barren land dotted with sage. At Rock Creek we waited for two hours while a derailed freight train was removed from the tracks. The stationmaster told us that sandy soil on this side of the mountains caused constant problems with bridges and track beds.

My attention was attracted by two smooth-shaven men at the end of the car. They'd been with us since Omaha, but had not joined in the general socializing. The older of the two was in his late twenties, taciturn and pinch-lipped. He stood about five ten, with light brown hair, a mouth pulled down as if in disapproval, a long elephantine nose, and protruding jug-handle ears that nearly rivaled Johnny's. He spent most of his time poring over a battered copy of *Pilgrim's Progress*. The book made an odd contrast with the long-barreled .44 Colt revolver strapped to his thigh. Weapons were common now, but he wore his with none of the showmanship that abounded out here. It seemed almost workmanlike, a hammer in a carpenter's belt.

His companion, about five years younger, was slightly shorter and leaner. He walked with a cane, wincing sometimes as he moved, but carrying himself so erectly that he seemed the taller of the two. He had short-cropped chestnut hair, dark eyebrows over pale hazel eyes, and a nervous blink that came every few seconds. Once, when he glanced up and caught me studying him, he smiled thinly and something icy emanated from him. I looked away. There was the same chill about the pair, especially the younger, that I'd felt from Le Caron; a menacing sort of charisma. Earlier Beard, the dry-goods merchant, had tried

[348]

to engage them in conversation. The older man had not looked up from his book; the other gave him the thin, icy smile and said, "We don't know you." Beard retreated in haste. Another time, when somebody referred to the Confederacy as the "Confabulated States of America," the younger one snapped, "Don't ever say that again." It was not repeated.

So I was surprised when he put aside his newspapers—he read stacks of them each day—and worked his way up the aisle toward me, employing his cane as if to keep from jarring himself. His companion watched fixedly.

"Heard tell you're a newspaperman." His voice was thin and nasal; a high-pitched twang and upward inflection made his words almost a challenge.

"That's true." This close I saw dark pockets under his eyes; his cheeks were gaunt, his skin pale.

"What paper?"

I told him.

"*Enquirer?* What's its politics?"

"Democrat."

He pursed his lips and nodded slowly, satisfied.

"What sort of articles?"

Before thinking to cover myself, I told him I was meeting the team in San Francisco.

"Red Stockings," he repeated, screwing up his face like a schoolboy in a spelling bee. "Read of 'em somewhere. Never endeavored that game myself. War busied me. And now there's the farming."

Again I heard a hint of challenge, as if maybe I thought there was something remiss in what he'd said. I didn't ask what a farmer needed with pearl-handled revolvers; the butts of them, protruding from crossed holsters, stuck out from his dark linen frock coat. They must have been encumbrances to such mundane things as sitting down.

"You get news of Western desperadoes up in Ohio?" He pronounced it "desper-A-does." The question came with studied casualness.

"Only what comes through St. Louis," I replied. "Which isn't much. Mostly Indian and troop movements."

He nodded judiciously. "Obliged."

I watched him move stiffly back to his seat. The older man lowered his gaze to his book once more. Was everybody out here media conscious? I wondered. Was the Old West populated by some whimsical casting agency?

That night I stared out the window at the Wyoming desert, a landscape so dreary that even moonlight didn't help. My lips were cracked, my eyes stung from the alkali dust that worked its way into the cars and powdered every surface. We stopped at Red Desert, Bitter Creek, Salt Wells. All aptly named. Johnny snored throughout.

I had a nightmare: Brainard was my father and Cait my mother; we huddled like terrified animals as Le Caron stalked my little brother, Timmy. I woke up sweating, thinking at first that I was back on Amtrak—that *everything* had been a dream.

I sent a telegram from Green River, our breakfast stop, grateful for the twin telegraph lines shadowing the rails. "Trip going well," I wrote on the dispatch slip, resisting adding, "Wish you were here."

A voice startled me on the way out. "Sendin' out a story?"

He was leaning against the wall, almost hidden behind the telegraph-office door. I stepped from the doorway and saw that he was sweating in the morning heat. The pupils of his eyes were dilated, his breathing labored.

"Just a message home," I said. "You okay?"

He eyed me as though weighing my words. I felt the menace again.

"Morphine," he said. "Always brings a sweat. Took a ball near my lung in the war."

That was a long time, I thought, to be using so dangerous a painkiller. At that moment the man's companion came around the corner.

"C'mon, Dingus," he said, ignoring me as he took the pale man's arm.

I thrust my hand out. "I'm Sam Fowler."

The older man paid no attention. The one called Dingus said, "J. T. Jackson, Louisville. This here's Colbourn, my partner." He said the names carefully, glancing back over his shoulder as he moved away.

What's with those two? I wondered.

We passed Cathedral Rock, where workers were replacing wooden bridge sections. All along the UP gangs were visible now—young and Irish mostly, dirty and bearded in dungarees and slouch hats, waving to us when their bosses weren't looking—replacing iron-capped wood rails, converting fueling stations to coal, reworking grades.

Rolling across the wastelands, I wondered if we would all be mummified by the heat and dust. At noon we stopped at Wasatch Station in the Utah Territory. Passengers craned their necks to spot Mormons, those goatsy old devils with harems of compliant wives. At the What Cheer Eating House we ate biscuits that must have been made with alkali.

We climbed through the rugged gorges of Echo and Weber canyons, staring at thrusts of red sandstone towering hundreds of feet above—

Devil's Gate, Devil's Slide, Witches' Rock—as we passed along ledges barely wide enough for the tracks.

The Weber River was spanned by a reconstructed bridge. The original had washed away. This one swayed alarmingly as the engineer stopped in midspan so we could look straight down into a chasm where the river flowed between rock walls three thousand feet high.

"This is worse than the circus high-wire act," Johnny said, looking away.

"Did you do that too?"

"Once."

In late afternoon we pulled out of Ogden. For the next fifty miles another set of tracks ran parallel to ours. In the frantic cross-country race for subsidies, the competing railroads had shot past each other. Belligerent Union Pacific gangs had attacked the Chinese Central Pacific workers with stones and bullets. Promontory had been selected as a temporary linking point—there the golden spike was duly driven, sparking a national celebration—but the permanent division was still in negotiation, with Ogden the strongest contender.

We reached Promontory an hour before sunset. At first glance it didn't seem different from other desert stations. We wrestled for our luggage and lined up at the ticket windows, only to learn that no connecting Central Pacific train departed until the next morning. Curses, threats, and offers of quick cash made no impression. We were all stranded in Promontory for the night.

"This whole place is on the wrong side of the tracks," Johnny commented, looking around.

Which about said it all. To our left squatted sun-bleached express buildings. In the distance a United States flag marked the site of the golden spike ceremony. To our right stretched a single line of canvas-topped structures with crude signs.

"Try your luck, gents?" Shills lounged in the doorways of faro and poker establishments. "Two dollars?"

"Could try *me* for that," a woman with orange hair said. "Wouldn't take much luck neither." After we passed she snorted. "Them two ain't likely stiff for anything!"

It got a laugh from men who eyed us like wolves inspecting the latest sheep shipment. Among them were knots of the ruggedest, most predatory-looking whores I'd ever seen.

After checking out several lodging shanties we decided on Sunny-side House, like the rest a flophouse where for steep prices you rented a cot in a canvas-topped room shared by fifteen others; but unlike the others it didn't double as a gambling house, and it promised "guaranteed protection" of luggage and valuables.

Since there was little else to do we ambled back up the street. "This is just an overgrown gambling hell," Johnny said, pointing at three-card monte and craps tables in front of doorways—convenient for fleecing travelers on a few minutes' stopover. Even our conductor, not overly solicitous of our welfare, had dropped hints that Promontory's whiskey was watered—or worse—and the whores who swarmed to greet each train were diseased.

In front of the Switch Key Saloon we ran into a man from our car who shamefacedly confessed losing forty dollars in less than fifteen minutes. We glanced inside and saw poker and faro games in full swing. Men clustered in the street around tables and lurched through doorways signed REFRESHMENTS. A few wore expensive clothes, but most were in typical plains garb: broad-brimmed hats with felt bands, wide leather belts holding guns and knives, thigh-length coats, pant-legs tucked inside high boots.

They were discharged railroad workers, miners, livestockmen; many were drifters now, dirty, ill-smelling and lice-ridden—I saw one whose *eyebrows* crawled. The sort who got their jollies watching dogs rip each other apart—which happened now in the street, prompting a rash of betting on which animal would survive.

Guns fired every few seconds and yelling was constant. I eyed the formidable weapons around us, thinking my derringer would intimidate few here. At least we didn't need to pretend Johnny was my servant. If a man had money he was welcome in all establishments, regardless of race. Everyone was ripped off equally.

"Let's get a drink," said Johnny. "I'm dryer'n dust."

We stood before a shanty modestly named the Palace Saloon. What the hell, I thought. Old West research. It was much darker inside. I paused beside the doorway to let my eyes adjust, first seeing only halos around the lamps. Beside me, Johnny muttered something.

"What?"

"Sam, it's them."

His tone puzzled me. An instant later, as something hard jammed into my back, spurring terrible memories of Le Caron behind me in the Newark station, I realized with sickening clarity who he meant. All my body systems seemed to hit the brakes.

"Move on up there," a voice growled in my ear.

We were prodded toward a poker table in the far corner of the room, where McDermott and Le Caron sat holding cards, eyes fixed on us. With them were four others, two I didn't recognize, and two I did: Jackson and Colbourn, the taciturn pair from our car.

"Attend to you in a wee bit, Mr. Fowler," said McDermott nonchalantly, as if I were his early-arriving client. To the one behind us he said, "Any shenanigans, kill the big boyo first, then the nigger."

Le Caron's jet eyes stared into mine. He smiled dreamily, as if all his fondest hopes had come true. I cursed my stupidity. Why hadn't I guessed that this would be the interception point? The only place between Omaha and Sacramento where everybody had to detrain.

The gun nudged my back, almost probing, in that same place. Something very strange began to happen to me. I thought I smelled earth and wet leaves, and my vision grew milky.

It couldn't have lasted more than a second or two, but while the images and sensations took over me, time stretched into an infinity. It's impossible to describe accurately, but at exactly the place where the gun was prodding me I seemed to feel my skin explode, the flesh ripping—but *outward,* as if a projectile were exiting, not entering—and then a bright tracer shone through my chest like a laser beam, impaling me, and I hurtled backward, arm flung high in a tunnel of light formed by walls of encircling greenery; for an instant before my body blended with the loam I glimpsed leaves and birds and a terrified face, a face I recognized though it was grimy and younger, the glass-blue eyes crazy above a smoking pistol. . . .

It's fairly unsettling to learn that your body seems to remember its own death and that your brain holds a picture of your killer. And now I was to die again. The gambling room was washed in milky half-light. Roaring filled my ears. I must have slumped, for the gun jabbed me abruptly—but in a different place. The pain presented a focus, helped bring me back.

"Some sort of trouble here?" The pale man was talking. Jackson. I squinted. He sat two places left of McDermott, across from Le Caron. On his right was the older one, Colbourn.

"No trouble." McDermott sounded expansive, jovial. "Not now."

Maybe I could yell. Scream they were going to kill us. Hope Jackson would do something. But although I was tracking better, speech seemed beyond my capacity. I realized that Jackson was studying me quizzically. He glanced away and with a lazy movement pulled his coat back to reveal the handles of his pistols. It was a gesture few in the room could have missed.

"A gun out in the open turns me skittish," he said softly.

"Play out the hand," McDermott said. "Then we'll be about our business." He nodded to Le Caron, who was dealing.

Speech returned to me suddenly. "Why'd he kill Colm?" The words erupted harshly.

McDermott stared in surprise, then grinned. "Who?" he said. "Me?"

"O'Donovan," I said. "Just like he sent you. But why'd he shoot Colm?"

"Oh, 'shoot' is it, now? You know that, too?"

"We playin' cards here or not?" Colbourn demanded.

McDermott waved a peremptory hand. Colbourn's scowl deepened.

"To your queries I'll say aye and leave you the why," McDermott said, laughing at his rhyme. "You'll have ample time to ponder it." His voice hardened. "Shoot the bastard if he opens his mouth again."

Jackson was studying him curiously. Colbourn still looked pissed. If only I could figure a way to get them on our side. I tried to forget the gun in my back and concentrate on what was happening before me.

Gold littered the table, a pot of at least five hundred dollars. The game was seven-card stud. Each of the six players had two cards down and three up: McDermott showed a pair of tens; Jackson two kings; Colbourn two clubs with nothing else; one of the others looked straightish with a ten, jack, and ace. Le Caron, already folded, dealt the fourth up-card around: no help for McDermott's tens, a third king to Jackson, another club to Colbourn, no help to the straight builder, who folded Jackson's fifty-dollar opener. McDermott raised fifty. Colbourn pushed his hundred in reluctantly, probably sitting on a flush but worried that he was already beaten. Jackson raised a hundred back. McDermott matched it. Colbourn folded his hand, eyeing the pot morosely.

I moved my head slightly to see the man behind us.

"Turn around."

I'd caught a glimpse. He was well back. I tried to catch Johnny's eye. He was oblivious, staring intently at Le Caron. No chance for signals between us. Jesus. My mind was thawing, but it came up with nothing.

Le Caron dealt McDermott and Jackson their final down cards. Jackson bent the corner of his up and peeked at it. His pallid face showed nothing, but his shoulders squared slightly as he spoke.

"I'll go five hundred dollars." He moved stacks of gold eagles to the center of the table.

"I'm thinking I'll raise you back the same," said McDermott, counting out a thousand dollars.

Jackson looked at Colbourn. Some message passed between them. Colbourn reached into his coat and produced a leather pouch from which he poured coins.

"Raise you the same again," Jackson said.

McDermott, who had not looked at his seventh card, now did so. His eyes flicked to Le Caron, then away. "It'll clean my pockets, to be sure," he said expansively. "But 'tis curious I am by nature, and I'll not rest till I know what you're holding so proudly." He pushed his remaining money into the pot and sat back expectantly.

Jackson turned over his cards: a full house, kings over sevens.

"A grand layout," said McDermott, leaning back. "Sure and should be a winner every time."

"Stop chinning, mister," Jackson said. "Turn up your cards."

McDermott did so, with maddening slowness. Two of his down cards were tens, making four in all. The room was hushed. McDermott reached for the pot.

"The deal's crooked!" Johnny yelled. "He's using a holdout!"

There was a startled instant in which everything seemed suspended. The man behind us snarled, "Shut up!"

I jumped involuntarily as an explosion came from the table. Each of Jackson's hands held a pistol. Smoke curled from the barrel of the one pointed upward. The other was trained on a spot behind Johnny and me.

"The nigger's got something to say." Tension gave Jackson's thin voice a higher pitch. "If you"—he moved the gun pointed our way slightly—"don't allow him a chance, you'll be the first dead."

Apparently it convinced whoever was behind us.

"That's good," said Jackson. Without shifting his eyes he said, "You set, Buck?"

Colbourn muttered something I didn't catch. He brought up his hands from below the table. They held revolvers.

I waited tensely, ready to spring in any direction. So many guns, so little time.

"Talk," Jackson told Johnny.

"It's a Keplinger holdout," Johnny said, his words running together. "Named for the fella invented it. Used to work in the circus. Did magic tricks. Saw him once and—"

"Whoa," said Jackson. "Just tell how it works, and we'll check this gent to see if you're right."

Le Caron sat like a coiled spring. Across from him, McDermott's face was ashen.

"It's a contraption with pulleys and cords and telescoping tubes. You spread your knees and a sneak—that's a little claw inside a double sleeve—moves down your arm to your hand. Close your knees, it goes back up. Makes cards appear or disappear. A Keplinger's safer than the type that just shoots a spring up your arm and pulls it back with a rubber band, see, 'cause you gotta bend your elbow to make it work, and suspicious folks look for that, but never the knees, of course—"

"And you're saying this gent is in cahoots with the dealer?"

"He fed his partner those tens," Johnny said, "and you'll find a fifth one—or maybe the fourth king you never had a chance of getting—in that holdout right now."

"It don't much matter what's *in* it," Jackson said, turning to face Le Caron, "but whether he's *got* one." He stood up and jerked the table back from Le Caron. "Okay, put your arms out in front of you and spread your knees, like the nigger said."

Le Caron raised his arms slowly, bringing them up even with his head rather than stretching them in front of him. Just as I wondered about that, a suspicion danced in my brain.

"Look out!" I yelled as he widened his knees and a card materialized in his left hand. "Watch his other—"

It was too late. As eyes fixed on the card fluttering from Le Caron's left hand, a knife blade flashed in his right. Positioned to throw, his arm blurred downward in a deadly sweep.

Gunfire exploded in the room. I spun low and dove at the man behind. Johnny had the same idea, wheeling a split second later but moving so fast that our bodies brushed as we hurtled forward. I felt a hot whisper on my scalp as a gun erupted. We slammed into him, toppling him backward beneath us. The gun went off again. I reached frantically for it, guts knotted and body writhing in anticipation of a bullet ripping into me. His knees came up, bucking Johnny violently. I slammed my right forearm into his face, still trying to grasp his gun hand with my left. Johnny got there first—just as the gun fired again. He yelped in pain and rolled away. Then I had the man's wrist pinned to the floor. I battered his head with short, brutal blows until his grip loosened on the pistol. Pulling Johnny in close, I propped the groaning, half-conscious man up as a shield.

I peered over him in time to see Le Caron crash through the room's only window. Jackson and Colbourn moved there quickly, their boots crunching shards of glass. They fired a volley through the window, reloaded, and stalked cautiously outside. McDermott lay against the wall, half covered by the overturned table, coins and cards spilled over him. He was groaning and his face was white. A dark flower of blood spread slowly on his coat below his right shoulder. Another man at the table lay still, facedown, on the floor.

Le Caron's knife, we learned, had passed between Jackson's left arm and his side, inches from his heart, grooving his flesh and thudding into the wall behind him. Both Jackson and Colbourn had sent bullets into Le Caron before he upended the table as a momentary shield. McDermott, on the floor, made the mistake of reaching into his jacket. Jackson shot him before he could free his weapon. Le Caron produced a gun from somewhere and fired wildly to cover his dash for the window. Jackson was positive he'd nailed him again on the way. With three bullets in him, they figured they wouldn't have much trouble tracking Le Caron down. They were wrong. He vanished in the darkness. In the morning we found a trail of blood leading out into the desert; and that too disappeared. I hoped he'd died under a bush somewhere.

Johnny had grabbed the barrel as the gun fired. The bullet tunneled through his palm. The wound was ringed by ugly powder burns. The doc, a cynical, shaky-handed old drunk resigned to treating gun-shot and stab wounds virtually every night, did a reasonably neat job of cleaning and bandaging it. He said the hand would never close as tightly as before and gave him a laudanum compound for pain.

McDermott got less sympathetic treatment. Cheating at cards—at least getting caught at it—was a greater wrong here than manslaugh-ter. McDermott was roughly patched and taken off to jail. The dead man was ordered hauled away by the sheriff. We were all questioned, and it was duly established that Jackson and Colbourn had acted in self-defense. The sheriff said he'd take a posse after Le Caron the next day. There was a reward for him; if we helped we'd have first crack at a share of the bounty. We didn't jump at the chance.

"Obliged to you'n the nigger," Jackson said as we moved along the street. It was after midnight. During the fight he'd looked quick and agile, but now he walked laboriously and used his cane. "My brother"—he shrugged slightly as Colbourn turned to scowl at him—"said we shouldn't get into that game, but I was of the mind we could hold our own." He laughed and said, " 'Man born of woman is of few days and full of trouble.' "

"Thank God you happened to be in there," I said.

"Looked like they intended you deadly harm," Jackson said.

"We had some problems back East," I said. "They came here looking for me."

"I don't guess they'll be fit to look farther. The half-breed's likely dead—we got him in places that don't heal easy—and that Irishman won't be laughing again for a spell." He chuckled softly, a nasal sound. "Tell you what, after you get to Frisco, come on down and pay us a visit, place called Paso de Robles. Know of it?"

Colbourn turned and stared.

"Paso Robles?" I said. "Past Salinas?"

Jackson shrugged. "County of San Luis, all I know."

"Christ, Dingus," said Colbourn. "He's a newspaperman, Yankee to boot!"

Jackson spun toward him, pointing his cane like a pistol. "Don't curse me, Buck." He waited a long moment, then reverted to his friendly tone. "We're fixin' to spend some time at our uncle's place."

"This ain't right," muttered Colbourn.

"Paso de Robles Mineral Springs," Jackson said, ignoring him. "We're wintering there to raise my health up. Hot mud, clear baths, iron and magnesia in the water. Take a steamer down from Frisco. You'd be welcome." His hazel eyes did their nervous blink. "Ask for us or D. W. James."

"Thanks," I said, thinking that hot baths or no, visiting these guys would be about as much fun as dancing with a cactus.

It wasn't until later, in the paling light of the false dawn, lying on my cot, surrounded by hellish snoring, my imagination conjuring vivid pictures of Le Caron skulking outside the canvas walls, that I heard Jackson say the name of his uncle again in my mind: *James.*

26

We traveled in elegance on the Central Pacific. Our Silver Palace car had dazzling white-metal interiors, spacious berths, private sitting and smoking rooms. Johnny was deep in laudanum-induced slumber as we stopped at stations scattered across the desert like rocks. Water lay in stagnant ponds so alkaline that cattle wouldn't touch them unless they were dying of thirst. Because alkali ruined boilers, special water trains had to run daily to supply the stations.

With no scenery to look at, passengers turned to each other to pass time. Jackson and Colbourn were in another car now—we exchanged nods at station breaks—and Johnny and I were sandwiched between two excursion groups. One consisted of ruddy Englishmen packing a small arsenal. They talked incessantly of the game they expected to kill.

The other group, merchants and wives, was from Washington. One of the Washington men came over just after Johnny had taken the last of his laudanum and nodded off again. In soft southern accents he said his name was Kramer. I got the feeling he was glad to escape his group—or maybe just his wife. A baseball enthusiast, he was curious about Harry and the Stockings. He responded to my questions about wartime tensions in the capital with anecdotes in which Lincoln figured as a buffoon. A staunch Democrat, he had little use for the martyred president or his ruinous policies.

"What about Grant?" I asked.

"A common drunk, glorified for butchery. The Radicals have him in their pocket." Kramer paused. "Have you followed gold?"

Only to Elmira, I thought. "No, why?"

"One in our party is close to Grant's son-in-law." He pursed his lips. "Close enough to hear things."

"Like what?"

"He's buying gold fast as he can."

"Why? Does Grant set the price?"

"No, it fluctuates in the open market. But what Grant does—or doesn't do—influences that market. Two groups are competing for his support: 'bulls,' who invest heavily in gold shares and oppose all printing of greenbacks; and 'bears,' who own millions in paper currency and fight anything that boosts gold—such as its greater use for money. Each group constantly lobbies the government."

"What's Grant done?"

"That's the point. Absolutely nothing. Everybody is waiting for him to take a position."

I thought for a moment. "So if you knew in advance, you'd clean up?"

"That knowledge would be of truly inestimable value to an investor."

"And so Grant's son-in-law—"

"—is obtaining all the gold he can," Kramer finished. "A consortium of powerful buyers is driving the price higher. People with gold certificates are getting rich."

"What's the risk?"

"Only one thing could ruin it: if Grant instructed the treasury to release gold reserves, deflating the market."

"That won't happen?"

Kramer shook his head. "He's so sick of being yammered at that he's privately decided to let the bulls and bears fight to the finish, *then* set his policy."

Johnny groaned and shifted in his sleep, his hand hurting him again. I worked a cushion beneath it. He was sweating. I fanned him until his breathing deepened.

"What if some of the big buyers dumped their shares?" I said. "Wouldn't that collapse the whole thing?"

"You grasp these matters quickly," he said. "The consortium's agreement is not to sell any shares whatsoever until gold reaches two hundred dollars."

"Where's it now?"

"One thirty-seven. Only two days ago it was one thirty-three."

"So it's already started."

He nodded solemnly.

"Are you in?" I asked.

"With everything I own," he said cheerfully. "Already I'm richer by fourteen thousand. If I cared to sell, that is, which I certainly do not. Keep your eye on things the next few days. There's still time to make

yourself a pile. Chance of a lifetime. And the more that go in, naturally, the bigger the profits for us all."

"I see."

He looked to the front of the car. "Pardon," he said, with little
discernible joy. "My wife requires me."

After that, whenever our eyes met, Kramer winked.

Elko, Nevada, was supposed to be only a supper stop, but with our
locomotive developing a "hot box"—an axle bearing overheating
dangerously from friction—we limped in for a longer stay.

Like Promontory, Elko was booming. A large Chinese settlement
lent it a different tone, but esthetically it still had a long way to go. The
ever-present alkali dust swirled in head-high clouds, stirred by mule
trains and eight-horse stages clattering off to the White Pines silver
mines.

Johnny stayed in our car to rest, his appetite blunted by the laudanum. Most of the others headed for a hotel restaurant. I held back,
having no stomach for more fried meat. I was about to buy some fruit
from a vendor when a Chinese boy walked by. He wore the customary
blue overshirt and pants, wooden clogs, and round hat from which a
braided cue stretched nearly to his ankles. Looking at him, I had an
inspiration.

"You wan' *my* food?" he said incredulously when I overtook him.
"Chinee food?"

I held out two silver dollars and nodded. He looked at them in
astonishment. Meals along the CP ran a buck and a quarter. To a
Chinese boy whose family lived on a fraction of what whites earned,
my offering must have seemed a small fortune.

"Not 'nuff," he said, eyeing me shrewdly. "Fo' dollah!"

The little bandit! The trouble was that suddenly I was ravenous for
Chinese food. I handed him two more dollars.

He led me through narrow packed-dirt alleys. I asked questions
about the settlement and gathered that it consisted mainly of discharged CP workers. Groups moving along the alleys or standing and
smoking cigarettes stared at us, the babble of their conversation slowing momentarily. I sensed no hostility, merely curiosity. There were no
women anywhere in view. He led me inside a frame shack where I sat
on the floor before a low bench.

The food was worth every penny: heaping bowls of steamed vegetables and rice, dumplings filled with spiced pork, succulent chicken and
duck, and apple-shaped pastries coated with melted candy. I plied my
chopsticks as fast as I could.

◇

Onlookers surrounded the repair crew. The harried engineer said it would take several more hours to fix the axle. I had a mug of coffee in the station and picked up a day-old paper with the caption ACTIVITY IN WALL STREET'S GOLD ROOM. Volume was heavy and the price had risen from 139 to 141 dollars an ounce. Hadn't Kramer said it was 137 dollars? I thought of Twain's thousand dollars. Wouldn't gold be more sensible than a flying machine?

I stopped by the telegraph desk. A boy about nineteen sat self-importantly behind the key.

"Anything about gold over the wire today?"

"You're 'bout the hunderth to ask."

"What'd you tell the other ninety-nine?"

"That's a dandy!" He slapped his knee. "What'd you tell the other ninety-nine!"

I decided he was simple, not putting me on. "Do you know today's closing price?"

"Up over one forty-two," he said. "Everybody says it's just the beginning."

"I suppose you're in too," I said

"Would if I had the cash." He grinned. "I know who *has* jumped in on the sly."

"Who?"

"Mrs. Grant, that's who."

Was the first family really so flagrant, I wondered, that every yokel in the Nevada desert knew their business?

I drank two more coffees and watched the uninspired panhandling of several ragged Sochoche Indians. Then I walked back to the train. The moon was just beginning to climb over the horizon. I took a gold eagle from my pocket and stared at it. It gleamed with the reflected radiance of ten thousand stars overhead.

Reno was the CP point nearest the fabulous Comstock mines, which for the past decade had channeled limitless millions through San Francisco into the world. The place was well-equipped for financial dealing. After breakfast I found a Wells Fargo office on North Virginia, where I learned that already the price of gold had risen fifty cents that morning. That decided me. With fourteen hundred dollars of my letter of credit, I purchased a certificate for ten ounces of gold.

I hurried back to the station thinking that the few times in my life I'd tried slot machines, I'd never hit for more than a handful of quarters. This time the jackpot would be bigger. Much bigger.

◇

With a second locomotive attached to our train—doubling the noise and smoke—we moved out of the Nevada basin upward into the pine-sloped Sierras. I saw yellow wildflowers that reminded me of backpacking trips I'd made near Tahoe. As we crossed the California border I felt my heart beat faster. This was home.

Evergreens covered the mountains like shaggy blankets, broken only by the log chutes used by timber crews to stockpile quick-hewn railroad ties. We climbed the twisting canyon of the Truckee and came upon a magnificent view of Donner Lake. Predictably, guidebook accounts of the ill-fated Donner Party, embellished with grotesque details, echoed through the car.

Near Cisco we lunged into darkness. The train butch laughed at our startled reactions. Lighting the car's lamps, he informed us we were in snowsheds extending the next fifty miles.

"Just when we get country worth seeing," Johnny said.

Snow here didn't drift like eastern snows, but lay in mammoth caps. The CP, at a cost of twenty thousand dollars per mile, was enclosing everything. Stations, tracks, water tanks, woodsheds, turntables, stalls for locomotives—all were to be roofed over before next winter's paralyzing storms. Fortunately for us, sections remained where we could see through unfinished walls.

At almost every station Indians, mostly Shoshones and Paiutes, climbed in and out of the baggage cars. One Paiute chief stalked through our car in stately fashion with a blue blanket draped around his shoulders and a ragged black hat on his head. The CP, tiring of attacks on its crews and trains, had showed more acumen than the UP by issuing free passes to tribal leaders; hostilities ceased immediately.

From the snowsheds only a hundred miles remained to Sacramento. Half of it was a roller coaster of straining ascents, breath-squeezing curves, and stomach-wrenching descents. Brakemen ran atop the cars spinning the brake wheels—air brakes didn't exist yet—adjusting to prevent the cars picking up too much speed. Or separating from each other due to uneven braking. Or going into a skid if wheels overheated from friction. Only two brakemen worked the entire length of bumping cars. Their thudding feet overhead reminded us how close we were to catastrophe.

We careened through Blue Canon and Dutch Flat and Gold Run, halted at Cape Horn to look down a dizzying abyss at the American River, a green ribbon two thousand feet below. We thundered through another stretch of snowsheds, where, reflected in the windows of workers' houses, I saw our axle boxes smoking and our wheels glowing like fiery discs.

After hours of it we finally leveled off and emerged into the brilliant sunshine of the Sacramento Valley. At our next stop we sniffed the air and gazed around in wonder at flower-strewn meadows watered by curving streams. After the desert wastes and the Sierra chill, it all seemed like paradise. We stood silently. Insects buzzed. Birdsong floated around us.

"We did it," somebody said. "Crossed the whole blessed country."

A woman started singing "America."

I have to admit it gave me a rush, goose bumps and all, as the rest joined in. Johnny and I sang too.

"Hurrah for the Union!" came the shout.

Simply by making the trip I felt I had achieved something powerful. I think we all felt it.

We rolled along Front Street toward the CP terminal, boggling at the sight of thousands of blooms. The guidebooks called Sacramento "Flower City" and "Queen City of the Plain." I'd forgotten the lushness of California's river valleys. In a single mile we passed orchards and fields teeming with apricots, cherries, apples, blackberries, strawberries, oranges, and peaches.

The dome of the state capitol reflected tracers of sunlight in the distance. Carpenters and gilders swarmed over it like so many ants. Somebody said it was nearly ready for occupancy.

"Who's governor?" I asked.

Nobody knew.

We moved along the oak-bordered river, where Central Pacific yards were heaped with rails and ties, and idled into a huge new twenty-nine-stall brick roundhouse. It was landscaped with eucalyptus saplings recently introduced from Australia. Funny to see for myself that the trees of my youth hadn't always been here.

We came to a halt.

And that was it. For many, this was the limit of their trip. They would visit Sutter's Mill, perhaps journey to Yosemite, and return home to recount their adventures.

Those of us pushing on to San Francisco still had 120 miles before us. With no direct rail link, we had three choices: ride the Western Pacific, opened just two weeks ago, to Stockton, then connect with Alameda and take a ferry across the bay; train to Vallejo and board a steamer; or journey by water all the way down the Sacramento.

From the ticket agent I learned that the Stockings had passed through earlier that afternoon.

"What a fuss!" he exclaimed. "Hundreds jostling to see, all the bigwigs on hand. Them with their little red stockings on their coats, fit and handsome. Why, that Harry's Wright's the very picture of a man!"

I agreed that Harry was and asked which route they'd taken.

"Steamed on the riverboat *Capitol*, their flag trailing out behind 'em in the breeze. A grand sight!"

"Can I catch them tonight?"

"Not till 'way after dark. Trip takes nine hours. Last boat leaves in a few minutes."

I started to turn away. "Oh, you hear anything about gold today?"

"Heard a whole lot," he said, grinning. "Got shares myself. Price jumped two dollars, up to one forty-five."

I grinned back. Today's increase on my modest holdings would more than cover the steamer tickets. I wished I'd bought more shares. Gold was a long way from two hundred an ounce, but things were moving fast.

Johnny and I stood on the deck of the stern-wheeler *Yosemite* beneath a black plume of coal smoke, watching the bank pass by lazily. A rust-red sunset tinted the river.

"You're quiet, Sam," said Johnny. "You got feelings about coming home?"

I didn't have an answer. I was definitely feeling *something*: a ball in my stomach seemed to combine expectancy and apprehension. Maybe dread. It was one thing to go off in time and geographical distance. It was another to come back to face the reality that "home" did not exist.

We slid past Benicia, its boatworks and fort barely visible in the darkness. We churned the dark waters of the Carquinez Strait between low treeless banks, and moved into San Pablo Bay. Finally we rounded San Rafael Point and were in San Francisco Bay. My chest tightened as I peered into the blackness.

Tiny lights glowed on a cluster of distant hills. I was confused by darkness to their right, where I was used to seeing the Golden Gate Bridge, but then I recognized the black humps of Angel and Alcatraz islands, and I knew where I was. I watched silently as the city's night-draped hills drew gradually closer. Sensing something wrong, Johnny stepped close and for a moment gripped my arm with his good hand.

I don't think I've ever felt lonelier in my life.

27

Johnny was up at seven. Wagons rumbled and men shouted on the docks outside. Instead of trying to find the team's hotel, we'd walked from the Broadway wharf and come upon the Blue Anchor, a seamen's rooming house, at the foot of Washington. It wasn't too bad if you ignored the fleas.

"Sam, I'm out of laudanum. Hand's paining me again." He pulled away the bandage. The wound was messy but seemed to be healing. "Someplace'll likely be open this early in Chinadom. Where is it?"

"Up to Grant, make a right, should put you—" I stopped, wondering if Chinatown was in the same place. "Tell you what, I'll show you."

"Why're you looking around so?" he asked me on the street.

"Lot of changes here." I tried to hide my bewilderment at not recognizing *anything*.

We walked up Washington to Montgomery. The plank sidewalks were thronged with fashionably dressed people. Brass plaques identified the Merchants' Exchange, Customs House, Post Office, Bank of California, Montgomery Block—all sandstone and marble and brick. Most of the city, I would find, was dull brown and fashioned of wood.

Farther up Washington we passed Maguire's Opera House; it bore no resemblance to the opera house I had known, and was in the wrong location. We entered Portsmouth Square, in my memory the peaceful refuge of elderly Chinese, pigeons, and winos. Now it was lined with city offices and saloons, and jammed with hacks. Omnibuses rolled through on a line between North Beach and South Park. Behind a high iron fence stood city hall; some of its windows were boarded and in places the masonry had crumbled badly. At the top of the square a gang of workmen sprayed the street to prepare for paving; others were replacing redwood sewers with brick. Smelly work. I detoured around them and turned at the corner.

"You said Grant!" Johnny called, pointing at the street sign, which read Dupont.

I could see Chinese signs ahead and a painted temple roof. We'd come the right way. "It's up there. You go ahead. I'll walk around a bit and get my bearings."

"You okay?"

"Sure."

"I'm gonna look for work," he said. "If something turns up, I'm thinking to stay on here. I'll be at the Blue Anchor at least a couple more nights. And I'll know how to find the nine."

I nodded, realizing there was no longer a reason for us to stay together. He had offered a graceful transition. I felt reluctant to say good-bye.

"Don't get shanghaied," I told him. "Stay out of the Barbary Coast."

He laughed. "That's where I'm headed."

I watched him walk up the street, a gutsy little man going against the odds.

I headed toward Telegraph Hill, surprised at the amount of open space. Irish shanties dotted only small portions of the hill. I made my way up slowly, my feet slipping on long grass. Coit Tower wasn't there, of course, but at the top I did find Sweeny and Baugh's signal station, a small wooden tower with a telescope and refreshment stand—not open this early—and thousands of initials carved on it.

I gazed at the bay. It looked larger than I remembered. Over the blue surface moved everything from tiny fishing craft to majestic windjammers. I checked familiar landmarks. The Golden Gate looked naked without the bridge. A small fort stood in the prison's spot on Alcatraz. Directly below, a line of three-masted schooners swayed at their docks along a section of completed seawall—the Embarcadero was evidently just being built. Hearing the faint sounds of voices and ships' bells and creaking masts and whistling lines, I felt a sudden exhilaration. The earthquake and terrible fires lay thirty-seven years in the future. This was how the city had *been!*

BOOM! I jumped as a blast of black smoke rose from the hillside below, where Montgomery met Broadway. I'd seen them quarrying there; they were carving Telegraph Hill into craggy terraces, using the soil blasted loose to fill the bayfront and build the seawall.

Trying to absorb everything, talking to people, I explored the waterfront, where lateen-rigged Italian feluccas and painted Chinese junks were moored, fishing nets spread to dry on railings, circular crab nets stacked on docks. Scow sloops were laden with cargo. Ocean-going vessels, their masts dense thickets overhead, discharged silks, teas, and rice from China, furs from Alaska, sugar from the Sandwich Islands, machinery and furniture from eastern factories.

In stretches where the seawall wasn't begun, flimsy wharves perched on rotting piles over tarlike mud. During BART's excavations I'd done a story on the discovery of skeletons and even an entire ship buried along the old seafront. At the time I'd wondered how they could have simply vanished beneath the wharves. Now I understood.

Ferries to Oakland, San Quentin, and "Saucelito" operated from separate wharves. I missed the old Ferry Building. As with the Golden Gate Bridge, the city would be improved by it. Which I couldn't say for most of San Francisco's future skyline.

In midmorning I walked up California, where men milled in front of brokerage houses advertising low commissions and high prices for silver and gold. The establishments were so crowded that I couldn't see inside.

"What's going on?" I asked a man on the outskirts.

"A bull run," he said. "Gold's shooting sky high!"

"Grant's thrown in with 'em," another said. "Greenbacks're worthless."

"What's gold at now?" I asked.

"One fifty-five—and climbing."

Jesus, I'd made 150 dollars on an investment of only 1,400. More than a month's pay in scarcely two days.

"The bottom'll drop out," a third said. "Mark me."

The first man laughed. "Sour asses like you'll stand by and watch the rest of us get rich!"

A Wells Fargo office stood on the next corner. It too was jammed. I pushed inside far enough to verify the price—now up another dollar to 156 dollars.

"What's the latest I can buy today?" I asked, and was informed that New York's Gold Room closed at one o'clock local time.

"Better get in now, it'll be over two hundred by then," somebody said behind me.

I started to reach for my letter of credit, then stopped. It was only ten-thirty. I'd give it a while longer.

Over coffee I scanned my all-time favorite paper. The Stockings' arrival was the *Morning Chronicle*'s page-one feature. The previous night a crowd of two thousand had met them at the Broadway wharf and escorted them to the Cosmopolitan Hotel. In the players' bios I was amused to see that Mac had tacked two years to his age, making him twenty-one. Probably Champion's idea. Hiring nineteen-year-old professionals might not look good. Tomorrow's contest with the Eagles, the city's top club, was expected to be a thriller.

The *Chronicle* also reported that an Arizona Indian chief was being held hostage on Angel Island against the good behavior of his entire tribe. I wondered if it were true. Already the paper showed a flair for the bizarre.

I walked down to Market, where New Montgomery was being extended to Howard. Hackmen there claimed this would soon become the city's poshest district.

"What about Nob Hill?" I said.

"Too steep for horsecars."

I realized then that I hadn't seen any cable cars.

Across the street stood a partially finished, enormous iron-and-brick-structure—the $400,000 Grand Hotel, scheduled to open early next year; it was secured by anchors, the hackmen said, to make it earthquakeproof.

"Hear about the big one this time last year?" one asked me. "Damn near knocked down Marine Hospital. Damaged the mint and city hall. Then there was the big 'un in 'sixty-five, same month. In heat just like this, too." He grinned maliciously. "Earthquake weather."

"Guess I'm just in time for it," I said, amused at being baited as a tourist.

I knew it was silly, but I walked along Mission to Fifth, passing gashouses and factories and weather-beaten frame shacks. The street was paved with wooden blocks that had been dipped in tar. Wagons made a swooshing sound as they passed. I shut my eyes and told myself that when I opened them again I would see the *Chronicle* building's familiar gray clock tower. For an instant I *did* feel something strange pass over me, but when I opened my eyes the plank sidewalk still lay beneath my feet and a horsecar moved on rails in the center of the broad street. I felt a pinch of disappointment.

A whiskey grocery stood on the Chronicle's corner. I looked at it for a while. Smells of stew meat and boiling potatoes were heavy in the air. Across the street was a large excavation. I wandered over and was pleased to see the beginnings of a longtime friend—the Old Mint. I'd looked down on it thousands of times. Workmen on break said that its cornerstone would be laid sometime next year.

I walked back along Market, passing the five-story business place of H. H. Bancroft, book dealer. From the basement of St. Patrick's, between Second and Third, boys in school uniforms boiled up and spilled into an adjoining lot. They had a baseball bat and a tape-covered ball.

"Dibs on George Wright!" A stocky boy waved the bat ferociously.

"Brainard!" another shouted.

"Andy Leonard!"

The kid imitating Brainard went into a contorted windup remarkably unlike the Stocking pitcher's. I realized again that without TV or movies or stop-action photography, the only images these kids could get came from seeing their heroes firsthand.

On Montgomery I passed the Occidental Hotel, where Twain loved the oysters, and in the five hundred block came on the current *Chronicle* office. Maybe I should go in and apply for a job. Check out old De Young—or had he already died in the famous duel? But I didn't stop until the next block, where I saw a sign above the sidewalk:

SAN FRANCISCO ADVERTISER
F. MARRIOTT
623 MONTGOMERY

A second-story window contained the same information in gold leaf. What the hell. Why not drop in and see about his airplane?

Tacked above the landing was an enormous advertisement: AVITOR NEXT IN POINT OF SPEED TO THE TELEGRAPH. The reader was urged to purchase stock immediately in this new wonder that would "bear men and messages through the air, while the railroad drags heavy burdens of freight." Entranced, I read every word that followed, enjoying Marriott's blowsy prose.

> *No savages in war paint shall interrupt its passage over and across our continent. No malaria or hostile tribes nor desert sands shall prevent the exploration of Africa, no want of water the examination of central Australia, nor ice floes the search for the Northwest Passage. No underground railways will be needed to accommodate the crowded thoroughfares of Broadway, no curcuitous passage to find a narrow isthmus between continents, no waiting for trade winds; no necessity of lying becalmed under tropical suns; no extortions for huge corporations who monopolize the great routes of travel. No tax for crossing New Jersey; no states under tribute to railway companies. Man rises superior to his accidents when for his inventive genius he ceases to crawl upon the earth and masters the realms of the upper air.*

Lovely, I thought, simply lovely.

There was also an announcement that daily flights of the *Avitor* could be witnessed at the Mechanics Pavilion in Union Square.

Just as I finished working through it all, quick footsteps and a rustling of skirts sounded on the stairway. I turned as a small figure yanked Marriott's door open and propelled herself inside. Before it slammed, I glimpsed blond ringlets and a thrust-forward chin. Interesting.

It grew more so by the second. Voices inside built in volume, one female and accusing, several male and placating. The female's built to a shriek. The males' grew urgent. I couldn't make out any words until a sharp crack resounded, followed by a shouted "No!"

It wasn't a gunshot—I knew that sound—but more like leather slapping a resonant surface. I stepped cautiously through the doorway. The sound came again. The outer office was empty.

" 'Indecent and nasty,' is it?" the female voice shouted from a cubicle to my left. The door stood ajar, FREDERICK MARRIOTT stenciled neatly on it. " 'Those who attend are a low *lot*'?"

The last was a combination of question and grunt. The cracking sounded again. There was a yell. I moved to the doorway and saw a shirtsleeved clerk cowering behind a desk. He looked at me imploringly. On top of the desk stood a middle-aged man. His eyes were riveted on the woman. She stood with her back to me, her right hand brandishing a riding whip, her left clutching a newspaper.

Crack! The whip snapped on the polished toes of his boots. He sprang with remarkable agility upward from the desktop.

"I didn't write it! You're demented!"

" 'No figure whatever'?" She waved the paper in circles, apparently quoting it from memory. " 'A pair of thin arms, huge hips, utterly out of shape. . . .' You bloody bastard!" The whip slashed down again.

"It wasn't me! Bierce wro—"

He jumped too late. The whip caught his ankles. He toppled to the desktop, more alarmed than hurt.

"You'll respect a lady, you guttersnipe!" She drew back the whip.

He raised his hands. "Wait!"

I grabbed her arm, gave it a twist, and yanked the whip away as she spun to face me.

I was staring into the furious eyes of Elise Holt.

She didn't recognize me. Or maybe she did. Without hesitation she launched a most unladylike kick at my groin. It had impressive extension, a dancer's, high and flamboyant. I stepped back barely in time, caught her foot on its way down, held it, and moved backward. She followed, hopping, her blue eyes blazing.

"Sam Fowler, remember?"

Tossing her head angrily, she twisted toward the man on the desk and hiked her skirts over the leg I held, revealing pale pink tights to her upper thigh. "Is this the 'wretched material exhibited'?" she demanded.

I regarded it critically, seeing nothing wretched; in fact, it was curvy and provocative. The tights and black boots could have graced *Police Gazette*.

She flounced her skirt down and shoved her hands under her breasts, swelling the blouse and short jacket. "Is this 'no figure at all'?"

A wave of pink washed Marriott's face. His gray-streaked hair hung in his eyes; his suit was rumpled. Though he looked mortified by present circumstances, it didn't keep him from staring at Holt's up-thrust breasts.

"May I descend?" he said finally, in British accents.

"And you're English!" she shrilled, struggling to free herself. "That's too bleedin' much for any—"

She lost her balance and started to fall. I released her foot and wrapped my arms around her corseted waist. Her bustle squirmed provocatively against me. I smelled her perfume.

"As I tried to inform you," Marriott said, climbing down warily. "I do not write the Town Crier column which so upset you, Miss Holt. Nor do I edit the *Advertiser*. I am merely its publisher."

I nearly laughed at that, but Holt seemed to be calming. Or at least accepting restraint.

Marriott regarded me. "Who are you, sir? I'm grateful for your assistance."

"Elise's old friend," I said, drawing a painful pinch on my arm. "Actually, I dropped by to see how *Avitor* stock was doing."

"Oh, you mustn't draw conclusions from what has just transpired," he said quickly. "You're an interested investor?"

"Interested," I said. "Probably not an investor. I'm with the Cincinnati *Enquirer*."

Alarm tightened his features. Holt looked up at me. "You *are?* How grand!"

She seemed tame enough. I let her go.

"The Aerial Steam Navigation Company is being capitalized quickly," Marriott said. "I expect Bill Ralston—Bank of California, you know—to become a primary backer. You've seen the *Avitor*, haven't you?

"Not yet," I said, turning to the door. "By the way, Twain sends his greetings."

"Is he behind this? Was this Clemens's prank?"

"No prank here," I said, glancing at Holt. "This was entirely serious."

In the corridor outside she gave me a long look. "How'd you happen in there? You follow me?"

"Just coincidence, but you should be thankful. If not for me you might be headed for jail."

"Speaking of thanks," she said tartly.

"Yes, thanks for getting your note to me. I hope it didn't cause you problems with Morrissey."

"None I couldn't settle."

"I'll bet."

She squeezed my arm and pressed her breast against me. I glanced down and caught her smile. She knew exactly what she was doing.

"Let's find this bloody flying machine," she said.

The Mechanics' Institute Pavilion covered ninety thousand square feet and was topped by a dome illuminated at night by thirteen hundred gas jets. A sign at the entrance told us that the Seventh Mechanics Fair was in its tenth day. People stared at Elise as we entered.

We passed a number of displays until we came to a long hall containing a roped-off oval track. At the far end the *Avitor* was in flight. Two men dogtrotted along the track below, holding guy ropes fixed to it.

I scrutinized it as it passed overhead. Basically it was a forty-foot cigar-shaped balloon encased in a cagework of cane. On either side a five-foot wing extended, and whirring on each wing was a two-bladed propellor driven by a small steam furnace heated by an alcohol lamp. Toward the rear was a steering rudder with four planes, like the feathered end of a dart, to direct the craft up or down or to either side. The rudder was tied in place now to keep the *Avitor* in an orbit corresponding to the track.

Well, it *was* flying, I had to admit. I wasn't sure how I felt about it. Impressed. Disappointed. The craft was by necessity so light that I couldn't figure how it would handle any wind whatever.

"How fast is it going?" I asked an observer.

"Six miles an hour."

"That its top speed?"

"The valves are entirely open, yes."

When the *Avitor* set down a few minutes later another drawback became evident: it held enough fuel to stay aloft only about fifteen minutes. To lift larger boilers and fuel tanks—not to mention passengers—would require an enormous balloon. And there just couldn't be enough thrust generated to keep it from being at the mercy of winds. *A for effort*, I thought. *Materials and technology aren't here yet.*

"Gonna invest?" I asked the man.

[373]

He shook his head. "In my view the pneumatic tube will supplant railcars as high-velocity transport."

"Really?" I remembered reading somewhere about a twentieth-century Japanese "bullet train" which shot cars through enclosed tubes at hundreds of miles per hour. Amazing that it was already conceptualized.

"Cheaper and more realizable than aerial carriages," he said firmly. "Wait and see."

We headed back to the pavilion entrance. Elise drew stares and whisperings. Mostly her skirts, I supposed, although to me they weren't particularly racy—they reached the bottoms of her calves. And of course there was her makeup—a "painted woman," no question. Quite a package.

"What are you thinking about?" she asked suddenly.

"You," I admitted, which caused her to laugh and press against me.

Outside, she pecked my cheek. "I'm off to prepare for my show. Come see it . . . wait!" She gave me an accusing glare. "I read that the ballists are attending Maguire's Opera House tonight."

"So?"

"Oh, Sam, they'd like my show ever so much more!" She clutched my arm. "Won't you come as my guests? Tomorrow night?"

"I'll see what I can do."

"Oh, yes, I'll put you in the dress circle—you must wear your lovely uniforms!—and I'll advertise in the papers too!" Oblivious to passers-by, she leaned close to kiss me again, flicking my ear with her tongue. "Then I might see you afterward."

I'd been thinking along those lines myself, but having trouble with it. Each time I imagined myself with Elise, an image of Cait filled my mind.

"I'm taken, sort of."

"Oh, well," she said brightly, "then we'll be chums."

She could at least have sounded disappointed, I thought sourly. "Listen, there's someone on the team I'd like you to make a little fuss over, all right? He thinks you're the greatest thing since popsicles."

"Since *what?*"

"His name's Andy Leonard."

"Wasn't he beside you on the field at Troy?"

"Good grief, you know the name of every man who stares at you?"

"When one looks at me like *that,* yes! He's a darling pup, isn't he?"

Her tone triggered a faint alarm in me. "You go easy on him."

She laughed and turned away, boots thumping on the planks, bustle swaying. When she vanished around the corner I felt a certain relief. But also that things abruptly had grown duller.

Gold was up to 164 dollars. That settled it. I forced my way up to the counter and showed my letter of credit.

"You have three thousand four hundred and forty-four dollars, sir," said the clerk. "How much are you putting into gold?"

"All of it."

"Very well." He filled out forms.

"Wait," I told him. "Keep forty dollars out."

"Certainly."

I instructed that a gold double eagle be placed in each of two new Wells Fargo accounts. In the names of Susanne and Hope Fowler. Maybe they would somehow, someday get them—plus interest compounded over 120 years.

I tucked the receipt for twenty-one more ounces of gold into my wallet. I was in up to the hilt now. So was Twain. I'd sell well before the price hit two hundred dollars, I told myself. And pocket my fortune.

As I walked I couldn't stop trying to remember where buildings would be in the future. It was dislocating to know that directly opposite Marriott's office, on the site of the four-story Montgomery Block, the Transamerica pyramid would rise. At California and Dupont I finally found an old acquaintance—Saint Mary's Cathedral, its bricks fresh and red, its stained-glass windows fewer and smaller than I remembered, its resonant bell booming over the neighborhood. I gazed at it for a long time, feeling absolutely lost. I felt an urge to seal myself between the bricks, a human time capsule.

"Sam! Where the devil you been!"

Andy was striding toward me. Behind him came the Stockings in their uniforms, looking for all the world like tourists. My mood brightened as I hugged Andy.

"Figured this time you got plugged for good," Brainard said dryly.

"He wanted to wager with us on it," Andy said.

They had just finished touring Chinatown. Allison and Gould did bad Chinese imitations for me. Harry asked if I wanted to suit up and play in my hometown, in front of my friends.

"They've mostly moved away," I told him. "But I'll stand in if you need me."

"Can you show us the main sights?" said Waterman.

"The ones you'd probably like most," I said, "we can see in Elise Holt's show tomorrow night."

Andy's face lit up. His whoop sounded over the others' wolf whistles.

Harry had worked them diligently all the way out from Omaha, Andy told me as we walked to the hotel. At every water stop they'd limbered their arms beside depots and sidings. To their considerable surprise, several times Indians had shown some facility for the game and even a knowledge of the rules. One group had wanted to play a match.

"How'd they learn?" I said. "Soldiers?"

"That's what we figured, but an old Injun who knew some English said a man with whiskers taught 'em when he passed through in a wagon, a generation or so back. Harry finally guessed that it must've been Cartwright himself, the old Knickerbocker who invented the game and later settled in the Sandwich Islands."

"Sounds pretty farfetched," I said.

"How else'd them Injuns know the New York rules from fifteen years ago?" Andy demanded.

"You got me there."

The Cosmopolitan stood at Bush and Sansome. It was five years old, with four floors and an elegant saloon. It was expensive, but Hatton was picking up the tab. Andy roomed with Sweasy, so I had to share quarters with Millar. I found him bent over a writing table in our room.

"I had to file several pieces for you," he said sourly. "I doubt the *Enquirer* is pleased, since naturally I didn't put in all the quality that went into my own."

"Naturally," I said. "Thanks. I'll have to get back on it right away."

"You most certainly will."

I lay down to rest a moment. I didn't realize I'd fallen asleep until the door opened with a bang and Millar came in bearing a stack of the latest editions.

"Big fuss up on Montgomery," he said.

"What, a fire?"

He shook his head. "Folks are running around like an earthquake hit. I guess that's how it feels to the banks and brokerage houses."

"I know," I said smugly. "It'll go on for a while, too."

"Yes," he said, "it certainly will."

"What's the price up to now?"

"We *are* talking about the gold market?"

"Of course, what's the price?"

"That's the thing," he said. "Nobody quite knows."

I sat up. "Why not?"

"The bottom just fell out."

28

They called it Black Friday. Two unscrupulous New York speculators, Jay Gould and Jim Fisk, had cornered the private market, possessing orders to buy every ounce of gold in circulation. As prices soared, their profits—and mine—would have been almost limitless had not Grant, reacting to charges of complicity, ordered the Treasury to sell five million in gold. As Gould and a few others sold short, dumping millions of shares, prices plummeted twenty-five dollars in less than fifteen minutes. Brokerage houses went under. Fortunes vanished. By the evening of that beautiful, golden day, I had lost thousands.

I walked numbly up and down Montgomery with hundreds of others trying to understand what had happened. Rumors abounded: Gould had raked in ten million; Fisk had been murdered by a ruined speculator; Grant had impoverished members of his own family. Nothing was certain—except that New York's swamped Gold Room had announced it would be closed on Monday. It would take days to sort it all out. I just prayed that enough would be left to salvage Twain's share.

Probably as a consequence of realizing I'd soon have to work for a living, I rose early on Saturday and knocked out some *Enquirer* pieces, mostly scenic highlights of the trip and chatty stuff about "our boys" in the Golden City. I mailed it early at the main post office at Washington and Battery, along with a long letter to Cait and Timmy.

At the Blue Anchor I rousted Johnny from bed. He'd been up nearly till dawn and looked it.

"Found a job," he said. "I'll be able to buy a new wheel in no time. There's racin' here."

"Where you working?"

"Pretty-waiter-girl place called the Bull Run."

"Maybe I'll come down with Andy and some of the others," I said, wondering what he did there.

"Champion'd have a cat fit," he said uneasily. "It's no church."

"In that case I'll come alone."

He frowned. "I wouldn't, Sam."

"Look, Johnny, if you had to take a job that bad, let me loan—" I stopped. I couldn't loan him anything.

"You've done enough," he said. "Time to stand on my own."

We talked a while longer. I told him I'd drop by in future days. Johnny said he'd get out to some of the games if he weren't too tired from working.

The Recreation Grounds' carriage gate on Twenty-sixth was hopelessly clogged. As we climbed down and walked to the main entrance on Folsom, we could see why. Wagons and carts lined against the fences offered vantage points for hundreds who refused to move. Adding to the growing area of gridlock were the aggressive yellow cars of the Omnibus Railway Company; they arrived every five minutes from the downtown Metropolitan Hotel, disgorging passengers who'd paid their gold dollar for the shuttle and admission package entitling them to be packed into the bull pens.

Police made a path for us. Hatton turned and grinned happily at Champion. If this turnout signaled what would follow in the week, it looked as if he would meet the high costs of bringing us here. Thousands were jammed into the ladies' pavilion alone, where seats cost two dollars in gold, two seventy-five in paper.

I sat at the press table. Again Harry had offered me the chance to play, but to do so would have been weirdly superfluous. I'd proven myself here already, playing before my grandparents and friends at Mission High, not more than ten blocks away.

The Eagles took the field in white flannel shirts and blue pants. They were the city's oldest club and victors in a recent championship series. I shared the Stockings' curiosity as to how good they could be, isolated as they were from the rest of the baseball scene.

Hearing that I was from San Francisco, one of the Eagles gave me some embarrassing moments by asking where I'd lived and did I know this person and that. After some fumbling, I said I'd actually grown up in Santa Rosa, fifty miles north, but said I was from this city because it was widely known. That was greeted with silent skepticism. I'd obviously been born before the gold rush, when few whites lived anywhere in California. Andy saved the situation with a good-natured taunt that no matter where I grew up, I knew my way around a diamond—which meant I must have learned to play at an *eastern* college; it provoked a good deal of intersectional needling.

Millar, beside me at the press table, said, "Do gamblers here truly shoot off guns to distract fielders?"

The Stockings had been told that it used to happen.

"Distract?" I replied. "Hell, usually they just shoot the fielders."

He seemed to realize I was kidding. With Millar you could never be sure.

George, Waterman, Andy, and Sweasy emerged from the clubhouse and went into their sleight-of-hand routine, getting the usual oohs and ahhs. I noticed that men and women in the stands wore bulkier clothing than in Cincinnati, and many carried heavy coats. The reason became evident soon after the game started. A wind rose abruptly, stinging us with sand particles. Papers blew in swirling gusts, and I was suddenly chilled. Shades of Candlestick!

Brainard was wild, but it didn't matter. The first Eagle went down on three swinging strikes. The second tomahawked a single on a pitch over his head. The next two fouled out.

When the Eagles took the field we saw how far behind the times, baseballwise, they were. Their hurler, working in what Harry called the "old style," stood flat-footed instead of striding forward with his release. George, leading off, was so surprised that he popped the first pitch straight back to the catcher, who dropped it. George whacked the next pitch on a line to the center fielder, who muffed the catch. Because the Eagles had no backup system—one defender moved while eight watched—George sprinted clear around the bases. It was a sign of things to come. At the end of the first inning we led 12–0. The contest ended 35–4. For us, a solid afternoon's work. For the Eagles and the watching thousands, a humbling revelation.

Money changed hands, but losers didn't seem chagrined. I heard several predict that local clubs would fare better now that they'd seen our style of play. Good luck, I thought, knowing that we hadn't played with much intensity after the first inning. Moreover, we weren't used to the Recreation Grounds' stiff winds. And we'd scarcely dipped into Harry's tactical bag. Playing their best, the Eagles would not improve much, if any, on their margin of defeat. I considered putting money down on us in Monday's rematch to recoup my losses—and had an immediate, near-sickening reaction. For a moment I actually thought I was going to throw up. My body was telling me, I supposed, that in the wake of the gold collapse it simply couldn't take any more gambling.

That night at the Alhambra Theater I felt something else, considerably more unpleasant. As the curtain rose I was suddenly sweaty and faint, my fingers shaking. The calcium stage lights seemed to pulsate, a strobe effect in my brain. I shut my eyes tightly. What the hell was going on? After long moments the sensations subsided. I thought the milkiness had been about to come on during the worst of it. I didn't like that one bit.

Around me, the Eagles and Stockings were resplendent in their colors. This era's ball clubs regularly wore their uniforms on public occasions. Here it helped Hatton boost game attendance. And it wouldn't hurt Elise either. With much pomp we had been seated in a dress-circle section set off by red bunting.

Elise's extravaganza was called *Military Billy Taylor, or Life in the Cariboos*. She played the title role of a Scotchman wooing the same woman as one General Jenks. Her antics got her into varying degrees of undress. The production numbers were filled with blondes in tights—particularly one called the "humbrageous humbrella tree," a gilded prop that spread itself each time the temperature reached 180 degrees, a phenomenon produced by Elise's dancing.

As she took her final bows she was presented a bouquet of roses. She glanced at the card, then waved grandly at us in the dress circle.

"I think she wants to meet you," I said to Andy.

He stared at me. "Oh, no, Sam, you didn't. . . ."

I took him backstage, where it didn't take Elise long to figure out that the flowers, from "A. J. Leonard, Cincinnati," were my doing. Since Andy was hopelessly tongue-tied, she did the talking, even to the point of asking about baseball. I could feel her assessing him, finding him attractive. He was lithe and muscular in his uniform, much more her size than I. His nervousness did not obscure his athlete's physicality.

"Would you buy a lady a glass of champagne?"

She wasn't looking at me.

"Why . . . uh . . . surely," said Andy.

"Guess I'll be leaving," I said. Her blue eyes flicked at me in amusement. Andy, I suspected, was in for a hell of a time. With tomorrow Sunday, and no game to be played, Champion was unlikely to run a bed check. Some guys got every break.

As I passed the Mercantile Library on my way back to the Cosmopolitan, my vision suddenly did its half-light trick again, and my pulse seemed to flutter. Something caused me to glance up at a passing carriage. I saw a moon countenance framed in its window, a dumpling face fringed with long girlish ringlets. I couldn't tell if the eyes were pale, but I would have sworn I was looking at Clara Antonia. The carriage turned up Montgomery and disappeared. The whole sequence took no longer than a few seconds, but I couldn't put it out of my mind.

Hatton arrived with coaches at noon. It was eighty-five degrees downtown. The Stockings grumbled that in any single day here they'd see every gradation of Cincinnati's weather from April to November.

"Where's Andy?" I asked Sweasy.

"Not feelin' tip-top." He flashed me a look. "Said he'd rest up today."

We moved away from the others.

"He didn't come in last night," Sweasy said worriedly. "Just sent a note saying to cover up for him. You think he got shanghaied?"

"Not in the usual sense," I said.

The Cliff House was a long, low, pyramid-roofed building bearing a huge American flag and standing exactly on the site of the larger establishment I'd known. Hundreds of rigs and teams were hitched at the racks in front. On a deck built on the ocean side Sunday couples sipped sherry and peered through binoculars. We walked to the edge of the bluff and watched combers surge against the shore. Below on the guano-encrusted crags of Seal Rocks, a family of sea lions, glistening like gray slugs, loosed occasional coughing barks.

"We've stood on both coasts," Harry said. "By the time we're home we'll have gone ten thousand miles."

Captain Junius Foster, owner of the Cliff House, greeted us warmly. We sat down to a meal of breast of guinea, terrapin, and hangtown fries. I eyed the elegantly dressed clientele drinking cocktails. The Cliff House was doing great business for a place so far outside the city, no bus or horsecar lines remotely near.

"The social set all patronize it," Hatton told me. "And young blades who like to race their flyers along the road." He nudged me. "Not to mention a certain fast breed of women who take pleasure in champagne lunching."

No sooner had he said it than heads began to turn. A lavish hansom, its brass and lacquered surfaces gleaming in the sunlight, pulled in beside ours. A uniformed groom hitched the horses. We watched in astonishment as Andy emerged. He offered his hand, and Elise Holt took it and stepped gracefully down. Arms linked, they walked toward us.

"Oh my," breathed Brainard, next to me. "Oh my!"

A low hum came from the others, then somebody clapped. Then we were all on our feet, applauding and cheering. Elise smiled winningly. Andy's face was strawberry red.

"Thank you," Elise purred. "I wanted to thank all you gentlemen for your patronage last night. And for your kindness in allowing Mr. Leonard to escort me here."

"Mr. Leonard," Brainard echoed in wonderment.

Elise marched up to Champion. "I wish you to know, sir, that Mr. Leonard speaks with utmost praise of your presidency of the Cincinnati club."

"I . . . thank you," Champion managed, twisting his napkin.

She complimented Harry in similar terms. He bowed in response. Beneath the straight face and courtly manners, I suspected that Harry was amused. Then Elise moved along the line of players, flirting with George, admiring Gould's and Mac's muscles, asking Brainard how he hurled the ball so fast.

"Thank you especially, Sam," she said when she reached me, and winked, prompting another mutter from Brainard.

Taking Andy's arm, she allowed herself to be escorted to the carriage.

"Jesus Q. Christ," said Brainard.

"Looks like the boy's gone and gotten himself involved," I said.

"Seems like she knows you pretty good, too," he said suspiciously. "You're some at stirring things up."

"From you, that's high praise."

Harry stood up as Andy returned. "My boy . . ." he began.

"I fancy her," Andy said. "And that's all I'm saying."

Harry regarded him intently. Brainard and I exchanged sidelong glances. At length Harry said, "Welcome to dinner, lad."

At that point Gould stepped close to Millar, pushed his chin up with one thick, gnarled finger, and said, "If this shows up in the papers, I'll break your bones."

"Me too," said Sweasy.

"Me too," said Waterman.

Millar reached up and carefully moved Gould's finger aside. "I saw nothing of note here," he said.

Even Champion smiled.

We spent the balmy hours climbing rocks and walking the beaches. Being on the western edge of the continent was exciting for the others. For me it was bittersweet, laden with memories that seemed as evanescent as the ocean spray rising in the afternoon sun. I watched two little girls playing with a puppy in the distance, dancing in and out of the waves. If only my girls were with me. I'd take them back to Cincinnati to make a life with Cait, or bring her and Timmy here. I wished that I could find a pathway from one family to another, one time to another.

Andy stayed close to me, talking excitedly of Elise. He would see her in the off-season, save money so he could travel to wherever she was playing. She was grand, wasn't she? Did I think she cared for him the same way he cared for her? Wasn't love the most awful and beautiful condition, all at once?

Finally he broke off and looked at me. "Sam, what's wrong? You got the blue devils?"

My fingers were shaking again. "Sort of."

"Seems like you're workin' awful hard at something," he said. "Is it something you can fix?"

I watched a squadron of pelicans skim the crests of rolling waves. "I'm not sure."

In the distance a snowy sail bobbed up regularly and was eclipsed by the combers; it moved toward the Golden Gate, gradually rounding the headland. Something seemed to speak to me from the ocean, some note in the rhythmic surf, a muted song in the wind that blew with increasing strength and chill in the waning afternoon. If it held any particular message, I didn't know what it might be.

29

T here was a good deal of betting in the Cosmopolitan lobby next morning. I finally went for a walk to get away from it. But there was no escape. Everywhere, I saw reminders of institutionalized greed. On Montgomery and California, following the Gold Room's lead, the brokerage houses were closed. The papers reported the suicide of an eastern banker. Here in the Golden City, even ferries carried such names as *Gold* and *Capital*. When banker William Ralston had opened his California Theater earlier this year, the first play had been titled, appropriately, *Money*.

The Gilded Age indeed, with everybody on the make.

Temperatures were in the eighties at the Recreation Grounds. A fair-sized crowd, smaller than the first, showed up. One interesting feature—a ten-minute intermission—came at the end of the sixth inning. Millar sniffingly said it was a dodge to sell more liquor and concessions. A ballpark bar was conspicuously open during games here.

The Eagles played less nervously than before, but it didn't matter. At the plate we were deadly, pounding out fifty-five hits and six homers and rounding the bases with dulling regularity. Brainard allowed only a handful of Eagle base runners. In the ninth we relented a bit—Allison went so far as to bat lefty—and they got a few gift runs.

The final was 58–4.

I should have bet.

In following days my periods of shakiness grew in intensity. At times it was a struggle to stay tuned in to anything around me. I had trouble composing my dispatches. I knew I appeared distracted, but I couldn't seem to do much about it.

On Tuesday the additions of Champion and Oak Taylor transformed the Stockings into a cricket eleven. Behind the bowling of Harry and George, they shocked a group of California all-star cricketers, decisively winning a seven-hour match. Champion moved surprisingly well for a man of his bulk. Harry had conducted a crash cricket seminar beforehand, and that, given the Stockings' fielding ability and George's formidable batting, proved to be enough.

The next day, winds near gale force whipped clouds of sand across the diamond, nearly blinding hitters and fielders alike. Opposing us were the Pacifics, who had narrowly lost the city championship to the Eagles. Diehard bettors expected them to outperform their rivals against us.

At the outset it looked like they might. In the first, a Pacific hitter spanked a ball off Gould's frigid hands and broke for second on the next pitch. Allison had him easily, but the ball soared on a howling gust over Sweasy into center. The runner scored when Brainard uncorked a gloriously wild pitch into the wind. The crowd hooted. The Stockings looked resigned. Throughout the long afternoon they staggered beneath windblown flies like a band of drunks—but managed to catch most.

The Pacifics got only two safe hits the entire game. Meanwhile, we went to work with a vengeance. Gould slammed two homers, George, Harry, and Andy had one apiece—Andy's a wind-aided grand slam— and the contest ended after six innings with darkness approaching and the score 66–4. I felt sorry for the Pacifics.

I talked afterward with the Shepard brothers, Pacific infielders who had played with Harry on old Knickerbocker clubs. Dedicated athletes, they were training for a ten-mile footrace at the Recreation Grounds the coming Sunday. Velocipede events were also scheduled. I decided I'd get Johnny to come out and watch them with me.

"The Base-Ball season has fairly commenced," reported the *Morning Call*, "and with an energy unknown before." Each day new clubs were formed: the Green Stockings, Silver Stockings, Gray Socks—a profusion of colors blossoming throughout the city. Others called themselves the Arctics, Young Bay Citys, Vigilants, and Young Pacifics, and were made up of clerks—often games started at six A.M., before work—businessmen, judges, bankers, draymen, and firemen; there was even a Fat Men squad whose players each topped 250 pounds.

Papers bristled with suggestions for improving hometown performance against us. Most involved imitating our play, but a few remained hostile. The *Golden Era* pointed out with some acerbity that, "The

Red Stockings are professionals who do nothing else and are paid for doing that."

Savvy entrepreneurs worked us into their newspaper puffs. One dry-goods establishment announced the sale of "Red Stockings and all kinds of underwear, shirts, ties, etc." The Cliff House crowed, "Those lionized Red Stockings went out to see Captain Foster's educated sea lions!"

Meanwhile, invitations to play poured in from clubs in Portland, Carson City, Cheyenne, Laramie, Denver, Virginia City, and Omaha; we were offered a gold medal to play at the State Fair in Stockton. Had it been up to Champion, we probably would have accepted all of them.

But the players were tired of being away from home, especially tired of San Francisco.

"We went through everything in three days," Gould complained. "Nothin's here but sand hills and Mongolians."

"Chinee're taking over everything," Sweasy said.

"Cincinnati is smoke-clogged, but I'd choose it over this damn cold wind," Waterman said. "No offense, Sam."

"None taken," I said, suspecting that he and Brainard found late-night outlets for their frustrations. The others, though tempted, were probably deterred by the risk. Except for Andy, who seemed to have tacit dispensation from Harry to float on love clouds to Elise's show each night.

The last day of September, a Thursday, dawned brilliantly clear. I had slept well and felt no signs of shakiness. Setting out from the hotel for the Blue Anchor, I saw that trees were beginning to lose their leaves. The air held a briskness I hadn't noticed before. It put me in mind of neighborhood football games I'd played as a kid. And watching the World Series on TV with Grandpa—who'd let me cut school when a game was *really* important. I didn't relish spending this vibrant day at the Recreation Grounds, watching the poor Pacifics get steam-rollered again.

Not finding Johnny in his room, I stopped at the California Coffee Saloon for the twenty-five-cent three-egg breakfast special and set off through North Beach, past Meigg's Wharf. The streets were a perfect grid, not yet slashed diagonally by Columbus. At Larkin, boundary of the Western Addition, I looked at the unbroken sand dunes stretching beyond.

Missing Cait badly, I opened my watch and gazed at the piece of yellow fabric for a long time. What was working on me so strongly in this city? I wondered. Something powerful enough to pull me from her? Again I sensed that whatever lay in store for me—maybe even the answer to why I'd come back in time—was waiting here, close by.

What I had to do was find it.

Fisherman's Wharf wasn't where I had known it, between Mason and Hyde, but instead stretched along piers at the foot of Union, Green, and Vallejo. There I saw Italian immigrants working on what looked like a large float. I stopped and asked them about it. Big celebration in two weeks, they said. The city's first Discovery Day.

"Discovery of gold?"

That brought a laugh. "Da whole country!" a woman said, "Cristoforo Colombo!"

The first Columbus Day! Well, all right.

"You come sing an' dance wit' us?"

"I'll be there," I promised.

As the words left my mouth I realized I'd made my decision: unless whatever was coming happened first, I wouldn't be going back with the team.

The clock in the Bank Exchange Saloon read one o'clock. Soon the Stockings would be heading for the ball field. I ordered a stein of beer and picked up a paper. To my amazement the feature story dealt with my alma mater, the University of California. It had begun its first classes. Ever!

I snacked on the Bank Exchange's cheeses and sourdough bread while I scanned the other columns. A gang of toughs had tied the braids of two Chinese together and beaten them savagely near Portsmouth Square; butter was scarce and dear at seventy-five cents a pound—why couldn't the Pacific Slope, prime cattle territory, produce enough of the stuff? And why weren't the gas company's lamplighters doing their jobs? With days growing short, lights weren't on in many streets until well after dark. Each item carried the same aggrieved tone.

I got up and went out from the thick walls and iron shutters of the Montgomery Block. My mind was made up: as a kid I'd cut school to go to games; today I'd cut the game to go to school. I walked to the ferry station at Pacific and Davis, where I took an open-air seat on the top deck. Crossing the bay, the boat's churning wheel and hissing boilers made an incessant racket. As the oak-studded east bay slopes gradually neared, I could see occasional stands of redwoods on the hilltops. I looked in vain for Berkeley. Where the town and university should be were only scattered fields and foothills laced with green creek lines.

"What's that near the shore?" I asked another passenger, pointing to a cluster of wooden buildings about where San Pablo Avenue should be.

"Ocean View," he answered.

Ocean View? I saw a wharf, several sawmills, and—perhaps the biggest surprise I'd found on the West Coast—a gorgeous mile-long crescent of white sand framed by marshes and two slow-flowing creeks. A beach in Berkeley. Lovely, lovely.

The university was in Oakland, a tranquil town of ten thousand. Broad dirt streets were lined with oaks and whitewashed fences and houses. I took a streetcar up Seventh from the ferry slip. At Broadway workmen were finishing the Central Pacific's impressive new depot; soon the overland journey would end here, not in Sacramento.

Near Lake Merritt—actually not a lake but an estuary named for the current mayor—stood a new girls' school run by the Convent of the Sacred Heart. Beyond it, projecting from a grove of oaks to the northeast, rose the cupola of a university building.

I walked slowly, trying to fit my mind to the lazy afternoon. I was starting to feel disoriented again, as if the milkiness were about to come on.

The campus covered the blocks between Twelfth and Fourteenth, Harrison and Franklin. Over the largest of the white frame buildings hung a Bear flag; a sign on the portico identified it as the College of California and offered the information that university courses were now added. In the hallway I found a class schedule and faculty roster. Physics Professor John LeConte—I recognized his surname from a Berkeley street—was acting president.

The building was empty. Classes took place between ten and two. It was now almost three. I was on my way out when an apple-cheeked boy appeared carrying books in a leather strap. I stopped him.

He introduced himself as George Beaver—"Eager," of course, to his classmates—and was a proud member of the freshman or "first" class, one of eight boys who had passed the grueling entrance exams. I asked what they involved.

"Oh, the customary," he said airily—a young Millar in the making, I thought. "Higher arithmetic, including metrics, square and cube roots, algebra as far as quadratic equations, the first four books of *Loomis's Geometry*. English grammer, U.S. history, and geography."

"Is that all?" I said wryly, impressed.

"Those're to enter the *regular* colleges," he said disdainfully, explaining that to get into *the* elite Harvard-style curriculum, one had to pass additional tests.

"Such as?"

"Latin Grammar: four books of Caesar, six of Virgil's *Aeneid,* six of Cicero's orations. Greek grammar: Exenophon's *Anabasis,* three books."

He rattled them off like items on a shopping list and added that so far they'd spent class time debating such subjects as who was the greater general, Caesar or Napoleon. "Of course, in the common university technical colleges," he finished, "standards are less exacting."

"Of course," I said, thinking that he seemed more like Stanford material. "How much is tuition?"

"Sixty dollars, plus admission fees—they said our yearly costs could reach five hundred."

Clearly not for the masses. He said that no dorms existed yet; students roomed with Oakland families. Freshmen had to be at least sixteen—his own age—and provide testimonials of sound moral character.

"Any women enrolled?"

He looked at me as if I were from another planet.

"Tell you what, Eager," I said. "Here's what I think. You've got to get some coeds in here, move the campus to Berkeley where it belongs, and start calling yourselves the Golden Bears."

"Golden Bears? Whatever for?"

"For when beanies and bonfire rallies come in."

He gave me the outer-space look again.

I got back to the city—already San Francisco was called that— around five and decided to catch the end of the game. Waiting for a horsecar at the ferry station, I glanced at a bulletin board. In stunned surprise I saw a flyer headed: CAPTAIN F. J. O'DONOVAN. It advertised the speech I'd heard him make in Cincinnati. It was sponsored by the local Wolfe Tone Fenian Circle and was to be held the next night.

McDermott and Le Caron had failed.

So he had come himself.

I arrived in time to see Sweasy field a bouncer and flip to Gould for the final out to nail down a 54–5 victory. While the teams cheered each other I looked over Millar's shoulder at the score book. "Is this right?" I said. "Eleven homers for us?"

"George alone had four." Millar gave me his owlish look. "Enjoy your day?"

"Mostly." I was trying to fight off thoughts of O'Donovan. "How about filling me in on the highlights?"

"Why me?"

"Hell, you know players can't be trusted to give us hard-working press guys the straight stuff."

"You know, Fowler, the *Enquirer* didn't have the slightest inkling of what they were getting in you."

"Aw, you're just saying that."

"No, I'm not."

The next morning, Friday, October 1, New York's Gold Room finally reopened. I cashed my certificates at Wells Fargo, barely able to cover Twain's thousand. I sent him a draft with a note saying I didn't think the *Avitor* was a good investment.

That afternoon we met the Atlantics, the third San Francisco club to test us. Only four hundred turned out—the result of cold driving winds and lack of excitement over the Atlantics' chances. Among them was Elise Holt, who caused a stir in her lacquered carriage.

She left after Andy's first time up. Which was just as well, for the game was truly awful. The Atlantics muffed everything. Their hurler issued eleven walks despite our desire to swing at anything in reach. With darkness falling and the contest only in its fourth inning, we went to ridiculous lengths. Allison batted with one hand and George leaped to swipe at pitches over his head. At last the requisite five innings were completed. The score was 76–5. Our record was a neat 50–0.

Next day we faced the California Nine, made up of the best players from local clubs. This was the contest many had awaited, and over three thousand turned out. Betting was heavy on whether we'd win by as much as a two-to-one margin.

The Stockings were ravenous for some genuine competition. All but Andy, that is, who was red-eyed and irritable. He told me that Elise's show would leave town that night.

"You know," I said tentatively, "there are lots of—"

"Don't start, Sam. I fancy her." He eyed me defiantly. "She fancies me, too."

"I'm sure she does, Andy."

He trudged off. I felt bad for him, guessing that he'd never before mixed love with sex. I wondered what Elise actually felt for him.

The all-stars came on as though they meant business, warming up with dispatch, winning the coin toss, sending us to bat, and sprinting to their positions. Unfortunately for them, George's lead-off double was the first of a string of solid hits, and the California Nine trailed 10–0 before even coming to bat—a deficit they could not overcome, although they played well. The final was 46–14. George slammed three homers and Andy, clubbing the ball angrily, added two more. Despite the offensive barrage, the contest moved quickly. For once we were out of the ballpark before sundown.

I carried the derringer. I scanned faces at the ballpark and around the Cosmopolitan. I didn't anticipate an attack as open as Le Caron's and McDermott's, assuming that O'Donovan wanted the money more than he wanted me. But I couldn't be sure. He had definitely arrived—the papers carried accounts of his speeches—and he could find me easily. What was he waiting for?

I busied myself working up a piece that compared George's individual stats for the six San Francisco games against *all* opposing players'. George came out ahead in every offensive category: 48 hits to their 45 (his in only 62 at bats, for a gaudy .774 average); 45 runs to 36; 106 total bases to 55; 13 homers to 0. His slugging percentage for the series was an incredible 1.710. Several Stockings, including Andy with six homers himself, were not far behind. I concluded that the message was as clear here as it had been around the country all summer: to contend with pros, teams would have to find outstanding players, skilled managers—*and* money enough to hold them.

Millar read it and scowled. He said it rubbed our courteous hosts' noses in their defeats. And what on earth was a slugging percentage?

Johnny's face was a mess. He'd been worked over, he mumbled, several nights earlier by a sailor.

"You gotta get out of that dive," I said.

"Pay's too good."

"What do you do for it?"

"Clean up, different things."

I parted the curtains. Sunlight poured in. Sunday morning. I'd come to see if he wanted to catch the velocipede races that afternoon. But he'd made it clear he didn't intend to get out of bed.

"You'll get yourself killed in the Barbary Coast."

He shrugged fatalistically.

"I'm coming down there tonight."

"You won't fancy it, Sam."

No smoking. No spitting. No standing. Strict limit of sixteen passengers. Well worth a dime—double the usual fare—to travel like that. The streetcar was normally reserved for ladies, gents riding only as escorts. And it existed strictly to carry patrons to Samuel Woodward's amusement park. Twentieth-century Americans take for granted padded seats, dirt- and spit-free surroundings—not to mention body soaps and deodorants. Back here I'd learned that anything reserved for women meant superior conditions. Even in horsecars.

Woodward's Gardens was a Victorian Disneyland; more aptly, a Xanadu. Picnickers thronged the sunlit lawns, flowered terraces, palm-shaded nooks. Children rode ponies and camels, were pulled in carriages by goats, petted tiger cubs, and threw peanuts to caged bears. The Second Artillery Band played on a platform decorated with streamers and baskets of roses.

In a different mood I would have enjoyed the picture-book world. Andy and I walked in silence past stuffed reindeer and grizzlies and watched giggling children leap to touch the end of the Chinese Giant's braided cue. With the other Stockings we sat in a pavilion and watched Major Burke's rifle drill, Japanese acrobats, and Jaguarine the Swordswoman.

"Let's get out," Andy said as Herman the Great was about to explode from a cannon.

At the edge of the lake, where men readied a balloon ascension, we watched a couple drift by in a boat. The boy plucked water lilies from the surface. He handed them to the girl, who smiled. I remembered first kissing Cait in such a boat. God, I wanted to be with her. Andy sighed. I knew Elise was on his mind. What a couple of lovesick wimps, I thought.

"Hey," I said abruptly, "I've made up my mind to stay out here a little while."

He looked at me. "Why?"

"Some business to settle."

"Does Cait know?"

"Not yet."

He stopped walking and faced me. "Are you coming back to Cincinnati, Sam?"

"Yes, of course."

"Season ends in only six weeks. I'll be heading for Newark. You'll be back before?"

"I imagine so," I said. "I'm sending Cait a telegram tonight."

"What is it you need to take care of here?"

"I'm not sure. I mean, it's still developing."

"There's a hell of a lot you're not sayin', Sam."

"If I understood it and could tell anybody, it'd be you and Cait."

He looked worried. "Are you wanted for not being on the straight?"

I was about to make a wisecrack, but he was in no mood. "No, nothing like that. I just need to sort out a few things, tie up some loose ends."

"Is it connected ʼ your life out here . . . *before?*"

For a second I was stunned, thinking he meant my twentieth-century life. Then I realized he meant my amnesia.

"I'm not sure, but I think O'Donovan's involved."

He pondered that. "Over Cait?"

"Partly," I said. "Maybe mostly."

He waited for more, then sighed noisily. "O'Donovan's mean, Sam. More than mean . . ." He hunted for a word. "He's twisted inside. Cait's been wise not to fancy him."

I said nothing.

"Okay, I'll let it drop," he said; then, a few seconds later, "Sam, you know how you have a way of disappearing? Don't ever forget to pop up again, you hear?"

"I won't, Andy," I said, moved by his earnestness. "I promise."

Even then I wondered if it was a promise I could keep.

◇ 30 ◇

The Barbary Coast, a maze of dingy alleys, lay between Broadway, Stockton, Kearney, and Dupont. As the area went into full swing around eleven, I set out down Kearney past noisy Mexican fandango joints where guitars twanged and boots stomped. More than once hands brushed my pockets as I was jostled on the crowded sidewalks. I gripped the derringer, glad I'd tucked my money inside my belt.

Stenches rose from pools and rivulets of slime. Rats scurried across the dimly lit boards. I stepped over a dead cat—and into a heap of garbage. A drunk lurched suddenly from a doorway; I pushed him aside. Saloons lined the street: cellar "melodeons" where reed organs and pianos added their notes to a din of shrill singing and guttural shouts; dance halls and concert saloons where heavy feet thudded. Whores on the sidewalk blocked my path, calling me darling and offering delights: a teaspoon of opium for ten cents; exposure of their intimate selves for fifty cents; various off-street services for a range of prices. Good luck, I thought, to anybody venturing with them into those dark alleys.

I turned at an intersection cluttered with cheap-john stores and made my way up Pacific, which ran through the heart of the Coast. Things grew even seamier, with rows of groggeries and deadfalls— dives selling the cheapest rotgut alcohol. The denizens here could have crawled out of *A Rake's Progress*. I asked several grizzled sailors how to get to the Bull Run Saloon. One spat and said, "Don't go there, mate."

"Why not?"

He looked me over. "You like fights with eyeballs rolling on the deck?"

"Not my favorite," I said. "Where is it?"

"Got a quarter?"

I flipped him one.

"Portside on Dupont, then again to Sullivan Alley. Big three-story joint."

"Thanks."

"Your funeral, mate."

One sign on the door said ALLEN'S BULL RUN, another, HELL'S KITCHEN & DANCE HALL. Even from the outside it reeked of stale beer. Inside, the sawdust was drenched, the humanity unwashed, and there were unmasked odors of urine and vomit. Dance stages were crowded in the cellar and on the main floor. Women headed upstairs frequently with customers.

At the bar on the street floor a sign proclaimed, ANYTHING GOES HERE. I tried to get a beer and was informed by a burly bartender that I'd have to order from a waiter girl.

So I moved to a small table and was accosted by an ill-smelling woman in her fifties who, calling herself Lydia, smoothed my lapels and draped a fleshy arm around my neck.

"Champagne?" It came out like a rasp.

"How much?"

"Five dollars."

I shook my head.

"Don't be stingy, a smash gent like you," she said, pouting. "A bottle of claret, then?"

"No." The bartender was watching us. "Just a beer."

Her fingers stroked my thigh. "At least a whiskey, honey? Maybe a little game of cards?"

"Lydia, how about me just sitting here, okay?"

Something ugly flitted across her face; I didn't like the glance she exchanged with the bartender. It occurred to me suddenly that leaving Sullivan's Alley might be a good deal more problematic than entering.

"While I'm waiting to see my friend," I told her, "maybe I could make it worthwhile for you to sit with me."

"How worthwhile?"

"What do you make here?"

She gazed at me for a long moment. "Beer for two!" she shouted, then, "Fifteen a week plus a quarter every turn upstairs." Her mouth turned down. "Used to get a damn sight more when I had my looks."

"I'll slip you twenty right now—you personally, not the house—if you'll just sit here and be a . . . companion."

She whooped and jumped to her feet. Raising a booted foot to my chair, she pulled up her skirts and exposed a flabby leg. Men around us hooted. I saw something resembling a diaper wrapped around her upper thighs.

"I'll do whatever you want," she said huskily.

"Sit, then."

She sat down slowly. "You a cop?"

Again the bartender was watching. "No, I just want to get out of here in one piece."

"Gimme the money, don't let it show."

I surreptitiously extracted a gold coin from my belt. It disappeared into her clothing.

"You gotta be more interested." Lydia replaced her arm around my neck. Her breath stank. "Else they'll know I'm not doin' my job. It'd go hard on me. On you, too."

"How so?"

"A flush gent's got to spend. Else he takes a club to the noggin when he leaves." She rested her head on my shoulder. "You're lucky I'm squarer'n most or I'd keep your twenty and set you for rollin' anyhow."

The beers arrived, a dollar each.

"Sniff it," Lydia whispered.

I tipped it to my mouth, pretended to drink, caught a faint tobacco odor.

"They put snuff in beer, plug juice in whiskey, morphine sulphate in mixed drinks, an' that ain't the half. Here, you gotta be interested!" She cupped my hand over her right breast, and then, giggling and snorting and writhing, made a show of pushing it away as if I'd gotten fresh. I glanced down at her. The caked makeup didn't hide pockmarks on her face. "Sure you won't go upstairs with ol' Lydia?" she cooed.

I shook my head. Old Lydia smelled like a stable.

"They throw in Spanish fly, too," she said. "My beer's got it, and surely yours."

"Spanish fly?" I recalled high-school tales. "Are you joking?"

"Cantharides," she said. "Makes folks jumpier'n goats. Thank the stars it don't affect me like some. But there's enough times they carried me upstairs drunk, to be screwed by fifty or sixty, one after t'other— and me not paid for even the first half dozen!"

She looked indignant. I took a deep breath. Rough trade here.

"All part of their damn hog show," she went on. "Get us out of our senses so we'll carry on like animals. Make us drink all night, don't even let us go to the joe."

Which explained the diaper, I thought. We watched dancing couples topple to the floor. Part of the sport. Men ringing the dance floor groped the women, yanking their skirts high.

"Things're heatin' up," Lydia said offhandedly. "Here, empty your beer in that spittoon on the sly and I'll order more. Then you tell me about your friend."

I managed it without the bartender seeing and began to describe Johnny.

"A nigger with red hair? Works here? You mean *Johnny?*" Scowling, she pointed toward the rear of the room. "That one back there?"

I peered into the gloom. Sure enough, Johnny had emerged with a push broom and dustpan. "That's him," I said.

"You're here to see the nigger clean-up boy?" Lydia looked me up and down, her face hardening. "I reckon you're a cop after all."

At that moment, shockingly, a bottle exploded against the brick wall near Johnny. He bent matter-of-factly and swept shards of glass into the dustpan.

Christ, I thought. I pushed my chair back, ignoring Lydia's clutching fingers.

Johnny saw me coming. He didn't look happy. "Go away, Sam," he hissed. "You'll cost me this job!"

"You didn't want to be a clown," I said, "so you work *here?*"

He didn't answer. His eyes were fixed over my shoulder. "Oh no, they're settin' you up!"

I turned and looked. Lydia was talking urgently to the bartender. His eyes were on me. Suddenly his hand lifted, cracking hard against her face. With startling abruptness she toppled to the floor. The bartender motioned and several men began to move toward us.

"Is there a back way out?" I said.

Johnny pointed to a door in the corner. "Somebody'll be out there too."

It couldn't be worse than here, I figured. I turned, but the bartender already was blocking our way, knife in hand.

Johnny pushed past me. "Wait, he's my—"

He didn't get a chance to finish. The knife flashed upward. Johnny leaped sideways barely in time to avoid being impaled.

I ran forward, yanking out the derringer. I aimed it between the bartender's eyes. He froze and slowly, very slowly, stepped aside. I wrenched open the door. Johnny slid through. I followed him into an alley that smelled like a sewer. Two men holding truncheons barred our way. I kicked one in the balls, swung around and gave the other a close-up of the derringer's business end. His club thumped to the ground. We sprinted frantically for the corner. Shots ricocheted past us.

We were chased through murderous alleys called China and Dead Man. Finally I turned and squeezed off a shot. It reverberated nicely in the narrow passageway, kicking up a spout in a stagnant pool. Our pursuers took cover, giving us just enough time to lose them in the next series of dark streets.

At length we reached the waterfront and the Blue Anchor.

"Jesus," I said, trying to catch my breath. "I can't believe you'd work in that dump."

"I don't anymore," he said shortly. "You fixed that."

"Am I supposed to feel bad about it?"

He was silent.

"Johnny," I said. "Tomorrow I'm going to look for a place to rent here. How about sharing with me?"

"You're staying on?" He looked at me levelly, his face hard to read. "How long?"

I had no real answer.

"A while."

Monday, October 4, the Stockings' last full day in the city, was chilly and gusty. I spent the morning looking for a flat and found a beauty on Russian Hill, several doors from an oddly familiar octagonal house on Green Street. Our rooms occupied the upper floor of a small mansion, its picture window overlooking sparsely settled slopes. The squat Montgomery Block loomed in the foreground, Telegraph Hill behind it, and beyond that the bay. The furnishings were cutesy but comfortable. I paid a month's rent of forty-five dollars and sent a note to Johnny at the Blue Anchor to meet me the next morning at our new digs.

The exhibition game that afternoon was played in a howling sand-laden wind that made each fly a fielder's nightmare. Sweasy chased one pop-up all the way from second into the crowd behind the foul line. Nonetheless, three thousand were on hand for a final look at the Stockings. The "Wrights," padded with four Pacifics, defeated the "Brainards," with four Eagles, 20–7.

That night the city's baseball clubs, their uniforms brilliant blocks of colors, treated us to a farewell dinner. Over three hundred of us crowded into a hall draped with flowers and banners and bunting. A string orchestra played during the five-course supper.

Then the toasts began: "To the Red Stockings: may they never meet the wash in which they may be bleached." "Our national game: may we never think it Wright to let our exertions come to a shortstop." On they went, corny and labored. Toasts to Harry, who blushed and mumbled, to Hatton, to the press, to the government, to the ladies. In a speech of thanks, Champion included a pitch for temperance. Too late. A good many ballists lurched from the hall.

[398]

The Cosmopolitan desk clerk informed me that a gentleman had called for me. He'd left no card, but the clerk recalled that he'd called himself a captain.

"O'Donovan?" I said.

"That's it," said the clerk. "He insisted that we find you before you departed the city. Grew angry when we couldn't tell him your whereabouts. Said his mission was urgent."

I felt the shakiness coming on.

"Yes," I said. "I imagine it is."

Pea-soup fog blanketing the Broadway wharf at 6:30 A.M. mirrored my feelings of dislocation.

"Come onto some flush new money game," Brainard said, "and cut me in."

I considered the five hundred dollars he owed me. "Okay, if you do the same."

He laughed and turned away.

" 'Luck, Sam," said Waterman gruffly.

"Get back in time to see us warm the Athletics," urged George, clapping me on the back, flashing his grin.

Sweasy nodded. Mac asked me to keep an eye on local mining stocks; he was inclined toward speculating. Gould crushed my hand. Allison twanged, "So long, bub."

"If you've a mind to work with us," Harry said, "I'll need help with the rink this winter."

"Thanks." It felt good to be wanted. "Maybe I can dream up some new wrinkles."

He smiled. "I have no doubt."

I hugged Andy hard. We had difficulty finding words. He stepped back and looked at me.

"You're coming back soon, then?"

I nodded.

"Want me to tell Cait anything?"

"Just that I think of her all the time."

I watched him follow the others. He turned and waved from the bow, above the riverboat's name, *New World*. Loneliness hit me like a fist. I felt an urge to leap for the retreating gangplank. The whistle sounded, steam hissed from the boilers, smoke belched from the stacks, and the great wheel began to turn. The craft inched from the dock. Kids waved and called to the Stockings. They'd been everywhere that summer: a generation that carried indelible memories of this matchless season. It felt strange to be standing among them. What on earth was keeping me here?

The watery slaps of the wheel faded and the steamer's silhouette blurred in the mist. I turned away, my footsteps echoing on the planks, the Stockings' song sounding inanely in my brain like a movie sound-track. Hero walks up the dock. Alone. Fade into the mist.

> *We are a band of ball players*
> *From Cincinnati City,*
> *We go to toss the ball around . . .*

Was someone calling?

"Mr. Fowler!" I heard a voice with high-pitched girlish lilts, familiar.

I peered into an alley. As nearly as I can remember—I've spent hours trying—it was off Broadway, between Stockton and Powell. In the gloomy passageway a figure materialized with a bundle extended to me. I stepped back involuntarily.

"For you, Mr. Fowler," she said. "From Caitlin."

I recognized Clara Antonia. So I *had* seen her that night. She put the bundle in my hands, bulky and soft. I untied the paper and stared at a patchwork coverlet. It was the size of the one from my childhood. I recognized some of the patches, several from Cait's yellow dress.

"Did she make this?"

Clara Antonia's ringlets bobbed below her bonnet. "For you."

"But there hasn't been time."

She smiled. "She intended that you have it."

"Cait sent you here to find me?"

She smiled again, the opaque eyes regarding me. "Your pain is nearly ended, Mr. Fowler."

I stared as she retreated into the murky alley. What did she mean by *that?*

"Wait!" I shouted.

She was gone. Dissolved in the mist. Exactly the sort of weirdness I needed right then, I thought. I studied the patches: fragments of Cait's dresses, curtains, tablecloths. She'd wanted to encircle me, warm me, with the shapes and colors of her surroundings. I pressed the fabric to my face, breathed—or imagined that I breathed—Cait's faint minty scent, and wondered why this had arrived.

The climb from Vallejo Street was long and steep. Over a shoulder of Russian Hill I saw tendrils of fog being swept before a brisk ocean wind. I stood at the edge of a high bluff. Far to the north the steamboat carrying the team looked like a toy. I strained to make out the stocking flag flying at its stern.

My vision began to change. I first I thought it was the sun emerging from the fog. The bay took on a milky, dazzling radiance. I rubbed my eyes and felt the vertigo coming. Not here, I thought. Not so close to the edge. Move away. But the dizziness muddled my sense of direction.

"Sam!"

Blurred as if behind a scrim, Johnny was running toward me, yelling urgently. I lifted my hand to wave. He shook his head, pointing to my left.

A figure stood several yards up the slope, erect against the gray sky. I raised my eyes slowly, puzzling over the familiarity of the green trousers. Above a wool topcoat, Fearghus O'Donovan's face regarded me with a thin, humorless smile. He held a gun aimed at me.

His smile broadened as my eyes focused on his. "Sure and you thought to make me the fool again?" The cutting voice sounded almost genial. "Not going with the others . . . did you think I'd be taken in?"

My hands trembled badly. I pressed them hard against my thighs. O'Donovan seemed wrapped in grainy light.

"I'll be having the money now."

Johnny moved into my truncated vision. He halted when O'Donovan moved the gun threateningly.

"It's gone." My voice sounded muffled.

His eyes were the blue of deep ice. "You're a liar."

"All gone in the gold collapse."

The sound of a boat's horn wafted up from far below, a flat, tinny buzz.

"No," he said. The gun wavered for an instant.

I realized then that I'd removed the only obstacle to his killing me. Would he do it? Probably. The whiteness thickened slowly, enveloping us. It was important to finish this.

"You'll never have the money," I said. "Or Cait."

He said nothing, but his eyes stared. Mad, brilliant blue. Out there. Nearly gone.

"It's not really the money you want." I heard a distant reverberation, like drumming wings. "McDermott and Le Caron couldn't do it, so you came."

"To do what?" he snapped.

"Finish me."

"Hush, Sam!" Johnny shifted his feet, looking, I knew, for a sign to spring at O'Donovan. He wouldn't get one from me. Death stood with us on the hillside.

Within the milkiness the drumming neared, a thrashing, whirring disturbance, gargantuan wings beating overhead. Or in my brain.

O'Donovan glanced upward. Did he hear it? Coming very close now: wings hammering the air, battering my face. Hard to breathe.

"Colm was murdered," I said.

"Murdered . . . ?" O'Donovan's face bled into the light. Only his eyes remained, cold blue beams. From the whiteness I heard him say something about McDermott.

I was borne backward in the milky light. Greenery floated on the peripheries of vision. My heart pumped lifeblood, a rhythmic exalted drumming.

"Sam!" Johnny's distant voice.

"You killed him." I floated rearward through a leafy forest, trunks of trees drifting past. "You wanted Cait." A wing touched my shoulder, pulling my arm upward. As if in a tide, hand thrust high, I struggled to stop receding, to take a single step forward. "Wanted my Cait!"

A rush of angry sound poured from O'Donovan.

"You killed Colm!" I screamed it above his voice and above the wind's roar and the wings and the rush of backward flight. "YOU MURDERED HIM!"

Then the wings were no longer wings but folds of a green banner, the light not milky but smoke-filled, and finally I was reliving it, all of it, and it was as starkly clear as if I'd always known. . . .

I carry the standard like a javelin, the folds of cloth snapping and rustling beside my face as I sprint through the smoldering aisle, hurtling charred stumps and saplings. Explosions erupt close by. The ground buckles and dirt rains through the branches. I run on, keep running, gaining on the blue-clad figure ahead.

I reach for him, my straining fingers grazing his tunic. He twists aside and wheels to face me, chest heaving, face smudged with powder. I see no recognition yet in the dilated eyes.

"There now, Fearg," I gasp. "Colm's here with you."

He shakes his head, his throat working convulsively, his eyes locked on the forest behind us where crimson flashes lace through billowing black smoke.

"They're butchering the lot," he croaks.

I clutch his arm as he gathers himself to run. "No, we're holding firm, Fearghus. We need you."

Flecks of cottony foam spray from his mouth. "Let me be, Colm!"

"They'll call you coward all your days!" I try to leech the anger from my voice. "Come back with me, Fearg, I'll see you through."

"I'll not." It is half-sobbed.

"Come, old lad."

"No."

I tug at him. He wrenches free with a violent twist and pulls his service Colt from his belt.

"Look at you with your damned flag . . . always gotten eveything."

I move toward him. . . .

"I hate you." His voice is choked.

I reach out, crooning, "Old Fearg . . ."

"Let me be!" It is high-pitched, keening.

"I'll help, Fearg."

The Colt rises.

"Fearg . . ."

Flame shoots through my chest and there is a spear of light in my brain. I careen back through the trees, the banner trailing over me. A solitary shaft of sunlight stabs through the greenery. I hear a bird's sweet, cooing note. And the earth rises like a solid wave. . . .

O'Donovan's finger was tightening on the trigger.

"No! Jesus, no!" screamed Johnny.

I grabbed frantically at my pocket for the derringer.

The sky darkened as throbbing wings closed on my shoulder again, lifting and thrusting me at O'Donovan. Face contorted, he tried to steady the pistol. A shape rushed at him—not Johnny, but a shadow in dark uniform. It seemed to merge with O'Donovan as the gun fired. Terrible noise split my body and hurled me to the ground halfway over the bluff's edge.

O'Donovan lurched forward as if dragged, his heels dug in. He leaned back desperately, his mouth a rictus of terror, and was drawn inexorably toward the cliff.

"COLM!" he shrieked.

His feet thudded against me. I saw his staring eyes fixed on the precipice. He plunged forward.

And disappeared over the edge.

Soon after, cradled in supporting arms, I felt myself floating slowly after him. A shadowy face near mine. Blue tunic, brass buttons.

I don't know whether he answered any of my questions. Possibly he did. In the end they seemed of little urgency.

We were together.

Moving backward. Accelerating. The bay a narrow river on the other side of which stood a knot of people. We raised our arms in salute, moving faster, air speeding through my chest.

Before the darkness came I looked back, just once.

Johnny bent over me, his yellow cat eyes gazing tearfully into mine.

I heard Cait whisper my name.

And I was gone.

EPILOGUE

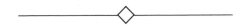

When I was younger I could remember anything, whether it had happened or not; but my faculties are decaying now and soon I shall be so I cannot remember any but the things that never happened.

MARK TWAIN, Autobiography

Quick, said the bird, find them, find them . . .

T. S. ELIOT, Four Quartets

The rumbling came from earth and sky, broken by a rhythmic beeping. My eyes focused on an ant moving across blacktop. I tried to raise my head. My face was stuck. Fearing I'd melted into the blacktop, I raised an arm and triggered a spasm of pain in my chest. Then I remembered the wind-raked bluff, O'Donovan's maniacal eyes, the flame from his gun.

I inched my hand upward. My beard was matted to the asphalt. I worked it loose with my fingertips. Things were gooey farther in. I raised my head a few millimeters and shuddered.

The sickening pain and gashed cheek, yes, the station outside Mansfield . . . but beeping? . . . the black locomotive had rumbled and hissed. . . .

A fearsome noise split the universe. I turned my head a few degrees and saw a vapor trail white against the azure sky. At its point sped a dart with tiny swept-back feathers.

Navy jet, I thought, heading for Alameda.

And then I thought: Oh, no. *Oh . . . no.*

The shock lifted me. The ground swam. In awkward stages I climbed to my feet. I noticed the breast pocket of my coat bulging oddly, then saw a small, blood-crusted hole in the fabric. Jesus. I tried to think . . . nothing. Breathe. Don't give in.

Shaky steps along the blacktop path stirred sediments of pain. I couldn't lift my head. Pine boughs swayed beyond the ivy, a faint whispering in the pervasive rumble. I stood before what looked like a bronze plaque. The words came slowly into focus.

INA COOLBRITH
First Poet Laureate of California
1841–1928

I thought it was a coded message. I stared at the 1928 and decided I couldn't decode it just then.

I tried a few steps uphill to my left. Too hard. I turned around. The beeping—shrill spikes of sound—drove into my brain.

Just do it, I urged myself. Lift your head.

I looked up, very slowly.

The asphalt path skirted a rocky outcropping. I was on Russian Hill. But the dirt bluff had been transformed—terraced now with beds of blooms. A flowering hedge stood where O'Donovan had plummeted.

I lifted my eyes all the way. Above a curtain of conifers rose the Transamerica pyramid. In the distance to its left, the Bay Bridge stretched eastward into a sprawl of glistening cities. Coit Tower stood once again on Telegraph Hill.

A roar below. A motorcycle streaking past at terrifying speed. A gridwork of streets. Traffic lights winking. Cars and pedestrians alternately moving and stopping. All bewilderingly fast. Wedged between the streets were masses of stucco and metal that hid the lines of the hills. The wooden buildings I could see were gaudy with bright paintwork; they looked tacky. It all looked tacky. The rumbling, I realized, was merely the city's normal commerce. A knot of emotions twisted in me. I couldn't have begun to sort them out.

I moved laboriously to a wire fence and looked northward. Where there had been forests of them, only the *Balclutha*'s yellow masts were visible. A tanker from Richmond moved sluggishly past Alcatraz, where the prison stood again. The rest of my view was blocked by a glass-and-aluminum apartment complex. A cement truck backed slowly at its base; the source of the beeping.

Too loud. Too fast.

I had come back. All the way back.

My chest aching with the effort, I reached the top of the Vallejo Steps, where elderly Chinese in gymsuits did t'ai chi exercises far below. Their slow, graceful motions were dizzying. I looked down the steep flights. No way I could make the long descent. Try for the street above.

I stooped over a drinking fountain on the walk but couldn't get my head low enough to drink. I wet my face with one palm, a welcome coolness. My hand came away pink with blood.

Nearby stood a grocery cart heaped with clothes and bottles and metal and cardboard. I came upon its owner several yards beyond, supine and snoring in juniper bushes, a wine bottle protruding from a paper bag beside him. He was unremarkable in every respect. Except one: Cait's quilt was wrapped around him.

I prodded him with my foot. Again, harder. He groaned and rolled onto one side. I bent and tried to pull the quilt away—and nearly blacked out from the effort.

"Wake up," I growled.

He groaned and looked up blearily, did a startled second take.

"I want my quilt."

His watery eyes shifted from my face to the hole in my coat. "You're dead."

"Hand it over," I said, with all the menace I could muster. "And help me up to the street."

The double message didn't threaten him. Even if it had, I realized, he could have escaped me easily.

"I'll pay," I said. "Ten bucks."

"You don't have . . ." Looking guilty, he stopped.

I checked my pockets. Empty. Things were getting blurry again. I unfastened my belt, pried loose one of the last gold eagles, held it out. He exchanged the quilt for it, eyeing the belt.

The blacktop spun. My mind was taken suddenly with images of Hope and Susy.

"Fella, about my girls . . ."

"Huh?"

"I've come back."

I don't know whether he edged away or just looked like he wanted to. By then little was clear. I hugged the quilt to me. Cait, I thought. Oh God, Cait.

"Get me to them," I muttered.

Beds are bolted to the floor in San Francisco Central's seclusion rooms. Bedding is minimal—self-strangling being a fairly serious no-no—and I couldn't have my quilt just yet, though they assured me it was being held. I asked for it each time somebody came to unlock the bathroom.

It wasn't what you'd call cheery. No windows. No TV. No sharp instruments, including pencils and pens. The walls held only fingernail line drawings: two sketches of genitalia, one perfect swastika. If you weren't already crazy, the place might nudge you closer.

On the other hand, my daily ten mils of Haldol kept me pretty groggy. With the quilt, everything would have been fine.

The bum evidently had a sense of honor. He'd taken my money belt but left the quilt and called an ambulance. At Medical Intensive Care my behavior—including, apparently, extensive descriptions of nineteenth-century life—was judged to be out of synch with consensus reality. Hence the funny room, with somebody looking in every fifteen minutes.

"What's the deal?" I asked an orderly.

"Fifty-one fifty, pal," he said. "Gotta do your time."

Section 5150 of the Welfare and Institutions Code permitted holding me for psychiatric observation up to seventy-two hours. An evaluation would determine if I were gravely disabled, perhaps a menace.

I waited.

Meanwhile, the big surprise was that although my chest was cut and bruised, there was no entry wound. I sought an explanation. Nurses patronized me and orderlies looked at me like I was, well, crazy.

Finally a guy about my age showed up, a shrink named Sjoberg. His friendly eyes and soft-spoken manner reminded me a little of Harry. That was probably why, like an idiot, I spilled everything. God knew, I needed to talk.

Sjoberg listened intently, nodded encouragingly. I talked and talked—and finally asked what he made of it. He smiled and said he'd defer "deep diagnosis" pending continued observation.

Which brought the abrupt realization that so long as I told the truth I wasn't going anywhere. Except maybe to the looney ward in a state hospital.

"Look, doc," I said. "Let's just say I was out there in fantasyland, okay?"

He looked at me with new interest. "Go on."

I told him of my daughters, my job at the *Chronicle,* the divorce.

"You've been through a lot," he said.

"I guess so."

He started to rise.

"Can you tell me what happened to my chest?"

"I'll check with Medical," he said, and went off to phone. "Do you own a watch?" he asked when he returned.

"Sure." I reached instinctively for my breast pocket. "Big pocket watch."

"It's still in your coat," said Sjoberg. "Badly smashed. If a bullet struck there as you claimed, it might have been deflected by the metal casing." He looked at me. "Which would explain the furrow on your cheek."

"No, that happened months ago."

His expression changed. Uh-oh. Three giant steps backward.

"Well, *something* happened," Sjoberg said.

Brilliant, I thought. "May I have the watch?"

"In due time." He chuckled at his pun.

Not funny. It had saved my life. I wanted it repaired. After Sjoberg left I said, "Well, little brother, you paid me back in full."

I looked at the door. Nobody observing. Which was fortunate. Since I was talking to Andy.

My condition was diagnosed as "adjustment reaction," a catchall category for inexplicable behavior on the part of accident victims and other traumatized types expected to recover over time. Not bad company, really.

My energy returned as the headaches and vertigo diminished. Sjoberg cut the Haldol and let me read paperbacks, probably testing me with vicarious violence. I devoured John D. MacDonald and Robert Parker. Great stuff, totally unavailable in the previous century. I ran in place, did sit-ups and push-ups, and thought of how I'd approach Hope and Susy. I tried not to think about Cait. Not yet.

I couldn't phone Stephanie. I wasn't sure I'd've wanted to. But Sjoberg had.

"We'll see you in three weeks," he said one afternoon. "I'm releasing you as an outpatient to your family. They're in the visitors' room."

I stared at him. "You mean I'm in my ex-wife's goddamn custody?"

"They're simply here to pick you up," he said. "You *wanted* to see your daughters, didn't you?"

"Well, sure. . . ."

He studied me. If it was a test, I was flunking.

"How do I get my quilt?"

I'd pictured it so many times, them laughing and hugging and kissing me. My heart swelled when I glimpsed them in their spotless dresses, hair brushed, faces scrubbed and glowing. Hope had just turned five, Susy three. Killer cute. My little girls. I burst through the doors and slid on my knees before them, calling their names, arms out to enfold them.

Hope hung back shyly. Susy hid behind her.

"Girls," said Stephanie, from above.

Hope climbed dutifully into my lap. Susy, clinging to her, followed suit.

I pulled them close and kissed them, smelling their freshness. "Glad to see me?"

Hope nodded.

"We got a new daddy too," said Susy, pointing to a man standing beside Stephanie. "Daddy Dave!"

I glanced up, half expecting Anchorman. But it wasn't. Daddy Dave was about my age, medium build, rust-colored hair. Three-piece suit—his a darker gray than Stephanie's—right out of *GQ*. A polo player. Or should be. He smiled with an appropriate measure of friendliness.

"Daddy Dave wants to 'dopt us," said Susy.

Jesus Christ.

"The wedding was last month," said Stephanie. "We mailed you an invitation."

I saw her gray eyes noting my full beard, registering details of my antique clothing. Very little would escape her, I knew. She looked thinner, cheeks almost gaunt, hair cut short. Streamlined. Best of breed. It was good to be able to look at her without the old anger.

"... naturally since we nor anyone else knew how to find you," she was saying, "or even if you were ..."

"I was alive," I said. "Working back East. Sorry about the support. I'll make it up."

Contempt flickered in the cool eyes, as if to say, "Who needs your money?" It occurred to me that she was probably enjoying this. Now I was not only an irresponsible, violent drunk but a full-fledged head case.

I didn't care. Stephanie had her own problems and vulnerabilities. And Hope picked that moment to reduce me to silly putty by creeping close and putting her arms around my neck and kissing my cheek. "We still love you, Daddy," she whispered.

Susy looked up at me and nodded.

Oh, lord.

Outside on the sidewalk Daddy Dave opened the door of a gleaming German sedan. The girls showed me a menagerie of expensive stuffed animals he had bought them and asked me to ride with them. Daddy Dave nodded neutrally.

"I don't think I'm up to automobiles yet, thanks."

Stephanie smirked and stepped in. A swivel of slender hips, a flash of pale stockings.

"I'll be in touch," I said.

Her lips curved ironically, eyes hidden behind dark glasses. Then the quilt caught her attention. She lifted the glasses. "Isn't that your grandmother's?"

"Almost." My glance fell on one of the patches from Cait's dress. The quilt had come through time unchanged: no aging, none of Grandma's patches. "Almost," I repeated. "Not quite."

I rented a place in North Beach. My previous landlord had put my stuff in storage. I retrieved it by paying five months' fees—easily done, once my credit cards were restored.

[412]

The Newspaper Guild prevented the *Chronicle* from firing me—which I suspect old Salvio would have preferred—but could not avert a major reassignment. I drew obits and nightside cop checks, the most dismal blood-and-gore beat imaginable. I worked four-thirty to midnight, often drawing the overnight shift till 3 A.M. Tuesdays and Wednesdays off.

Everybody was surprised that I didn't complain. Cubs usually got stuck with the night police beat. It was punishment. I didn't care. Day or night or what sort of story made little difference. I worked thoroughly, mechanically.

Sjoberg asked repeatedly about my father during our sessions. There wasn't much I could tell him.

I assumed, as a working hypothesis, that either I had been summoned by Colm, or in fact had once *been* Colm. That was my best guess and that was how it felt to me during the experience. *Why* it had happened I didn't know. That's what I wanted Sjoberg to help me figure out.

The trouble was that no matter how fascinating he found my accounts, no matter how inexplicably detailed, he could not help viewing them as manifestations of deep-rooted problems. He invariably returned to my father, suggesting that I was sublimating feelings of rage and rejection through complicated fantasies. Once he even hinted that I had abandoned my daughters in retaliation for my father's abandoning me, and then subconsciously concocted the time-travel stuff to stave off guilt.

It was too deep for me. I knew what I had experienced. And that was all I knew.

After six months I stopped seeing him. We weren't getting anywhere. And I felt okay, in the sense that I was coping reasonably well, not suicidal, not drinking. Most of all, with each passing month, I knew more clearly that I wanted to go back again.

The watch ran erratically, though it didn't look bad. Too many makeshift parts, the repairman said. I wound it faithfully each day with Andy's key, resetting it frequently.

It became clear that although Hope and Susy were central to my new life, I was an adjunct to theirs. Stephanie at first refused to budge on the terms of the custody order: one *visit* per week, during which she seldom strayed farther than the next room. In time she loosened and let me take the girls out.

It was a losing proposition. I got one day a week; Daddy Dave got them all. By the time I saw their day-care papers, he'd already lavished praise. If I bought dolls, he'd buy a whole damn dollhouse. I had the impression he couldn't have kids of his own. He loved mine deeply and was a hell of a competitor. It was probably good for the girls—not so good for me.

Or maybe it was. It kept me from feeling guilty over the longings I felt to be with Cait and Timmy.

They listened patiently at Wells Fargo Bank without asking why, lacking receipts, account numbers, any record whatever, I believed deposits had been made in 1869 in the names of Susanne and Hope Fowler. They did ask if I were a descendant. I said I was, sort of—and realized I hadn't thought this through at all.

They explained that mergers had occurred, that banking laws permitted the transfer of accounts to the state after a lapse of a number of years. I could check with the Superintendent of Banking in Sacramento to see what laws might have applied. But even if the gold pieces had remained in special accounts opened in 1869—similar to placing them in a safe-deposit box—they would have drawn no interest. Their value would lie only in what a coin collector would pay.

So much for that.

Pizza—like TV and a good many other modern cravings—turned out to be not such a big deal. Now I missed the clatter of horse-drawn vehicles; the sight of men wearing tall hats and high collars; women with bustles and parasols; even dirt streets with their raw stinks.

At work I stared out the window at the Old Mint for long minutes, remembering the morning I had walked by and seen its foundation being prepared.

Before long I was spending all my spare hours at the public library poring over 1869 newspapers on microfilm. I discovered what I was looking for in the October 6 *San Francisco Call.*

IRISH SPEAKER FOUND DEAD

The body of Capt. F. J. O'Donovan, noted Fenian lecturer and organizer, was found at the foot of a precipice near Vallejo Street yesterday. The body bore marks of its fatal descent, the head and neck injured terribly. This tragedy is but another lamentable example of the City failing to provide safety railings in mountainous sections—a needed reform long urged in these columns.

I stared at the smudged gray words. *Fatal descent . . . head and neck injured terribly. . . .*

It *had* happened; I hadn't fantasized it.

But that was all I could find. No hint of foul play or mention of witnesses. Nothing about Johnny or me. No coverage at all in other papers.

Rereading accounts of the Stockings' San Francisco games made me feel part of it all again. Hungry to know what happened to them, I haunted UC's Bancroft Library, where I cranked through reel after reel of the *Cincinnati Enquirer*—jolted by the occasional sight of my own dispatches.

The Stockings had demolished foes as they headed back across the country. At home again, they beat the Philadelphia Athletics and New York Mutuals, each making one last-ditch try at knocking off the unbeaten Stockings. There was wild celebrating in Cincinnati the night they concluded the perfect season: sixty games without a loss. Champion awarded them fifty-dollar bonuses on November 15, the day their contracts ended.

I felt an odd moment of trepidation when I ordered the reels for 1870. Time had gone on. What had the next year brought?

By late January the Stocking regulars were "reengaged without change," the *Enquirer* noted. Harry's lineup would be the same—although the substitute was one Ed Atwater. In April they toured Dixie, winning seven games in New Orleans and Memphis. In May they notched eight victories in Ohio and Kentucky, then in June invaded the East again, taking nine straight in Massachusetts and New York.

Then it finally happened. On June 14 they finished nine innings against the Brooklyn Atlantics with the score 5–5. The rules allowed ties, and the Atlantics, content with their performance, drifted from the field. But the Stockings stayed—I could picture Harry grimly commanding them to hold their positions—until the Atlantics returned from their clubhouse.

With Brainard tiring, Brooklyn got runners on first and second in the tenth. But George snuffed the threat by dropping a pop-up to start a double play. Brainard doubled and scored in the eleventh, and George, coming through in the clutch as ever, singled in another run. The 7–5 lead looked decisive.

But the Atlantics' leadoff man blooped a hit in front of Andy and took third on Brainard's wild pitch. The next hitter drove one into the right-field crowd. By the time Mac plowed among them and dug out the ball, the run was home and the hitter stood on third. Waterman took a hot grounder cleanly, held the runner, made the throw. One down. The Brooklyn captain, Ferguson, normally a right-handed batter, hit lefty to keep the ball away from George and managed a dribbler between Gould and Sweasy. The tying run scored. The next Atlantic drove a smash at Gould, who knocked it down to save the run but had no play. Ferguson alertly moved to third. A grounder went to George. He fielded it and threw to Sweasy at second to begin a game-saving double play.

Sweasy dropped the ball!

He scrambled, picked it up, threw desperately to Allison. Too late. Ferguson crossed the plate and was carried from the field by his teammates. Brooklyn went crazy. And an eighty-four-game win streak came to an end.

Eleven innings. 7–8.

Sweasy, you son of a bitch, I thought. But then I felt sorry, knowing how wretched he must have felt. I was sorry for all of them.

Champion sent a telegram home: "Our boys did nobly, but fortune was against us. Though beaten, not disgraced." The newspaper said that he cried in his room that night.

It wasn't the same afterward. George hurt his leg and the Stockings dropped more games—including narrow losses to Chicago's new White Stockings and our old hungry rivals, the Rockford Forest Citys—and ended at 68–6.

A sensational record for anybody else. But not the Stockings. At the end of the season there was mention of discord among the players and even instances of open drinking—it wasn't hard to figure who—and an alleged conspiracy by the Wrights to force salaries higher. In the end the club decided it was all too wearying and expensive; they voted to return to amateur status. Harry and George went on to Boston with Mac and Gould and, later, Andy. The others played for Washington in the first year of the new Professional Association.

And so it all came apart.

In late May of 1870, the front pages of the *Enquirer* were filled with the Fenians' invasion of Canada. Troop movements were reported from dozens of American cities. General O'Neill personally led the assault. I read every syllable of the Cincinnati coverage, praying I wouldn't see Cait's name among those killed, assuring myself that a woman wouldn't have been permitted near the fighting. I wondered what she and Timmy had done . . . *were doing.*

The unlikely invasion had a comic-opera end. O'Neill's advance force ran into withering fire from thirteen thousand alerted Canadian militiamen. Grant, disappointing the Fenians' hopes as he had the gold bulls', issued a proclamation forbidding American citizens to violate the neutrality laws. When O'Neill regrouped his men and moved back to his own lines, a United States marshal calmly entered his quarters and ordered him at gunpoint into a waiting carriage. O'Neill was driven ignobly through his own army to prison. Within a few days the operation collapsed.

In *Leslie's* an engraving depicted the capture. There was O'Neill as I remembered him in Cait's parlor: round-faced and black-browed, with a drooping mustache; he wore his officer's tunic, IRA visible on his belt buckle, gleaming spurs fixed to his high boots. All dressed for war—and gazing forlornly into the barrel of his captor's gun. In several histories I read that the debacle had exhausted the Fenians' remaining credibility; the organization faded away. Poor Cait, I thought.

"Oh, Daddy," complained Hope as we crossed Portsmouth Square. "Do we have to go to that old church again?"

"Not for long." I squeezed her hand and tried to steady Susy, bucking like a pony on my shoulders. Around us Asians gambled and winos sprawled on the grass. A couple in matching polyesters studied a tourist map. I pictured the rows of saloons, the horses at the hitching rings, the old city hall frequented by portly, top-hatted, cigar-smoking men.

"Daddy, I'm *talking,*" Hope said.

"It's a good place to go," I said.

"But we see the same things every week—that mint building near where you work, then here, then the church—"

"Old St. Mary's!" interjected Susy.

"That's good, Suse," I said, bouncing her.

"—then to ride the horse 'n' buggy," Hope finished.

"Oh, boy!" Susy bucked vigorously. "Horsey!"

"Why don't you take us to Great America like other daddies?" Hope said.

"I will, honey." Only five, I thought, and already she knew how to twist the knife. "But see, there's this other kind of great America— how things used to be, how people used to live."

"We *know,* Daddy," she responded. "You tell us all the time."

I bought ice cream cones as we walked along Grant through Chinatown. We ate them sitting on the grass in St. Mary's Square. Across the street rose the cathedral, once the highest, most massive structure in the city. I told the girls that. They didn't look impressed.

"What are those words?" asked Susy, pointing up at the inscription below the bell-tower clock.

" 'Son, observe the time and fly from evil,' " I read.

"What does it mean?"

"Sort of a warning," I said. "For boys." A row of whorehouses had stood where we were sitting. The Barbary Coast had been only a stone's throw away.

"See all the bricks?" I said. "They came from New England. And the stones were cut in China and shipped all the way here. Those big crosses—see up on top? They weren't put there till the church was rebuilt after the earthquake."

"You know lots about everything, Daddy," said Susy, her words muffled as I wiped ice cream from her chin.

"How about Marine World?" asked Hope.

"Another day," I said. "It's a long way out of town. Right now, let's wait to hear the bells strike three. Did I tell you how the old bell was so loud that people all over the city told the time by it? And how the neighbors complained? How they switched to this sweet-sounding one after the earthquake?"

Both girls nodded. In a few minutes the bell chimed. I closed my eyes for a moment.

"Okay," I said briskly. "Now, what say we hit the aquarium in Golden Gate Park. Then a coach ride. Who knows, maybe you'll be handling one someday. Have you noticed all the drivers are women?"

"Okay, Daddy," said Hope, resigned.

Later, as sunlight filtered through the trees near the Japanese Tea Garden, another fringe-topped surrey clopped past ours. I caught a momentary glimpse of its driver's profile and my heart stopped: a pale cheek and a mass of jet hair partially caught up over a high lace collar.

Cait!

I may have yelled it. For an instant I was inside the milky radiance. Then I saw our driver swiveling in the front seat, smiling expectantly at me—she in Victorian costume, standard for the park's carriages—as I held the girls tightly.

"Did you want something?" she said.

"That driver we just passed—do you know her?"

She leaned out and peered behind. "Sure, my friend Rosie Renard going in for her last fare."

"Please," I said, "would you mind . . .?"

"Following her?" The smile was less friendly.

"Yes, I think she looks—"

"Familiar?"

"More than that. Please?"

With visible reluctance she reversed direction in a turnout. The other coach had halted before the tea garden. I saw the driver step down, her booted foot reaching to the pavement from a long skirt. The jet hair was Cait's, I was certain. She was slender, her movements graceful. *Cait* . . .

"Daddy, what's the matter?" said Hope.

The woman turned as our driver called to her. With a plummeting heart I saw that her eyes were blue, her mouth too thin, her face . . . not Cait's. I couldn't speak. I waved our driver on.

"Are you acting funny, Daddy?" said Susy.

"Shh," Hope told her sternly.

"What?" I said.

"Mommy says we must tell her if you start acting funny," Susy said.

"It's okay," I said to Hope, who looked mortified. Disappointment burned in me, but I was surprised that the milkiness had been so close. So attainable. "That would certainly be a very good thing to tell Mommy."

"Well, *are* you?" Susy persisted.

I gave her a squeeze. "Daddy's fine."

"Not funny?"

"No, not funny."

I found a history of theater that included early burlesque performers. In a chapter dealing with the British Blondes I found a stagy photo of Elise Holt. She didn't look nearly so sexy as in person. Maybe my taste had already modernized. What shocked and saddened me were the parenthesized dates beneath her picture: 1847–1873. Twenty-two when I had known her. She died only four years after. No cause was given.

The account mentioned Holt's feud with the *Advertiser*. I smiled as I remembered her encounter with Marriott.

On an impulse I looked for material on the *Avitor*. A thick history of California aviation offered the information that it had made the first lighter-than-air flight in the western hemisphere on July 2, 1869. Despite setbacks with creditors, Marriott and his backers had raised enough money by 1875 to push ahead with plans for an "aeroplane." Eventually a company was formed to produce a triplane to be called the *Leland Stanford*. But a crushing blow fell in '83, when the Patent Office rejected it as an impossibility. Profoundly hurt and discouraged, Marriott died the next year.

I closed the book, depressed. For the first time I realized—emotionally—that they were all dead. They had been dead for a long time. Longer than my grandparents.

Dead.

◇

I phoned the National Baseball Library at Cooperstown and learned that they had biographical files on thousands of ball players.

"What about the early ones?" I said.

"How early?"

"The 'sixty-nine Red Stockings."

"Oh, well, that's a famous bunch, you know. I imagine we have more on them than most others from that era. You weren't kidding, were you? Those are *real* old-timers."

"Yeah, I guess so." I pictured Andy, George, Mac, Allison—young, fresh-faced, exuberant, loving their music and laughter and horseplay. I felt infinitely older than all of them.

"You want copies of anything in particular sent out to you?"

"No," I said. "I want to come and see it all myself."

One starlit night I lay with the quilt pulled up around me, looking out my window at the Transamerica pyramid glowing even larger than usual. I remembered the Mongomery Block which had stood there. And I thought of Cait, imagining her arms around me, recalling details of our night at Gasthaus zur Rose. Mustn't let the sense-memories slip away, I thought. They might have to last a long time.

For the first time I seriously considered writing to Hamilton County. Had a marriage certificate been issued to Caitlin Leonard? Perhaps a death certificate, if she'd remained in Cincinnati. If not, then maybe Newark. And there was Timmy, too. Not to mention the possibility of descendants still living.

I started to cry.

I knew I could never write to those places.

But a month later, taking some earned vacation time, I flew to Cooperstown. It is reputedly a charming village, but I didn't pay much attention. I headed straight for the Baseball Hall of Fame. And my first disappointments.

The plaques of Harry and George aren't bad—if you can believe that somebody in bronze bas-relief ever actually lived—and it was nice to discover that they were the first brothers in the Hall of Fame.

But so *little* remained. A single trophy ball, filthy, naturally, from 1869. Another ball—a sad relic, to me—from the Stockings' loss to the Atlantics in '70. A few faded club ribbons that players wore on their uniform sleeves. A scattering of ornaments and badges; an Eckford banner that brought to mind the hot June afternoon we'd faced them in Williamsburg.

And that was about it. No bats, no uniforms, no trophies. What had happened to Harry's cups and medals and plaques? To George's already-impressive collection of silver inlaid bats and victory cups that must have grown enormous over his career?

All gone, I was told. Dispersed to relatives. Lost in fires. Gone.

I spent only one morning in the library. Apart from Harry's and George's files, not much existed in the individual Stockings' folders. What I did find was more than enough.

I skipped over their baseball careers. Only George and Mac played on into the National League era to any extent, after they, with Andy and Spalding and Ross Barnes—the latter two recruited from the Rockfords—had powered Harry's Boston Red Stockings to four consecutive Professional Association pennants.

Instead I hunted for clues as to how their lives had gone. The fragmentary information I found held few surprises. George founded a sporting-goods company, grew rich, married well, played tennis and golf and cricket, the perennial sportsman. Andy worked for him in his Boston factory.

Mac migrated west and settled in San Francisco—back home again I would phone every McVey in the book but find none related—where he played ball and married; in the '06 quake his wife was badly injured; there is a touching 1914 letter in his file, written by Allison, then living in Washington, appealing to the National League for aid and medical care on Mac's behalf, saying a mine accident had left the former star "down and out."

Waterman and Brainard each married Cincinnati women and eventually deserted them. Sweasy got into trouble on several ball clubs, developed rheumatism that ended his career, and became a huckster in Newark. Gould and Waterman spent their later days in Cincinnati's West End, scene of their greatest glory, holding menial jobs for the most part. Hurley—how glad I was to find a clipping about him!—played briefly with the Washington Olympics, then drifted home to Honesdale, Pennsylvania, after "getting in dutch" in pro ball, according to hometown sources, who admitted him to be "quite a boozer." He taught school for a while, captained the Honesdale ball club, and held down second base for years. He was still alive in 1903, the last mention of him.

My old nemesis, Will Craver, was kicked out of baseball permanently for crooked dealings. I couldn't muster much sympathy.

In 1919, exactly half a century after the establishment of professional baseball, the Cincinnati Reds hosted the World Series opener at Redland Field. Matched against them were Chicago's White Sox—soon the infamous Black Sox. Guests of honor were George Wright, Cal McVey, and Oak Taylor: the only surviving Stockings. I thought I could imagine some of what they must have felt that day, proud relics of another time.

And even then, fifty years later, the crowd had stood and roared for Captain Harry's boys. . . .

Reading of their deaths devastated me.

Brainard went first, of pneumonia, in Denver, where he was a saloon keeper. He died in 1888—year of the Great Blizzard—only forty-seven.

Harry went in 1895, at age sixty, after a long illness; beloved and respected to the end, his passing prompted "Harry Wright Day" in ballparks across the nation.

Champion died within a month of Harry.

Waterman went in '99.

And then Andy, in 1903, in Roxbury. I held a copy of his death certificate with trembling fingers. Gastric ulcer. Fifty-seven. A *Boston Herald* obit said he was survived by his wife and several grown children. There was a picture: I stared at a much older Andy, with full mustache, fleshy cheeks, receding hairline. My God.

Sweasy went in 1908.

Allison in 1916.

Gould in 1917.

Mac in 1926.

George was the last, passing peacefully in Boston, August 21, 1937. Ninety years old. In baseball, Joe DiMaggio was already in his sophomore season. My grandparents were still fairly young, my parents only teenagers. And George had still been living.

I rose and moved blindly toward the door.

"Something wrong?" asked the young assistant who had helped me find what I wanted.

"They're all dead," I blurted.

As I pushed through the door she said, "I'm sorry."

For a long time I was bummed, preoccupied with death and dying. It got so bad that I went back to see Sjoberg. I really thought I was going off the deep end. He told me my morbid period was actually a sign of growing health. Grief represented a stage of acceptance and accommodation following disbelief and anger. I was getting in touch with myself.

And just what was I coming to accept? My friends' deaths? No, he said, the distinction between *that* reality and *this*. His meaning was clear: I was finally distinguishing the here and now as opposed to my time-travel delusion.

What about Cait, then? Why hadn't I chased down every trace of her?

Still protecting in some areas, he said. To be expected.

Protecting what?

Innocence, ideals, he suggested. The cherished idea of a pure and blameless mother. One I (conveniently) had not known and therefore found easier to love and protect. At a distance. As with Cait.

What the hell was I accepting, then, my father?

Yes, perhaps. Coming to terms with an indifferent universe in which innocents suffered neglect and abandonment—sometimes even violent death.

I told him I thought it was a crock of shit.

He may have been partly right, though. My perception *was* changing, but not the way he thought. With the passage of time I began to realize that, from this perspective, of course they would all *have* to be dead now. But it wasn't from *here* that I had known them or existed with them. A simple realization. But it felt profound.

And something more dramatic was happening too. On several more occasions I mistook women for Cait. Each time the whitish light broke around me, and each time it seemed more accessible. Discovering it wasn't Cait became less agonizing with the awareness that the line between that reality and this *was* blurring, becoming somehow navigable. I didn't understand the process, but I felt that I was slowly gaining control of it.

What made me surer was seeing Clara Antonia. Not mistaking somebody for her. *Seeing* her. I was entering the *Chronicle* building one evening when I heard my name called. I turned and saw her waving to me from in front of the Old Mint. I recognized her instantly, even in conservative wool business suit and running shoes. She looked a bit thinner, though her face was still on the pudgy side and fringed with little ringlets. I grinned and returned her wave. When I took a step toward her she turned and walked around the corner. I didn't try to follow.

A validation, I thought. And a promise.

As for baseball, I occasionally watched games on TV till I got too bored. Once I went out to Candlestick with guys from work, but the amplified sound bothered me. So did the slow pace, the players' stylized posturings, the elaborate equipment, the succession of specialists. The professionalization of the sport—a process refined by Harry and Champion—had come too far in my view. Give me teams who sing as they ride to the ballpark in horse-drawn, pennant-bedecked wagons. Who play with spirit and sit down to banquets with opponents afterward.

I get more honest feeling for the sport at the diamonds in Golden Gate Park, where the field is banked like old-time grounds, and where the players show up out of love. I spend quite a bit of time there.

Where the Recreation Grounds stood, at Twenty-fifth and Folsom, is all residential grid. I went there once—and felt nothing. For me it's mostly the carriages in the park, old St. Mary's, and Chinatown. And every once in a while I go up to Coolbrith Park and stand in the spot where O'Donovan fell to his death, where Colm saved me. I feel the milky light close by and hear Cait whisper my name.

It's been almost a year since I returned. I feel pretty good. The job's okay—not exciting, but it's enabled me to stash a fair amount of money in an account for Hope and Susy, with very specific legal instructions and protections. I've told Stephanie what to do should I vanish. She appreciates my attempt at responsibility. All the while thinking me nuts.

I've spotted Clara Antonia twice in recent weeks. There's no particular cause, no pattern that I can see. She didn't call out again, but our eyes met. Once she waved, once nodded.

I keep the tiny piece of Cait's fabric inside my watch. It's always in my pocket. I take the quilt with me everywhere in a locked carrying case. They tease me at work about it. I don't care. I'm packed and ready to go.

I see them clearly: Cait and Timmy and Andy and Harry and Johnny and George and Brainard and all the rest.

In the autumn of 1869 the world is younger. And yes, more innocent. They are waiting.

My lovely Cait is waiting for me.

I don't know when, but I know I'm going back.

I can feel it.